D0077924

THE TIDINGS OF MISFITS

WHISPERED TALES SERIES

JORDAN DUGDALE

ISBN-13: 9798987221112

Cover design: Franziska Stern - www.coverdungeon.com - Instagram: @coverdungeonrabbit

Interior art & formatting: Etheric Tales – www.etherictales.com -

Map: Joshua Dugdale

Library of Congress Control Number: 2018675309
Printed in the United States of America

For everyone who never stopped believing in me.
For my family, who always supported me.
For Matlin, my love, the voice of this story.
For Josh, Ellie, Quinn, Mitchell, and Hannah—you are the heart of the
Misfits.

**For those out there who have never felt like they've belonged.
The Misfits will always have a place for you by their side.**

Trigger warnings

Sexual content (all consensual, multiple partners, mention of genitalia, nudity)
Violence (standard fantasy violence - gore, blood, murder, body horror, mutilation of corpses)
Slavery (very brief in the beginning, and then mentioned in conversations later)
Bigotry (brief situation)
Violence against children (brief situation, non-sexual) / Child death
Abuse (emotional)
Cults
Alcoholism
Trauma

Isles of Mirað

Lyvira

VILANTHRIS

Kreznov

Volreya

Spine Mountains

Volendam

Amajin

Wolstadt

Fraheim

Nantielle

Rovania

Wilhaven

Halvðarc

Hestia

Kythera

Daesthara

Shoma

Dalasae

Prologue
Cassius

The smell of blood woke Cassius from his long sleep.

The pain of consciousness was excruciating. Blood stained his lips. Every time his tongue darted out to taste it, his bloodlust sent him into a fit of panic and rage. His mind fractured into a million pieces as he scrambled to cling to his memories, but they were slow to return. The rush of blood flowed through him, reanimating his corpse as it pulled fresh skin over bones where it rotted and decayed. He could not see as darkness consumed him, making him even more aware of how hungry he was. His fangs ached, longing for the soft flesh of a neck or thigh to bite into. Oh, how sweet and succulent the taste of blood would be between his lips if he could just muster the strength to move.

A soft whimper echoed off the stone, and it was only then that Cassius realized he truly could not see. It wasn't the darkness that blinded him as he reached up with shaking hands to sockets devoid of any organs. A breath shuddered through him, the first breath to move new lungs that had regrown from the dust of his previous body. He knew the salvation from his rotting corpse: blood. Only the curse of his vampirism could save him now. He tried to cry out, to seek whoever had woken him, but no sound passed his lips; there was nothing more than a desolate exhale of air.

"Drink," a woman said. Her voice was soft, like waves crashing against a shoreline. Her fingers slipped behind the back of his head and lifted it to the supple flesh of a wrist. Was it her wrist? No, he could sense her steady heartbeat behind his right ear. Whoever was being offered to him was frightened, her heartbeat matching the pace of a terrified deer caught in the eyes of a wolf. "Drink, Cassius. Set yourself free," the woman whispered.

As his fangs brushed against the wrist, his mind was lost. A frantic feeling built in his chest. It thickened like sand—suffocating, clawing, itching, burning. He was a slave to its nature. He quelled the desperate attempts to resist such nature, drowning in the maelstrom of bloodlust that consumed him. A soft cry bubbled between his lips as he bit down. The blood pooled in his mouth, and the world turned to color again. The blood coursed through him, awakening his lungs, heart, and stomach. He felt it travel all the way to his toes as they curled against the chill of the stone. Tears poured down his cheeks as his eyes reformed, the body he exsanguinated coming into a blurred view.

A loud gasp echoed against his cheeks as he pulled away, the body of the woman he had just murdered falling to the floor. The other woman's hand was gone from the back of his head, and his eyes adjusted quickly, revealing the dusty tomb they had confined him to. In the back was the shuffle of feet, the quiet cries of several people as they moved to get as far away from his coffin as they could. Cassius expected them to scream, but none of them did.

Leaning over the stone, he threw up until his stomach spasmed and tears blurred his vision. His fingers curled over the coffin's edge, his heart unsteady against his chest. His lower stomach cramped as he gagged, but there was no more blood left to purge. He did not want to feed again, did not want to see the light fade from their eyes, but knew it had to be done, for he hated the husk of a creature he became without the blood.

"More." His voice came out no louder than a whisper. "Need more." A person leaned down to grab a rock from the floor and flung it at him, and it hit the wall behind him and bounced off. The noise startled Cassius, and he hissed, his lips pulling back over his teeth as his fangs extended. One human started to cry, and Cassius turned his head away, realizing that whoever had fed him before was no longer in the room with them. If he wanted to feed more, he would have to do it himself.

Strength returned to him slowly as he pushed himself out of his coffin. His arms gave out during the first attempt, and he hit the ground hard, grunting as pain shot through his right hip. His hunger for blood kept him moving; his eyes trained on the humans huddled in the corner. He was a predator in the darkness, and their heartbeats betrayed their livelihood.

"I'm sorry," he called out. Was he sorry? Guilt swam in his chest, calling out to the quiet, gentle boy he had been so long ago. That softness was nothing but a ghost that haunted him from time to time, and he had attempted to strangle it decades ago. Still, sometimes it was insistent, as it was now. It swam into his lungs, curled around his heart, and squeezed without mercy.

"Truly sorry."

The sounds of their screams were the last thing he remembered before instinct turned over, and he blacked out.

He wasn't sure how much time had passed since he regained consciousness. Hours? Days? Weeks? His hunger had faded to little more than a pinprick at the base of his skull. The stone was cold against his fingertips, sticky with dried blood. As his head cleared, his gaze caught sight of the massacre.

Shame crashed down on his heart as he looked into the lifeless eyes of those around him. Moonlight filtered through the door on the opposite end of the tomb. Someone must have pushed the stone door aside when he'd blacked out. It was strange to see a peek at the outside world. The wind whistled through the opening, a quiet urge to free himself, but he was not yet strong enough.

Pushing himself into a seated position, he looked about the room. It wasn't a large room by any means, no larger than his office at his estate, but it was far less pretty. The unpolished stone housed a thin layer of dust. Thick cobwebs decorated the room's corners as spiders danced across their homes, waiting for the innocent fly to stray too close. There was no light except the full moon pooling a few feet into the tomb, and it was enough to grace the room with the blood he'd shed from the bodies strewn about.

A quiet hum echoed through Cassius as a shudder of magic settled into his right arm. His arm was no longer rotted and scarred flesh when he looked down at it. He noted no irregularities as his finger grazed over the scar he'd gotten fighting Vera before she had turned him into a vampire.

Staring at it sent a wave of nostalgia and regret coursing through him as a memory shifted to the forefront of his mind.

It had been nightfall when Vera had come. His maker was a strong-willed woman, her presence demanding attention the moment she walked into a room. He'd felt it hit the back of his neck as he'd sat at his desk. He remembered the silence, thick and tense. It had been some time before he'd dared to turn and stare into the blue-gray eyes of his maker.

"Was it worth it?"

Her question haunted the halls of his heart, twisting his gut until he clenched his fist to stem the pain. He did not regret defying Dmitry's orders. The head of the Sanguine Order should have known Cassius would not carry out the task of killing a child.

"That child has to die." Cassius recalled Dmitry standing on the wall overlooking the mountain pass at Dragon Keep when Cassius had sought him out. Dmitry was the face of the Sanguine Order, his beard peppered with silver, his dark eyes under thick, slanted brows. Turning

into a vampire later in his life didn't stop him from being a force to be feared on the battlefield. He had slain many influential leaders in his time in defense of the high vampire families under the guise of humanity.

"Why?" Cassius had asked, falling in line to stand next to him at the wall. It had been a chilly night as they braved the wind, the Keep overlooking a clearing that stretched as far as they could see through the mountains.

Dmitry's sigh still echoed in Cassius' head, heavy and full of the weight of regret. Regret for what? Cassius didn't know. *The why matters little, Cassius. You will do as I command. There is no other option.*

Dmitry had left Cassius standing on the wall that night with no chance for an argument. It hadn't taken long for Cassius to decide he would betray his Order and seek his own morality by sparing the boy.

Vera's question haunted him again as he pulled himself from his recollection. *Was it worth it?*

Yes, he thought to himself, rising to his feet. *It was worth it.* Even if the child was dead now, he had made peace with his decision.

The moonlight drenched his face in a soft glow, and he resisted the urge to shiver. Hunger was a low rumble in the bowels of his belly. The smell of smoke off in the distance clogged his nose. He could sense heartbeats, a faint pattering that almost sent him back into a frenzy.

He stood in a clearing surrounded by woods, his tomb unmarked except for several necromantic runes carved into its stone sides. Cassius recognized them as warding runes, likely to keep him inside but also to keep those too curious for their own good from opening the door.

Someone or something had left three jagged marks through the runes, breaking them.

Cassius. No louder than a whisper, a soft voice called out to him from beyond the trees. Cassius stilled, but it did not seek him out again, so he thought nothing more of it. His hunger was too demanding, and a sudden itch on his left arm urged him to look down.

At first, nothing appeared out of the ordinary. His skin had returned to a dark olive hue thanks to the blood and illusion magic coursing through his veins. He blinked as an opaque object slithered through the veins in his forearm, but it disappeared before Cassius could inspect it.

Don't go insane now. You only just came back, Cassius thought as he stood alone in the meadow behind his estate. They had granted him his last request to carry out his punishment on his own land. The tall walls of his estate peeked over the tree line, beckoning him inside.

One thing at a time. His clothes were in shambles, and he was desperate for a bath. It was all he could think of as he left the meadow and headed into his home.

Chapter One
Cassius

Come, Cassius. Find us. Set us free.

It started as nothing more than a feeling, a tickle at the back of his mind, an urge to go to Volendam. He wasn't sure why he wanted to go—he hadn't been to Volendam since he was a young man. Perhaps another vampire was calling out to him, or maybe it was his unconscious state telling him he needed a vacation. It felt almost like hunger. He was familiar with hunger, the constant ache that cradled the base of his throat, ushered him forward, and motioned him to act without thought of consequence. He was familiar with its insistence to be noticed, which commanded much of his life. He teetered on the edges of being consumed by its beast-like rage should he ignore its demands. Instead of demanding him to feed, this hunger was gentle—a quiet temptation to follow its request. With it came a bitter feeling in his gut, so he did his best to ignore it. But the voices were constant, and he knew it was only a matter of time before he fell prey to them.

Moonlight filtered onto a countryside estate. To the human eye, it looked abandoned, the landscaping unattended, and the windows dark. The children of Wilhaven all whispered of its haunting and the monstrous man who lived alone inside. "People go there to die," one child whispered, prompting a nod of agreement from his friend.

The estate sat on a cliff-side, overlooking Wilhaven's flowing farms and vineyards. The vast majority of the small town was lush and green, with winding grapevines that created the best wine out of Rovania. The estate on the hill had a small vineyard of its own, but no grapes grew, and the vines had long been dead.

The only room currently occupied within the estate was the bedroom. Cassius Antonia lay awake, staring up past the canopy. The lovers he had taken to bed just hours before snored in a symphony around him. Someone had thrown the sheets to the floor, where a naked woman lay. Sleeping in a pile of pillows, the moon's light illuminated her milky skin. A man's arm was slung across Cassius' waist as he breathed heavily into Cassius' ear. When Cassius moved to slide out from under him, the man mumbled something and turned to sleep on his side. The woman on Cassius' right snored softly, her arm cast over her eyes to shield them from the moonlight. Cassius moved silently from the bed and avoided waking any of his sleeping guests. He stepped over their bodies and stopped before his large cathedral-style window to peer down to the gardens below.

Abandoned in his absence, the sight of the dead flowers and shrubs filled him with a bitter sadness as he prided himself on tending to the estate with excellent care. Exiled for five years, the sour taste of regret fouled his tongue as he stared at the fountain in the middle of the barren garden, the statue of a rearing horse staring up at him with unseeing eyes. Leaves littered the walkways, and dead branches groaned as the wind filtered through them. Cassius' heart squeezed painfully in his chest. If his uncle were alive to see the estate…but no, his uncle was dead, and even if he wasn't, he hadn't cared for anything other than his horses and wine.

"I'd pay to know where your mind wanders off to." Cassius turned as the woman from the bed came up behind him, her scent a mixture of their lovemaking and sweet perfume. She pressed against him and wrapped her arms around his waist, the heat of her body chasing away the never-ending cold that consumed him. Her fingers wandered across his chest, and he remained stoic and silent as she laughed against his neck. "You are silent as always, my lord."

"It's not information I give away lightly," Cassius said, a soft sigh echoing against the hollow of his cheeks. He turned as the woman's fingers slid gently across his skin. He made eye contact with her, his expression guarded. Her skin was bare and pale in the moonlight. Light hair cascaded down in curls around her shoulders, and she stared at him with pale blue eyes. Two puncture marks cradled the base of her throat, but her expression was clear. Cassius' compulsion must have worn off.

The woman chuckled, her hand trailing down past his navel to grab him with a firm grasp. Cassius' mouth parted as desire erupted like a forest fire in his belly. She peered up at him through long eyelashes, her mouth forming into a pout. "I let you put your cock inside me. Does that not warrant a fair bit of trust?" Her breath tickled his lips as she drew closer, and he lowered to meet her, kissing her deeply. Her heart beat wildly in her chest like a hummingbird tempting him to feed. He ignored it, wrapping his arms around her waist to pull her in.

It wasn't long before she pulled away, her fingers reaching up to splay against his cheek. "Cassius," she whispered, her voice insistent. "Tell me what is wrong." Hesitation made itself a home in his expression, whittling away his thoughts. She was nothing but a mortal, one gifted with mortality. Her failures, her trials – they were fleeting. How could she possibly understand?

"I wonder if I will ever feel full again," he admitted, searching her gaze for an answer. Since someone had opened his tomb and liberated him from its prison, he hadn't felt sated by blood. The confinement had left him with a touch of madness he hadn't been able to cure, no matter how many people he'd drained dry. "I wonder if I'll ever feel like me again." The woman's eyes were beautiful up close, like glittering pools of sapphires. It reminded him of home, his human home in Verenzia, of water so clear he could watch the schools of fish dart through the shallows. There was something cold within them, too, intelligence that should not be scorned. Perhaps confiding in her would not be so unwise.

He did not find answers in her expression, nor did she answer, so his fingers reached down to run over her breasts, worshiping her nipples. A gasp escaped her as her fingers closed around his cock once more. He could not stifle the groan that passed his lips, his eyes flickering as he bent down to press his lips to her ear. "I'd love to taste you again."

A hand moved to grip the nape of her neck as his lips marked a pathway of kisses along her jawline. A stroke of her hand and another moan lodged itself between his teeth.

"Oh dear, sweet Cassius," the woman breathed, her voice sultry and low. She drew out all of the primal feelings within Cassius, and his hand moved to slip between her thighs. "You're a monster," she uttered, and as she pulled back, metal flashed in Cassius' peripherals. He moved to grab her wrist, but he underestimated the woman's strength, and the stake sank into his chest. He cried out in pain, the edges of his vision flickering on darkness. The hilt was wrapped in silver, and the woman heaved breathlessly, the passion in her expression replaced with cold dark hatred. A startling realization struck as he stumbled back and hit the cool glass of the window, sweat collecting on his brow. The weapon had missed his heart but barely, and the woman growled, twisting the stake and forcing Cassius to hiss as the pain washed up his chest.

"They told me if I killed you, your blood would aid in Gorvayne's rising."

Red magic snaked through the veins around the woman's eyes as the point of the stake found Cassius' heart. Growling, his human illusion dropped, revealing the monstrosity underneath. His canines elongated to fangs as his face rotted and sank, his cheeks hollowed, and his nose pressed up to mirror a bat's. His eyes glowed a faint red, and his skin went from olive tone to ashen gray as he towered over her. His hands turned from fingers to talons. His hair, undone from its usual ponytail, was lifeless and dark. She thought him to be a monster? It was a pleasure to show her how monstrous he truly was.

Knowing her strength, he slammed his head forward right into the woman's nose. She cried out as she flinched away, stumbling over a man sleeping on the floor. The man woke in a panic as the woman hit the floor, holding her broken nose as it gushed blood over her lips and chin.

"No!" the woman shouted as Cassius pulled the stake from his chest. The silver would have burned his fingers had he come from the bloodline of lower vampires, their curse contracted through necromancy instead of being blessed by their god. Cassius had come from a long line of high vampires, and the pain of silver did not bother them. A mere prickling sensation dissipated the moment he flung the stake away.

The woman's eyes burned with anger as she glared up at him. "No, no, no. The Whispering Lord must rise! Only he may carry us into the light. You must cooperate, or you will see. You will all see." The ramblings of a mad woman—Cassius had heard rumors of these cultists in the heart of Halvdarc to the southwest but hadn't had the time nor care to investigate it. The fact that there was one in his estate now was a cause of more significant concern. She didn't look like a cultist at the party he'd been attending the night before. She'd approached him on her own with offerings of Rovania's finest red wine and a radiant smile. Taking her back home with him had taken little convincing, and now he was facing the consequences of not looking more deeply into her background. Cassius wasn't confident he even knew her name.

"You speak in tongues," Cassius said, bolting forward quicker than the eye could follow. The awakened man screamed as Cassius grabbed the woman by the hair and shoulder, bearing her neck to him. He hoped whatever dark god she worshiped would grant her mercy as he sank his teeth into her throat and drank deeply. She struggled until the venom that slipped from Cassius' fangs hit her bloodstream, and then she went limp. Loosening his grip, he shuddered, the sweet taste of blood sending him into a dizzying high. The man beside him scrambled backwards on his hands and knees, still screaming, and Cassius pulled away, his eyes bloodshot and his pupils so wide it hid the brown of his irises. The wound on his chest wept black blood as he stood, but it felt like little more than a bee sting as it healed.

"Shut up," he hissed, drenching his words in compulsion magic as his gaze whipped around to look at the man. The man did as he was told, tears slipping down his cheeks, but it was too late. The rest of the room erupted into chaos as everyone woke in a fit of screams and cries.

Several tripped over blankets and pillows to get to their feet, rushing the door with little care that they were completely naked. A shadow of supernatural movement, Cassius blocked them with a snarl, gnashing his teeth as he stood in front of the only exit.

"I cannot allow you to leave," he said, shutting the door behind him. A madness consumed him, reddening his vision as a woman to his left broke down crying, falling to her knees.

"Please, please don't hurt us. I just want to go home," the woman sobbed.

Cassius stared down at her, cupping the side of her face with a gentle touch. He felt nothing but a touch of madness within him, beckoning him to sink his teeth into her neck. The woman's voice echoed in his head. *Monster. Monster. Monster.*

Breaking the girl's neck, his knighthood training took over as he moved towards everyone else in the room. Several froze, like rabbits caught in a corner with nowhere to go, while others attempted to fight him off. It mattered little, and soon silence drenched the air. Once more, he was a prisoner of his isolation.

Falling onto a bench in front of his bed, he stared at his blood-soaked hands in horror. He did not care to re-illusion himself into looking human, for what would be the point in hiding amongst the dead? It was not as if they could rise again and accuse him of their murder. His hunger sated, guilt blossomed through him like spring forging a flower, and he hung his head. The wound on his chest was no longer bleeding, but it was an angry wound and would likely scar. His father would have been so disappointed by his lack of control. His father would have been disappointed in a lot of things. The ghost of Dominic's stern words echoed in his head, but Cassius shoved them away and moved to clean up the mess he'd created.

Movement from the floor to his left caught Cassius' attention—the twisting of a corpse. Reanimating the dead was something all vampires could do, but the two high vampire families looked down upon it, seeing it as blasphemy to their image. He did not use necromancy when he didn't have to—another assured way he would have disappointed his maker had she been there. He could hear Vera's voice in his head, chastising him as he watched the woman push herself to her knees in a seated position. Perhaps I called out to her in my loneliness, Cassius thought as he studied her. He used to do that when he was a younger vampire, and the guilt of killing consumed him. Unlike some, whose strengths were in the reanimation of corpses, Cassius' gifts in necromancy dealt with the spirit, and it had been a long time since he had last conjured the ghost of the recently departed.

When cast, necromancy felt like an uncomfortable shift across the skin, like something was not right in the air. There was no such tension in the air now, no feelings of ghosts resting on Cassius' shoulders. As the woman moved to stand, his heart thumped painfully in his chest, resuscitated by the blood he had just drunk. She reminded him of a ghost, the edges of her skin peeling away to smoke. A traditional black and white kimono covered her form. She was spared of blood, her eyes amber-hued and thin. She had small facial features, and her hair was loose and dark, framing her face in waves.

"I did not call for you. Begone," Cassius said bitterly, waving his hand at her.

Despite his dismissal, she did not dissipate, her eyes imploring. She was painfully beautiful, and Cassius stared at her, trying to decide how he had forgotten a face like hers. She looked like she had come from the east, over the Spine Mountains, where people practiced old magic through the martial arts of Amajin. The energy of their magic flowed through concentrated movements versus the spoken word like it was in much of the western world. The Silent Fox ruled there in his bamboo forests. It was rumored he was one of the oldest vampires in the world, hailing from one of the founding families cursed with vampirism.

What was one of his kin doing here?

"You look like you've seen a ghost, Cassius." The woman purred his name, drawing closer. Her lips were a dark ruby red, and she radiated with power, which Cassius respected. A long black nail traced Cassius' jawline as she leaned close, and the moment she touched him, Cassius felt the familiar ache, the urge to go. What was happening to him? He had felt that itch since the moment he had awoken inside his tomb, the door open and insistent he free himself.

"Who are you?" he asked, pulling his illusion back over himself in shame. The Hestian roots from when he'd been human presented itself once more. His skin darkened, his hair an inky black as it cascaded around his face.

"That matters little." A pout softened her features as she grabbed his chin, forcing his expression to meet hers. "You are far better than that little fit you had, hm?" Her tongue clicked at the roof of her mouth as she looked upon the surrounding bloodshed, shaking her head. "You are a Knight of the Sanguine Order, a vampire fit for the Armory of Ebony Fang."

"The Armory of Ebony Fang?" Cassius questioned, furrowing his brow in confusion. "I've never heard of such an arsenal."

The woman smirked. "You already have one piece, and another calls to you. Why do you fight it as you fight your hunger? It isn't healthy." She ran a finger along his forearm, and Cassius moaned in pain as his blood secreted from his skin and formed a flintlock gun. Shadows slipped off it in waves as it solidified, fitting into his hand like it was made for him. Guns were not a standard weapon in Vilanthris, an invention privy to a few of the Royal Guard in Wolstadt. It was beautifully made, though, with a dark metal that was cool to the touch. A soft hum of energy radiated from the gun as a fox's crest with nine tails devoured a bat formed on its side.

"How did you do that?" he breathed, staring at the woman with a thoughtful expression. He'd never seen the gun before, but his forearm had burned and itched every time something called out to him from beyond the Spine Mountain. Sometimes it was nothing more than an urge to follow. Other times, it was a woman's voice calling to him, much like the woman who stood before him. Since leaving his tomb, whatever was calling to him had been insistent in quiet nature, something he had attempted to ignore. Now that the woman stood in front of him and the gun was resting in his palm, the urge to get up and leave was almost painful.

The woman curled her fingers around his wrist and squeezed, pressing a kiss to the corner of his jaw.

"I did no such thing, Cassius. You called it forward because your destiny demands it. Stop fighting the urge to travel northwest. Seek the next piece in Volendam." Stepping back, she folded her arms across her chest, gesturing with one hand around her. "Or continue to suffer alone. The choice is yours."

"But–" Cassius said, but the woman and the gun both faded away, shifting into shadows and blood that ran back up his arm and slipped into his skin. Silence greeted him, followed by that itching in his chest. A quiet hunger plagued him far worse than his hunger for blood.

Standing, he ran his hands through his hair and swept over to his closet, where he pulled on a pair of breeches and a tunic. He found the red ribbon his brother had given him so long ago and used it to tie his hair back into a ponytail. It would take him the rest of the night to clean his bedroom, but come morning, he'd purchase himself a new horse and make his way to Volendam.

If that was where the answers were, he had to seek them out.

He could resist the temptation no longer.

Chapter Two
Cassius

The sun greeted the following day too quickly for Cassius' liking, and as he rose from his freshly cleaned bed, a sigh passed his lips. The appearance of the strange woman had left him skittish, for it was apparent she had something to do with the urge to go to Volendam. Did that mean she was responsible for freeing him from his tomb? It did little to soothe his anxieties, having no answers to his questions. He shoved simple traveling clothes into a backpack he hadn't touched since before his imprisonment and stared at the empty bedroom. It had taken him all night to clean the bedroom thoroughly enough that he wouldn't be suspected should someone break into his estate while he was away. Another bout of guilt twinged his chest; he didn't like to kill if he could help it. Since he had liberated himself from his tomb, it had been more difficult to control himself.

Hefting his rucksack over his shoulder, he headed downstairs and grabbed his sword that rested near the hearth in the sitting room. His armor stood on display behind a glass cabinet, which was the only thing that saved it from the dust that collected on every other surface in the home. Cassius pressed his fingers to the glass, a longing gripping his gut with little mercy. He hadn't worn his armor since the Sanguine Order had exiled him, and the guilt of his crimes turned him from his armor. The travel to Volendam should not warrant the use of full plate armor. *I will be fine*, Cassius assured himself, reaching the front door.

He left his estate the moment dawn broke over the horizon.

It was uncomfortable being out in the sunlight. While it could not kill high vampires, if he remained in it for too long, a headache would set in, and his need for blood would come more frequently. It also made him sluggish, like swimming through mud. Autumn and winter sunlight were far more tolerable, and Cassius was grateful for the autumn weather as he approached Wilhaven's stables.

While Wilhaven was known for its wine, it also served as a fruitful farming town. The lush forest of Daesthara to the south of Rovania stretched its fertile soil northward, and the farmers of Rovania benefited from most of their harvests. He approached the stables now, heading towards a man in nice clothing.

"Ah, a familiar face I did not expect to see." Korvus was the stable master of Wilhaven, and to whom the locals went for livestock or horses. He was an older gentleman with speckled gray in his beard and lines that aged his face. He wore the same clothes as always—a simple gray tunic cross-stitched and layered over dark breeches.

"I've been away for quite some time, I know," Cassius agreed. The stables were immaculate, with great care taken into their cleanliness, and stable hands bustled about the stalls, tending to the horses.

"Some time? Cassius, you were gone for five years." Korvus snorted, one hand pressed to the nape of his neck as the other waved for Cassius to follow. A hearty laugh left his lips. "But it is not my business, friend. You're here now. Are you in need of another horse?"

Cassius nodded. "Indeed. One equipped with the journey through the Spine Mountains. I am to take the mountain pass to Volendam."

"The mountain pass? Why not take the road through Wolstadt and Nantielle? They will be safer than the mountains," Korvus asked with a raised eyebrow.

Cassius shook his head. The main road would be too busy, too full of people. Guilt from his indulgence of blood the night before was still too heavy a weight to chance it. Plus, there were whispers of vampire hunters about; Cassius would rather chance dwarves than come into contact with a Blodrägr, humans blessed by their god with divine magic that could easily take down a vampire. Cassius had narrowly survived a Blodrägr's attack a few years after he'd become a vampire. The encounter left him with a scar on his right hip and nearly took his life. He could live the rest of his undead life, never crossing paths with a Blodrägr again. "I will take my chances."

Korvus nodded. "I have just the horse. She's nothing to brag about, but she's surefooted." Korvus stopped at a stall where a young mare was grazing the hay. Her tail flicked at flies, and her chestnut coat was shiny and recently brushed. Cassius reached his hand out. Even as a vampire, horses didn't seem to flinch away from him. The mare nibbled his fingers before returning to the hay, and Cassius turned to Korvus.

"How much?"

"One hundred and twenty skaels," Korvus said, gesturing to one of his stablehands. "Ta, get Jia ready to ride. Cassius is buying her."

Cassius pulled the coin purse from his side and counted the small silver coins. He felt like he was sitting several inches out of his skin, and his urge to go was impatient. Hyper-aware of Korvus' and Ta's blood, his hands shook at the temptation. Staring at Korvus, he watched the vein pulse at the curve of the stable master's neck, hidden slightly behind a beard. Ta had a fresh cut on his finger, bandaged but intoxicating to Cassius as he rushed forward, mumbling to himself. Cassius swallowed, reminding himself he had just fed in abundance the night before.

Turning to Korvus, he said, "I can saddle her, Korvus. It's no trouble."

Korvus nodded and waved Ta away. The saddle was well-used, worn leather, and simple in design. "This saddle has been well loved, Cassius, but it comes with Jia. Take good care of her now."

Entering Jia's enclosure, Cassius ran his hand fondly over her neck. "I will," he promised. He had always been fond of horses; their gentle willingness to work was admirable. The horse snorted as Cassius moved to put the saddle on her back, and Korvus watched from outside the stall.

"And Cassius? Travelers have been speaking ill of the road. Strange folk have been wandering the wilds. Best be careful on your journey even if you take the mountain pass." The quiet fear in Korvus' tone caused Cassius to look at him. Korvus shook his head and smiled, patting the side of the stables with his palm. "Never mind that. You were a knight once! Surely you can handle the threat of bandits."

Cassius said nothing, only smiled. Korvus lowered his head in respect before turning to leave. Cassius stood still for a moment as a strange feeling passed through him—a strange sort of trepidation like he was standing at the edge of a cliff.

The feeling was fleeting as he mounted Jia.

One worry at a time.

The transport system across the plains of Rovania was well maintained—simple dirt roads that were easy for herding livestock. Cassius' travel to Fraheim, the capital of Rovania and the nearest city to the mountains, was brief and uneventful. He did not run into any strange folks like Korvus had been worried about. Cassius was a quiet man who enjoyed his solitude, and the empty roads were not unwelcome. A day out from Fraheim, a pair of farmers stopped him, desperate for his help catching their cattle which had spooked when one of their wagon's wheels slipped off its axle.

Drain them dry. An intrusive thought whispered in Cassius' head, but he ignored it, locating the cattle and steering them back to the wagon. He helped them lift the wheel back onto the axle, ignored their offerings of bread and soup, and continued on his way.

It was mid-afternoon the following day when the grand wall of Fraheim approached in the distance and Cassius paused on a hill to appreciate its glory. Rovania housed good relations with the dwarves of the mountains and often used the mountain pass to travel through, offering trade and resources to them. The wall was a reminder of a time when that wasn't the case, and the king in the mountain was enemies with those who ruled Rovania. That was a long time ago, and peace with the dwarves was thriving. Still, it was a sight to behold, stretching for miles and wrapping Fraheim in a protective layer against the mountains. The urge to continue through the city to Volendam did not allow Cassius to marvel for long, and he pressed Jia forward as the sun hit the tip of the mountain peaks.

Vendors and businesses were being locked up for the night as Cassius rode into town, steadying his horse with a small click of his tongue. Jia protested softly and continued forward until Cassius hitched her in front of the Pig's Trough Inn. The outside was worn down, weathered by the fierce storms Rovania experienced in autumn, and only a few other horses were hitched to the wooden posts in front of its doors. As Cassius walked in, his nose scrunched in disdain; the inn smelled of livestock and sweat and was not an establishment Cassius was one to frequent. A small squat man with a thick mustache stood behind the counter, and he barely glanced in Cassius' direction, even when he walked up to the counter.

After renting a room for the night and with a glass of wine in his hand, he ignored the stares of the other patrons and found a dark corner to drink in. The itch to move forward was quiet, and he sipped his wine as he listened to three traders haggling over their livestock and grain. No one glanced his way after his initial entrance, and he retired as the night grew dark and the fire dimmed in the hearth.

The following day he left before the sun rose. The city guard paid him no mind as he wandered out of Fraheim through the gate facing the mountainside pass. The stretch of mountains went on for miles, keeping the valley cool in the early autumn days. The cold did not bother Cassius as he stared at the mountains with contempt. They hummed with the same magic that fueled his curse, and their ominous peaks put him on edge.

During his stay at the Dragon Keep, where the Sanguine Order he'd been a part of resided, he remembered how much magic seemed to soak the earth, how the air was electrified with energy. It felt like the mountains pulsed with their own energy source, something Cassius had never felt anywhere else. He could never pinpoint what he feared about it but remembered the first night he'd stayed in the Dragon Keep. He hadn't been able to get a wink of sleep due to the thrum of a heartbeat that coursed through the ground and jarred his bones. Vera and the others had taught him how to tune out the feeling during his knightly training there, but it still sent a thrill of fear through him.

He looked to the northeast, where the Dragon Keep resided. Tucked away in the mountains, its location was hidden from everyone but the Sanguine Order's knights to preserve their numbers. They were an order of vampires, and had their location been leaked, Dragon Keep would have been eradicated long ago by the likes of Blodrägrs.

Would they force him back into his tomb, should they find him again? Or would Dmitry just demand his execution outright? He shuddered at the thought of seeing the disappointment cross Vera's face again. His maker had placed her trust in him, and he'd failed her. He hadn't been a part of the Order for close to seventy years, which was short for a vampire's lifetime, but it was long enough for his disobedience to bring him dishonor.

Cassius shook his head and urged Jia forward. He did not want to shake the dust off those ghosts.

The mountain pass was winding and merciless. The fauna and flora were as hardy as the dwarves, surviving on little to none. Fir trees dotted the inclines as Cassius passed through the forests, and it wasn't until nightfall that the trees started to thin, only to be replaced by rocks and tall ravines.

There were moments when Cassius was confident Jia could not cross, the pathway almost too narrow for horseback, but he managed to coax her forward on foot, leading her with gentle words and reins.

On the third day, Cassius came across a lone traveler. Bent over a small stream, he hummed a soft but lively tune, his horse tied to the nearby tree. He greeted Cassius with a genuine smile, and the way his eyes went from joy to horror haunted Cassius as he drained him dry.

Blood pooled in the water, turning it red, but the relief he felt as the blood brought his body back to life chased away the guilt.

On the fourth day, it rained. Cassius slipped his hood over his head and pulled his cloak around him, staring sullenly at the sky as it wept. His forearm burned all day, accompanied by the increasingly distressed whispers urging him to move forward and to stop taking rests.

"What do you want from me? I can only travel so quickly!"

He screamed out into the darkness that night as the pain became overwhelming. Raindrops hit his face in a steady downpour as his horse grazed on tough grass, his hunger for blood spurring on his irritation. There had been nothing to feed on besides that lone traveler he'd passed, and the longer he went without blood, the more his body decayed. It felt like he was back in his tomb, months without food, his sanity ripped from him.

His hunger forced him closer to the main road through the mountains. He'd been avoiding it in the slight possibility he'd run into another vampire from the Dragon Keep, but he needed to find someone to feed on. His lungs felt as hollow as his stomach.

"Why are you urging me to Volendam?" he shouted. He was miserable, wet, and hungry, with no apparent reason for being drawn to Volendam in the first place. A headache had set in behind his right eye, insistent and pulsing, and he growled as he looked to his arm, where the woman and the gun had disappeared into. If he wished it hard enough, perhaps she would reveal herself and give him the answers he sought.

The voices did not answer. Quite the opposite–they went silent. Cassius' relief was brief as the soft patter of a heartbeat called out to him in the darkness. It was too fast to be a dwarf's. It sounded human, and he spoke up before waiting for the stranger to step forward.

"You cannot hide from me. Reveal yourself; I will give you only one chance." Hunger brushed his throat as the human's smell wafted over, making his mouth water. The scent was exotic, ripe with spices and a hint of incense. The human smelled like he hailed from Shoma, the desert land to the southeast, full of sultans, nomads, and thieves. It reminded him of his human estate and the spice crates his mother had received in her trading empire.

Laughter trickled from the shadows momentarily before the human materialized out of the darkness. He was tall and wiry with a thick silvery beard adorned with beads and leather. Atop his head sat a turban clasped with a jeweled skull, and the sight of it infuriated Cassius.

"What's a shoma'kah doing so far north and in the mountains?" Cassius asked. Shoma'kah hunted in the deserts of Shoma, raiding caravans and enslaving any outsiders they thought they could make money from. He didn't know they left the sands of Shoma.

The rain stopped, the clouds parting to reveal the stars as they twinkled merrily in the sky above them. The shoma'kah studied him, his expression hidden by shadow.

"I could ask the same thing; vampires are known to avoid mountains. Can you feel the lack of corruption here? Does that weaken you, I wonder?" The shoma'kah sneered, the metal staff he walked with resting comfortably within his grasp. The voices that had carried Cassius here were still silent, and Cassius scoffed. Vampires allowed the rumor that mountains weakened them to fester. Most low vampires stayed away from the mountains, the necromancy that fueled their curse fighting with the raw magic of the mountains. Cassius was a high vampire and did not succumb to such weakness. Not when the bone marrow of a dead dragon coursed through his veins. He could still remember the day Vera had told him where vampirism had come from, how Ruxandra the White Dawn had sought out whispers of a dead dragon in the East. The dragon had granted her the power that she desired, but in doing so, vampirism and necromancy were born. It wasn't until much later that the Razvan family and their experimentation caused low vampirism to flourish through necromancy. The number of low vampires in the world vastly outnumbered the number of high vampires, and their weaknesses were common knowledge. Those weaknesses did not harm high vampires, but better to let the enemy underestimate them.

"Still strong enough to overcome you. I'm certain you're smart enough to never underestimate a vampire." The magic thrummed through Cassius' veins, urging him to use his deadly tools. In his resistance, he eyed the shoma'kah, attempting to gauge his next move. The slaver leaned casually on his staff, and perhaps it was the way the man smirked that infuriated Cassius. Or maybe it was his growing hunger, or because he'd been led to these godsforsaken mountains by voices that no longer spoke to him. Regardless, he found himself moving forward, drawing his sword, eager to kill, anxious to feed.

Raising his sword, Cassius struck out with expert swordsmanship, but his blade was met with the metal of the shoma'kah's staff and parried away. Shifting his sword down, he blocked the staff as it attempted to sweep his feet out from under him. He curled his lips back and snarled, his illusion bleeding away.

The shoma'kah did not flinch at Cassius' true visage, his mouth merely uttering tongues that deepened the shadows around them. Sleepiness drove itself into Cassius, but he fought it, knowing the mage was attempting to cast a spell on him.

"Have you no honor?" Cassius hissed, raising his sword again. He loathed fighting mages, their moral codes erring on the side of winning no matter the cost. Sick to his stomach, he fought the urge to spit at the shoma'kah. The Sanguine Order prided themselves in the sense of honor in battle, and Cassius did not see a hint of it in the shoma'kah's expression.

"Do the dead pay homage to honor? Do your victims praise your mercy?" The shoma'kah sneered.

A sickening fury swept through Cassius as he lunged. The shoma'kah sidestepped quickly, his heartbeat slow and steady. Pivoting, Cassius barreled into him, shoving him onto his back. The shoma'kah's staff flew a few feet away as Cassius dropped his sword and grabbed the side of the shoma'kah's head and right shoulder, pulling them apart to reveal his neck. The shoma'kah's pulse was a drum of temptation beneath his fingertips.

"Pay homage to your god," he breathed as he sank his fangs into the shoma'kah's neck. It was intoxicating. The magic that flowed through magic users preyed on Cassius' curse. The stronger the magic user, the stronger the blood's effect on Cassius. He felt dizzy moments after the blood touched his lips, but still, he drank, even as the shoma'kah struggled.

A sudden pain blossomed from the back of Cassius' head, and everything went black.

Chapter Three
Cassius

When Cassius woke, he snarled with his teeth bared. It was daytime, and he was inside an open cage. The walls were metal and barred, and red runes hummed at the top, suspended in the air in a line surrounding the cage. His prison was settled next to the right of two others, situated on an open wooden caravan. One of the other cages was occupied, and the rest of the caravan was filled with two types of humans: slavers and slaves. The latter had their ankles and wrists bound in metal as they sat on a bench lining the entire length of the far wall. There was no pattern regarding who the slavers captured to sell: the caravan was peppered with different skin colors and ages. The only similarity was they were all human. Their clothes looked like they hadn't been washed in some time. While there was still a twinkle of hope in one or two expressions, many wore the heart of defeat on their sleeves.

Nearly a dozen shoma'kah walked alongside the caravan as three stepped up to walk between the cages and the slaves on the bench. Most wore scarves to hide their faces, and all carried whips at their hips. A quick glance around the caravan and he could not see his bag or weapons. Perhaps on the other caravan or up front with the rider.

A young girl with dirty cheeks and white hair studied Cassius. She sat between a woman from Shoma and a man who was somehow granted the use of a flask. She observed Cassius with one large brown eye, and the other was unseeing as three jagged scars blinded it. Her skin was tanned and muscled, but she didn't look older than nineteen.

"Wonder why you're locked up and we're not," she said with a thick Kreznovian accent. Her voice was soft and kind, something Cassius did not expect, as Kreznov's people were hardy and serious. Her seeing-eye glittered with a silent curiosity as one of the shoma'kah walked past, ensuring all of the slave's bindings were secure. "Can't be magic. They could have just bound you with these." She held her chains up. "Keeps those magically inclined from performing magic."

Cassius ignored her. He wanted to slaughter the entire company, prisoner and slaver alike. The metal was cool to the touch and did not budge under the stress of his strength. Electrical currents burned through his fingers as the runes glowed brightly at the top of the cage.

"No point. Sealed with magic." A voice in the cage beside Cassius distracted him from his ire. It was a greka, a small member of the drikoty—a species of lizardfolk to the west. They were not known to dwell in this part of the world. He was small in stature, no larger than a seven-year-old human, and he sat with one ankle propped up on the opposite knee. His scales ranged in varying shades of blue, the ones on his snout teetering on black, and he had a thin line of spikes trailing down his spine beginning at the base of his neck. How had a group of shoma'kah gotten hold of a greka? They were small, slippery to catch, and tended to stay in Lyvira, their homeland. It was strange to see one in this part of the world.

"Been trying for days," the greka continued. "Gonna kill that one first when I get out." He gestured to the man driving the caravan, the same man who'd overwhelmed Cassius and put him in his cage. A spike of anger shot through him, but he dropped his hands off his bars.

"You're going to have to fight me for that right," Cassius said, bitterness streaking through his tone.

The greka shook his head as he studied the runes at the top of his cage. "Somehow managed to sneak up behind me. Hit me with a stick. Didn't like it." The greka rubbed the back of his head and looked at the empty space beside him. "I know, Ekalas. Watch back. Don't trust anyone."

Uncertain about who the greka the speaking with, Cassius eyed him warily. "Where did he grab you? I did not know drikoty left their continent," Cassius asked.

"Came across sea. Nasty storm—blew us off course. Ended up in Amajin, scurried south to get away from vampires. Ended up in desert. Took my krok'ida out first." The greka pointed behind Cassius and growled. "Never seen someone take a krok'ida down so fast."

Turning away from the greka, Cassius saw the krok'ida in question taking up the caravan behind them. They were another of the drikoty, only much, much larger, similar to that of a crocodile if they could walk on two feet and hold weapons in their hands. The krok'ida matched the greka in terms of color, only their scales shimmered more in shades of blue-green. They stood at eight or nine feet if one were to measure them from head to toe.

Massive metal shackles ran over the width of krok'ida's back, nestled between his shoulders and back legs. A muzzle kept him from opening his mouth. Cassius had only fought one or two in his ninety-four years of life and knew the shackles were the only thing holding the krok'ida back from murdering everyone.

Hunger gripped his throat, demanding to be heard. The urge to find the Arsenal of Ebony Fang the woman had spoken of was still silent. He longed to be back inside the comfort of his estate, restoring it to its former glory with wine in hand and women and men pressed to his sides. Yet here he was, surrounded by the Shoma'kah, with nowhere to go.

"Hey there, gorgeous." One of the Shoma'kah, a man with dark skin and a peppered beard, came up from the back of the caravan and halted in front of one of the woman slaves. At first, Cassius thought it was the white-haired girl, but then the shoma'kah turned from her to stare at the woman next to her. She was gorgeous, her skin light brown, her hair inky dark in a braid over her shoulder. A thin trail of silver cloth ran through the braid, and her expression was half tucked behind a scarf. She eyed the shoma'kah with a cool, collected study as he crouched next to her.

"Th' name's Basam. 'M thinkin' I'll buy you at the selling point. You'd make a beautiful wife." Basam ran his finger over the woman's cheek, and Cassius tasted the hatred radiating off her skin. She remained silent, and the man sitting near her laughed.

"The first place she'd stick your cock is up your own ass." The urge to laugh was compelling, but Cassius resisted as he studied the man who spoke. It was the man to the right of the white-haired woman—the one with a flask. He was rugged, his brown hair cut short, and his beard no more than a shadow. The stench of alcohol clogged his breath, and he had a hardened expression that had seen many horrors in the world. One of his eyes had been blackened—it was half swollen shut, and a cut fattened his lip. Still, unlike the rest of the slaves, his clothes were clean, his face free of dirt. It also looked like a paste had been applied to his wounds to help them heal.

Basam bristled, his hand flying to the small whip at his side. "You know better than to say such horrid things, Rooster. Do you need some more lashings to remind you of that lesson?"

Laughter echoed among the shoma'kah as Rooster stared at Basam, a cocky smile gracing his lips. "You wouldn't want to hurt me before my next fight, Basam. Who will win you more skaels? Amir would not be happy if you were to permanently damage your best fighter." Rooster gestured to the man who had incapacitated Cassius.

Basam stared at him as he worked it over in his head. The caravan hit a bump in the road, and Cassius stared sullenly as it rattled him around in the cage. Finally, Basam spoke again as his hand left his whip. "You're lucky you have Amir's favor, Rooster. Hope you're ready for tonight." Basam's smile was wicked as he retreated towards the back of the caravan. Rooster pressed his flask to his lips and drank deeply, and Cassius leaned forward to talk to the Shoman woman.

"I did not know shoma'kah enslaved their own people."

"They are not our people." The woman's accent was heavy. Her hand closed around the jeweled blue and silver eye hanging around her neck. *Wonder why the shoma'kah let her keep that*, Cassius wondered as she stared at the front of the caravan, where most of the humans were silent. Their heartbeats beat erratically around him and to his left, the greka muttered to himself as he waved his hands over the runes of his cage.

"They are not from Shoma?" Cassius asked.

The woman shook her head. "They are, but my people call them 'shoma'kah,' which loosely translates to 'people of the cursed sands' in Vilris, the common tongue. If you were to pull back their sleeves, you'd see a slavers mark branded into their skin. The leaders of Shoma pretend to exile them but take their money and turn a blind eye all the same." She frowned.

"Sounds like every bastard that drinks the poison of power," Rooster commented, running a hand over his head. "They're willing to turn a blind eye to evil for their own happiness and heavy pockets." The sun had started its descent behind the mountain, and with it went the warmth, but Cassius was glad for it. His headache was already dissipating, and he found his senses sharpening.

The woman remained silent, so Rooster turned to Cassius. "I know Ayla and Helai here," he said, gesturing first to the woman from Kreznov and then to the Shoman woman. "What can I call you, friend?"

Cassius eyed Rooster in thoughtful regard. "Sir Cassius Antonia, if it pleases you."

"You're a knight then?" Rooster asked.

Cassius nodded slowly. "Was." His exile left his knightly status hazy. Once a knight of the Sanguine Order, always a knight of the Order, but he felt too guilty of his disobedience to hold on to his title.

Helai hummed, leaning back against the caravan. The scarf had slipped from her head when another bump in the road jarred the caravan. Behind them, the krok'ida growled in irritation.

"And you, greka?" Cassius asked, turning to look beside him.

Still muttering to himself, the greka didn't glance over at him as he raised his voice to speak. "Don't see why it matters. Not going to know each other much longer." Irritation rang through Cassius at being dismissed, but the greka did not seem interested in Cassius' offense.

Helai gestured to Rooster and Ayla. "The three of us have been captured for quite some time, but you are the first person they put in a cage beside the greka."

Cassius shrugged. "I gave the slaver a difficult time." He quickly changed the subject. Didn't need them asking too many questions. "Kreznov is in the north, no?"

Ayla nodded. "I was visiting a sick family member in Verenzia, and the slavers ambushed me on the journey home." The mention of

Cassius' human city made his heartache. He hadn't returned to Verenzia since his father sent him to live with his uncle.

One of the shoma'kah on the road hit the caravan behind Ayla and Helai.

"Quiet. No talking unless you all want lashes."

They fell into silence after that, and Cassius watched the shoma'kah pull the caravans into a small open area where they stoked a fire and set up camp. The day had officially turned to night, and the wind was jarring. Several prisoners shivered in what little clothes they wore, and the shoma'kah made no move to remove Cassius and the greka from their cages. The krok'ida was also left on the other caravan, and his tail pulled against his confines as the fire was made and the shoma'kah settled down around it. They spoke amongst each other in tongues Cassius did not understand. A shoma'kah tugged Rooster to his feet by his bindings, and Rooster sighed, winking at Cassius as he passed.

"Wish me luck," he said.

Helai spat at the ground as Rooster was led over to a half-ring of people.

"What are they doing?" Cassius asked.

"Fighting rings. Very popular in the sands of Shoma. The winner is usually seen as honorable and can make a name for himself out of it— unless you are enslaved by the shoma'kah. Their rewards for your successes are usually food and booze."

Cassius watched Rooster roll his shoulders as the shoma'kah pulled off his binds. Rooster gripped his wrists as he assessed the man standing before him. Rooster was not a very broad man but broader than the other fighter. The shoma'kah were not bothered with being quiet, and Cassius wondered if the vampiric Order or the dwarves living below would come for them. Dwarves were known for their hospitality, given the right crowd, but the Sanguine Order was wary of strangers straying too close to Dragon Keep.

"Where did they pick you up?" Cassius asked Helai, who was watching Rooster circle the other fighter. The light of the fire flickered as the shoma'kah surrounded the fighters in a ring, and a low chant in Shoman echoed through the clearing.

"Off the coast of Dalasae. They caught me trying to board a ship," Helai replied, offering Cassius her gaze. Metal clinked as people shifted and stood to watch the fights. Ayla stood too, but her eye was on Cassius again as she steadied herself in her chains.

"Stare any longer, and I will have to seek payment," Cassius said.

Ayla did not smile. "You said you were a knight. What Order?"

Cassius did not hesitate. "White Dawn." The Sanguine Order came up with a name to keep Blodrägrs off their scent and was also the title their founder carried.

A flicker of recognition crossed Ayla's face. "They are renowned, blessed by the gods with long life for their servitude to the light. You served with them?" She nodded towards his cage. "Now I know why you are in there."

Over their heads, through the front of the caravan, Cassius turned away from Ayla's meddling to see Rooster's opponent charge. The man tried to grab Rooster around the waist, but Rooster brought his elbow up and slammed it down on his opponent's back. Cassius was disgusted by the fight and looked instead to his cage. The runes still glowed in the growing night, and every time his hand drew close to the bars, magic hummed, warning him not to touch.

"Greka," Cassius whispered. "How close are you to figuring out how to disarm these wards?" The greka next to him had not turned once to the fight.

"Shoma'kah magic—very good. Will take time," the greka said in Vilris. Pacing the confines of his cage, he stared up at the runes on his own bars, now speaking in lizard-tongue. Occasionally, he raised his hand. A current of electrical energy zipped through the air. He halted every time one of the shoma'kah guarding their caravan looked over, but he was relentlessly seeking out a weakness amongst the wards.

In mere moments, Rooster managed to choke the life out of the man he'd been forced to fight. Breathing heavily, he rolled free. Blood poured from his nose and caked into his beard, mixing with the dirt. A shoma'kah woman approached him, helping him to his feet. Pressing his flask in his hand, she and several other shoma'kah shouted in Shoman. When Cassius glanced at Helai, her expression was stern.

"Rooster joined us a couple of nights later," Helai commented, watching Rooster sit by the fire and drink. "It's been a long journey."

"Too long," Ayla said mournfully. "I have been trying to figure out if we could fight our way to freedom for some time now." She glanced around, lowering her voice as shoma'kah passed by the caravan. "I think if we can figure out how to break those runes surrounding the cages, we might stand a chance."

"Working on it," the greka muttered firmly. Cassius hadn't seen him sleep once. "Almost got it, I think. Have a few more tests."

The rest of the night was uneventful. Rooster was given access to the fire and did not return to the caravan until the following morning. No dwarves came for them that day, and Cassius never once felt the presence of another vampire. It was eerie. He wasn't sure how the shoma'kah were getting away with passing through unnoticed nor where they meant to sell them. Volendam, perhaps. Cassius had heard stories of some of the nobles of Volendam and their love for the slave trade. It filled him with a quiet rage that simmered at his core as he sat in his confines.

Hours turned to days, which turned to weeks. The hunger scratched at the back of Cassius' throat, pulling at the edges of his illusion, threatening to put his true visage on display. A silent scream sat in his molars, a panic that he would lose control and kill himself, trying to escape to feed. At one point, he looked down at blood pooling down his fingers from where his nails had dug into his palm. Fractured memories of starving in his tomb resurfaced to torment him.

"Feeling weak?" A shoma'kah stopped at his cage one morning as they prepared to leave, and Cassius could not stop the frenzy of madness that consumed him as he bolted forward. He managed to grab the shoma'kah before she could get away. Slamming her against the bars of his cage, he ignored the pain that shot through his arms as his wards flared up and extended his fangs, sinking them into the shoma'kah's neck. The taste of her blood etched relief into the hallows of his cheeks as he drank deeply. The shoma'kah's attempts to fight him off were feeble and easily resisted.

It took two other shoma'kah to pry their companion away from Cassius, and even then, the magical resistance around his cage bent under pressure as his bloodlust urged him forward, but it did not break as he shot back and heaved. Blood dripped down his chin as he calmed, straightening his shirt and ignoring the frightened stares of the other slaves. Helai glared at him from her seat, and Ayla stared at him with ill-concealed awe.

"The cage really makes sense now," Rooster said, chuckling, running a hand over his head.

"Steel chains would not keep me from killing them," Cassius agreed, wiping the blood from his face with the back of his hand. The longer the days went on, the grimier he felt. His mood was soured despite the pleasant hum that zipped through his body from his meal, however temporary.

"What?" He snapped at the greka, lowering himself to sit in the middle of the cage. The runes no longer glowed in protest to his attempted escape, and the greka stared at him too. He felt on display, like a specimen for everyone to view.

"Vampire. Makes sense—gotta get some of your blood when we're free," the greka said, muttering.

Cassius did not respond but shuffled further from the greka all the same. The rest of the day was far less uneventful. The shoma'kah did not stop, save to rest for the night, where fighting rings ensued. They did not have Rooster fight each night, but he fought often enough to bloody his face and force his silence.

Something forced them to stop on the last day of the fortnight.

As the caravan halted, an unease spread through the party. Cassius wasn't sure what it was, but a magical hum vibrated the ground, so slight in nature that the others did not react. Helai hadn't spoken to him again since learning he was a vampire. The shoma'kah had taken care to keep away from his cage since he fed from one of them, and his insides felt hollow like he was nothing more than an animated husk. It left him on edge, like he was standing several inches outside his skin, and he couldn't stop pacing.

A low shudder erupted beneath the ground, vibrating up through his caravan.

"What is going on?" Rooster asked one of the shoma'kah, who ignored him. Several others moved forward, disappearing out of sight as they rounded a corner, and Cassius glanced back at the krok'ida. His tail slapped against the caravan as he attempted to free himself from his chains, and when he made eye contact with Cassius with the left side of his head, his pupil was dilated in rage.

Quiet chatter and a throaty laugh sounded off to the right, along with the shuffle of shrubbery. Cassius stared at it long and hard, but nothing appeared. There was another heartbeat, separate from those of the caravan's company—Cassius had never heard a heartbeat so fast. It had been some time since Cassius had felt the tremble of fear, but it sank into him now. He steeled himself despite it.

For several moments, nothing happened. The wind whistled through the mountain pass, and trepidation soaked the air with a poorly concealed warning. Beside him, the greka twisted his fingers in a way that forced the runes above his cage to fizzle and fail. The smile on the greka's face was one of relief and mischief, and a crack of lightning from his fingers broke the lock on his cage.

"Greka," Cassius hissed. "Free me."

The greka ignored him, his eyes fixated on the shoma'kah Rooster had called Amir. "Little busy. Gotta murder." The greka spared Cassius a glance then. "Name's Intoh. You know my name now." The whisper of teeth gnashing together echoed somewhere off to Cassius' right once more, hidden in the shrubs. Quick, breathless laughter came from behind a tree, followed by squeaking, but Cassius could not see anything when he looked. He only heard the shuffling of bushes and felt the heartbeats of countless others lurking in the shadows.

"There's something—" a muffled explosion went off, and then another. The ground in front of the caravan shuddered and opened up, splitting apart. The crack shot towards them, and Cassius braced himself in his cage. Intoh threw himself from his and levitated, slowing his descent as they were swallowed by the darkness. Chains snapped as prisoners, and shoma'kah slammed into the rocky terrain below, their screams echoing in the void. Caravans smashed into pieces, freeing the chains from their walls. Moans and cries of pain erupted around him.

As Cassius' cage slammed into the ground, pain exploded in his back and legs under the cracking of bone. His cry lodged in his throat as a gasp escaped his lips. His vision flickered as consciousness threatened to leave him. He could not move for some time until his vampirism slowly cured him. The stench of blood was overwhelming. Gurgled grunts and whimpers faded, their heartbeats snuffed out by the dozens. The moment he could, Cassius lifted himself from the shambles of his cage.

Basam lay several feet away, coughing on his blood as a stalagmite stuck out of his belly. "Vampire, help me," Basam wheezed, and Cassius knelt next to him, his eyes glowing red in the dim cavern. "Please—"

Basam was the first victim as Cassius lost himself in his bloodlust, the sight of his pleading eyes darkening when Cassius tackled him, low growls pathing melodies in his lungs. It did not stop with Basam, as his blood only spurred Cassius' desire to completely sate his vampirism, and he moved on to others, silencing their dying cries as he sentenced them to a quick death.

He came to as he dropped the body of the shoma'kah woman he'd fed on a week ago, her blank stare upturned towards the ceiling. His mind felt clearer than it had been in weeks since he had fed from all of those lovers he'd taken to bed. It was liberating, but his relief was short-lived; with clarity came the sight of Helai holding a dying, unnamed slave in her arms.

"No, no. It's okay. Look at me." Helai ignored the blood on her hands as she rummaged around the ruins of the caravan. Dried blood caked her hair to the side of her face as she muttered to herself, tearing off the cloth of a dead slaver to press against the slave's wound. The moment pressure was put on her abdomen, the slave threw up blood, and her eyes sought out Helai's as she attempted to inhale, but Cassius heard the moment her heart stopped.

"She's dead, Helai."

Helai did not seem to hear him as she stroked the slave's face. A quiet prayer in her native tongue was whispered against her cheek as Helai set her down, and it was only then that Cassius noticed that Helai was missing her right pinkie, cut at the middle knuckle.

"Get away from me, dead-walker. What do you know about death?" Helai's voice broke as a sob ripped through her. Her shoulders shook once as she composed herself, her hands reaching down to close the woman's eyes.

"Far more than you, I imagine," Cassius said bitterly.

Helai glanced up at him, opening her mouth to respond, but a screeching noise above them caused them both to look up.

Overlooking them on one of the outcroppings of rocks was the silhouette of an enormous bipedal rat. It stood upright and brandished a small sword, the steel gleaming as the sun bathed the cavern in light. It stood nearly six feet in height with pus-filled sores coating its arms and right leg. Its other leg had been replaced by metal. Crudely done, it hummed with a soft purple glow.

Several more rats appeared at the lip of the crevasse where they'd fallen, shouting in chattering tones Cassius did not understand. It sounded much like the whispering he'd heard before, and he quickly found a sword on a shoma'kah corpse and pried it from its sheath. Its lightweight and curved edge was not something he was used to, but Cassius gripped it all the same.

Scurrying forward, the rats feasted on the dead horses and attacked those too hurt to move. Screams filled the cave as it erupted into chaos and bloodshed.

"Stupid man-flesh-things! We will kill-eat you and chew on your skin-bones," a rat hissed as it appeared from the shadows with a small horn held loosely within its grasp.

The rats' stench was so overpowering that Cassius struggled not to gag as the one in front of him raised the horn to its lips and blew. To Cassius' left, Helai slipped into unnatural shadows, a bloody hand pressed to her side. He hadn't sensed magic in her, but it did not surprise him—the magic of the shadows was difficult to pinpoint in a person and not widely practiced.

Giant rats poured in from behind rocks and through tunnels leading into their small room. Some ran on two feet while others crawled on all fours, and many of them chattered in tongues. Some of them were covered in sores, a soft purple glow secreting from their wounds like sap, clinging to their fur in sticky residue. The closer they got, the more repulsive they became.

A rat stepped on top of the wreckage of the caravan, its eyes shielded by a cloak that had seen better days, stained with dirt and dotted with holes. Its tail curled around a piece of wood jutting out of the caravan. "Fellow rat-things! We must skitter-scamper to the chosen! Mark their flesh-skin with the brand. Let them see-sniff their path to salvation." The rat spoke in quick tongues, its voice hoarse.

Figuring it was time to go, Cassius moved to disappear down one of the tunnels, but something pressed against his lower back on the right side. It was white-hot and burned worse than anything he'd felt since the night he'd died and been reborn. His low cry pierced the air as he turned and decapitated the rat that had snuck up on him under all the chaos.

As a branding iron dropped from its hand, the rat's head rolled a few feet away and hit the corpse of a shoma'kah. It stopped, staring up at Cassius as it appeared to laugh at him, its mouth parted in an eternal snarl. The brand still burned against Cassius' skin, but he had no time to investigate as more rats approached him with swords and spears.

Helai's scream caused Cassius' head to turn. Two rats trapped her against a wall. As she fought off one with a small dagger, the other darted behind her and stuck her with a hot poker without mercy, screeching in tongues. She fell to her knees, and Cassius fought his way towards her. After stabbing the rats surrounding her, he offered her his hand. Burned into her back was nothing more than a black circle with three squiggly lines running through it diagonally. Her skin was red and angry.

She froze as she stared at him. Fear and disgust mingled in her expression. "I do not need your help," she said, pressing further into the wall. Her heartbeat was elevated, and tears still stained her cheeks, running trails through dust and dirt that collected on her skin.

"Don't be ridiculous. Look around us. Have I given you a reason to fear me?" Cassius asked, hand still outstretched. The sounds of rat hearts thumped all around them, and his patience wore thin.

"Yes," Helai admitted, but her gaze flickered to the space behind his shoulder. Grabbing his hand and tugging him towards her, she shot around him and stabbed a rat in the neck as it tried to sneak up on Cassius, and it went down with a low hiss.

"Thank you," Cassius said.

"Just stay away from me," Helai replied, fighting her way through the rats towards Rooster. Several other caravans survivors attempted to fight, but it was apparent in the uncoordinated movements that most were untrained. Many of them were overwhelmed by swarms of rats. One accidentally killed his comrade as a rat redirected his blow, stabbing her through the head. Chaos infected the room, and Cassius raised his sword, steeling himself against the unit of rats that spilled out of every hole in the cavern.

Rooster stood off to the right near the wall. He favored his left leg, which was mangled and broken, but otherwise, he appeared uninjured. He fought with a small, curved dagger, and despite his drunken state, he fought well, keeping the rats at bay. Cassius still felt a surge of annoyance rip through him at Rooster's intoxication. *What little honor,* he thought.

The krok'ida fought beside Rooster without a weapon—tooth and claw were used as he bit into a rat's neck and slammed it against the wall, snapping its spine instantaneously. The giant drikoty fought without mercy, killing anything that got too close to him, human and rat alike.

"Do not let him get away," Intoh shouted, throwing small magic bolts at Amir, who shuffled through the wreckage to salvage what tools he could. He picked up a lamp, and Helai cried out.

"We can't let him take that!"

Cassius was too overwhelmed by rats to move. Intoh fought desperately, his hands thrown out to shoot magic around him, keeping the rats off his back. He moved quickly and efficiently, but it still wasn't enough.

Amir made it to the other side of the room, one hand full of items, the other swinging in a large circular motion as a doorway of magic opened up. He did not even spare a glance backwards before the exit swallowed him up and closed behind him.

Intoh screamed out in frustration, killing several rats near him, and Cassius cut down another rat as it drew near, dodging its sword and parrying with knightly grace. A dagger sang through the air, whistling as it flew past his ear, and he glanced at Rooster and Helai in offense. He did not know which one threw the dagger.

"Watch where you are throwing things," he shouted. Rooster laughed, adrenaline coating his tongue, and pulled another dagger from where he had shoved it at his waist. To his left, Helai knelt on the ground while Rooster covered her. She was rummaging through a bag on one of the dead shoma'kah, muttering to herself. A few moments later, satisfaction gleamed in her eyes as she pulled out a bomb. As a rat closed in on her, she lit the bomb in a panic as she stood to throw it.

"Careful, you'll send the whole mountain down upon us!" Cassius shouted, his tone sharp. He made his way towards her to... do what? Pry the bomb from her hand? Chastise her up close? He did not know. Only he did not wish to die in these mountains.

Helai spared him no glance as she threw the bomb into a pile of rats feasting upon corpses.

One of the rats hissed as the grenade landed at his feet. "Stupid man-filth. You will kneel before claws and teeth and beg for your life-breath." Picking up the grenade, it charged through the crowd and ran at them, its jaw poised as saliva dripped from its two front teeth.

Cassius cursed the situation. He cursed the shadow woman in his forearm. He cursed the Sanguine Order for condemning him to his tomb. If he had known he would die here, he would have fucked more people before leaving his estate.

Intoh shot behind the wreckage of one of the caravans to find cover, and the krok'ida turned to run, finding a reprieve from the rats to make his way towards Intoh. Rooster saw the rat running towards them and kissed the blade of his dagger for good luck. Without saying a word, he flung the dagger with a flick of his wrist and dove behind a pile of dead rats, hiding him from view. The dagger pierced the rat between its eyes, and the rat fell, landing on top of the bomb. Guts and gore exploded everywhere as the bomb went off, and Cassius and Helai were thrown back against the wall. Cassius' head hit something sharp, and then he fell unconscious, his last thoughts but a flicker before the darkness greeted him.

Fucking mortals.

Chapter Four
Helai

Helai lay in a sea of sand. It did not take long to recognize her home, the land of Shoma, the Desert Sea. The sun swam in the horizon's haze, casting a brilliant orange in the air. Helai blinked, her eyes bleary as two figures stood before her. One, she could not quite make out—her older brother Massoud, perhaps, with his lean stature. The other was of a more petite build, with dark hair spilling over his shoulders.

"Aryan?" Her voice rasped as if she had not drunk water for several days. She felt too weak to stand as she lay in the sand, its warmth cradling her in comfort. She felt so tired like the desert was pulling her in, urging her to rest, but she didn't want to lose sight of him. She had spent so long looking for Massoud, but Aryan pulled at her heartstrings painfully, a lost love she hadn't seen in quite a long time. He had been sent away by Massoud.

"He is too close to your heart, little sister. It will serve you both best if he is sent away," Massoud had said, and by the time Helai had learned Aryan was to leave, he'd been gone.

She hadn't seen him since.

Aryan stood just out of her vision as she blinked, and a blurred hand reached out to her, deeply tanned and scarred. "Come, Helai. It is not yet time."

"Time for what?" Confusion set in, and Helai struggled to focus as her vision cleared. Aryan still looked like a mirage, swaying in the sand, but she would have remembered those large, brown eyes anywhere. Her heart ached for him, and she longed to reach out and grab his hand, but no. She had not seen him for years. It would not be right. "Aryan, Massoud said we are to scatter. We are tasked—"

Aryan shook his head and then his hand, his impatience clear. "No time. Come, Helai. You must get up."

A weariness settled in her bones. Perhaps she could find peace if she stopped resisting and let the sand claim her. She had been running for so long, trying to liberate her people, and she deserved a rest, did she not?

"Just—Aryan, please just give me a moment. I need—" Her voice sounded far off, and she looked behind Aryan's shoulder at Massoud. His hair was embellished with jewels and silver trinkets that freed his hair from his face, and he was clean-shaven, something unusual for Massoud. A soft sadness crept into his expression, but he was silent.

The desert called her name and called her home. She needed to reclaim her right among her people. If she could not help them gain their voice, who would?

"Get up, Helai. Get up. Do not follow Zahra into the darkness. The sun–" Aryan paused, pressing his palm to his brow and glancing at the sky. "Seek the sun's warmth." Aryan's voice had gone from a command to a whisper, the vision of him fading as the sun's brilliance overcame him. Helai squinted, staring up at him. He was nothing more than an outline against the horizon's haze. He was right. Her task was not complete. Her people were still ruled by a murderous tyrant, her land ravaged by those who thought it was their birthright to claim. She could not rest until her people were liberated.

As she stood, the sun swallowed her whole.

She woke in the cave, gasping for air. Aryan and Massoud were gone, replaced by two drikoty. The attack returned to her as she groaned and pressed two fingers to the back of her head tentatively. Wincing, she found where her head had connected with the rock. She didn't notice the pain on her left side until she attempted to move. A fire of pain licked down her arm and waist. A soft cry passed her lips as she forced herself into a sitting position, and Intoh scurried over to her from where he had been healing Rooster's leg, which looked far better than when Helai had seen it last. He knelt, studying her wounds. The krok'ida moved away, killing anything that made noise, and Rooster stood over Cassius, who had not yet woken.

"Hit with shrapnel. Need to pull out metal," Intoh said, holding his hand over her side.

"Do what you must," Helai said through gritted teeth. Intoh's palm was warm to the touch as he hovered it over her arm. His eyes dilated, do what you must, do what you must, do what you must, do what you must, do what you must.

"The vampire is dying," Rooster called out, causing Helai's eyes to fly open. Rooster kicked Cassius' side softly and moved out of the way, revealing his corpse. Cassius was lying there, but no more illusion was woven into his features. His nose was pushed up like a bat's, his leathery skin a shade of gray. The corners of his lips showed rot, and his hair was dry and brittle.

"It's unnatural for him to be alive." Helai's expression was sour as Intoh dropped the metal spikes from her arm and moved to her side.

"May I?" He held the bottom of her shirt, and she nodded, lifting it to reveal her midriff. The cave was cool, and she repressed a shiver as the greka worked to remove the metal there. She hissed as Intoh's hand slipped, and the shrapnel dragged through her skin, a painful pinprick that made her eyes water. His gaze had turned from her to stare at Cassius, and as he returned his attention to her, no apology left his lips.

The krok'ida ambled over, staring over his shoulder at Cassius. "Smell dead," he said in broken Vilris. "Don't like."

"That's because he is," Intoh spoke without looking up, and the last of his magic swept over Helai. It felt like water slipping over her skin as her wounds healed. The pain from the back of her head even disappeared, now nothing more than a slight twinge that could easily be ignored.

"Thank you," Helai said as she climbed to her feet, looking at all the death and destruction around her. Intoh immediately scurried over to Cassius, poking various parts of his body for any signs of wounds.

"Must study—much to learn." Intoh reached up and pulled Cassius' upper lip back with his finger. His teeth were all razor sharp. Intoh's eyes gleamed as he tapped one of the fangs with his fingers, darting his hand back as some sort of liquid secreted from the tooth. "A venom, perhaps?" He questioned aloud, patting his legs and standing.

"I need to look for survivors," Helai said, turning away.

"Will accompany. Aid where I can. Also, look for our things. Need a vial. Much to learn, much to learn," Intoh muttered, glancing at Cassius one more time before scurrying off with Helai.

Helai wasn't sure of the greka's company but welcomed it all the same as she knelt down, feeling for the pulse of anyone who looked to be breathing. Many of them were dead or too far gone to aid, and Helai eased their suffering, slipping her dagger between their ribs. Their gratitude only sent sadness coursing through Helai, but she continued onward as Intoh rummaged through wreckage and bodies, piling items in a group on the ground in the middle.

"He—help me," a quiet whimper cut out through the room. The world slanted on its side as Helai got lightheaded, her gaze falling on

Ayla. Rats had feasted on parts of her, leaving a mess of a woman behind. Her entrails had been pulled from an open wound in her belly, and her blind eye was gone, eaten away. How she was still alive was lost to Helai as she rushed over.

"Intoh, please," Helai called behind her, kneeling down to pull Ayla into her arms. Blood gurgled up Ayla's throat, bursting through her lips as she was moved, and she stared up at Helai with fear in her remaining eye.

"I do not want to die," she said. She began to cry.

Helai hushed her quietly, brushing Ayla's hair away from her face as Intoh bent over, hovering his hands a few inches over Ayla's body as he muttered in tongues Helai did not understand. After a moment or two, he locked eyes with Helai and shook his head so quickly that it was a blur of motion.

Helai pulled Ayla closer. "It's okay," she whispered as Ayla continued to sob. Helai hummed a quiet melody. It stemmed from a faint memory of the lullaby Massoud used to sing to her in the sands of an abandoned building they slept in to keep out of sight of Shoma guards or when she was sick. It was a song his mother sang to him when he was a child, and Helai hoped it could bring Ayla the slightest of comfort as she passed.

Her hand reached up to squeeze Helai's wrist, but it never made it, falling limp as the light faded from Ayla's eyes.

She was dead before Helai finished the song, and a sob shot through her as she cradled Ayla in her arms and rocked her. She had failed–it was all her fault. She should have done something, should have protected her somehow. The hurt blossomed through her chest like a flower unfurling, her breath shuddering in waves.

"Must go. Think more are coming," Intoh whispered, pressing a hand to her shoulder. Faint screams could be heard in the distance, and Helai closed Ayla's eyes, steeling herself against the grief as she moved Ayla to the floor.

"Right," she said, glancing at the small pile Intoh made on the floor. Another sob ripped through her, so she closed her eyes until she could find herself again. "Is this everything you could find?" She reached over to rummage through it, wiping the tears from her eyes with the back of her hand. She was pleased to find her pack. It was only then she remembered Amir stole her lamp, and her heart plummeted to her throat.

Before she tried to leave, she had stolen that lamp from a mage in Dalasae. There was a jinn inside, a being of elemental powers beyond understanding. She intended to use it one day to kill Mohalis, the head sultan in Shok'Alan. He was a vile man and a cruel ruler who allowed slavery to go unchecked and his common people to die in the sands without resources under the pretense that it was the will of their new god, Qevayla, the dragon of mirages.

Helai spat at the ground and stood, hefting her pack over her shoulder and grabbing her other things: two daggers, their sheaths, which she strapped to her waist, and a halberd Intoh must have plucked off one of the dead rats. Its blade was slightly curved and rusted, but Helai tested it in her hands, and it still seemed solid. She studied the krok'ida, who still stared at Cassius' form with a vague sense of mistrust, and then moved to approach.

"Can you wield a halberd?" She asked. "We should stick together." A slaver pulled himself from a pile of corpses off to her left. He was bleeding heavily from his arm but fled down a tunnel, not even sparing a glance in their direction. His dying screams sounded a moment later, and Helai suppressed a shudder. He died too close to them. They needed to get moving if they wanted to avoid more contact with whatever those rats were.

The krok'ida looked down at Helai and snorted. "Too small," he said, pondering for a moment and reaching out. "Give anyway."

Helai handed the halberd over to the krok'ida, which was much too small in his grasp. Still, it was better than nothing.

"Perhaps we should wake him," Rooster said, glancing down at Cassius. "You said so yourself—we should stick together. He was a good fighter."

"If he kills us when our backs are turned, all of this fighting won't matter," Helai said bitterly, but a sigh latched itself in her lungs as she knelt next to Cassius. He didn't *smell* like he was dead.

Helai still stared at Cassius hesitantly. She hadn't known about the existence of vampires until she'd met Masika, a woman from Shoma who hunted *Almkin*, Shoman mages who performed dark magic that mutated their lower forms into that of giant snakes. Masika had told her vampires were creatures of the night, cursed long ago by Jaleer, the first god of Shoma. They were gifted immortal life but at the price of the insatiable need for blood. She'd only seen a vampire one other time when she was thirteen. Massoud had been off somewhere in Balqas, likely smoking iisha with the pretty male bartender he had eyes for at the local tavern. Aryan had convinced her to go out stealing that night, and they had been on their way to Iron's Belly to steal some daggers when a flicker of movement in the dark alley stopped Helai in her tracks.

As he dropped his victim to the ground, the vampire's dark, glowing red eyes had carved a home in her mind, never to be forgotten. She wasn't sure how she had gotten away from the alley before the vampire noticed she had seen, but she ran as fast as she could anyway. That vampire caused many sleepless nights for her after that.

Her stomach lurched, and she dug into her bag to find a vial that had miraculously survived the fall. Within it was a wisp of white smoke, and Rooster watched her with curious eyes.

Helai looked to Rooster. "Are we sure we should wake him?" she asked, gesturing to Cassius. Her reservations held strong, but her morality plagued her, a quiet insistence that it was her bomb that had gone off, and Cassius seemed different from the vampire in the alley somehow.

Rooster nodded. "I do not imagine his wounds are of the fatal kind. It would be better for us to wake him. Otherwise, he wakes up on his own, finds out we left him for dead and comes after us in his ire." While Rooster was right, Helai still felt a sense of hesitation. Masika had always warned her to keep her distance from dead-walkers, but Cassius had yet to give her a reason to be frightened. Uncorking the vial, she knelt down next to Cassius. Massoud used to wave a vial like this under her nose when she'd been young and sick with a cold. She hoped it would boost the vampire's healing enough to wake him.

Gently lifting his head, she ignored the compulsion to gag and pull away. His skin was bone cold and leathery to the touch and did not feel real under her fingers. A moment or two was all it took before the vampire's brown-black eyes shot open. They glowed a faint red but not nearly as strong as the other vampire Helai had come in contact with. The krok'ida tightened his grip on the halberd he was wielding, and Rooster took a step back as Cassius' mouth opened and fangs slipped past his lips. His hair was in disarray, half pried from the ponytail he wore.

"I *warned* you to be careful," Cassius said, standing at a speed her eyes could not follow. His anger rang through her as if it were her own, and she pulled away from Cassius, pressing the cork back onto the top of the vial and slipping it into her bag.

"A sense of gratitude for saving your life would be appreciated," Helai hissed, her anger pounding at her temple. A Shoman prayer was uttered in her native tongue, asking for patience, but it was met with silence.

"Gratitude for saving me from what my body was already in the process of doing?" Cassius scoffed, and as he rose, youthful features hid the monster he truly was. He must have been quite handsome as a human. Helai couldn't see anything now but the beast. "Saving me from a bomb you set off? I think not."

His words fueled the flames of anger in her belly, but she swallowed the words that rose to her throat and turned away, waving her hand at him in dismissal. "We do not have time to argue. There could be more of those rat things in the tunnels, and we've been hearing screams of dying survivors for several minutes now." She pointed to Intoh, who had just finished putting salvageable items into a pile. "Intoh's been putting things in a pile for us. I suggest you rummage through it, and then we go the opposite direction of where those rats poured out of."

Teeth clicking against each other sounded off in the tunnels just as Helai finished speaking, and her hand immediately flew to her hip against the hilt of one of her daggers.

"We hurry," Intoh said, scurrying through the dead. He carried a short staff, built for his size, and he used it to climb up the krok'ida and balance on his shoulders, sticking the end of the staff against the krok'ida's back to steady himself. If it bothered the krok'ida, he did not show it.

No one said anything after that. Rooster and Cassius rushed to the pile, pulling swords and packs from the mass of things Intoh found. Rooster pried a simple bow from the pile and a quiver with a handful of arrows. Helai hurried towards the tunnel that didn't have the sound of rats coming from it, and she kept a lookout until the others approached. Rooster had tied a cloth around a small piece of wood and dipped it into a small fire that had started from the bomb. Helai was grateful as she stared down the dark tunnelway.

"Let us make haste," Cassius said, disappearing into the tunnel. Everyone was eager to follow them, and even as the light from the cavern disappeared, Rooster's makeshift torch stopped the darkness from swallowing them as they plunged deeper into the mountain.

When Helai no longer heard the rats, she turned to the krok'ida. "What is your name?"

The krok'ida looked at Helai. "I am Lindrz'kt. Just call Linda."

Rooster cocked an eyebrow. "Linda? Isn't that a woman's name?"

A large exhale flared at Linda's nostrils. "Linda is lizard. Linda no gender. Linda is Linda. Linda she. Linda he. Linda they. Linda not care."

Rooster and Helai glanced at Intoh, who shrugged. "We choose our own gender in drikoty culture. Use whatever you'd like for Linda. Been using 'they' for them. Refer to me as male."

Unrest ripped through the party as a magical current sang through them. The brand on Helai's back burned, and a hiss passed through her teeth. It burned like fire through her blood, a heat that licked the inside of her skin rather than the outside. A quiet whimper hit the back of her teeth. She hadn't seen the rat circle her and wasn't sure what she had been branded with or why. Her gaze flickered to Rooster as he turned, and she noticed the same brand on his back, just under his shirt, slick with sweat and crusted with dried blood.

"You were branded too?" Helai asked, gesturing to the brand on his back. He turned, trying to look, and nodded. "One of the fuckers stuck me. Hurt like a bitch," he muttered, pulling his shirt down.

"Happened to me, too," Cassius said. "I wonder why they branded us if they just meant to kill us."

"Linda and I have one too. Can conclude they wanted us for something," Intoh said, approaching again while gesturing to Linda's inner thigh, where their brand shone brightly against the lightness of their underbelly. Her own brand burned, but it was bearable. Still, she felt dizzy and weak and could nap for days if given a chance.

They walked in relative silence after that. The brand burned for several minutes before quieting down to a pinprick as if Helai had allowed her foot to fall asleep, and she ignored it as they came up to a crossroads. One tunnel veered off to the right. When Rooster stuck his torch into the opening, they could not see where it veered off again. The other continued forward, stretching for as long as the torchlight revealed.

"I'm continuing straight. That looks to go deeper into the mountains, which would be unwise," Cassius said, glancing down the right path before taking a step forward. Helai shook her head. "Maybe we will run into dwarves, and they will know the way out."

"If they do not imprison us first," Cassius said. He stopped and turned, raising an eyebrow. "I do not care who follows. I am going straight."

Helai glanced down the right tunnel hesitantly, but the others were already following Cassius down the main tunnel.

I can't continue by myself, Helai decided, turning away from the right tunnel to catch up to the rest of the group. She needed to get out of these mountains, find Massoud, then Aryan, and then the rest of her Ghosts of Light.

She took a deep breath and exhaled in frustration as she followed the rest of the group into the darkness.

Chapter Five
Linda

The cavern they had fallen into had been full of stalagmites and stalactites, rough and rocky, but these tunnels were smooth and carved out, easy to navigate. Linda huffed as they dragged their feet, ambling through this dark place and wishing for home. Linda couldn't remember when they were born, only that it was long ago. Life before traveling with Intoh had been much of the same: guarding the cities built by drikoty. Krok'ida were used to protect and build for the greka as they tended to the study of knowledge and magic. It filled Linda with a low rumbling ire every time magic was performed; it reminded them of each and every time a greka would hit Linda with a small magical bolt for disobedience. Linda had protected the city of Ko'kala for hundreds of years without failure. Then, one day, dark things came out of the forests and butchered Linda's home. Ko'kala was a peaceful village, their leader a small shamanic greka named Mi'k that loved krok'ida as much as his own kind. When the dark eldrasi slaughtered him and burned their village to the ground, Linda returned the favor when the other krok'ida charged to protect the innocent people of Ko'kala. They murdered each other, and Linda was the only one left. Linda wasn't sure how long they sat, staring at the ruins of their beloved city without a purpose. Then one day, Intoh burst out of the woods, eyes wild.

"Come with me. Protect me," Intoh had said, and Linda had obeyed without question.

This time, they would not fail.

Rooster's torchlight depicted runes that decorated the wall near the ceiling and floor, but Linda had never learned to read Alkazed, the language of the dwarves, and could not tell what they meant. The runes were faded, and Rooster hummed as he raised his torch to look at them.

"These tunnels must be abandoned. They don't look like they've been tended to for quite some time."

"Beautiful," Helai commented, leaning down to trail one of the runes with her fingers. "I've never met a dwarf."

"Let us hope we don't cross their path," Cassius said. "They believe strongly in home and hearth, and you two will find immediate hospitality from them, but Linda, Intoh, and I will be greeted at the end of a blade. We should avoid them, if possible. These tunnels, if dwarven made, should spill out at the top sooner or later."

"But the dwarves might have some explanation for those rats. Why they were mutated, why they spoke, what their purpose is," Rooster said.

"And why do you think they would tell us anything?" Cassius argued.

"My charm and good looks might be able to sway them," Rooster retorted, swinging the torch towards Cassius to get a better look at him.

He shrank away in anger. "I think not."

Linda stopped listening after that. They didn't care to hear any longer as their stomach protested loudly. "Hungry," they said. "Want food." As Linda watched Rooster and Cassius continue to bicker at each other, they contemplated eating one of them. Perhaps they would eat the loudest one, or maybe they would just eat both. Cassius was bulkier, but Linda was confident they could find room in their stomach for the both of them. Oh, maybe just Rooster. He smelled better than Cassius did.

"You will bring more rats down upon us if you don't shut up," Helai said with a warning look.

Cassius and Rooster fell into silence once again.

The sound of dripping water called to the krok'ida's neverending desire to be near it, but Linda ignored it, turning their attention instead to the soft sound of gnawing and a fast heartbeat. Intoh sat on Linda's shoulders, his fingers curled tightly around the thick of their neck, and he whispered about someone named Ekalas as they drew near an opening to the right. Intoh spoke to Ekalas a lot, but Linda wasn't sure what Ekalas was since they had never been able to see them. The one time Linda tried to ask Intoh had gotten terribly angry with them.

Cassius sidled up to the side of the doorway as Linda approached. Peering through the door, Linda bent over to pluck a small stone from the ground.

Two of those enormous rat-like beasts stood hunched in the middle of the room. They stood on two legs but were curled in on themselves, coming up to Linda's chin. If straightened, the krok'ida was certain the rats would be near them in height. One was missing nearly all of its fur; small tufts of black burst from its back and head. The other twitched as if it wanted to keep still but could not. Both wore breastplates forged from scraps and gleamed like they had not been worn long.

"No, no! We must eat, eat-gorge. Consume flesh; give us strength for the above world. Yes, good. Let us consume-feast."

Linda did not enjoy the sound of their voices, like rocks sliding across more rocks. Raising their arm, Linda threw the pebble in their hand, striking one of the rats in the shoulder as it happened to turn. The rat hissed and cowered before turning and lunging at the other rat, its hackles bristling in rage.

"You will die-kill! I eat you now."

The rats scuffled, their claws tearing at each other, scraping against armor as they each attempted to dominate. Linda stepped forward, hungry for combat, and Intoh could not stop them in time before the rats stopped fighting, sniffing the air and turning to look at Linda with beady red eyes.

"You! You threw the rock-stone. Time to eat-die!" One rat yelled, charging forward.

"Such a shame; it would have been easier if they had just killed each other." Cassius sighed from behind Linda.

"No worries," Linda said before pausing. "I kill now." The halberd Helai had given them was drawn from their side, crudely made and rusty.

"Wait! Wait, wait, wait," Intoh said, using magic to levitate off Linda's back towards the edge of the room. He waved his hand. "Proceed."

Linda charged forward, their halberd slamming one rat into a wall. A crack resounded through the air as the rat's body broke on impact. A gurgle exhaled from the rat's lips as Linda quickly stabbed the rat through the heart. Its body decayed at an accelerated pace, its skin rotting as it festered and slipped from the halberd to the ground. The other rat jumped back, a purple luminescent breath trailing from its mouth in a foul taunt.

"No, no!" the rat screeched as Linda dodged its blade and bit into the rat. The overwhelming taste and scent of rot assaulted their senses, death tasting on their tongue, and something they could not identify— raw energy that tempted Linda to taste more. The rat struggled, biting at them with gnashing, jagged teeth, but it could not pierce through Linda's scales. The krok'ida tightened their mouth around the rat's throat until the thing went limp, and then the room met silence.

Linda hissed in disgust as they let the rat drop to the ground. Had the rats not smelled so bad, they might have eaten the corpses. Instead,

Linda held their mouth open, hoping the smell would dissipate. The others entered the room, barely large enough to fit everyone comfortably. Cassius delved further into the room to make way for Rooster and Helai. Flies swarmed a rotting pile of corpses in the corner. It was evident that the rats had been feasting on the bodies before they'd arrived. Cassius knelt next to the massacre and picked up one of the severed hands. A ring was wedged on the swollen finger. To Linda, it bore no interest, but Cassius looked at it thoughtfully.

"We could use this. This looks far too valuable – if we run into any dwarves, we could tell them whoever this was was still alive when we found him. They might grant us passage if we tell them he told us to deliver such a message."

Helai chewed her lower lip and shook her head. "That would be dishonorable to his spirit, and we should let him rest."

Rooster shrugged. "Either way—we should take the ring. Whoever it belonged to, their family would want it back. We can decide what we do or do not tell them if and when the time comes."

Cassius nodded, tore the ring off the finger, and placed it in his pocket.

Ambling over, Linda took the severed hand from him.

"No, no, Linda. We don't need you to eat this one," Intoh said, forcing Linda to halt. Linda snorted and dropped the hand, disappointed. They were still hungry. Eating the rat corpses was out of the question, and a few sniffs from Linda revealed there was no viable food in this dark place except for the two humans. Intoh would scold them if they ate the humans, though.

"Do you guys hear that?" Despite them growling another warning, Cassius brushed past Linda and pressed his fingers to the wall, his head cocked to the side to listen. Linda raised their head, and after a moment, they heard it too. It was small and faint, but it was all the same, like thunder in the distance.

"I'm going to go and look. Stay here." Cassius disappeared in the shadows, and Linda could smell the rot of his dead body.

Good, they thought, *he reeks.*

"Linda, twist your ring. Must conceal ourselves in case dwarves come." Intoh tapped the ring on his finger, nothing more than a glint of silver, and then gave it a twist.

A shimmer of light so quick it could have been mistaken for a trick of the eye passed over Intoh, and then he resembled a human of small stature with golden brown hair and blue eyes. He wore simple clothes, a white tunic over brown shorts, but his smile etched the same devilish nature. "Come on now."

Linda huffed out a breath, then shook their head. "Linda no like. Linda like Linda."

A twitch of impatience crossed Intoh's face as he reached out and turned Linda's ring for them. "Like Linda too, but not everyone does. Must do what it takes to ensure survival."

The magic that slid over Linda was disconcerting. It was like their skin was stretched too thin over their scales. A warmth shuddered through them before going away completely, but Linda growled at the feeling nonetheless as they shrank down a couple of feet. The first time they had seen their human form, they had been tempted to fight their reflection—--a tall, broad-shouldered human male with dark hair peppered with white and eyes a mixture of sea green and blue.

A sharp exhale sounded behind them, and Linda looked to Rooster and Helai. Helai looked confused, and Rooster weary. The brand on Linda's thigh burned, and they felt Helai's and Rooster's emotions as if they were their own. Unsettled, Linda shook their head, attempting to eliminate the feelings.

"What just happened?" Rooster asked.

"Illusion magic? I have seen my big brother wield it efficiently but did not know drikoty were able to use it," Helai said, moving forward. "I cannot even tell you are anything but humans."

"Well, you see—" Intoh started, but his explanation was cut off as Cassius stumbled back into the room. His hair was in complete disarray, and his expression was wild. The stench of those rats rolled off him now too.

"I found a potential way out, but we're going to have to be quiet," Cassius said. He composed himself, though he still looked shaken. Linda was eager to see what caused his fear; Cassius didn't seem to get startled easily.

A peculiar look crossed his face as his eyes fixed upon them and Intoh. "You are the lizards, are you not? Those illusions must have cost you a fortune."

Intoh had plucked them off a vampire whose magical shop had whirred and spun with fascinating lights and magic. The vampire had nearly killed them both, and Intoh had lost his tail in the process, but they'd managed to escape. It had taken Intoh's tail two months to grow back.

Intoh grinned. "Didn't pay a single skael."

"Fascinating," Cassius said, circling Linda. "How does it work? I merely hide my undeath under a faint illusion, but the illusion can still be broken. This is so…solid."

Intoh held up his ring. "Plucked these off a merchant in Amajin."

Cassius' eyes flickered in alarm. "The Silent Fox domain? Those are some powerful vampires you aim to displease, Intoh."

Intoh waved his hands in dismissal. "Got away. Will handle if they come looking. For now, benefit from rings."

Rooster studied Linda for several moments, saying nothing. Leaning down, he picked up a small rock on the floor, aiming for where Linda's head used to be. Throwing it, the rock shot through the space above Linda's human head, hitting the wall behind them with a slight sound.

"I imagine only Amajin's high vampires were able to make illusions strong enough to bend the will of physical form. It is the only reason I believe you," Cassius commented, watching the rock sail over Linda's head.

"And your clothes changed," Helai commented, finding the courage to draw close to Linda. Linda decided they liked Helai and did not snap at her with their jaw, choosing instead to stay perfectly still. Helai studied their clothes, reaching to feel the fabric under her fingers. She inhaled quietly in surprise. "It's real," she whispered.

"Clothes change and come back between forms. Don't wear clothes in greka form," Intoh murmured impatiently. "Should move on. Come, Linda."

Eager to be out of this damp, dark place, Linda followed him. They did not like the underground; it felt as if the walls were closing in on them. Selfishly, they wished for the ocean, where they could swim and bask in the sun. The dream was quick to fade. They were on a mission for Intoh; other desires could wait until Intoh figured out how to live longer. He didn't share much with Linda, but sometimes Linda heard him muttering to himself when he thought they were sleeping. If they defy sickness or injury in combat, Linda could live forever, but Intoh's life was short, shorter than three decades. Linda didn't know how old Intoh was but could not imagine a life that was so fleeting.

Chapter Six
Rooster

As they walked, Rooster took a swig of his flask and studied it again as he pulled it from his lips. The shoma'kah had given it back to him after he'd won his third fight, and he'd been wracking his brain over the initials faded on the brown leather since.

"C.W.?" Helai asked, walking alongside him.

Rooster hummed in acknowledgment. "They're initials, but I still can't remember if they're mine or someone I murdered before I lost my memory."

Helai did not laugh, but he thought he saw the corner of her lip twitch in a suppressed smile. "And that? What is that?" She gestured to a tooth attached to a leather band wrapped around the mouth of the flask. "Is it a tooth?"

"I think so," Rooster agreed, unwrapping the tooth from the flask. The leather was long enough to wear as a necklace, so he slipped it around his neck and tucked it into his shirt. "I'm not sure what of, though. A large snake, maybe?" He struggled to keep the frustration out of his expression, but Helai saw right through him.

She placed a hand on his forearm and forced him to look at her. "Your memories will return, Rooster," she said gently.

Rooster laughed, a bitter noise, and shook his head. "We both know the gods aren't merciful." Helai smiled sadly as Rooster clipped the flask back to his belt and moved ahead to stand next to Cassius.

"I think I see something," Rooster said. Off in the distance was a faint and slow pulse of purple light, and it drenched an opening of the tunnel in its glow. Rooster glanced at Cassius before putting out his light.

"It is what I saw earlier," Cassius said quietly, reaching for the sword at his hip. "I did not investigate further, but I heard more of those rat creatures." Rooster walked in front with Cassius, the others lingering behind, and they urged forward, curious. Helai muttered her doubts behind him, but Rooster ignored her.

The glow faded, masking them in darkness. It was long enough for Rooster to reach out to touch the tunnel's edge. He suddenly regretted putting out his torch, and as they moved forward, Cassius lashed his arm out, halting Rooster in his tracks.

"Stop!" He cried out in hushed tones.

Everyone froze in the dark, uncertain of Cassius' warning, until the purple light pulsated again, revealing that they stood on the edge of a hundred-foot drop. Rooster's stomach leaped into his throat, and he glanced over at Cassius in silent gratitude.

"It's quite the fall," Rooster called back to the others, noting a small pathway to the left that led down to the ruins of an abandoned dwarven city carved deep inside the mountain. Their designs were immaculate even in their ruinous state, carefully sculpted to suit their magnificence. The buildings were forged straight from the rock, utilizing wood where rock did not suffice. Constructed close together, they dotted up the cliffside of the massive room, and old, worn-down wooden bridges strung them together. There was no wall, and on the floor of the city were buildings constructed mainly as what appeared to be forges, mine carts strewn about and knocked over.

"A mining city, perhaps?" Cassius pondered, and Rooster shrugged. His mind was a haze of unfamiliarity. He couldn't even remember his name, much less the politics of dwarves.

A statue was knocked over in the city's center, destroying several houses. It bore the likeness of a female dwarf wielding a pickax, her free palm holding a mound of gems. The gems were real and gleamed from a constant purple light that covered the room. The winding path led towards a bridge that would take them across the cavern towards another tunnel entrance or into the city. Rooster's skin crawled at the thought of going into the city.

"Something festers here. We should be careful," Cassius said as the purple light faded.

Rooster blinked in the vampire's direction. "Really? I was thinking of running and shouting to see if anyone was home. Perhaps to get the taste of dwarven ale and roast lamb?"

Cassius' expression deadpanned. "I do not enjoy your sarcasm, human."

"Silence. Look," Intoh said, pointing to the far side of the city as the purple light resurfaced. Rooster and Cassius moved towards the side to give the others a way to move forward. The light source appeared to be pulsating from under a nest of rats, crawling over whatever it was like cockroaches. The light fluctuated, the energy surging from it in waves, and each time it lit up the room, it highlighted the number of rats climbing over each other. There had to be hundreds of them. They had built makeshift buildings and homes over the ruins with mud, claiming the city as their own. The sight sickened Rooster to his core.

"We go now," Linda said, urging Rooster forward. He didn't need to be told twice. His nose clogged with rot and desecration as he led them, followed by Cassius, Helai, Intoh, and Linda in the back.

It did not take long to reach the bridge. Ancient scripture embellished the sides of the bridge, lavished in gold and infused with the purple glow of magic. It stood soundly, and Rooster was sure-footed as he stepped on it, confident he wouldn't plummet to his death.

"Uh...do you think those dwarves are friendly?" Rooster asked, halfway across the bridge as he spotted a couple of dozen dwarves across the cave stepping out of the shadows on a cliff overlooking the ruined city. More followed them to the sound of a low drum until several regiments lined the other side of the ravine. Low drawls of their war cries echoed off the walls, and the rats hissed below, their attention snared by the pounding of fists against shields.

Rooster watched them with his heart in his throat. If the dwarves were to attack the rats now, what would stop them from being in the crosshairs? Glancing behind him at the path they had just traversed, a thought crossed his mind. He owed nothing to the others, save for maybe Helai, who had been nothing but kind to him since the shoma'kah picked him up. They could sneak away and leave the drikoty and the vampire to fend for themselves. The way back would be deserted if the rats were busy fighting off the dwarves.

No, he decided. It wasn't the type of man he was, or so he thought. Anxiety crept through his skin at the unknown. He didn't know who he was before the amnesia, but he didn't want to desert now. Not really.

"We should run," Rooster said as the rats scurried up the cliffside towards the dwarves.

The dwarves shouted in a language Rooster did not recognize as they moved forward over the bridge. Balls of flame flung from the front ranks of the dwarves, cascading down the wall of rats and lighting them on fire. They screeched as they burned, several of them plummeting to their deaths. Rooster was not close enough to see how the dwarves utilized their flame. Magic? Tools of war? He shook his head and began to run, leading the group with Cassius across the bridge.

It did not matter. So long as the dwarves distracted the rats, then perhaps they could slip across the bridge unnoticed.

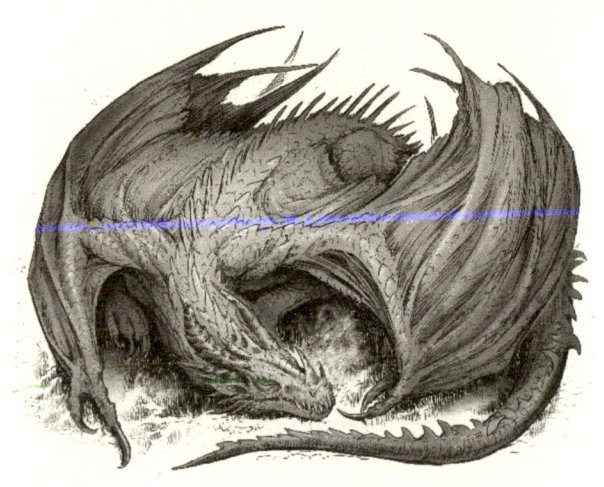

Chapter Seven
Intoh

This wasn't the first time Intoh found himself cursing his circumstances, his legs only moving so fast. He still remembered the exhilaration he had felt when he and Ekalas had decided they were going to murder their leaders to free themselves from their imprisonment. The day it had finally happened, Intoh had never felt so free. It was too bad that Ekalas had to pay the price that day with her life. The other greka had been Intoh's dearest friend–they had been seeking the gift of immortality together. Now it was up to Intoh to finish the task.

Calling out to Linda, he scurried up to them as the krok'ida passed. "I know I said to cloak, but need you to twist ring again. Bite more powerful in true form." Reaching forward, he twisted Linda's ring, uncloaking their lizard form.

Pulling himself up Linda's spines, he climbed onto their back and perched on their shoulder. There was no way he would outrun the horde of rats tailing them otherwise. Using his magic, he camouflaged himself in invisibility. He also attempted to cloak Linda, but he had used too much magic without rest in the initial cavern. Sweat gleamed along his brow, and his chest ached. It would be a shame to strain himself too much with magic use and pop a blood vessel in his heart, so he preserved his strength. Linda could handle themself.

Helai slipped on a rock, but before hitting the ground, Linda reached over and scooped her up. They threw her over their other shoulder. A soft noise of protest passed Helai's lips, but she did not struggle.

As they crossed the bridge, several dwarves moved to the cliff's edge and began to chant, their voices echoing off the walls. They wore nothing more than black pants tailored at the knee, and their bodies were covered in tattoos similar to the etchings on the walls of the tunnels they'd traveled through. The tattoos lit up in a soft purple as they continued to chant.

"What are they—" The ground exploded behind them, rocking the bridge. The screeches of rats dying were high-pitched and music to Intoh's ears. Turning his head, he watched with horror as the start of the stone bridge collapsed. The stone beneath him rattled, and he clung to Linda's neck fearfully.

"Run!"

It was desperation mingled with fear that got them across the bridge before it managed to collapse beneath their feet.

"This way. Through here!" Cassius shouted when they reached the other side. He ushered them through the opening in the cliffside. The room they now found themselves in was large, dimly lit, and empty except for four giant metal plates on the floor with dwarven runes etched into their surface. Even up close, Intoh could not discern what each rune did, only that they were all the same. An archway sat on the opposite wall, leading up. Perhaps it was the way out Cassius had spoken of before.

A giant rat fell from the ceiling, hitting the ground with such force that it left the party unsteady on their feet. Explosions sounded off in the distance, muted by the walls.

The rat's fur was stark white, and stood at least eight feet tall, nearly mirroring Linda in height. Its features were grotesque, mutated, twisted, and deformed. One of its legs was useless, but the rat had strapped a metal brace to keep it functioning, with cogs forged at the knee to give it mobility. A purple fluid ran through tubes decorating the metal plate work, and the rat parted its lips to reveal several rows of jagged, uneven teeth. Armor covered the rest of it, metal armor that kept it well fortified. Intoh cursed in his native tongue and hissed from behind the safety of his invisibility.

Linda did not hold back. An ear-shattering roar left their lips as they set Helai down and charged, halberd at the ready. Intoh jumped from Linda's back and watched the party break off—Helai slipped into the shadows to flank, and Cassius turned as four smaller rats fell from the ceiling. They disappeared into the darkness as they, too, masked their presence within the room's dim light. Rooster lifted his bow at the ready next to Intoh, nocking an arrow.

"You. Die. Now!" Linda roared in lizard-tongue, their halberd connecting with the rat's shoulder, disconnecting the armor and exposing the flesh underneath. The rat hissed out a curse and lurched back as the room darkened, magical energy ripe in the air. It made Intoh's scales crawl, a compulsion to retaliate with his magic.

"Did anyone see where it went?" Rooster held the nocked bow at his side, his eyes darting through the dark. Whispers came from the shadows as Cassius decapitated one of the smaller rats, his sword slick with its blood.

"There, to your right!" Intoh shouted. Surprise forced him out of invisibility as a flurry of white fur revealed itself from the shadows. Rooster shot without hesitation, an exhale sending his arrow across the room as the rat attempted to charge him. The arrow pierced the rat in the shoulder, but it only enraged the creature, who continued to charge. In an act of pure instinct, Intoh threw out his hand.

"*Asmit!*" A burst of light fled his fingers, sent onward by his word, striking the rat in its good leg and throwing it off target. It veered to the left, slamming into the wall and screeching in pain and rage. Rooster glanced in Intoh's direction, his eyes unfocused as he wasn't sure where to look.

"No need to thank. Know I am best." Intoh's heart pounded, adrenaline and magic coursing through his body. His fingers felt prickly like electricity was biting the tips, and his head spun, but he shook his head and forced himself to focus. One of the runes lit up, and a pillar of flame shot up towards the ceiling. The flame killed a rat on impact, its screams dying as it burned alive.

"Watch out. Plates on floor, very dangerous," Intoh warned, just as the one in front of him and Rooster lit up. The heat blistered his underbelly and sent him scampering back as Rooster flinched away. "Don't think dwarves care if they kill us," Intoh said, his eyes following a rat as it ran up to its master, who was still favoring his leg.

Intoh called to his magic once more, sending another shot of light at the two rats. The smaller had removed a syringe hanging from its side, the vial filled with a vibrant green liquid: aumbur in its purest form. It was a chemical that coursed through eldrasi and granted them their magic. In its natural state, aumbur was orange, but the green indicated it had been fused with herbs to create a healing concoction.

Intoh's magic hit the syringe, shattering it into pieces. The albino rat roared angrily and grabbed the smaller rat by the throat, lifting it up. The rat squeaked in pain and terror, its tail darting erratically as it clawed at the albino rat's hand. "Useless you are-are." Squeezing, the albino rat broke the smaller rat's neck and dropped the body to the ground.

"*Liiiiiiinnnnnnddda!*" Intoh shouted as Cassius struggled with a rat. It pounced on him, gnashing its teeth in his face, and Rooster quickly shot an arrow into the back of its neck, severing its skull from its spine. It went limp, but Cassius had no time to voice his thanks before another rat raised its steel at him. Helai appeared from the wall's shadow to stab the second one in the back before it could attack Cassius from behind.

Linda's head reared up and roared, charging into the albino rat before it could attempt another attack. Pulling out two knives, the rat faced Linda. One of the knives made contact, piercing Linda's shoulder. Linda's rage urged them forward, and they pinned the rat to the wall, grabbing its other hand to keep it from stabbing the other knife into their hide.

Linda shouted in the rat's face before clamping down on its shoulder and neck where the armor had slipped away. The rat had no time to scream before Rooster let loose another arrow. Its head slammed back against the wall, an arrow sticking out of its eye. A sizable chunk of flesh was freed from its shoulder as Linda pulled away. Their eyes still swam with rage and the hunger for combat.

But combat seemed to be concluded for the moment as Cassius liberated the remaining rat's head from its shoulders. Eyeing it with disgust, he dropped his sword to his side. Helai looked equally repulsed but remained silent, falling in step with Cassius to return to the party's side.

Intoh clapped his hands together, and small bolts of electricity danced between his fingers from the friction. "Well, that was fun. Wish to leave here and never come back again." He still did not know where the mutated rats had come from and hoped it was merely a small anomaly he'd never have to deal with again.

Rooster nodded. "Right. One... one second." He gestured to Cassius' sword, "Can I borrow that?" Stepping away, he approached the albino rat slumped across the floor. Hacking its head off, Rooster held it at his side. "This one seemed to be in charge, so I'm thinkin' it might gain the dwarves' favor and grant us hospitality should we run into them. Can't imagine they fancy the awful things we saw back there."

"What did we see back there, exactly?" Helai asked.

A shudder passed through the party as Intoh imagined rats scurrying over each other. When he and Linda had traveled the edges of Spine Mountain, he had read stories of dragon magic haunting the halls of the mountains. He had written it off as nothing more than myths, stories festered from fear that dragons laid dormant in the ground, doomed to return one day.

"Not sure I care to know," Rooster said, rubbing the nape of his neck.

Intoh shook his head. "Strong source of magic. Can feel it pulling at me here, now." The hum of magic sang stitches in his veins, compelling him to turn around and join the rats in their worship. He resisted the compulsion as his stomach growled. "Used a lot of magic today. Could use food and sleep."

"I, too, am beginning to get hungry. I don't suppose either of you wants to offer me your wrist out of the kindness of your hearts?" Cassius' eyes gleamed, his mouth parting to reveal a hint of fangs. Rooster shook his head, and Helai's brow furrowed in horror.

"No," she said. Intoh was thankful he'd never appeal to a vampire's appetite.

Now that the rats were dead, the runes faded from the metal plates on the ground, and steady footsteps echoed in the distance. Dwarves shouted in Alkazed, and Intoh scurried behind Linda in his human form.

"Linda, your ring," Intoh shouted in warning, but he was too late.

"Do not move. By orders of King Stoneheart, you will lay down your weapons and yield." Intoh did not know which dwarf spoke as dozens of them poured into the room, armored and carrying the flags of the mountain and their king. Many of them bore the same hardened expression, and none of them were without beards, grown long and wild. Intoh's hands went up in surrender, just as the others dropped their weapons.

"Tell your king we have so kindly liberated this great rat's head from its miserable shoulders in his name. We do not mean any harm to your kind." Rooster held up the severed head of the albino rat, its maw still open in mid-snarl.

One of the dwarves pushed through and spat at the ground near the rat's body. He was taller than Intoh with a fiery red beard and clear eyes. Braids donned his hair and beard, and he carried a crossbow, his arms covered in a dark purple cloak. "Damn rakken infesting our halls. They grow by the numbers each day." He glanced at Rooster and nodded in affirmation. "I will plead your case when you meet the great King Stoneheart." A gruff hum pressed his lips. "I'd wager his favor. We've been hunting these rakken for weeks. Come."

The dwarves encircled them, trapping them within their flanks, and Intoh felt the pull of fear tugging at his belly. Were they walking to salvation or a trap?

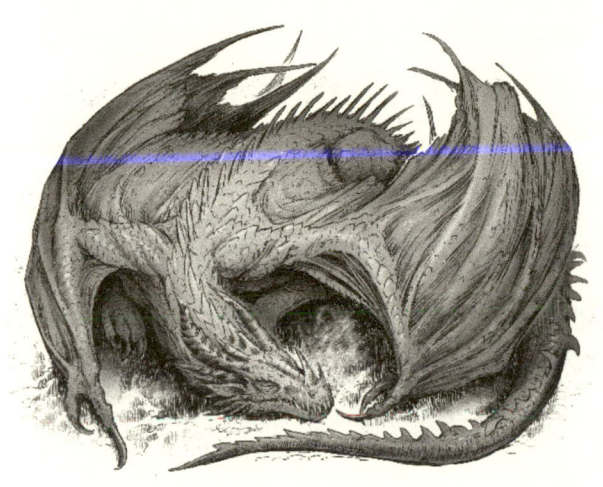

Chapter Eight
Linda

Linda did not know how long they walked, only that it was long enough for their limbs to feel weary and their patience to fade. They wondered when Intoh might grant them the chance to taste the tiny creatures that reminded Linda so much of the mountain around them. The dwarves reeked of earth, and that electrifying spice Intoh often smelled of, and Linda's stomach groaned loudly in protest. A soft growl passed their lips in response, and one of the dwarves spared them a glance, her eyes narrowing in suspicion. Linda took it as an act of dominance and stared back, their jaw parting in a challenge.

"Hey, none of that," Intoh spoke quietly, laying a hand on Linda's side in a warning. Linda looked at Intoh, their mouth snapping shut. *You lead with no cause*, Linda thought sullenly, though they dared not speak it. Intoh never cared to explain why they should stay quiet or why they shouldn't eat anyone that irritated them.

Several of the dwarves up front shouted in what Linda could only assume was Alkazed as they approached a new cavern rich with dwarven architecture. Stalagmites littered the floor. Glittering pools of bioluminescent water filled the numerous craters in the ground. On the opposite side of the cavern, a cathedral was etched into the side of the wall, brilliant beyond comparison. The builder in Linda was impressed. Its architecture was embellished with sharp lines and decorated with large dazzling gems. Two dwarves were sculpted on either side of the door, which reached heights Linda could not discern. They wielded hammers and shields of great splendor, the shields' centers bearing an amethyst of epic proportions. A bridge separated the army from the cathedral. The town before it was abandoned and in a state of ruin but no less magnificent in size and splendor.

Linda slowed as they neared the bridge, their weariness seeping like quicksand in their bones. Sometimes, the krok'ida wondered what would have happened had Intoh not asked them to follow him after his city erupted into chaos, their leader dead on his throne. Sometimes, Linda just wanted a big rock to lie on with the sun beating against their back. It was so dark and damp down whatever horrible place they had fallen into, and frustration halted Linda's steps.

A dwarf poked Linda in the back with the end of his ax. "Oi, keep movin'."

Linda thought about eating him first once Intoh gave the okay. It filled them with enough purpose to move, and soon, Linda stood at the cliff's edge before the bridge, staring down into the abyss. The bridge was wide enough to carry massive equipment to the other side. Large contraptions and pulleys graced the cliffside, and dwarves worked hard in forges chiseled right alongside it. When Linda glanced down, they could see nothing, the forge's smoke masking whatever sights lingered on the trench's bottom. However, Linda could sense something substantial down there, even if they couldn't quite smell it under the smoke. The air was thick with heat.

"What down there?" Linda asked, turning to a dwarf.

The dwarf did not respond, and Linda huffed, following Intoh. None of the party spoke a word as they crossed the bridge. The closer Linda got to the cathedral, the more they realized how large it was. The door could have easily accommodated Zhalzor, who had stood at several hundred feet by the time the ancient krok'ida had finally been slain in battle roaming the frigid wastelands of the North. Linda's kind never stopped growing, and Linda strived to be as big as Zhalzor one day.

The dwarves shouted as they halted in front of the door. There was a moment or two of silence before the doors opened, allowing them passage through. The army parted to let the dwarf with the dark hood through. He seemed to be in charge, and Linda wondered if Intoh would kill him, too, just as he had his clan leader back home. When Linda glanced at Intoh, they could not tell what he was thinking, though he did not seem to enjoy being down below ground any more than Linda.

The cloaked dwarf turned to look at them. "Welcome to Kaldrom. You will follow me, and I will lead you to our king."

The cathedral's interior was just as immaculate as its exterior, with swirling obsidian design and vast hallways. Within it housed a small city, and the dwarves had built structures and homes from the inside. Dwarves stopped to jeer and glare at Linda as the krok'ida passed.

"What Linda do?" Linda remarked, hissing in anger. "Linda just Linda."

"They don't take kindly to you because your kind kills mercilessly on the battlefield. Try not to take it so personally." It was Cassius who spoke, tucked safely behind his illusion. Linda started to regret not having twisted their ring. "If it makes you feel any better, they like vampires even less." He stared at the dwarves with ill-concealed disgust as they were led up a staircase towards another door.

A rumble passed Linda's lips as dwarf guards shouted in Alkazed. The hooded dwarf leading them responded, and the dwarf guards stepped aside as they walked through.

Inside the great hall were guards perched along a wall bearing little decorum. Tables lined the aisle, but they were empty, and at the opposite end stood an obsidian throne. Amethyst and other sparkling gems were crafted within its arms and dotted the head of the chair in the form of a dragon. Rooster was ahead of them, allowed more freedom with his movements, and he turned to walk backwards and marvel at the architecture carved into the ceiling that seemed to sing praise to the dwarven gods. A dragon was breathing fire on the forges of their ancestors, bringing them gems and weapons aplenty.

"*Kakurni! Kor ka vu keen.*" The dwarves stomped their right foot in unison and then beat their right fists twice in quick succession over their hearts. Through a side door emerged another dwarf, his beard dark, flowing, and embellished with silver clasps and amethyst beads. He was also clad in heavy plate armor, his dark eyes curious and unyielding beneath his helmet.

"King Stoneheart, what a pleasure. It is a shame dwarves don't see too far past their mountains, else, we might have made an acquaintance already." Cassius spoke first, his brow furrowed, his chin high. A quiet hush fell upon the room, silence infecting the air so quickly that Linda shifted on their feet.

King Stoneheart spat at Cassius' feet, his expression lit with rage. "You will do well to silence that tongue, *vampire*. I know the stench of your kind, and not once has one been allowed safely within my walls. Your human compatriots are granted permission to speak." A wave of fury passed through Cassius' expression, but he remained silent as Rooster stepped forward.

King Stoneheart turned to Rooster. "Tell me what has transpired and why there is such strange company in my halls. Humans mingling with *nicktkulvers* and krok'ida. Very strange, indeed."

Cassius' illusion slipped ever so slightly. Rot and death bled through, etching decay along the skin of his face, and his eyes glowed red as his monstrosity edged forward. Linda snorted at the stench, their nostrils flaring in disgust, and Rooster laid a hand on Cassius' shoulder to steady him.

"Sad to say it, Mr. Dwarf King, sire, but this vampire helped with your rat problem. He's kind of an asshole, but he proved his worth out there today. We were being transported to fuck knows where by slavers up top, and something caused us to fall into your abandoned tunnels. We're just trying to find our way out, but we ran into those…." Rooster shuddered. "Things."

King Stoneheart heaved a sigh. "Have you heard of rakken, lad?" The dwarves around them did not move, but the air in the room shifted. It was unsettling, and Linda's tail beat against the ground. Several guards lifted their axes, but King Stoneheart held up a hand to loosen their stance.

"I have not," Rooster said.

A hum sounded low in King Stoneheart's throat. "They're not just giant rats, as you might have guessed. We believe them to be a manifestation of humanity's greed, possessed by demons. They infest cities the most, but my grandfather's grandfather died fighting them."

Helai opened her mouth to speak, hesitated, and then stepped forward. "I don't know if this bears any significance to you, but we found this on one of the rats—or rakken—we killed. Or rather…" She paused for a moment, growing quiet. "We found it on a hand they were eating."

At her gesture, Cassius moved forward and revealed the ring he had plucked from the hand, and silence had never felt so loud. King Stoneheart stared at the ring for some time before he moved to take it.

"That's Hjaldor's ring." It was the dark-cloaked dwarf that spoke, his hood falling back over his shoulders to reveal untamed hair. His hand stroked his beard, and Helai looked between him and King Stoneheart with a worried expression.

"So you do know whose hand that belonged to?"

"Aye, lass. That was the king's eldest son. Hjaldor and his younger brother, Faerdren, have been missing for many weeks now. We held out hope…." He trailed off as the king pocketed the ring.

Stoneheart gave a long hard stare at Cassius, then did the same with Linda before he turned to the other dwarves. "The krok'ida and vampire are to be treated as guests in my kingdom." He gestured to the cloaked dwarf, who stepped forward. "My nephew, Obrand, will escort you to somewhere you can stay. With luck, you will not be here long, but the rakken have blocked all paths to the surface, and unfortunately, we cannot spare the men to escort you."

Rooster held up the albino rat's head. "And this? What do you wish to do with this?"

King Stoneheart gestured to one of his guards, who stepped forward to take the head from Rooster. "That rakken has been evading us for weeks. I'll see that you get paid for killing the beast." He spoke quickly in Alkazed to the guard beside him. The guard nodded and left, returning a few moments later to hand Rooster a hefty-sized pouch.

When Rooster shook it, coins clinked together, and Rooster's smile grew.

"Thank you, Your Majesty."

King Stoneheart waved his hand. "It's the least I could do for ridding us of that problem, even though there are still dozens more to take its place. I gave you skaels so you may use them in whatever human city you end up in. The choice to stay is yours. I have men to lead." With that, the king turned, speaking in Alkazed to his command. They all fell in line without question, disappearing back through the door they came in from, leaving only Obrand.

Linda was saddened to see the king go. They had a sudden urge to challenge him to combat. He looked to be a worthy fighter.

A hearty smell wafted through the halls from off to the right. Linda inhaled deeply, their stomach rumbling. It smelled of meat Linda couldn't identify, soaked in the salt of the sea. If Linda could figure out some way to be quieter, like they'd seen Helai doing during the rat fight, perhaps they could sneak away before anyone noticed.

"Come, Linda," Intoh said, and Linda looked off to the side room mournfully. Inside, dwarves roared with laughter, and Linda felt compelled to join them. Instead, they turned towards Intoh, following him away from the noise towards the front entrance where they'd come in.

Next time, Linda promised themself.

Chapter Nine
Helai

Helai twisted her fingers in her palm anxiously as they followed Obrand out of the throne room. The outside of the cathedral was a ghost town, the majority of dwarves fighting to reclaim the rest of Kaldrom. Intoh whispered in Linda's ear, who snorted and shook their head. Cassius was silent as stone, his eyes trailing the length of the cave system, likely seeking a way out. Helai could not discern Rooster's thoughts. He fiddled with the tooth necklace around his neck, something Helai often found herself doing with her necklace.

A low hunger pounded at the base of her skull, a quiet ache she couldn't place. It didn't feel quite like the hunger she was used to, but it demanded attention all the same. She rubbed the nape of her neck and tried to ignore it.

"Is that an armory?" Rooster asked, gesturing to an open building with an anvil and forge. It appeared deserted, but the coal in the forge was still warm, glowing a cherry red. Someone had used it recently.

Obrand looked to where Rooster pointed. "Aye. Smithy likely went off to fight the rakken. She'll gladly take your skaels if you have some to spare."

Rooster nodded, absentminded. "Later, then."

Obrand continued leading them up the cliffside and into a tunnel, where rooms had been carved out of stone. Torches lit their way, casting shadows about the walls, and Obrand finally stopped, gesturing to several of the rooms. "Take your pick—you're welcome to stay in any of them for the night. Most of this hallway is not being used, so you'll have privacy."

"Where can we find you should we need you?" Cassius asked, peering inside one of the rooms. Helai couldn't place the source, but the tunnels smelled of brimstone and rich earth, and she inhaled deeply as she splayed her fingers across the wall, peering inside another room herself. It was empty, save for a small cotton bed and table, but it would do. A small curtain of fabric was tied to the side, ready to grant privacy. Weariness settled in her bones, and it was only then that she realized just how tired she was.

"You lot will be alright, yes?" Obrand asked, glancing at each of them. "I have several matters to attend to, but I can find you later this evening. It's best if you don't wander around until there's time for word to get out of your pardons." His gaze lingered on Linda and Cassius, and then he nodded, hefting his cloak more securely around his shoulders.

"I'll make sure they'll stay out of trouble," Rooster said. Linda opened their jaw towards Rooster as if to take a bite out of his shoulder, glanced sheepishly at Intoh, and then shut their mouth again. Helai suppressed the urge to laugh.

"You're a good lad." Obrand clapped Rooster on the shoulder and turned to leave. The silence was thick after he left, and Cassius turned back, his shoulders square and tense.

"Where are you going?" Helai asked.

"This is ridiculous. I will find a way out myself."

A current of rage ripped through Helai. "And leave the dwarves to their fate? They told us the surface is blocked."

"Cassius right—it is ridiculous. Could find faster way out," Intoh argued, twisting his staff in the dirt. "Not our fight."

Helai threw her hands up in exasperation. "They could have executed us for trespassing or sent us along to face the rakken alone without any warning as to what we're up against, and you want to abandon them?" Shaking her head, she lowered her hands. The torchlight that soaked the tunnel in a faint glow illuminated Rooster's skin as he stared at her in contemplation.

"I agree with Helai. They've given us a good amount of skaels—do we not owe them one fight? Especially if it will bring us to the surface anyway." He winked at Cassius. "Plus, maybe they'll pay us more if we do a good job. I've seen you kill—I know you would be invaluable on the battlefield."

Cassius' shoulders relaxed as he turned, but his face was stone hard. "I will not risk my life for dwarves, and I would not recommend you join me, for I am famished." Rotted flesh mottled the corners of his lips, his eyes a faint glow of red as he retreated down the hall and disappeared around the corner. No one moved to stop him.

"By the gods, I hope I never have to run into him again," Helai muttered, pulling her braid apart only to redo it, twisting it to hang over her left shoulder. Her head throbbed as her headache worsened. She was glad to see the vampire go.

"Still think we should seek our way out. Want to go to Volendam," Intoh said, eyes glued to where Cassius had rounded a corner. "Feel more urgent lately." Helai touched her necklace thoughtfully. Intoh's claim wasn't too far off—she had felt more desperate to get to Volendam as of late. The urgency pooled in her belly, a dull weight that, while insistent, had been relatively easy to ignore.

The brand on her back burned.

"Want to fight," Linda said. "Kill rats." They seemed to ponder for a moment, their head cocked towards the ceiling. "Chew their bones."

Helai stared at Linda. She often couldn't tell if Linda was kidding when they threatened to eat everything in sight. "I think aiding the dwarves could benefit us, and being on a king's good side is better than him thinking us cowards," she said, locking eyes with Rooster.

Rooster shrugged. Helai couldn't tell what he was thinking as he stumbled a bit, leaning up against the wall of the tunnel. "It doesn't matter what we think. 'S not like we're a team or a group of mercenaries. Cassius proved that by leaving." He gestured down the hall to where Cassius had disappeared. "I think it would be good money—could use the skaels if they have more to spare. It's why I'm staying."

Helai scowled. Money was a strong motivator for a lot of people, but money changed them. She had seen it poisoning the minds of her own homeland for many years. Skaels would not decide her fate. Turning to Intoh, she gestured to the darkness of the hall behind them. "Have you ever traveled through these mountains?"

Intoh patted the side of Linda's leg and shook his head. "No."

"As we've seen, these tunnels are a maze—their paths are known only to the dwarves that traverse them. Seeking a way out yourself would find you lost or killed by those rakken. It would be better to stay, fight, and seek the dwarves' help getting back to the surface." Her headache grew more insistent, accompanied by a soft demanding tickle at the back of her throat. She exhaled sharply, pinching the bridge of her nose with her fingers.

"Perhaps right. Don't want to die to rats," Intoh said, picking at the wood of his staff. He glanced up at Linda and heaved a heavy sigh himself. "Will stay and fight."

Linda roared in response. The walls shook, and Helai's headache pierced her temple. She needed the quiet of darkness.

"Yes, will fight," Linda said, nodding. The torchlight gleamed off their scales as Helai sighed happily, waving her hand at the others as she turned towards her room.

"If we are to wait for Obrand, I will take advantage of these rooms and have a nap." She turned back to look over her shoulder. "Don't wake me unless we are being attacked or Obrand has returned."

It didn't take long for Helai to greet sleep, a welcomed venture that she had been desperate for the moment she took notice of the bed. It was almost too comfortable, having slept on the ground most of her life, but her head pounded with such demand that her weary mind pulled her into an immediate sleep.

She wasn't sure how much time had passed when she was wakened by the gentle shake of hands. How dwarves told day from night was lost to Helai. *Their eyes must hate the sun*, she thought to herself as she blinked, waiting for her eyes to adjust.

It was Rooster that woke her. "The dwarves have returned victorious. Obrand has come to tell us that they have set up camp outside the cathedral—they mean to celebrate tonight if we wish to join them." Helai sat up. Up close, Rooster had a deep scar in the stubble at his chin that she had only just noticed. She wondered if he had gotten it fighting in the pits during their enslavement or if it had happened before. She couldn't imagine not having her memories to recall.

"Did you tell Obrand we would remain to fight with them?" She asked.

Rooster shook his head. "Not yet. Cassius also returned a few hours after you went to sleep, and he hasn't said a word to me other than he would remain."

Confusion crossed Helai's face, but she didn't say anything. The vampire's motives were suspicious, and she didn't trust him. A quiet hum graced her lips in response as she threw her legs over the side of the bed and bent to pull her boots towards her. She felt the most rested she had been since the shoma'kah took her, her headache nothing more than a minor ache at the base of her skull.

"How long was I asleep?"

Rooster shrugged, watching her put her boots on. "It's difficult to tell down here. It's been quite a while, and I slept a bit too." He paused. "Is that necessary?"

Helai glanced up at him, confused. "What?"

He gestured. "Your boots. Do they need so many buckles?"

"Are you judging me right now?"

Rooster held up his hands, laughing. "I'm just saying–that seems like a lot of unnecessary work."

Helai ignored him and moved over to the rest of her things, which she had set on the small table that decorated the opposite wall. The air was stale, but a comfortable warmth seeped through the walls, lulling Helai into a relaxed state. If she listened hard enough, she heard the faintest of hums in the air. Magic, perhaps? She pressed her hand flat against the wall, where the humming vibrated vaguely against her fingertips.

"I feel it too," Rooster said behind her in a much somber tone. Turning, she found him watching her. "I don't know what it is."

"The mountain itself, maybe," Helai said, stepping away. "I have heard stories of these mountains having potent magic in their earth. It feels like stepping into the holy city of Shok'Alan, but stronger." Unease plummeted to her stomach. "We shouldn't keep Obrand waiting."

Rooster looked to say something more, only to change his mind at the last minute. Following Helai out of the room, they ran into everyone in the hallway. Obrand studied a scar trailing over Linda's snout, laughing.

"You fought a *Bruka?* Those bears are massive. You're lucky to still have a jaw at all, lad." Seeing Rooster and Helai exit the room, his attention shifted.

"Cassius tells us you mean to stay and help us." Helai narrowed her eyes at Cassius, who stared back at her with a calm, collected expression. He looked freshly fed, and Helai refused to think about who he might have fed on.

"We do," Helai said, focusing back on Obrand. "With the understanding that we will have our freedom to the surface soon."

"Payment would also be nice." Rooster piped up, folding his arms across his chest. He looked especially rugged, his eyes clear of any alcohol. They all looked like they could use a bath. Intoh's hair stuck straight up on one side.

"Payment would be up to the king, but my Rangers and I would be glad to take you to the surface. We mean to reclaim a mining town about a day's march from here that has been overtaken by rakken." Obrand grabbed his beard thoughtfully. "Our victory will ensure your safe passage under the mountain."

"Then it is decided." Cassius finally spoke, reaching up to brush the hair from his face.

"Indeed," Obrand murmured, clapping his hands together. "I wish to celebrate. Let us sit by the fire and drink our worries away, aye?"

"I would kill a hundred rakken for some good ale." Rooster agreed, tipping his flask to reveal it was empty.

"Ale? What is ale?" Linda questioned, earning a laugh from Obrand.

"Come on, lad – I'll show ya!"

Chapter Ten
Helai

It didn't take long to reach the camp the dwarves had set up since reclaiming Kaldrom. Fires stretched for miles, with dwarves drinking merrily around them. The warmth felt good against Helai's skin as they drew closer, sparking her homesickness. She missed the feeling of sand between her toes and the sun's heat on her back. Obrand wove through the camp, and they followed until they came to a stop at a campfire with seven cloaked dwarves surrounding it. Two of them were women, and they all had a mug in their hands as they roared with laughter.

"Obrand! Come and drink with us before Eirmus drinks it all for us," one dwarf shouted. Eirmus, one of the female dwarves with wild blonde hair and dark eyes, shoved the other dwarf before downing the rest of her drink.

"Oh, come off it, Kolin. You're just jealous because I can out-drink you every time. Stop being such a *Guvtek*." Several gasps echoed throughout the dwarves as Obrand took a seat next to Eirmus, clapping her on the back as she chugged the rest of her ale. Kolin grumbled in Alkazed, but his smile was genuine behind a thick, dark beard. His hair was heavily braided on one side and soaked in blood. No one seemed to notice their war-torn state, or if they did, they did not care, and Helai found herself comforted among the easygoing nature of the dwarves.

"Cut the lad some slack. Give him a chance to redeem himself," Obrand said. Quiet laughter shuffled around the group as Obrand gestured for Helai and the others to join them. Cassius took a seat away from the fire, and Rooster settled between Obrand and a dark-haired dwarf with thick eyebrows and a thicker beard.

"This is Drithan," Obrand said, gesturing to the dwarf next to Rooster. "Don't speak much Vilris. You met Kolin and Eirmus." In response, Kolin and Eirmus raised their mugs, and Drithan sipped at his drink silently. Obrand pointed at two dwarves sitting across from him. One was another female with fiery red hair and wild, ice-blue eyes. Her smile had gaps in it, her expression wild. The male next to her was broad-shouldered with tattoos lining his face. They looked like runes, similar to the ones they'd seen on the walls of the tunnels, but Helai couldn't recognize any of them. "Those two are Jaera and Ryzuk."

Rooster lowered his head in a bow. "Won't remember any of that, but we're just here to drink, yeah? I'm Rooster." He waved his hand in Helai's direction. "This is Helai—the one with entirely too many buckles on her boots."

Helai frowned, exasperated. "I do not."

Rooster ignored her, introducing everyone else. "Cassius, Linda, and Intoh. We had the pleasure of falling into your tunnels and meeting the rakken firsthand."

Pulling a book from his bag, Intoh settled against Linda, waving a hand when Obrand offered him a mug. Linda took theirs eagerly, and Obrand chuckled as he moved over to give Cassius a drink, which Cassius gladly accepted.

"Leave it to Obrand to familiarize himself with you lot," Kolin said. Attention was diverted as Helai was handed a mug herself, which she took gratefully. It had been some time since she had enjoyed alcohol and had never had the chance to try dwarven ale. The wine was the drink of choice in Shoma, sweet reds that stocked the cellars of nobility. The dwarven ale had an earthy smell, a mountain herb of some kind. Its taste was unforgiving. Helai coughed, hitting her chest as the ale burned down her throat.

"Dragon's Breath Ale isn't for the weak, lass. It will take the edge off and fill your belly with warmth, though," Obrand said, raising his mug to Helai. The other dwarves laughed, ale slipping out of the sides of their mugs and staining their beards.

"No, I like it." Helai wheezed as she drew the mug close to her lips. Her words were genuine—the smoky taste of the ale was pleasant, and it was easier drinking it the second time. "Is all dwarf ale like this?"

"Some dwarves in the southernmost cities of the Spine Mountains brew lighter ale, but we prefer it dark and hardy up here, where the chill can be kept at bay by its consumption."

"Aye, and we like it strong!" Eirmus beat her chest with a fist, turning a playful gaze to Kolin. "Ain't that right, Kolin?" Kolin responded in Alkazed, and Eirmus laughed, guzzling the rest of her ale before moving to pour herself another.

"And you lass—what is the drink of choice where you come from?" Obrand asked. Linda took a tentative sip of their ale before huffing loudly and downing the rest in one massive gulp. The other dwarves seemed weary of Linda but cheered when Linda finished their drink, their appreciation lighting the expressions of unease on their faces.

"Wine," Helai responded simply. "I traveled with a group called the Ghosts of Light for a time, and wine was the drink of choice among us."

"Ghosts of Light? Sounds dramatic," Jaera said. The rest of the group had quieted to listen. Cassius stared out into the darkness, and Helai could not tell if he was listening. Rooster eyed Helai with a sense of laziness, his eyes half shut as the fire glinted off his skin.

"As dramatic as a band of thieves can be, I suppose." Helai shrugged. "We were just a group of people trying to survive. It was a long time ago." Half-truths and a lie; she had been with the Ghosts just six months ago, and while they *were* all just trying to survive, their purpose was much more significant. Killing the tyrant, Mohalis, was no light task. Still, she knew it would not be wise to spread the news of their intentions to those she wasn't sure she could trust, so she smiled softly behind her mug and waved her hand.

"Anyway—wine is one of the biggest trade items in Shoma."

"Was never a fan of wine. Too sweet," Obrand said, shaking his head. He stood, moving across the campfire to reach the keg, where he refilled his mug. "To each their own."

"Not all wine is sweet," Cassius said finally, turning his attention towards the campfire. "The dry reds of Hestia might suit you better."

"Can a vampire even drink wine?" Helai asked before she could stop herself.

Cassius' gaze burned daggers into her. "So long as the curse is healthy and thriving, I can enjoy simple pleasures, same as anyone."

A heaviness settled in the pit of Helai's stomach at the thought. She turned away from Cassius, ignoring the feeling of his eyes on the side of her head.

Obrand shook his head, gesturing to the keg. "I'll leave the wine-drinking to you, nightwalker." A sigh escaped Obrand's lips as he sat back down. "In other regards—I am grateful that you remain. Rakken are nasty creatures that reproduce at speeds we cannot keep up with. It will be good to have seasoned fighters at our side."

"You say rakkens are demons that feast on human greed. Why have I not seen them before? I have been to large cities like Fraheim, and any city in Nantielle is rich with greed. Why are they not overrun?" Cassius asked, one leg bent as he leaned against the wall. He sipped his drink, and Intoh peeked over his book as he tuned in to the conversation.

Obrand stroked his beard. "We're not sure, lad. If you ask humanity, most will write rakken off as a myth, something that does not exist."

Cassius' laughter was bitter. "I just killed enough of them to know humanity is full of shit, but with how many we just witnessed? There is no way they have hidden away."

"We've not had to deal with them for several hundred years, lad. I don't know where they went or why they're here now, only that something's woken them, and they hunger for Draugmin."

"Draugmin?" Intoh asked, staring at Obrand. "Never heard of it."

Jaera leaned forward, her eyes honey-soaked and bright as the alcohol tinged her skin red. "You know the sap that collects on the trees of Daesthara?"

"Aumbur?"

"Aye, lad. Draugmin is similar; it comes from dragon scales mined from the Spine Mountains. They are gifts from our god." Obrand raised his mug, soon followed by all the other dwarves in the vicinity. "Praise Kurzda." The dwarves all shouted, "Praise!" and drank deeply. Cassius shifted as Linda downed the rest of their drink and handed it off to Obrand. The name sank into Helai's bones, a heaviness that felt elevated from the ale.

"More?" Linda questioned, and Obrand filled it eagerly.

"You look large enough to drink a keg on your own, lad."

Linda hummed in agreement as Obrand laughed.

"The draugmin is what gifts us with magic, as we are not like the eldrasi with their aumbur, nor do we have saelic running through our veins as the humans, and those wee lizardfolk do."

"It is why you use runes. They are a focus," Cassius said, his expression turning thoughtful.

"It is. We don't have a fancy magical muscle to flex like these humans here, hmm?" Kolin said, gesturing to Helai and Rooster. "It's the safest way to cast without hurting ourselves."

The company went quiet after that, content with talking amongst themselves. In the campfire next to them, a male dwarf sat with a small child. A toy rested within their hands, made of stone and carved into the likeness of a dragon. Its maw was outstretched, and the child squealed with laughter as her father pressed his finger to a rune on the dragon's side, and a small spurt of fire shot out from its mouth.

Helai turned to Linda. "It's Lindrz'kt, right?" Helai struggled with the pronunciation, and Linda nodded, returning to a seated position. Helai twisted her hair into a braid. It was the first time she had been near Linda outside the threat of battle. Old scars ran along Linda's scales at their snout and legs, a testament to former fights. "What did you do for fun back home?"

"Just call Linda. I... like Linda." They pondered Helai's question. "I fought. I built. That all."

Without looking up, Intoh interjected, "Krok'ida are used to fight wars and build cities. Otherwise, they sit, they sleep, they find water to bathe in."

Helai pressed a finger to her chin. "Sometimes simplicity can be a good thing."

Linda shrugged.

"And Cassius—" Helai turned to look at the vampire, who had contented himself staring off into space. "Are vampires capable of having fun?"

"Ah, yes." He leaned forward, the fire dancing off the gleam of his teeth as he smiled. "We indulge in sex, wine, and politics. Blood orgies are frequent, and sometimes the thrill of the hunt is so pleasurable we can hardly stand it. Is that what you wanted to hear?"

A quiet hush fell over the company as Cassius leaned back, his expression stony and absent of his earlier smile. The answer did not please Helai as her hand went to clasp the pendant at her neck.

"Like necklace. Make one someday," Linda commented, leaning down to peer at the eye.

"You would have to have a long string," Helai said, staring at the thickness of Linda's neck.

Linda hummed, a low guttural sound as they leaned back and repeated themself. "Make one someday."

Soon enough, the dwarves began to exchange stories, and Intoh fell asleep with his head pressed to Linda's side as Rooster told tales of his time enslaved to the shoma'kah. Helai contented herself with watching the dwarves around the campfires. Most of them were soldiers, but some were dressed in regular clothing.

"Oi?" Rooster shouted, gathering Helai's attention. A raven-haired dwarf lowered his head, speaking to Obrand in Alkazed. Obrand laughed and gripped the other dwarf's shoulder.

"Drithan doesn't know much of Vilris, you see. He's been learnin', but he ain't too confident." Obrand laughed again.

"Oi," Linda shouted. They parted their maw and attempted to lift their lips like they had seen the others do many times. Helai stared at Linda.

"Are you trying to smile, Linda?" she asked.

"Hah!" Obrand and the other rangers laughed. "A lizard's first smile. It must be euphoric. Don' go an' break a tooth, lad!"

Linda stopped, deflating in defeat, when Helai protested, "No, wait. Do it again. You almost had it." Linda complied, pushing their tongue up against their teeth and opening their jaw. Squinting their eyes, they received another flurry of laughter from the dwarves. Linda looked over at Helai again, who gave them an encouraging nod.

"You'll get it one day," Helai said.

"Aye, that you will, lad! Now it's time for drinking and stories to lift our spirits before we dive head first into more rakken," Obrand shouted, holding his mug high.

Drithan gave Obrand a shove, murmuring something in Alkazed. Obrand tilted his head back and grinned as Drithan pulled out a pipe and packed it with tobacco.

"Who here would like to hear the story of how me wife and I single-handedly slew a gront, one of the mighty giants of the north?" Obrand asked.

Rooster took a swig of ale, a coy smile crossing his face. "Go on then. You can't lead with suspense and then hold your tongue," he said.

Obrand continued as Drithan puffed on his pipe, offering some to Rooster. "It all began when my wife—who was no more than another soldier to me at the time—pulled me aside and showed me a set of tracks leading away from our regiment. She had a thirsty gleam in her eyes, an accurate tracker at heart, and she asked me to help her hunt the beast. A part of me wanted to deny her offer, but what kind of warrior would I be to turn her down?

"So I followed her into the forest, her steps silent as we moved close to the ground. I was miserable—covered to my neck in mud, and it rained the whole time we were gone—but it was worth it when we entered a clearing and spotted the gront. It must have been ten feet high, reaching up into the trees to find a good branch to pick food from its teeth. Diandra—that's my wife's name. She was *mesmerized.*"

"How the fuck did you manage to bring down a gront that size, just the two of you?" Rooster asked, puffing away on Drithan's pipe and then handing it back.

"Giants aren't magnificent on their feet, you see. They are too large, and their legs are too gangly. We managed to trip it on a trap, and Diandra shot it straight through the eye. She looked so beautiful that day." Obrand marveled quietly, his eyes glazed over in memory. "We had giant stew for weeks after, didn't we, lads?"

Ryzuk waved his hand in dismissal. "We all know you didn't kill any gront, Obrand. Diandra kicked your arse in a fight and wouldn't accept your courting for months. You only won her over because of that thick head of yours." Laughter filtered around the campfire as Obrand shook his head in protest.

"My story rings true. Do not listen to Ryzuk. I have the scar to prove it." Obrand leaned over and pulled his shirt away, revealing an uneven scar that ran from the back of his neck to his shoulder. A growl of approval passed Linda's lips.

"Worthy opponent," Linda said.

"Worthy indeed." Obrand nodded in agreement, clinking mugs with Drithan beside him. "Truth be told, I've never felt so exhilarated from a fight since." Downing the rest of his ale, he offered another to Helai, who gladly took it. The ale was starting to make her head buzz, but she felt warm, a comfort she hadn't truly felt since leaving Shoma.

"And these rakken?" Cassius asked, forcing the campfire to quiet. "Are they truly a threat?"

Obrand glanced Cassius' way. "These abominations seek to consume the world in their filth, but they are not difficult to kill. The only advantage they truly hold is their sheer numbers. One day we will push them back into the darkness where they can rot in peace."

The group went silent after that as everyone settled for the night. Helai had moved to speak with Drithan, and she sat across from him, teaching him words in Vilris. It filled her with a sense of peace despite knowing the coming day would probably bring more bloodshed and death.

Clear mind, clear soul.

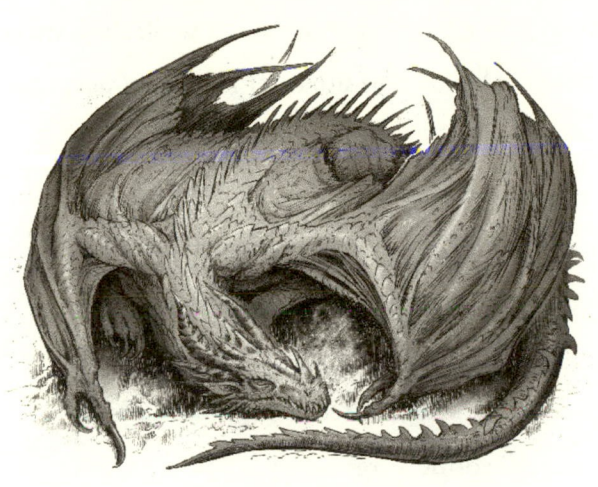

Chapter Eleven
Linda

In the morning, Obrand led them to a forge right outside Stoneheart's hall, and the process was fairly painless. Aerkron was a burly woman with large muscles and was tall for a dwarf. Her hair was long and thick, a curly red she had twisted up on her head to keep it free from her face and the fires. Her forge was nothing to be impressed by, and she gave Linda a foul look when they walked in.

"By order of the king, the party is to be outfitted by your best," Obrand said. Aerkron glanced at him curiously and then looked the party over.

"Don't have anything fer th' krok'ida. Have some vambraces I could make to fit 'em. Already got some leather armor to fit th' lot 'f ya," Aerkron said, gesturing first to Linda, then to the rest of the party.

"Go on then, Obrand. These lads will be here a while, 'n I know ya've got things ta attend to." Aerkron grunted. "I hope you have the skaels to spare."

Obrand nodded at Aerkron, and then looked to Rooster. "We'll be by the campfires again once you're done spending your skaels." He gestured beyond the stairs, down towards the door of the cathedral. "Look for the purple cloaks. Any of my Rangers will be wearing one."

Rooster nodded as Aerkron started to measure Cassius, who stood perfectly still. Helai walked the forge, staring at the various weaponry dotting the walls. The quiet conversation sounded outside, and calls of celebration began as laughter and music broke out over the camp.

"Linda want hammer." Linda turned to look at Aerkron, who did not look up from her measurements. Intoh clicked his tongue against the roof of his mouth as Linda stepped forward, reaching for a hammer lying on a shelf on the wall.

"Linda takes what dwarf blacksmith gives them," Intoh said.

Aerkron hummed in the back of her throat and turned to Linda. "I can give you a halberd. Best I can do for ya. My hammers are m' best work. I won't be givin' one ta th' likes 'f krok'ida."

It was getting exhausting, the desire to eat everything they couldn't have, and they found themself once again wondering if they could get away with it as Aerkron left Cassius' side and went over to the wall, where she pulled a halberd from its place.

Linda studied it quietly in their hands as Aerkron went back to outfitting the humans with armor. It was a little too light in Linda's hands, but it would do the job until Intoh could purchase them a hammer to wield.

"I hope ya don' have somewhere ta be. Yer gonna be here a while," Aerkron said.

Linda admired their new vambrace as they left the forge. Everyone had been given leather armor despite Cassius' mutterings about fighting better in plate armor, and each had been given the weapons they'd requested.

Rooster had a new crossbow strapped to his back, its base a beautiful dark wood surrounded by black metal work, and a new short sword in his grasp. Helai had been outfitted in a cloak of dark blue, with several straps housing various daggers. Intoh had refrained from everything but a cloak, and Cassius also had a new sword at his hip.

Linda was still sad they hadn't been given a hammer, but perhaps in the next town, Intoh would buy one from the blacksmiths there. Aerkron had only had enough material to make Linda one vambrace, and it was nothing more in design than simple silver, but Linda felt like they finally had a piece of the skin they had been missing.

Rooster swung his sword, the blade whistling through the air as he admired its movement. "The dwarves really do know how to forge beautiful steel." He marveled, running fingers over the flat part of the blade as he sheathed it.

Helai hefted her cloak over her shoulders. "I lost some things from the shoma'kah—I might try to find a general goods store."

"I'll go with you," Rooster said. "Might be the only time I'm in these mountains, and I might as well see what kind of goods they sell."

As they walked off, an exclamation sounded behind Linda. They turned as Cassius lunged out and grabbed Intoh around the throat. Intoh struggled, one hand reaching up to scratch at Cassius' grasp, the other holding an empty vial. A thin line of blood ran along Cassius' arm, but the wound had already healed.

"Stick me again, and I will not hesitate to break your neck," Cassius hissed.

"Linda... help..." Intoh gasped, his face turning red.

A silent rage overcame Linda as they reached forward and grabbed Cassius' arm. It was strange—the moment their claws curled around the softness of his skin, Linda felt the urge to go. They couldn't decipher where they were supposed to go, only that there was a quiet ache in their chest as the brand on their leg burned.

"Let go," Linda growled. They ignored their pain despite it radiating up their leg, opening their jaw as they breathed hot air into Cassius' face.

After a few tense moments, Cassius' grip on Intoh lessened, and Intoh fell to the ground, sputtering and gasping for air. The vial he had been holding shattered, scattering glass amongst the ground, and several dwarves eyed them as they passed by but did not approach them.

Linda immediately let go. The moment they did, the strange feeling in their chest went away. They stepped back as Intoh cursed at Cassius in drikotyian.

"Need to know how you live forever," Intoh said, switching to Vilris.

"That would be the vampirism," Cassius retorted as his irritation cut through his tone. It came off of him in waves that sank into Linda and whispered at their impatience.

"No fighting," Linda complained, turning away from the argument to scan the room. The open cavern was massive, and Linda eyed the pools of water in craters on the floor. "Could take bath," they suggested.

"I do not think the dwarves would appreciate our undressing," Cassius said.

"Already naked," Linda replied sadly, but perhaps the vampire was right.

"It's okay, Linda. Once we are back on the surface, we'll find the nearest creek for you to swim in," Intoh promised, eyeing Cassius remorsefully as he came back into Linda's line of sight. His right hand was bleeding from the broken glass, but already he was weaving his fingers as a faint white light stitched the wound close.

"Want more ale," Linda said sullenly. No one ever listened to what they wanted. It was exhausting, being nothing more than the one that guarded Intoh.

The feeling was fleeting as Intoh patted Linda's leg and gestured towards the campfire. "Wish to go and read more of my book."

"Fine with me," Linda said.

Cassius had followed Linda and Intoh back to the campfire they had entertained around the night before. It was surrounded by Obrand and the other Rangers, who were all enjoying more drinks and food that slow cooked over the fire. The food looked like some kind of meat rolled and soaked in a sweet glaze. Whatever it was, it made Linda's mouth water. Linda's stomach rumbled loudly, and Obrand laughed before offering them some.

"Here you go, lad. Though I expect it's not much for someone your size!"

As Linda tipped the plate back, Helai and Rooster returned.

"There you are," Helai said, rushing forward. "Please tell this drunken fool—"

"I prefer the term 'handsome vagabond'—" Rooster cut in.

"Drunken. Fool." Helai squinted her eyes at him. "He claims I am a bad haggler, but I know for a fact the owner of the general goods is just an old bastard with no eye for a good deal."

Linda lowered their plate, savoring the rich taste of the meat, and looked at Intoh, who shrugged from behind his book.

"Is she awful?" Cassius asked, gesturing to Helai. He had been silent the entire time, nursing a mug of ale. A tired look in his eye was accompanied by a vague hunger, and Linda shuffled away from him. Rooster nodded, his hand pressed to the nape of his neck.

"Worse than a troll trying to tie a shoe," he said in an exaggerated whisper.

Helai protested as they all settled in for the night. Many stories were told as Intoh rested against Linda, content with his book. Cassius was as silent as always, and Rooster exaggerated a tale of his past, which confused Linda. They thought he couldn't remember his past.

A weariness hit Linda, but they were too tired to fight it as they fell back and shut their eyes. Perhaps the next few days would bring worthy combat, and the confusing feelings would disappear.

Chapter Twelve
Rooster

That morning, they marched.

As they departed, they stuck close to Obrand and his rangers, hefting weapons over their shoulders and preparing for the long march ahead. They walked for the better part of the day. Rooster thumbed the tooth necklace around his neck as he walked, anxiety hanging low in his belly due to the upcoming battle. He did not fear a good fight, he did not even fear the thought of death, but something about dying without discovering who he'd been before his amnesia sent a cold wave of horror coursing through him. He did not pray to any god for mercy or salvation, and his numbness caused him to shuffle forward to Obrand.

Jaera leaned over to Obrand, whispering something in his ear. He laughed, clapping Jaera on the back, and turned to Rooster. "Are you ready for a good fight, lad? I expect it won't be too long."

Rooster nodded, tugging at the chain around his neck to show Obrand the tooth. "I meant to ask you last night but got caught up in the festivities. Do you know what this is?"

"Let me have a closer look," Obrand said.

Rooster tugged it over his head and handed it to Obrand, who studied it closely. Turning it over in his hands, he hummed, offering it back to Rooster. "Looks to be a hydra tooth. They're considered rare, so it might be worth something to an alchemist." Obrand eyed him curiously. "Alchemists don't often sell items that could be worth more in their potions. Where did you manage to get your hands on a hydra tooth?"

Rooster shrugged, pulling the necklace back down over his head and tucking the tooth underneath his shirt. "I'd love to know that myself," he admitted. He wasn't sure why he thought Obrand would have answers. Perhaps he hoped the knowledge would spark some memory in his head, but there was nothing. No spark, flashback, or flurry of remembrance when he looked at the hydra tooth. He sighed in frustration and took a swig from his flask, which had been filled with dwarven ale from the night before.

Helai fell in step beside him. She gave him a sidelong gaze. "You remind me of a friend of mine. You both drink like you'll never get another drop. I always told him it wasn't wise to drink so much before a battle."

Rooster laughed, drowning the last of his alcohol and then wiping his lips with the back of his hand. "Oh? And what excuse does your friend give for his alcohol-loving habits?"

Helai deadpanned. "Alcoholism, my friend." She paused, her head turning to watch the dwarves as they marched on. Rooster's gaze followed hers. Obrand leaned over to say something to Linda, who roared in groveling laughter. It was strange to see a krok'ida partake in such things. He'd never met one before, but Linda struck him as unusual for their kind. Softer, almost.

Helai continued, "He'd always say, 'Oh, but quite the opposite, little sister, for it dulls the demons and leaves plenty of room for thinking.' I always thought it was an excuse, but what do I know?" She shrugged, her gaze forlorn. Rooster struggled to refocus on her before steadying his feet. He would never grow used to dwarven ale and its strength.

"Hmmm. I think I like your friend. You must miss him," Rooster said.

"Massoud? Yeah, I do. I haven't seen him or the rest of my group for some time now." Helai's voice sounded far off. "He told me to meet him in Volendam if we ever got separated. I hope he waits for me there."

Rooster placed a hand on her shoulder. "We'll be out of here soon, and you can go looking for him. You seem resourceful."

Helai offered a smile. "Thanks, Rooster."

Rooster nodded, then left it at that. He could feel it, the rumbling of war. Drums echoed, and the sounds of screeching and dwarven cries filled the air. Obrand fell back into step with Helai and Rooster.

"Oi, Rooster. I reckon this is your last opportunity to take our offer and leave. This isn't your fight to bear."

Cassius spoke before Rooster could. "We are here now, are we not? Let us prove our honor and be done with it. What fools would we be to turn tail and run now?" His gaze pierced Rooster's, and then he nodded. Rooster found a smile forging against his lips as he responded in kind.

"You heard him. I can't argue with that logic."

Obrand gave a grim nod and beat his fist against his chest. "So be it. Let us make our ancestors proud."

They marched forward, the hallway diverging into a wasteland of devastation. It was an open cavern like before, with a cliffside offering a vantage point. Off to the right was the abandoned town, which lay in ruin. Several buildings no longer stood, their stone walls jagged and desecrated. Minecarts were abandoned, and dwarves lay dead in the streets. Some were half eaten, feasted on by the rakken.

Crimson stained the battlefield, eyes unseeing as corpses stared up at Rooster from beyond their grave. The artillery sat in front of them, massive cannons manned by dwarves wearing spyglass goggles atop their heads. The air was thick with smoke, and Rooster tasted the sweetness of magic in the air.

Obrand turned to address his rangers, his crossbow raised. "All right, lads. This is it. This is the time to show these bastards what we're made of. If you fall, fall with honor and dignity and greet your ancestors in the afterlife knowing you fought for something."

Obrand's rangers shouted in Alkazed, and Rooster felt drunk off dwarven ale and exhilaration. He gripped his sword at the ready as he stormed forward, flanking Linda and Cassius. The two of them paved the way forward, brushing up against the back ranks of the dwarves. Cassius fought with the structure and grace of a trained knight, killing rakken with every blow of his sword. Linda fought beside him, but they swung with reckless abandon, nearly cleaving dwarves with their halberd as much as rakken.

The rakken came in droves from every opening in the small cavern. They crawled on the ceilings and poured over each other through the tunnel openings. They did not fight in tight formations like humans and dwarves but threw themselves at the dwarves without regard for their own life. They fought with aggressive desperation as their teeth gnashed in unyielding determination.

"Cassius, Linda, the right side is caving. Help them reclaim it." Obrand gestured with two fingers to the right flank. There, swarms of rakken fought to overtake the dwarves with gnashing teeth and rusted swords. Purple saliva oozed from their mouths as they cackled and chanted in a chattering language.

"Rangers–to me." Obrand barked orders and everyone followed without question. "Rooster, you'll be in the back with the other ranged soldiers." Rooster's heart pounded in his ears as he gripped the sword more tightly in his hand, took a deep breath, and threw himself into the thick of the fight.

A rakken jumped in front of Rooster, a crude dagger in its hand. It looked him in the eye, a jagged white beard curling from its chin. Beady red eyes sparkled with malice. "Yes, good, man-flesh-filth. We eat-feast."

"Gods, you stink." Rooster grunted, swinging his sword. The rat hissed as it died, but the victory was short-lived as two more replaced it. The rakken seemed to fight with their overwhelming numbers rather than their ability to coordinate, and despite his best efforts to carve a path to the artillery, Rooster could not kill enough of them. The dwarves around him fought valiantly, but they were struggling—their exhaustion was written clearly in their expressions and slowed movements.

A bright lightning bolt hit the ground a few feet from Rooster, killing a rakken on impact. It was close enough for the hair on Rooster's arm to stand on end, the stench of burning fur clogging his nose.

"Saved your life," Intoh called out, scurrying close to Rooster. "You're welcome."

"You almost hit me," Rooster protested. The small greka was like no one he had ever met. Even in human form, he moved like a lizard, lanky and graceful. Intoh did not look pleased being surrounded by battle, his brow furrowed as he tucked himself behind Rooster.

"Keep me safe," he demanded, and Rooster rolled his eyes as he ducked under the swing of a rakken's sword and pierced it through the shoulder. It hissed and jumped back, but Rooster bullied it until he could break past its defenses and stab it through the heart.

"Just stay close," Rooster instructed. A wave of determination surged through him as Intoh scuttled behind him, and together they made their way towards the artillery. "Have you ever even been in a battle?"

Intoh took some time to reply as he urged little zips of electricity from his fingers, shooting them out at rakken that swarmed the dwarves. "Once or twice."

Rooster pushed aside a dwarf that fell against him, blood spurting from his lips as a rakken screeched, chattering in tongues. His heart pounded as he approached the dwarven artillery. Several of the dwarves screamed at each other. The one wearing goggles led them, shouting and gesturing to the back flanks.

"*Forvka!*" the dwarf shouted, and each cannon fired. Fear shot through Rooster at the thought of the mountain coming down upon them, but the cavern held large enough to brave the trembles of cannon fire. Rakken piled over each other, and the corpses of their dead as the cannons took them down in droves. Off to the right, Linda pushed back the rakken's ranks as Cassius shouted to the dwarves around him.

A purple light flashed beside Rooster, piercing the belly of the goggled dwarf. His mouth twisted in pain as purple lit up the dwarf's veins, quick as fire. Groaning, he fell to his knees, his flesh festering and mutating. It made Rooster gag as Intoh ran up to him, whispering into his hand. A small white glow pooled over his fingers as bile rose to Rooster's throat, but it seemed too late. Intoh's healing magic did nothing as gurgled words fled the dwarf's lips, his twisted hand floundering in the air. Rooster raised his sword at him for a mercy killing, but the dwarf gasped and widened his eyes, jerking away as his hand smashed at his goggles.

"Intoh, get away from him," Rooster gasped, swallowing the bile in his throat and ignoring its burning descent as he pulled Intoh away and plucked the goggles free. The dwarf's eyes rolled up into the back of his head, and then he mutated beyond recognition, sores etching across his skin as they grew and exploded, secreting a purple pus. The pus zipped with some electrical current, filling the air with magical energy, and Rooster stumbled away from it immediately, clutching the goggles in his hand.

"Thank you. Do not want that to touch me," Intoh said, staring at the dwarf. Rooster did not want whatever it was to touch him either, and they both approached the other artillery as Intoh watched their back, sending lightning to any rakken that got too close.

With the goggles in his hand, Rooster did not know what to do with them. He started to put them in his pocket, but a dwarf shouted at him in Alkazed, miming him to put them on. His stomach, in a knot of protest, Rooster slipped the goggles over his eyes. Suddenly he could see as if great distance meant little to him. Reaching up, he fiddled with the spyglass that covered both eyes, increasing his sight, and his nausea was forgotten. His grin was wicked as he sought out where rakken were pushing the dwarves back. As the dwarves loaded the cannons, he threw his hand forward.

"*Forvka!*"

The cannons rolled back as they all fired in unison, a deafening noise ringing in Rooster's ears as his joints ached in response. Each cannon round met its target, and as rakken were flung in the air by explosions, the dwarves pushed forward. Deep in the thick of it, Helai wove through the masses to deflect a sword meant for Kolin, who was bent over a dying dwarf.

Intoh drew close as Rooster pried off the goggles, pressing them into a dwarf's hands. The dwarf looked at him in confusion, and Rooster pointed to him and then the goggles.

"Better in your hands," he said, unsure if the dwarf spoke Vilris. Still, the dwarf seemed to understand as he pulled the goggles down over his head and turned away. Sheathing his sword, Rooster pulled his crossbow from his back and looked at Intoh. "Think you can cover me if any rat bastards get too close?"

Intoh nodded, fingers curled as electricity shot through them. "Yes."

Rooster took a deep breath as he stepped away from the cannons towards a line of dwarves shooting crossbow bolts. The line was still thick—the dwarven swordsmen had done an excellent job at keeping the rakken from tearing them apart.

Still, Rooster knew the battle was far from over.

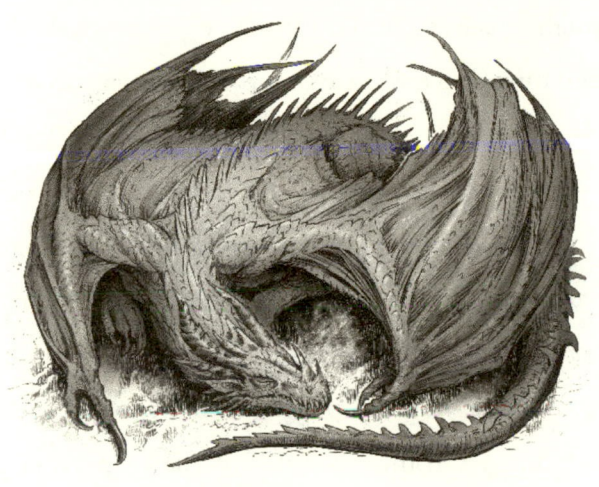

Chapter Thirteen
Cassius

"Keep a tight formation. Don't let them overwhelm you. Work with your fellow soldier as you fight. Trust each other." Cassius barked out commands despite himself. Some of the dwarves ignored him, knowing what he was, but some took his orders to heart after seeing him fight.

His right arm ached for a shield, but he made due as he ducked under the swing of a rakken's sword, lashing out with his own to pierce the rakken. The rakken screeched, and it rang in Cassius' ears long after he moved forward.

An ax came down on Cassius' side but was deflected by a dagger thrown to hit it and knock it off course. Helai's eyes met him for only a moment before she wove through the battlefield, wielding a dagger with expert grace.

Thick, wet laughter echoed in the halls. The fighting halted as the dwarves and rakken turned to look at an approaching mass that walked out of the tunnels, dragging a bruised and broken body behind it. A massive rakken materialized from the shadows atop the cliffside, bearing a small piece of draugmin and wearing blue robes, a hood cloaking most of his face. His snout was long and deformed as his hand curled, weaving some form of magic. Pulling the body up from behind him, he threw it at the cliff's edge, displaying it to the two armies.

It was a dwarf dressed in the shambles of ruined royal clothing. His head and chin were poorly shaven, and his arms and legs were riddled with wounds. Several of them secreted a purple pus, and his face was nearly unrecognizable as he heaved in broken breaths.

"Faerdren," the king shouted. A hush overcame the battlefield as the rakken mage stood above them, keeping the prince hostage. The magic he weaved earlier encompassed Faerdren in soft blue light, raising him to suspend in the air. Cassius' expression hardened as he tightened his grip around his sword.

The rakken mage gnashed his teeth together as saliva dripped from the roof of his mouth. "Dwarf-thing wandered where it should not go-go-travel with kin. First, dwarf-thing would not beg-cry, and this one scream-yell only when we shaved his beard-hair. Now," the rakken rasped, a wet grin stretching across his face, "you will watch him die-die." The rakken mage turned, pulling a dagger out of his robes and slitting the prince's throat.

Rage poisoned the room as the rakken mage flung the prince's body off the cliffside. As the king screamed, the dwarves around

Cassius beat their chests with their fists, shouting in Alkazed. Cassius' heart sank as the rakken mage backed up and lifted the draugmin in his paws towards the ceiling, swaying and chanting in tongues.

A portal began to open up behind the rakken mage.

The battlefield broke into chaos as the dwarves surged forward, shouting. Metal clinked together as the fighting resumed, and Cassius swung his sword as he moved forward to join the ranks in front of him.

A body barreled into his side, throwing him into the stone wall of a ruined home. He crashed through the stone, and it crumbled around him as a rakken fell on top of him, dripping saliva against his chest. "Chosen-chosen-marked you are! Skitter-flee away. One taste. One bite." The rakken muttered quickly to itself as it went to bite Cassius.

Cassius reached up to snap the rakken's neck, but a thunderous heartbeat echoed through him, jostling his bones. Before his fingers could make contact with the rakken's neck, it was lifted and pinned to the wall by Linda's halberd as Linda shoved the blade through the rakken's shoulder.

The rakken screamed as it struggled, purple-black blood soaking its fur. Cassius quickly moved to his feet and grabbed his sword, which had been thrown several feet away. The rakken's screams were silenced as Linda raked their claws over its throat, killing it quickly. Pulling their halberd from the wall, the rakken sank to the ground, blood gushing from its wound and soaking its chest.

"Thank you, Linda," Cassius said, peering around the house he'd fallen into. It looked to have been abandoned suddenly–wooden plates and bowls were thrown about what looked to be a small, one-room house. The table was broken, and mining tools rested in the corner.

"Should stick together," Linda suggested, gesturing outside. Where the dwarves' rage had won them a moment to push forward, the sheer number of rakken was overwhelming, and dwarves died by the masses.

A sickening feeling swept through Cassius, quick and merciless. They were losing.

Cassius looked up at the rakken mage. He was still chanting, and the portal behind it looked half-opened. He could not see what was on the other side, but they couldn't let it open.

"Linda, can you help carve a path to the cliffside and keep rakken from following me? I need to get up to that rat mage." He pointed to the chanting rakken. They stood a chance if they snuck through the ruined town instead of fighting through rakken.

Linda nodded, hefting the halberd in their hands. "Can try."

Together they moved forward, cutting down any rakken they came into contact with. Even in ruin, the simple mining town provided just enough cover to shield their presence from the main bulk of the rakken army. Cassius pressed a hand to Linda's side to stop them at the outskirts. Many more dwarves lay slaughtered in the open cavern before them. The smell of blood-drenched Cassius' senses, but his curse only craved the blood of humans. He pushed past the scent, the throb of heartbeats, and screams of rakken to look up at Linda. Heat rolled off their scales as they exhaled, their eyes trained on the battle.

"Ready?"

Linda nodded, and they both charged, their weapons poised at the ready. It was a massacre—the rakken were succeeding at pushing the dwarves back. The smell of death made Cassius' eyes water as he fought with Linda to get to the front lines. Cassius had lost count of how many rakken he killed, his armor slick with their blood.

"Go," Linda shouted as they made it to the cliffside. He was prepared to climb; it was something his father had taught him at a young age. He could not remember the number of times he had almost fallen to his death. The rock was just jagged enough for him to climb with ease, and Linda protected him from below as he pulled himself up the side of the cliff. He almost fell once, catching himself as some rocks slid from under him. He looked down to see them almost hit Linda, and they glanced up at him and roared.

"Sorry," he called down, his fingers finding purchase against the top of the cliff. As he pulled himself up, he was stopped by a horrible stench and the sound of quick, shallow breathing. He looked up to see a rakken approaching, its mouth open to strings of saliva stuck to buck teeth. He managed to get onto the top of the cliff just in time to roll out of the way of the rakken's attack, his teeth gritted in frustration. He lashed out, grabbed the front of the rakken's fur, and used his strength to pull the rakken off the cliff.

A small needle of pain whittled its way into his temple, accompanied by the low hunger in the base of his throat. He hadn't had any blood since he nearly left, and he was beginning to feel it, his body weakened by its absence. He could go without blood for perhaps a week before his curse would drive him to kill, but his bones ached, and he felt like he could lay down and sleep for days if he could.

Two more rakken came after him, but he cut them down quickly, his eyes trained on the rakken mage behind them. The mage did not acknowledge him. His paws raised to the ceiling as purple tendrils of magic sank out of his fingers and trailed to the portal. An electrical current soaked the air, the hair on his arms standing on end as he pushed forward. The air reeked with the stench of war as Cassius raised his sword to strike through the rat mage.

Laughter clogged in saliva left the rat mage's lips as he stopped chanting and looked at Cassius, a paw flinging towards him. "Filthy man-filth. You will be a gift-honor to the gods."

A magical resistance hit Cassius, throwing him back. He felt the cliff's edge, dropping his sword to catch himself before falling. His stomach plummeted as his fingers found purchase on the cliff's edge, and he glanced down, noting Rooster now fought alongside Linda with a sword of his own.

Get up, Cassius told himself, throwing his elbow up to pull himself up. There were no more rakken to greet him, and he pulled himself up again with ease, dragging himself forward until his feet no longer dangled off the edge.

"Fool!"

Cassius looked up. The rakken mage held a squirming Intoh, his face turning red as he clawed at the rakken's grasp around his throat. He almost felt pity for Intoh, who had found himself in that same position just the day before when he had tried to steal some of Cassius' blood.

"You will die-die to appease Mother Sickness," the rakken mage said, tightening his hold on Intoh. The portal was wide open behind them as rakken poured through, slipping past the rakken mage to join the fight.

Cassius exhaled sharply as an itching sensation raced up his arm. Looking down, his blood coalesced into a gun, the gun that had slipped out of his arm at his estate. It was cool in his hands as he curled his fingers around the grip, and he stared at it for a moment before pushing himself to his feet and pointing it at the mage. He was no bowman and had never fired a gun before, but it was as if the woman in his blood urged him forward and steadied his hand.

He pulled the trigger.

It was like a dam broke inside him, releasing a wave of magic that coursed through his veins. The power was exhilarating as the gun fired. A bolt of red light shot out the barrel as it met its target between the rakken mage's eyes. His screech echoed through the cavern as the bullet pierced through the mage's head straight out the other side.

Intoh pried himself from the rakken's loosened grasp and fell to the ground, gasping and clinging to his throat. A relief overcame Cassius as the mage died and, with it, the rakken army's resolve. The portal behind the mage grew unsteady, crumbling to dust as rakken that poured through it were cut in half, their guts spilling over the ground as they died on top of each other.

The gun sank in on itself as it returned to the blood, sinking back into Cassius' skin. He flexed his fingers as the itching dulled to a tolerable notion and he rushed over to Intoh, who groaned and muttered in drikotyian.

"It over?" he asked, reaching forward to grab the piece of draugmin off of the mage's body. It was gnarled like it had been chewed on, but it still burned a bright purple and burned Intoh's hand when he touched it. The greka hissed and dropped it, looking around for anything he could use to grab it. It seemed the cloth on a dead rakken would do, and Intoh took greater care picking it up a second time. It did not burn him this time, and Cassius watched with vague interest as Intoh stuck it in his pocket.

"It would seem so," Cassius said, walking forward to peer over the cliff. The remaining rakken had lost their courage as their leader fell and turned back into the darkness. The dwarves felled them as they retreated, cornering them so they could not seek solace in the tunnels. The cries of the dying were thunderous as the last of the rakken were slain.

King Stoneheart fell to his knees in front of his son, weeping openly as he swept the corpse in his arms. A hushed sadness was thick in the air as Intoh brushed past Cassius, murmuring under his breath as he jumped off the cliff and levitated down.

"Fucking mages," Cassius muttered to himself. The dead only heard his annoyance as he bent to pick up his sword and sheathed it. Turning, he lowered himself over the cliff's edge and climbed down.

When he reached the bottom, Rooster approached the king, his hand on his shoulder.

"I will see you again, my boy, as the deep underground halls of our fathers welcome us home. Rest now. Be with your brother." The king pressed his lips to Faerdren's head and then forced himself to his feet, his expression grief-stricken but clear. "Our losses are heavy on this eve, but we are victorious nonetheless. The rakken flee further into their tunnels, waiting to be eradicated. Each day we push them back more, but soon, there will be nowhere for them to go. Two of their leaders are dead, and now we must act on that opportunity. First, we will tend to our wounded and bury our dead."

Cassius could find a newfound respect for the king. His care for his people ran deep, and Cassius bowed his head as he passed.

The king walked a few feet before turning to address them again. "My gratitude is unyielding. You will always find a home in our halls and safe passage through our tunnels, should you need it," the king said as Obrand approached. His face was somber and pale beneath the gore of battle. Tears stained his cheeks, but he was no longer crying, his head cast downwards as he spoke to the king in Alkazed. The king grabbed Obrand's arm and pulled him into an embrace.

"There is great value in dwarf hospitality. We won't keep you from grieving," Rooster finally said, stepping aside to let the king pass. "We only ask for a small escort to the surface."

Nodding, Stoneheart picked up his son's body and cradled it as if Faerdren was still a baby. "My nephew and his Rangers will see to your safety through Stone Flame pass. It's half a day's journey down that tunnel," he said, gesturing deeper into the tunnels with a nod of his head. "I don't expect the rakken to try anything now, but it will be good to have them, just in case."

The thought of seeing the surface so soon tore at Cassius' patience as he looked to the tunnels the king spoke of. The king whispered something to Obrand, who nodded.

Cassius lowered his voice as his fingers shook. "I do not mean to rush the party, but if it is to be a half day's journey, it would be wise to make haste. There is only so long I can go without food, and I don't think you want me to insult the dwarves by draining one of their kin." Even mentioning it sent a wave of disgust coursing through him. He had only tasted dwarf once not long ago and would be happy to go the rest of his long life without doing so again.

Rooster frowned. "Right," he said. "You look like shit, Cassius."

The vampire's face soured. "All you fucking mortals are the same."

Rooster gave a small, mocking bow. "That's me. You'll have to talk to the others about traveling without rest."

Cassius turned toward Helai as she approached with Kolin at her side. Her hair was half torn from her braid, her face dirty, and her cloak worse for wear, but she was free of wounds. "If they don't want to get eaten," he said, "we'll go immediately. It's as simple as that."

Parts of Kolin's hair were singed off, and he was also covered in gore, his belt housing several different vials of spiraling colors.

"Ah, Kolin, glad to see you well." Obrand reached out to Kolin's forearm, gripping it tightly as the medic nodded, his jaw tight.

"Much bloodshed today," he said.

Helai looked at all of them. "We managed to treat some of the wounded, but I am running low on supplies. I heard it is only a half-day travel to the surface?"

Rooster nodded.

An excited gleam hit Helai's gaze. "What are we waiting for?"

The other rangers approached as Obrand took a small step forward, his face strained. "Aye. The others have work to do. Let's leave them to it. We should set out while the rakken's courage fails them."

Cassius' relief was short-lived as they set out. The constant ache of hunger at the base of his throat was little compared to the urge that coursed through him, desperate for him to seek out Volendam.

Chapter Fourteen
Helai

They'd neared the mouth of the tunnels when Obrand collapsed.

It was sudden and without warning. Light filtered through the mouth of the tunnel enough for Helai to see him fall, but Drithan reached out and caught him before he hit the ground.

"Is he okay?" Helai asked, kneeling as Drithan lowered him to the ground. Obrand's breathing was shallow. A thin sheen of sweat crossed his brow, and fresh blood coated his shoulder, oozing a dark purple-black. It looked infected, webbing through his veins around the wound.

"Never mind, I've answered my question. He needs medical attention, and I fear we won't make it to the post."

Cassius looked worse for wear, his illusion slipping away as his fangs poked out beneath decaying flesh. His eyes tinged with the glow of red. She knew they were working within a dangerous time frame, but Obrand would not make it unless his welfare became their priority.

Obrand murmured in Alkazed, his eyes darting frantically around the tunnel.

"The rakken use the same magic as dwarves. Why is it poisoning him? Have any of you seen something like this before?" Helai asked, glancing up at Drithan and the other rangers.

Drithan shook his head, hesitating. "...No..."

Obrand moaned as Helai peeled back his shirt. The center of the wound was cut deep in his shoulder, a minor laceration that would have healed fine had it not been infected.

"I've never seen a wound like this," Helai said, glancing up at Kolin.

Kolin hmphed under his breath, kneeling beside her. "The rakken are doing something to the draugmin, mutating it. This poison is corrupting the blood. It may be too late for him, lass."

"I won't accept that." Helai's memory sent her back to the desert, her hair whipping in the wind, the sun beating against her back.

"I promise," Helai had said, clasping her pinky with Zahra. *"We'll all make it out of this. You just have to trust me."*

Helai spared no glance at the others as she attempted to calm her shaking hands. The space where her right pinky finger used to be ached, a phantom of a limb that had been there before she'd cut it off. Her promise that day had been hollow, and she'd paid for her mistakes in blood.

Pulling a vial from a small bag at her hip, she sent a silent prayer to Dalnor, the god of shadows, to steady her hands. The liquid was yellow and thick like sap, and Helai did not know if it would work. She just knew she had to try.

"This liquid is from a flower called *Niemat Alharara* by my people or 'Grace of Heat' in the common tongue. If it works, it will burn the poison out of him." She didn't mention that too much could cause blood to boil. He would die if she didn't try.

"Hold him down and keep him still," Helai instructed calmly, and Rooster moved forward to help the dwarves pin his arms and legs to the ground. As she poured the liquid over the wound, Obrand attempted to convulse as he cried out in pain.

"How long will it take to know if it's working?" Intoh asked, peering around Linda.

Helai dumped the whole vial onto Obrand's wound and then ruffled around her pouch until she found a salve that was light green and cool to the touch. When she slipped some over the injury itself, it began to close despite the darkened veins still being very apparent against Obrand's pale and sweaty skin.

"Lift his arm," Helai said.

Drithan lifted Obrand's arm as Helai wrapped it in bandages, her brow pressed with worry. The poison wasn't receding, and Obrand's breathing was still shallow. Standing, she finally focused on Intoh. "We'll know pretty soon if it starts to work."

The next moments were tense, the other rangers not leaving Obrand's side. They were close to the mouth of the tunnel, but Helai feared moving him.

"I can wait no longer. I worry for our companion but fear I won't last much longer without feeding. I must move ahead." Cassius stopped pacing, his eyes glowing through the darkness. The sight of his decay beneath his illusion sickened Helai, and she nodded.

"I will feed quickly and then alert the post that we have someone who is injured," Cassius said, slipping away towards the mouth of the tunnel. A dark tension lessened in the air at his departure. Intoh glanced up at Linda.

"Before we are greeted by strangers, perhaps it's time," Intoh said, gesturing to Linda's ring. A low sound rumbled deep within Linda as they complied. Their illusion slipped over to a man. Several of the dwarves flinched away, muttering in protest.

"What dark magic is that?" Kolin asked, his brow furrowed, but all their attention was diverted to Obrand when his breathing started to even out. The poison receded, slinking back towards the bandages, and one of the dwarves clasped Helai on the shoulder in relief.

"Do not move him until help arrives," Helai said as Drithan spoke rapidly in Alkazed.

One of the female rangers offered her hand to Helai, helping her to her feet. "Drithan says you did good, and he's not the type to give compliments. Quiet and observant he is. The name's Dagrun—Dagrun Marblebreaker. You have our gratitude." She lowered her lips to the back of Helai's hand and then let go, moving to kneel next to Obrand.

Helai let them tend to the king's nephew, her hands still shaking at her side. The image of Zahra was still fresh in her head. They had lost her to the sand years ago, yet it still felt like it had happened yesterday.

Remember to breathe, little sister. One foot in front of the other, and you'll be taken where you need to go. Meet me in Volendam. It's a trade city, and our skin will not be a beacon for those who might seek to condemn us. Those had been Massoud's last words to her before they had all split off to better hide from Mohalis' men scouring the streets of Dalasae to find them. Massoud had kissed her temple and sent her to the docks to find passage to Hestia. She hadn't even made it to the ship; the shoma'kah had been waiting for her at the docks.

"Come, Helai. Help has arrived," Rooster said, shaking Helai from her thoughts. Several human guards rushed down the tunnel with Cassius, carrying a stretcher between them.

Helai would worry about finding the others once she reached Volendam.

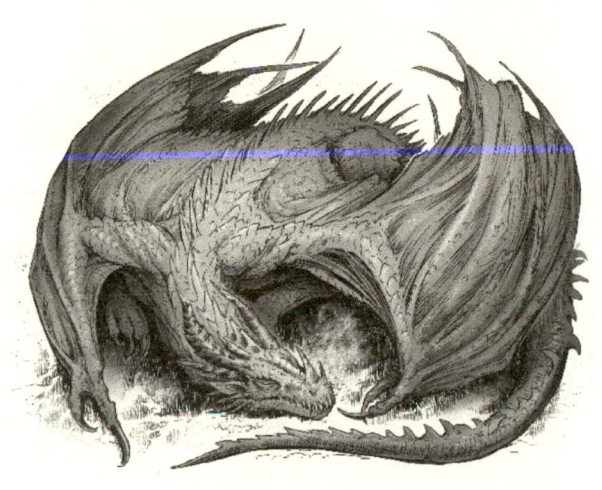

Chapter Fifteen
Intoh

The sun was disorienting as they left the tunnels. Intoh had to blink several times before his eyes adjusted to the sun's glare, but thankfully, it was reaching mid-afternoon, and the glow would soon disappear behind the mountain pass. A chilly wind wove through the trees, and Intoh resisted the urge to shudder. He was not accustomed to the cold weather of this side of the world. It made his joints stiff and stole his appetite. Still, he tried to find the comforts in it like Ekalas would have. There was a quietness that settled in the mountains, a sense of peace, even as they approached the outpost. Helai spoke quietly to the humans carrying Obrand on a stretcher, her brow pinched. Cassius was silent, this face calm in thought. Unrest settled within Intoh; he wanted to go to Volendam. He had heard revered tales of the mage college and its library–perhaps he could find tomes on extending life. He still hadn't managed to get a drop of Cassius' blood, but that was only a matter of time.

"Welcome to Emberfoot Refuge." A human man approached, garbed in simple plate armor. His helm gleamed; it must not have seen much of war. His face was kind as he stopped the party and rangers at the door. The humans Cassius had brought back to carry Obrand moved towards a separate building.

"The King's Rangers are welcome, as are those who seek their company. I am Garen; it was I who was notified of Obrand's injury by your friend here." Garen gestured to Cassius as he stepped forward. Cassius' illusion was tucked back into place, and there was a pep to his step that hadn't been there before. Intoh could no longer feel the insistent scratch of hunger at his throat, as he had before Cassius fed. It was strange; he had never been able to feel such things before. He wondered if the brand had anything to do with it.

"Ah, Drithan. *Heik*," Garen said, switching to Alkazed as Drithan approached. Intoh lost interest in the conversation, watching the guards change shifts, replacing those at the door. Some of them were dwarves, but most of them were humans. It was strange for humans to defend the entrance to a dwarf kingdom, but Intoh did not care enough to ask as Drithan nodded, and Garen turned back to address them.

"Come. I'm made to believe there is a celebration to be had," Garen said, gesturing to the door. Cassius stopped him, a soft frown gracing his lips.

"Is there a place where I might get a bath? We have been underground for too long, and I wish to shed the stink of war."

Garen nodded, turning to the other guard at the door. "Kiva, do you mind taking Cassius to Saela? Tell her Garen sent you, and she'll draw you a bath." The relief that crossed Cassius' face was immense, and he allowed Kiva to lead him away as Garen led the others inside.

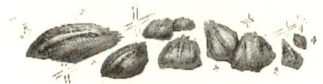

The evening was a blur. Intoh felt light, having cleaned the blood off his skin and changed his clothes. He wore a light woven tunic now, and the small hall was bustling with music played by the bard on the dance floor. Intoh discovered that Emberfoot Refuge was also a stopping point for travelers and traders through the mountain. The hall was thick with people as they drank, danced, and ate until they could no longer.

They had all been greeted as heroes. It was a foreign feeling, the pride that swelled in Intoh's chest whenever someone clapped him on the back, thanking him for keeping their tunnels safe from rakken. But it was also exhilarating and fueled his desire to seek it more often.

"Intoh, get tattoo," Linda said, pulling Intoh from his thoughts. Several dwarves pounded the table as the bard concluded his song, shouting in Alkazed, and one chugged a beer so deeply he fell back and hit the ground hard, rousing laughter from those around him. Across the bar, a woman eyed Intoh with an expression he could not place.

"Here ya go. Lass paid for your drink." The bartender slid a mug at Intoh and gestured to the woman, who smiled at him. Intoh smiled back nervously, hopped off his stool, and looked at Linda. "Tattoo? Sure, why not." *That woman looks like she wants to eat me. Must flee.*

Linda ambled through the crowd, grunting as dwarves patted them on the side in celebration. Linda was no stranger to the celebration of victorious battles, and Intoh was thankful they did not try to bite the heads off of everyone foolish enough to touch them.

Linda led Intoh to a small corner where the rangers were nestled together. Obrand had joined them sometime in the evening, his bandage gleaming brightly under his tunic. He no longer looked as if he toed the line of death. A pipe graced his lips. Rooster held the back of Helai's shirt down as Drithan inked her shoulder blade with a pointed object. The tattoo resembled a dwarf, his beard embellished with knives instead of hair. Rooster was shirtless, his tattoo proudly inked above his heart. His was of a rooster with Alkazed words written beneath it.

"Hmmm." Intoh hummed in contemplation. "What say?" He gestured to Rooster's ink.

"Bird of the tunnels," Rooster explained. Hers was nearly done, and Drithan guzzled down his ale and wiped his beard clean as he put on the last finishing touches. The other rangers watched Drithan work, speaking in hushed tones in Alkazed.

"Oi," Drithan said, admiring his work as he finished the last line.

"All right, who's next?" Dagrun shouted, raising her mug in the air.

"Go, Linda." Intoh urged them forward, his brow furrowing. Whispering, he added, "Must tattoo underbelly. Ink won't pierce scales."

Linda spared Intoh a glance, then twisted their ring despite his protest. As their form shifted, several people nearby shouted in shock, and men and women grabbed swords and spears. Obrand rushed to his feet and winced, holding his hands out.

"The krok'ida's with us. No need to get alarmed," he shouted. "Go back to your mead and mind your business." After a few tense moments, things settled, and the celebration continued. Obrand sighed as he fell back in his seat. "Warn a lad next time, will ya?"

Linda opened their maw, revealing several rows of uneven, sharp teeth. They turned to Drithan and pointed at their tongue.

Drithan stared at Linda with uncertainty and turned to Obrand for instruction. Obrand raised a fist in the air, nodding.

"Give 'em the runes of the ancestor's lad. You know the ones."

Drithan shook his head and grunted, rolling his shoulders. Finishing his ale, he hesitated once more at Linda's open mouth and gazed up at them, working his jaw over with his teeth. "Don't…eat," he said. Muttering in Alkazed, he leaned into Linda's mouth and got to work.

Obrand leaned over to Intoh. "Those runes will condemn whoever enters your scaly friend's mouth to Byrvka, the Wastelands of the Dead. When dwarves of our culture are condemned, their souls are doomed to roam those wastelands in the afterlife, barred from the halls of our fathers. They are left with no honor to pass down to their descendants." Turning to Linda, he cupped his mouth. "So you best make sure they're worthy of such a trial." The other rangers beat their fists against the table, and Linda huffed as Drithan etched the runes into their tongue.

Curious, Intoh leaned up to study the runes. They were similar to those he'd seen in the tunnels, and they all centered around a circle, which housed a single rune in the middle.

"Interesting," Intoh muttered, tucking the information away. Helai took a seat next to him, sighing softly. Her hair was down, cascading around her shoulders, and the small twine of silver fabric curled around a lock hanging over her shoulder, tied at the bottom.

"It's good to be out of those tunnels," Helai admitted, pressing her palms to her knees.

"You don't like the tunnels, lass? I take offense to that," Obrand said, narrowing his eyes at Helai. A small squeak passed her lips as Obrand roared with laughter.

"I jest. The halls of my people aren't for everyone. Still, I hope our hospitality makes up for it."

Helai's laughter was hesitant. "Yeah, of course. When we weren't being hunted by rakken." She leaned forward, her eyes lit with curiosity. "You say they've only been a problem recently and are waking up. Do you know why?"

Obrand's smile sobered. "Nay. There are rumors, but... I'd hate to ruin the mood with such foul talk. Tonight's for drinkin'." He raised his mug in the air, and the other rangers joined him, drawing a reluctant smile from Helai.

Intoh had to admit he was disappointed too. His curiosity burned like a forest fire left unchecked. "Rumors?" he asked. "What kind?"

Obrand glanced over, frowning. "I'll say this once, and then we drink until the sun comes up. Agreed?" At Helai's and Intoh's nods, he lowered his mug, setting it on the table in front of him. He was silent for several moments as he stared at his ale. "There's whispers of cult activity. We know it festers in the north, where demons frequent the chilly wastelands of Volreya. But now it seems cults are forming in the south, coming out of Hestia."

Helai's expression turned anxious. "I have heard of demons laying waste to Hestia, but for evil to be seeping through the wards the Inquisition put in place? That's hard to believe."

"Inquisition?" Intoh asked, drawing the gazes of both Helai and Obrand.

"You have heard tales of Ji'noa's fall, right?" Helai asked, and Intoh nodded. He'd read about the holy city of Hestia and how it had been desecrated by demons. He did not know much about why; only that day, the sky had wept blood, bathing the city in red. Portals had opened up to demons, who'd left almost no one alive. There were holy bunkers that had saved a handful of Hestians, but the city still suffered to this day.

"The Inquisition was forged after Ji'noa's fall. It is told that their god's name is lost to them, ripped from the minds and libraries of Hestia by the demons, and the Inquisition seeks to reclaim the name before the god fades from existence," Helai said before waving her hand in dismissal. "Anyway, they put up a ward around the city to keep the masses of demons from pouring out into the world, but now and again, they manage to slip through."

"I don't know, lass. It is probably all rumors. Enough talk of it. I wish to drink. My people lost much today, but we managed to kill two of their leaders." Helai and Intoh exchanged looks and said nothing as Obrand turned away to engage Dagrun in conversation.

"Can I steal you for a dance?" A voice had Intoh looking up into the woman's gaze from the bar, her smile radiant. She gestured to the dance floor, where humans and dwarves alike moved in a pattern unfamiliar to Intoh.

Nervous laughter echoed from Intoh's cheeks. "I don't think so." The woman's lower lip poked out into a pout as she moved forward, her finger coming up to run along Intoh's chest. "Perhaps we could skip the dancing then and have some fun back in your room?" The look she'd given him from the bar returned, and Intoh's heart pounded. Her expression hungered like a predator that had just caught sight of her prey.

"*Lindaaaaaa!*" Intoh cried out, garnering the attention of everyone around him. The woman straightened, color flushing her cheeks. Intoh stood suddenly, knocking his chair over, and he backed up, holding his hands out. "If you plan to eat me—"

"My friend is kidding, of course." Rooster appeared in front of Intoh, his smile wide and friendly. "The name's Rooster. Intoh here—" Rooster slung his arm across Intoh's shoulders. He was so close he could taste the alcohol coming off Rooster's breath. "You see, he's a eunuch. Doesn't like to talk about it." Rooster turned to whisper in Intoh's ear. "She wishes to mate, *mate*. Don't worry. I'll get rid of her."

Understanding gathered in Intoh's expression as Rooster pulled away. Other species mated; it was how they reproduced. Drikoty were born from goo left by their gods. They had no need or want to reproduce.

"Oh." The woman's face lit up. "I see. I'm so sorry. Excuse me——"

"I could buy you a drink if you'd like." Rooster winked at Intoh and pressed his hand to the small of the woman's back, leading her to the bar.

Intoh sighed with relief.

One of the dwarves leaned over, his whispering not so much a whisper as it was a quiet shouting. "You really a eunuch, lad?"

Intoh shook his head vigorously, causing the dwarf to laugh. Next to him, another dwarf downed the rest of his drink and slammed his head against the table, passing out before he hit the floor.

Drithan grunted and backed up, admiring his finished work on Linda's tongue.

Linda opened and closed their mouth as if they could taste something foul and then thumped Drithan on the back. Drithan coughed as he was thrown forward but grinned gently up at Linda.

"Well, as fun as this has been, have book to finish studying." Intoh started to back away, but Obrand caught his arm.

"Celebrate with us. You can finish your studies when we deliver you to the edge of the mountain."

Intoh hesitated, looking at the disaster lying before him. Many patrons had already passed out, and the dancing was going full force. Drithan approached Helai, asking her to dance in broken Vilris, and she accepted, taking his hand and allowing him to lead her away. Fleetingly, Intoh wondered if they would mate.

He found himself caving. "One drink. Won't hurt."

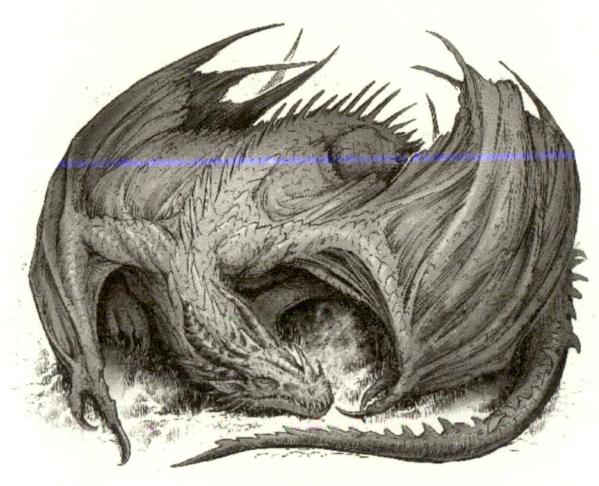

Chapter Sixteen
Cassius

Quiet settled around Cassius like a warm blanket as he sank into the bath, a low hiss seeping from between his teeth as the brand on his back burned from the contact of the water. It itched mercilessly, and Cassius fought the urge to scratch. The servants that the guards had granted him made sure the water was hot, and steam trailed off the water to chase the chill away. He offered the servants a dazzling smile of thanks as they continued to pour hot water into the bathtub. Sounds of festivities went on in the tavern next to him, the shouts of dwarves and humans alike a distant echo as Cassius closed his eyes and descended until only his eyes and forehead were above water.

Hunger still stitched itself into the back of his throat, but he ignored it, drowning its demands in his goblet of wine. It felt good to clean the grime and filth of those tunnels. He still felt the pull towards Volendam, the quiet hum of the city calling to him. The sooner he could be free of its shadow, the better.

"Room for two?" A voice, sultry and low, shattered the silence, and Cassius' eyes shot open, meeting the gaze of a woman standing in the doorway. Her hair tumbled in loose curls around her bosom, a plunging dress fixated perfectly against her curvy form.

He recognized her immediately. "Gabriella, what are you doing here?"

Laughter echoed at Cassius' question, her eyes never leaving his as she tossed back her hair and opened her mouth to flash her fangs. Gabriella was an ambassador for the Sanguine Order, and he hadn't seen her since his exile. His hopes of evading the Order entirely during his travels through the mountain immediately evaporated.

"To see you, of course, dear Cassius. It's been far too long. Have you been avoiding me?" She stalked towards him, her head lowered in a hurtful pout. The servants behind him stood, unmoving near the back of his head. He didn't have to turn to know their eyes were unfocused; she had compelled them not to move or speak.

"Now, now, Gabriella. That's not fair. You know full well why I haven't been around." Cassius fought to keep the steadiness in his voice. It had been months since he had been liberated from his tomb and years since the Sanguine Order had put him there as punishment for his defiance. If Gabriella was here, that meant the Order knew he was free.

"You could come back, you know. Dmitry has been asking about you." Gabriella's expression turned thoughtful as she knelt, pressing her chin against her arms as she slipped them over the lip of the tub. The servants still did not move, and Cassius scooted up, so he sat with his back erect against the tub. "He won't say it, but the Order's numbers grow few, and you are a decent knight. You have to understand. There are rules in place. He only did what he had to."

Cassius' expression darkened. He remained silent. If Dmitry asked for his presence, he should not disobey. He was the head knight of the Sanguine Order, placed there by the founder Ruxandra and her wife, Louelle.

A twist in his stomach forced him to grimace. "I cannot," he said.

Gabriella's smile was sad. "Then why come through the Spine Mountains? You know your presence would not be hidden from us. Vera felt your freedom the moment you took it, but Dmitry was content with ignoring your tantrums until you passed too close to the Keep." She paused a finger drawn to her lips as Cassius opened his mouth in anger. "Something is stirring, Cassius—an ancient feeling that calls to us. Have you heard it?" Her finger darted over the surface of the water.

Cassius wondered if she felt the same hollow hunger in her chest urging him to Volendam. Something within him kept him silent. If she felt it, she would be in Volendam, not chasing Cassius through the mountains.

"Still not much of a talker, Cassius?"

"I was just admiring the view." The words left his lips before he could help it. He and Gabriella had found comfort in each other's arms several times in the solitude of Dragon Keep. Their relationship had only ever been physical, and Gabriella's silence during his sentence of exile had been noticed. He told himself he would scorn her if he ever saw her again, and that promise died when he looked into her eyes.

Gabriella's head tilted as she stood, snapping her fingers at the servants. They reacted without hesitation, setting the vases of water on the floor and kneeling on either side of Cassius. Bearing their wrists to him, they remained silent.

Cassius eyed them for a moment before his gaze was back on Gabriella, who had slipped entirely out of her dress and stood naked before him. He was unable to look away. "How many times must we do this dance, Cassius? When will you tell me what's going on in that head of yours?" Her words sent a current of deja vu coursing through him of the woman in his estate who tried to kill him. She had asked him the same question, and now she was dead.

"You're the one who keeps seeking me out, Gabriella. Can't say I'm disappointed to see you, though." Cassius' head lolled to the side as one of the servants leaned forward and pressed a damp washcloth to his chest. The other still offered her arm to him, and Cassius kept eye contact with Gabriella as he opened his mouth and bit into the servant's wrist.

A quiet sound slipped from the servant's mouth as she sank against the tub, her wrist shoved more insistently against Cassius' mouth. Her blood was sweet as it hit his tongue, and he pulled her in to drink more deeply.

Gabriella's nostrils flared, and she slowly raised a leg over the lip of the tub and slipped into the water. The sound of celebration still sounded outside, but it had faded, drowned out by Cassius' hunger and Gabriella's insistence of his attention.

"I'm afraid I must come with a warning too, Cassius. Your punishment in that tomb was carried out, and Dmitry no longer has any quarrels with you. Still, we are to keep a close eye." She scooted closer, her hand sidling up his thigh to rest teasingly while she pressed against him. Cassius dropped the arm of the servant as his fingers moved to ghost along Gabriella's back. Her tongue darted out to taste the blood staining the corner of Cassius' mouth before her lips etched pathways up the side of his cheek to rest against the cusp of his ear. "If you do anything to challenge the Order, we will show you no mercy." Teeth dragged lightly against his earlobe, and Cassius did growl then, his arm moving to wrap around Gabriella's waist. His eyes lit up with lust and fury. Gabriella's lips parted as Cassius pressed her against the tub, her smile coy.

"You needn't worry about my intentions, for they are innocent. That, you can tell Dmitry himself." His fingers curled around her neck but did not tighten as he tilted Gabriella's head to the side so he could press his lips to her ear. "I'm no man to be threatened, but I mean no offense. Can't a vampire enjoy the delicacies of wine and a bath after dealing with dwarves and rats?"

His words drew laughter from Gabriella's lips, and she spread her legs. He sank lower against her. Her hand reached up to drag a nail along his cheek while the other reached down between his thighs, forcing his breath to hitch.

"Oh, Cassius—" As her eyes narrowed playfully, her fingers gripped his chin roughly, pulling him closer. "There is still much for you to learn of the world." She kissed him passionately then, teasing him beneath the water as she let go of his chin and snapped her fingers, commanding the servants closer.

Cassius' head grew dizzy with lust and hunger, and the scent of human blood preyed on his curse as his eyes darkened. He pulled away from Gabriella, his fangs descending in response to the blood. He could hear the voice in his head again, quietly now, urging him to give in to his temptations, to fall prey to his lust.

He bit into the servant's wrist as Gabriella kissed along his neck, and the quiet sound of the woman behind the gun called out to him.

Cassius. Come to Volendam.

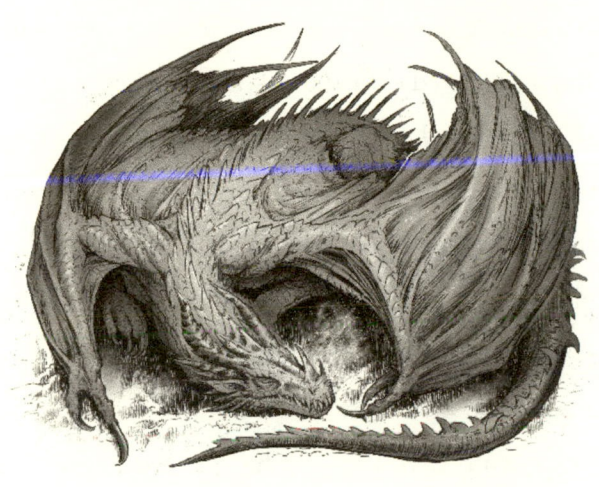

Chapter Seventeen
Helai

Helai's head was a haze of alcohol and the exhilaration of dancing as she pulled Drithan with her through the tavern towards the stairs. She did not know which rooms were vacant, but she got lucky; the first one she tried was empty.

Drithan followed her willingly, silent and stoic. Helai had never met a dwarf before, and Drithan intrigued her. Shoma culture was full of rich colors and living free in the sands, but dwarves differed with their mountains, sense of honor, and tradition.

"Perfect," Helai breathed, tugging the window open. Despite the chill of mountain air, she welcomed it. She had been trapped underground for days, and the fresh air was a relief. The room was large enough to furnish a double bed and a small table but no fireplace. She shivered, and Drithan shrugged off his cloak and offered it to her.

"Are you sure?" she asked. Silent, he reached over and draped her shoulders with it. He was tall for a dwarf; she was only a few inches taller than him, and his breath tickled her chin as he pulled the cloak around her. The cloak was heavy and warm and smelled of war and the mountain. Still, it chased the chill away, and she curled into it as he stepped away to stare out the window.

"I didn't bring you up here for—" She glanced at the bed, her cheeks flaming. Clearing her throat, she glanced at him. He was staring at her now, the glow of moonlight highlighting the hard lines of his face. She noticed a thin line of freckles dusting his cheeks, and she ran her finger over the grain of the table, trying to find the right words. She hadn't been alone with a man since Aryan; a giddy feeling sat in her stomach. She didn't bring him here to bed him, but she would be lying to herself if the temptation didn't lie deep within her belly.

"Obrand…" Drithan hesitated as he spoke, his accent thick on his tongue. "Obrand has been teaching me Vilris. I'm sorry if my Vilris is poor." He hummed, his hand moving to run through his hair as he muttered in Alkazed and sat across from her. "Will listen."

"I had to learn the common tongue too. When I was a teenager, my big brother taught me so that I would be prepared if we needed to flee my home country. It gets easier the more you practice." She still lost words in her head, but it came to her as second nature now.

"From Shoma?" Drithan asked.

Helai nodded. "It is a beautiful country, truly. When we aren't warring with the neighboring countries and the cities aren't occupied by soldiers, the sights are truly spectacular." Her heart ached for home, of weaving through the ribcage of Shok'Alan, the holy capital built within the skeleton of Qevayla, Shoma's most worshiped god besides Jaleer. She ached for the sweet taste of jif'ta, a desert usually served one month out of the year when the whole city made offerings to Qevayla. She'd only had it once when she'd been very young and her parents were still alive.

"I think I just wanted some quiet and company. If I've pulled you away from the celebrations, you are free to go," Helai said, wringing her fingers nervously in her hands.

Drithan shook his head and sat at the table, kicking his foot over his ankle. "Do you mind?" he asked, pulling a pipe out of his pocket. When Helai shook her head, he started to pack it with tobacco, hitting the bowl against his open palm to clear it.

"I miss home," Helai said, looking out the window. She watched Linda slink across the ground on all fours, hunting a mountain boar grazing in the distance. Linda was truly terrifying in their krok'ida form.

"I understand."

Helai turned to see Drithan watching her. A heavy sigh left him as he ran a hand through his hair, dragging on his pipe. Massoud used to smoke iisha, but Drithan's pipe tobacco had a harsher smell as it wafted through the room, slipping out of the window into the night sky. Helai watched it dissipate for a moment before she turned back to the dwarf.

"The rakken took my home from us, and we only just reclaimed it."

"You must feel so relieved," Helai said softly.

Drithan nodded, the heat of his pipe illuminating his eyes. "Fighting against them for months. They crave the draugmin and have a heavy supply of it in Kaldrom. Why they come."

Helai raised an eyebrow. "You speak Vilris very well for claiming otherwise."

Drithan's smile was sheepish. "Know it better than I claim. Just haven't found anyone worth talking to." A quiet thrill sang through Helai at the compliment, heating her cheeks. She coughed and looked away towards the melodic trill of a mountain canary.

"I'm glad you were able to get your home back." Oh, how relieving and joyous it must feel. Envy was a snake in the garden of her heart, a shallow feeling that she smothered before it could fester. Jealousy would not free Shoma of its tyrannical ruler.

"Helai, what is wrong?" Drithan's question brought her gaze back to his, and she hesitated. She had not brought him here to speak of such heavy topics. Why had she led him up here? Perhaps, among the chaos of the party, Drithan's grounding presence had kept her from panicking. Maybe she just craved some form of conversation.

Pain shot through her back, radiating from where the rakken had branded her. She flinched in her seat, hissing, and Drithan stood, his pipe lowering from his lips. "Helai?" he asked, moving around the table.

This wasn't going at all as she'd hoped. Anger heated the blood in her veins as she gritted her teeth. "It's nothing. I'm fine." The anger fueled a quiet… hunger, an itch towards Volendam. A flickering lust. A desire for blood. Some sort of silent fear. A craving for knowledge. The thunderous joy of winning some duel. All the emotions filtered through her in a frenzy, and she pressed a hand to her brow as they all dissipated at once, leaving an emptiness swelling in her chest.

"I'm sorry. That was weird. I felt strange suddenly," she said, laughing breathlessly and looking up at Drithan. "This may be inappropriate, but can…can you look at something?" Helai asked, stumbling to her feet.

Hefting the cloak off her shoulders, she laid it on the bed and turned around. "When we first came into contact with the rakken, one of them branded me. Can you make sure it's not infected?" She turned to gaze over her shoulder at him as he moved forward. "If you don't want to—"

But he was already lifting the shirt she wore under her armor, exposing her midriff. The air from the window chilled her back, but Drithan's touch was warm, sending a flurry of excitement through Helai, settling at the bottom of her belly.

"I do not recognize the sigil. It looks like it is healing, but it will leave a scar. You said a rakken did this to you?" His hand strayed, etching the brand with his finger, and Helai suppressed a shudder, forcing herself to step away. Drithan cleared his throat and clasped his hands behind his back.

"Yes. I believe they did it to several of us. It doesn't look infected?" Helai asked, ignoring the heat of her cheeks. Drithan shook his head, and Helai sighed with relief. That was the last thing she needed.

"Does it hurt?" Drithan drew closer after setting his pipe down on the table.

Helai turned, shaking her head. "Not anymore. If it's okay with you, I don't wish to speak about it any longer."

"All right," Drithan said, and silence passed between them. For several moments, neither of them said anything, and Helai began to braid her hair, anxiety a hum in her chest that fluttered, unforgiving.

"What would you like to talk about?" Drithan asked finally, and Helai smiled.

"Tell me about the other rangers. What are they like?"

Drithan's gaze lit up, adoration a wildfire through his expression. He sat on the bed, his hands moving in the air in wild gestures. "Obrand is our leader. He's the king's nephew; I don't know if you know that. He demanded to lead Stoneheart's personal ranger unit, and we are Kaldrom's best scouts. Kolin is our medic and a damn good one too." Helai turned one of the chairs around as he spoke, sitting across from Drithan.

And it was where she sat for the rest of the night as she and Drithan exchanged war stories, rogue missions, and other little insights into their lives.

For the first time in a long time, Helai did not shoulder the worries of the world. It was just her, Drithan, and the little room they were tucked away in.

Chapter Eighteen
Rooster

The sun was unforgiving as it rose, waking Rooster from a deep slumber. Bleary-eyed, he blinked, prying his arm from the naked woman it was slung over. She didn't stir, and with sobering clarity, Rooster realized it was the woman who had been flirting with Intoh. They had somehow made it onto the roof of the fort.

No one can say I never did anything for anyone, Rooster thought. Pulling his pants on, he moved to the roof's edge to look at the ground below. Men and women replaced guards on post for their morning shifts, and the fort bustled with life.

Rooster pressed his fingers to the stone wall and groaned, his head pounding with little mercy. He hated this feeling of clarity; it made him remember just how little he knew about his past.

He watched Linda stir near the creek running through the mountainside, their maw bloodied as dead mountain boars lay in a pile around them. Rooster watched several people approach Linda but stop some feet away, muttering amongst themselves.

Behind him, the woman shifted. Rooster cleared his throat and returned to her side, grabbing his shirt and slipping it on. Red hair cascaded over the woman's shoulder, shielding her naked back from the morning breeze, and a moment of deja vu gripped Rooster so tightly it made his head spin.

"Wait, where are you going?" The woman sat up, a palm pressed to the makeshift bed of blankets they had made in their drunken passion the night before.

Rooster spared her a glance, his smile apologetic. "Last night was fun, but I must go and find my friends."

The woman pouted for a moment but seemed to decide otherwise, for she nodded and began to dress as well, giving Rooster a friendly nod. "Indeed. I should probably report to my post. Maybe I'll see you around again sometime."

Rooster was silent as he watched her leave. He had to admit, things rarely went that smoothly. He doubted he'd ever see her again, and as he pulled his shoes on, his head pounding from his hangover, he felt a great heaviness settle in his stomach. Gods, he wanted a drink.

Trudging down the stairs, he watched Helai exit a room, Drithan following closely behind her.

Rooster grinned.

Helai's expression darkened as she caught Rooster's gaze. "I don't want to hear any judgment from you. I saw you leave with that redhead last night." She gestured to Drithan. "He wanted help with his Vilris."

Rooster held his hands up defensively, eyeing Drithan with an ill-concealed smile. "You won't hear anything from me." Drithan remained silent next to Helai.

"By any means, I think we should find the others and leave. We have quite the trek ahead of us," Helai said, quickly changing the subject.

Rooster agreed with a nod. While the mountains were beautiful and the celebration last night was one he meant to commit to memory, he was eager to free himself from this place.

"Come on then. I saw Linda outside. I'm sure the others will find us," Rooster said.

Helai nodded, turning to Drithan. "Thank you for talking with me last night," she said. Drithan smiled fondly, and Helai snuck several glances back at him as they left him outside the room and descended the rest of the stairs.

The post loomed over their heads as they approached the creek.

Yawning, Linda ambled over to them. Rooster still wasn't accustomed to how large Linda was. They had cleaned the blood off them in the creek, and their scales shimmered brightly in the sun. "We go now?" they asked, ignoring the whispers of those around them. Cassius had reappeared, looking the same as when he'd left them the afternoon before. He was well fed, his eyes shining, and his skin youthful and smooth—no sign of death or decay to be seen. He remained silent even as he fell into step next to Rooster. Helai shied away from him, but if that bothered Cassius, he did not show it.

"Yes," Rooster said to Linda, glancing around. "We need to find Intoh and Obrand, and we can make our way to Volendam."

They didn't have to search for the two at the stables long. Three horses were saddled and ready to go as they grazed the ground for its craggy flora. The horses were miniature stout mountain horses, and Rooster reached out to scratch the velvety nose of the chestnut one closest to him.

"We have prepared the horses for you," Obrand said. "We'll ride out with you until the edges of the marshes but will go no further. You will have to walk on foot from there on." Obrand eyed Linda. "We don't have a big enough steed for your friend here, so they'll have to walk."

Guttural laughter left Linda. "It fine. Used to walking," they said.

"Let us not linger. I was ready to leave these mountains behind days ago," Cassius said, mounting his white horse gracefully. The other rangers approached on small ponies of their own, and Drithan attempted subtle looks in Helai's direction. Rooster suppressed an urge to laugh, hiding it behind a cough.

Giving Cassius a calculating look, Obrand huffed. "Let us go then. We have quite the journey before us."

Chapter Nineteen
Rooster

It took a week and a half to traverse the mountainside, but no trouble met them. The rakken stayed underground, and no more rifts opened up to swallow them. Cassius was on edge, and Rooster watched him pace the edges of camp every time they stopped for the night. He felt a quiet itch for Volendam that had been absent until they encountered the rakkens that had branded them, but he paid it little mind. Perhaps he was reading too much into it.

Rooster contented himself with scribbling in a journal he'd gotten at the general store in Kaldrom, drawing the fauna of the mountains and rough sketches of his companions. The mountains were chilly at night, and they made small fires just so they wouldn't freeze to death, but it was tense when the roar of wind sounded like the chitter of rats.

Rooster was thankful when they began their descent, and mountains turned to stretches of flat plains and then into marshlands. The mountains loomed over them, but they were behind them, the clouds sheathing their tips from view.

They halted at the edge of the marshland. Banks of land dotted the pools of water, and a great fog hid the wetlands from view. The horses pawed the ground, snorting nervously, and Obrand rode beside Rooster.

"Be careful traversing these marshlands, lad." Obrand nodded, staring out into the fog. "We've lost many men to these wastes. If you head west for several days, you'll hit the coast, where you might find a safer passage."

Cassius shook his head immediately. "I have a dire need to go to Volendam, and this way will be quicker."

Rooster hesitated. Obrand's words were wise, and he would know these lands far better than them. They had spent many days fighting for their survival. Still, a low hum echoed in his belly, a quiet urgency to get to the port city. Helai peered through the fog into the marshlands. The others seemed on edge.

"The quicker I get to Volendam, the better," Helai agreed.

"Split off—go to road. Don't want to fight anymore," Intoh said. "Might take few more days. Fine with me." He rested against his new staff as Linda swatted at a butterfly attempting to land on their snout.

"It would be wiser *and* safer if we stick together. You will have an easier time getting Linda into the city if you're with us," Rooster argued, gesturing to himself and Helai. Rooster's brand burned as if in agreement, and Intoh scowled, rubbing where his own brand was.

"Can see logic," he said. "Will stay."

Obrand's expression sobered. "I trust you all to know how to keep your head and wits about you."

Rooster dismounted, leading his horse over to tie to Obrand's pony. Reaching up, he took Obrand's forearm in his grasp. "Maybe our paths will cross again. I hope to be in Volendam for some time if your travels find you there."

"It was nice to have met you, Rooster. Nice to have met all of you. We travel to our embassy in Volendam from time to time for political talk and trade, so we'll look out for you if we find ourselves there." Obrand bowed his head as they led their horses back to the mountains. Exhaling slowly, Rooster could already feel the unsettling nature of the marshes.

"I've heard tales of this marshland," Helai said, reaching out a hand. The moment her hand slipped through the fog, it almost disappeared. "One of the people I used to travel with said beasts hunt these lands, and the fog is so dense the concept of time is lost."

"Let's not lose our heads then, yeah?" Cassius said.

A gust of wind brushed past him, and the smell of sea air assaulted Rooster. All of a sudden, he wasn't standing beside the others at all. Disoriented, he looked down and noticed he stood upon a small eldrasi sailboat. The sails billowed softly in the wind, and it was nearing sundown, the sun drenching the sky in a hue of pinks and golds.

"Sailor, are you all right? You look like you've seen a ghost." Rooster turned to see a woman staring at him in concern. The sight of her took his breath away, a longing piercing him so suddenly it left a physical ache in his chest. She was petite, her eyes so deep a blue he'd be happy to drown himself in them. Her hair was loose, tousled, and a deep brilliant red tucked neatly behind pointed ears. She was an eldrasi of Míradan—an island nestled in the southwest between the two continents, made up of woodland folk ostracized by the eldrasi of Daesthara for wanting to adapt to the modern world. The eldrasi of Dacsthara were often mistaken as plants—shepherds and caretakers of the forest—while the eldrasi of Míradan were cursed to don a more humanoid appearance.

"Of course, my love. I thought I felt the boat rock." Rooster spoke as if he were reliving a memory or a dream. The edges of his vision were blurry as if he were peering through a spyglass, and the woman grinned at him, her fingers grazing pathways down his cheek.

"You need to learn to relax, sailor," she said.

A smug look crossed his face. "I am the master of relaxing, and you should know this."

Laughter slipped past her lips, and she looked at him with a teasing judgment. "Your ineptitude is acceptable because I love you." The gentle sound of waves lapped up against the side of the boat as Rooster pulled her close, embracing her. Her hair smelled of sea salt and an intoxicating aroma of some flower he couldn't quite place. He found himself not wanting to let go. *I don't want to lose you again.*

"I love you too," he said, his words muffled by her hair.

The woman kissed him gently, her fingers threading through his hair. Her skin was warm and sun-soaked as stars lit up the night sky. Desire heated his belly as her fingers raked his back. She pulled away even as he chased her lips with his own.

"Are you certain you must leave?" she whispered as his kisses fell against her neck. "We could just stay in Vitreuse, build ourselves a lovely home away from the world."

Rooster hummed against the woman's neck and sighed. "I have to, Igraine. I'll regret not going if I stay." As he pulled away, the woman stared at him sadly. His heart throbbed painfully in his chest, but as he opened his mouth to speak, he was drawn from the memory. Her large sad eyes were the last thing he saw before he blinked and was back at the edges of the marshlands.

"Rooster, we go now." Linda bumped him gently on the back of his head with their nose as the others stared at him, Helai with concern and Cassius with ill-concealed curiosity.

"Where did you go?" Helai asked.

Rooster blinked and shrugged. "Got lost in my thoughts for a second. Doesn't matter. I don't like the feel of this place. The quicker we get through it, the better." Rooster still felt disoriented from the memory, the edges of his mind desperate to remember but unable to hang on. It grew as fogged as the swamp that lay before them. Still, he clung to the woman's appearance with a stubbornness he wouldn't yield from.

"For once, I agree. I can detect heartbeats in the fog, but it's too difficult to tell where they are. We must tread carefully." Cassius rested a hand on the hilt of his sword, his brow furrowed.

Helai pulled two daggers from her belt and held them loosely. "Into the fog, then?"

Intoh twisted his ring and climbed onto Linda's back, a greka once more. Linda opened their maw, a low hiss passing their teeth, but it was silenced by the fog. Unease gripped the nape of Rooster's neck, forcing the hairs to stand on end, but he was the first to tread forward, allowing the fog to swallow him up.

He did not know how long they walked. He found a small game trail to follow through the fog and gestured for the others to follow. It became almost comforting, the repetition of white as they traversed through. The marshes often gave way to shallow bodies of water, leaving the party wet and miserable. Rooster did not know how many bugs he killed against his skin, and the air was so dense at times he thought he might choke on it.

At one point, he called forth the magic humming inside him, beckoning a small flickering flame that rose a few inches over his open palm. It did little to light the way, but it brought him small comfort.

"You know fire magic?" Intoh asked, staring at the flame as it glinted off his scales.

Rooster nodded slowly. The heat from using magic colored his cheeks red, and he shrugged. "Nothing more than little flames to light the way. I cannot recall where I learned it, now that you ask, and I don't like using it. The magic is too chaotic for my tastes. I'd much rather learn the ways of the water or nature healing."

Intoh hummed, studying Rooster's hand closely. "Should teach me sometime."

Cassius stepped away from the flame with a small scowl but said nothing.

Rooster nodded. "Maybe. Fire magic is difficult to teach, and I don't think I'd be the best teacher." After that, the party fell into silence, and the flickering flame led them forward.

Rooster could almost taste his relief when they finally broke through the fog and spotted a small island. One lone tree rose from the soil, its bark dark and twisted. Bones collected at the base, and Rooster wasn't sure what kind of creature they'd come from.

"By the gods," Helai whispered with a sharp intake of breath. When they drew closer, Rooster saw what hung from the tree's branches.

Corpses of dead dwarves stared out into the fog with unseeing eyes. They had only begun to decompose; whatever had killed them was not long gone. Three squiggly lines had been carved diagonally into their faces.

A low growl of frustration fled Cassius. "The heartbeats are still too strong, lost in the fog. I cannot tell where they are coming from or what they are," he said.

A chill ran down Rooster's spine as he noticed all the hair on the dwarves had been sheared off. It was a great dishonor in dwarf culture to lose one's hair. The tree itself wept a sickly black substance that oozed over the dwarves and scratched into the side of the trunk was a language Rooster did not recognize.

Whispers echoed off the branches in a low tone, inviting them to come closer.

"I would not go near," Cassius warned.

"I was going to go touch it," Rooster replied sarcastically, stifling the flame in his palm. A collective intake shot through the party as Rooster's brand flared in pain. A sickening rage coursed through him, building with every moment he looked upon the tree.

"Come on. Let's get away from it," Helai whispered, moving forward. Linda and Intoh had already moved ahead, their silhouettes in the fog barely visible. Rooster did not look back at the tree when they moved, yet he could still feel the gazes of the dwarves as he walked away. It was some time before the anger within him faded and longer still before the brand on his back stopped aching.

"What do you think could have done that to them?" Helai spoke in hushed tones after the tree had disappeared in the fog.

"Whatever it was, I'm sure we don't want to run into it. Dyrvak, perhaps. Or maybe the rakken came out of the mountains to haunt this place," Cassius said.

"What are dyrvak?" Helai asked, horrified.

Cassius stared out into the fog. "The people of Wilhaven speak of them as monsters that dwell within the forests of Daesthara. They're said to worship old things and steal children that stray too close to the forest's edge." Cold seeped into the air at the mention of dyrvak, and Rooster shuddered.

"More likely beast things. Doubt rakken come out this far. They seem to like cold dark places," Intoh replied, still clinging to Linda's shoulder.

Rooster didn't like the thought of either option—or an equally terrible one.

"Wait," Cassius commanded, his arm shooting out. "Get down!"

Everyone obeyed without a second thought, slipping behind trees as the sound of marching echoed through the fog. Linda and Intoh slid into a deep puddle of water off the bank, naught but their heads breaking the surface. The bark pressed through Rooster's shirt as he eyed Cassius and rested a finger against his lips. Gesturing with his other hand towards the source of the noise, Cassius nodded, quietly unsheathing his sword.

A few moments passed before Rooster could make out their forms. The fog broke away as if it were clearing a path for the herd. Rooster inhaled sharply.

Hooves thundered against the ground as they marched, their eyes brutal and unforgiving as they came forward in droves. Their approach left dread coursing through the earth as if their very presence was wrong. Bodies of enormous deers and elk, their upper halves were humanoid in appearance, their faces still bearing some semblance of the woodland realm. Massive deer-like ears twitched as bugs invaded their space, and their horns were twisted and shaped in various and unique ways, decorated with small trinkets and fabric.

Their leader wore braids in his beard that met in the middle, resting over his bare chest. He shouted in a harsh tongue, and the herd halted, their nostrils flaring. Several of them still held bloodied scimitars at their sides.

Silence etched itself into the air, strangling the party with bated breath. One of the beasts pawed the ground, snorting as their leader held up a fist, his ears twitching. Heads of dwarves hung from his waistband, and anger swelled up inside Rooster. His fingers dug into the tree trunk in front of him so hard that tiny beads of blood slipped from the cuts forming on the tips.

Rooster caught Cassius' eye.

Dyrvak, Cassius mouthed. Another chill coursed through Rooster.

The leader shouted again, yanking his other arm forward to show a dead dwarf being pulled behind him by his beard. His head was split open, and his eyes bore into Rooster's, begging Rooster to liberate him from beyond the grave. Rooster was not a religious man, but he hoped wherever the dwarf was, he could find peace. Helai mouthed a silent prayer as the dyrvak conversed amongst themselves.

Many tense moments passed before the herd moved out, their hooves leaving indentations in the soft ground. Rooster's shoulders didn't relax until the sounds of their war cries were no longer heard. He exhaled.

It was several minutes more before anyone dared to speak.

"I do not know why they left, but I do not care to stay around and find out," Cassius said. He carried his sword at his side and did not resheathe it as Intoh slunk out of the water, shaking his scales free. Linda still floated there, their maw breaking the surface.

"Linda eat?" Linda rose, water sliding off their scales as they fixed their stare at the fog towards where the dyrvak had disappeared.

"Not a good idea. Find you something large and worthy to eat," Intoh promised.

That seemed to satisfy Linda, and Rooster rolled his shoulders, eager for Volendam and the closest inn. He was going to drink himself beneath the table the moment they arrived.

"Volendam can't be far now," Rooster said.

Cassius gave him a pointed look as if he didn't quite believe him. "So long as we don't lose our way." He wiped some dirt from his arm, staring off into the fog. "This place is strange. We just saw those beasts, and yet... I cannot feel their heartbeats." It was unsettling, seeing someone like Cassius so off guard.

"Why would dyrvak be up here? Cassius, did you not say they were creatures of Daesthara?" Helai asked

Rooster was ready to be out of these marshes.

"I do not know," Cassius admitted quietly, glancing over his shoulder. "Something is not right. I do not see us finding any answers in the middle of the marshes, but maybe someone in Volendam will know." He sniffed, his fingers shaking. Rooster didn't know how long a vampire could go without eating, but Cassius always seemed to push it. Not that there were many options out in the marshland. He was surprised Cassius hadn't asked or attempted to compel him or Helai for a feeding.

"What did you say earlier about not losing our heads, Cassius?" Rooster called out.

An arrow shot past his head when the words left his lips, and it missed narrowly, embedding in the tree trunk in front of him. Everyone reacted instantly, using the trees for cover, and Rooster turned just as a smaller horde of dyrvak materialized from the fog, shouting in their language.

"Well, shit," Rooster shouted as more arrows flew. "If they want a fight, who are we to deny them?"

Chapter Twenty
Helai

A quick prayer was sent to Dalnor as Helai drew low to the ground, her hair plastered to her face from the humidity. Cassius disappeared somewhere in the fog, and Rooster kept his body pressed against the tree on her left as he loaded his crossbow. Linda stood at her right, Intoh perched on their shoulder once more.

She noticed something unsettling on the dyrvak. A mark was branded on their side and matched the brand on her back, the brand on all of them. She turned her head and rested her face on the cool earth, her eyes latching onto the brand on Linda's thigh. Small red veins radiated from its center, snaking out in all directions.

The dyrvak in front of Linda chucked a spear that pierced the krok'ida's shoulder, sending them into a fit of rage. Luckily it missed

Intoh, and he jumped from Linda's back the moment they charged, shooting at a dyrvak with electricity. As the electricity pierced the dyrvak's skin, it shrieked, convulsing as the shock prevented it from moving away. Linda slammed into the dyrvak and bit down on its neck, ripping it open and feasting on its blood.

Darting forward, Helai struck out with her daggers as she came up on another, slicing through his tendon at its knee and ankle. It collapsed in a cry of anger and pain, and she drew back, plunging the dagger through the dyrvak's eye and killing it quickly. A dyrvak nearby attempted to grab her, but she ducked, using the fog and shadows to cover her.

The leader pried a horn from its side and blew into it. The noise cascaded through the fog in all directions and sounded eerie amongst the wall of silence. A chill of horror gripped Helai as another horn sounded not too far off.

As the leader lowered the horn from its lips, it spoke in broken Vilris. "Dying here would be kindness. Coming chaos."

Rooster shot around the tree, his crossbow cocked and ready. "Right. Whatever you say, big guy," he said, shooting the dyrvak attacking Intoh. The bolt hit the dyrvak in the shoulder. Shouting to its fellow dyrvak, it charged. Cursing, Rooster dove to the side, almost ending up in a pool of murky water. As the dyrvak neared, it reared up, and Helai ran to help, sure it was about to crush him beneath its hooves. But halfway there, she stumbled to a stop with a cry of surprise.

Bursting out of the water, Linda dragged the screaming dyrvak down into the depths.

Turning her head, Helai saw the first dyrvak who'd shot Linda now in pieces on the ground, and a trail of blood circled to lead into the water at the other end. Shock and horror mingled within Helai. Linda moved so silently for being such a giant beast.

A moment later, red bubbled to the surface where Linda had just taken their newest victim. Off in the distance, the sound of hooves thundered closer.

"I will *not* be getting on their bad side," Rooster said, looking at Helai as he gestured to Linda in the water. "Did you know they were in there? I did not know they were in there." Shaking his head, he slid his foot into the cocking stirrup and loaded another bolt.

"Horrifying," Helai agreed. As she pulled from her satchel the orb she had stolen from a rakken's corpse after the battle, the purple mist within it stirred as if beckoned by her touch. *Please don't miss*, she thought, chucking it at the two remaining dyrvak. She aimed for the one armed with a crossbow as it raised it to shoot at Intoh.

The orb flew through the air, hitting the dyrvak in its chest with pinpoint accuracy. It exploded upon impact, sending a sea of amethyst smoke around it. The dyrvak immediately dropped its weapon and collapsed as its flesh bubbled, burning away to reveal the gleam of bone. It screamed to whatever god it worshiped as it died.

The leader turned a hateful gaze to Helai, but before it could move to attack, a bullet of red shadow shot through the side of its waist. Turning, the dyrvak glared at Cassius, who stood in front of a tree, the flintlock in his hand still smoking as it retreated into the shadows. Crawling up his forearm, it sunk into the skin. Helai wondered what kind of weapon that was and if it belonged to Dalnor, her god. It would make sense for a gun of shadows to belong to the shadow god.

Surely not, she thought. *A vampire would not follow Dalnor. They only followed Drausmírtus, the god of death.*

The leader charged at Cassius now, blowing its horn.

Before Helai could react, a net was flung around her. She hit the ground, a frustrated exhale passing through her as a dyrvak broke the treeline and picked her up. It charged, throwing her toward the water. She took a large breath just before she crashed below the surface, where everything was murky and dark. The water was warmer than she'd expected, and Helai saw Linda's form in the distance, struggling with something.

Pulling a dagger from her side, she attempted to cut through the netting, but it seemed infused with magic and would not yield. Panic crept up in her throat as the net continued to drag her down, and she fought against it. The edges of her vision blurred as her throat tightened and a dark mass approached her. At first, she thought it might be Linda, but then Cassius' face appeared before her, and he was pulling her to the surface. A wet cough escaped her as she gasped for air. "Can't cut it," she rasped as Cassius fought to tear a hole through it with his bare hands. When that was unsuccessful, he moved to find the clamp that shut the net around her.

"Stop struggling," he said. A moment later, the net around her loosened, and she could kick away from it, swimming to the water's edge. She did not have time to thank him as four more dyrvak joined the fight, and they were forced to their feet.

Stumbling, his head bleeding, Intoh threw out his hand, and a bright burst of light hit a dyrvak attempting to run him through with a spear.

Helai turned as a centaur threw another net over Cassius. As the Dyrvak chanted in low tones, the net heated to a dark red, and Cassius' sword slipped from his grasp as he fell to the ground and struggled to regain his composure. The leader stomped the ground with one heavy hoof.

Cassius fought beneath his net, his fangs on full display, his face decayed. The leader laughed as it picked him up by the throat through the net. Blood secreted from the corner of the dyrvak's eyes, dripping down onto his hand and slithering up towards Cassius. Helai stared at it in horror as she stumbled away. She had never seen magic work like that. It looked to be moving on its own accord, and she feared what would happen if it were to touch Cassius.

"Gorvayne awaits you. His reckoning will be heard," the leader rasped. Helai moved again to help, but another dyrvak stepped in front of her, shielding them from view.

Helai flinched back as the dyrvak swung its sword down, cutting her shallowly in the shoulder. She shot under his right arm and stabbed to the side with her dagger. The dyrvak cried out, and Intoh flung a beam of light towards its eyes. The dyrvak reared back, and Helai locked gaze with Intoh.

"Blinded it. Your chance," he called out. Reacting without hesitation, Helai stabbed the dyrvak in the neck until she was certain it was dead. Linda had pulled their kill up on shore, leaving it to charge another that stood on the edge of the fighting, a bow in its hand. It let loose an arrow just as Linda brought it down, but lucky for Rooster, the arrow missed, flying past his head into the fog.

"These beasts should stick to swords and nets, eh? Not much of a good shot," Rooster called out. Despite being in the midst of combat, Helai couldn't help but smile. He reminded her so much of Massoud at times. Her brother could never help but crack jokes during trouble, either.

With relief, she looked up and saw Cassius removing himself from the net, ire stitched in his expression. The leader was dead, with a crossbow bolt sticking out of the back of his head. When the dyrvak leader hit the ground, its blood stopped moving towards Cassius. Rooster lowered his crossbow and stepped out of the shadows.

It didn't take long for them to kill the rest of the dyrvak, and after a few moments, they all gathered, heaving and covered in blood.

"Is everyone all right?" Helai asked, her fingers trembling. She clung to her dagger, allowing an exhale to soothe her nerves. Adrenaline roared in her ears as the humidity suffocated the air around her. She could say with certainty that she preferred the dry heat of her homeland to this wetness. Wringing out her clothes, she sighed, cursing herself for not having a spare set. Rooster pulled some clothes out of his bag and threw them at her. "Here—we'll put your clothes by the fire to dry when we stop for the night. I don't think it would be wise to stop here." Helai caught them and opened her mouth to respond when Intoh groaned.

"Ah..." Intoh said, clutching the side of his head. "One got me good with their pummel. Hurts pretty bad. Can conclude I may have concussion."

Helai went to his side, pulling a salve from her satchel and ignoring the throb from the wound at her shoulder. Luckily, the salve was in a waterproof vial, sealed shut with magic. Her fingers gently pried his hand away to assess the damage. The scales at his temple were cracked open, and green blood seeped through. "You are lucky," Helai said, dropping his hand. "It looks like your scales protected your skull. This salve should help with that. It might make you a bit sleepy, but you should try to stay awake if possible."

"Hmm," Intoh hummed, patting Helai on the shoulder. She took that as gratitude, given he didn't verbalize such, and when she finished applying the salve with her fingers, she went around to the others and assessed them as well.

"Linda shoulder hurt," Linda said, gesturing to where a dyrvak had sliced their shoulder open. The wound wasn't too deep, and Linda remained perfectly still as Helai cleaned and wrapped it. As Helai patted their shoulder, Linda leaned down to press the bottom of their snout to the top of Helai's head. It was oddly comforting, even if buried under a thin layer of fear. Linda was so large up close.

"You're bleeding," Intoh pointed out, gesturing to Helai's shoulder. "Come here—will take look."

"Did any of you understand anything the dyrvak said?" Helai asked as she knelt next to Intoh. "He mentioned the name Gorvayne. Have any of you heard that before?" Helai shuddered as the mere mention of the name sent a chill down her back. The fog seemed to dip and wrap around her, drawing her into a sense of comfort and home. Perhaps it was merely the magic that wove through Intoh into her skin, sealing the cut at her shoulder.

Cassius' brow furrowed at the name, but otherwise, he remained silent.

"I have not, but that doesn't speak for much. Got a memory for shit, as it were," Rooster said, tapping a finger against his temple. "It was likely just some god those beasts worship, and we shouldn't pay it any mind."

"I believe I know of some cultists that worship Gorvayne in Halvdarc," Cassius said, clearing his throat. "I came into contact with one about a month back." He rubbed at his beard, his illusion back in place. "I do not know who Gorvayne is, but I know his worship goes beyond the dyrvak."

"Volendam has college. It's why I travel there. We can research. For now, would like to leave this place," Intoh muttered, rubbing his head as he pulled away from Helai and leaned against Linda.

"Can you purify this, Intoh?" Rooster asked, gesturing to the net that had ensnared Cassius. It was still reasonably intact, and she wondered how he'd managed to free himself. "Could come in handy if we need to trap something."

Helai couldn't argue with that logic. She had seen Masika do it once from an item they'd stolen from the Almkin. Helai had watched as Masika bent over the dagger and whispered something in a tongue even Helai did not recognize. Black tendrils had been pulled from the metal, and it no longer bred a sick feeling in the pit of Helai's stomach.

Intoh shrugged and used his staff to get to his feet. Tiny shallow breaths left him as he wove magic over the net. Plumes of blue danced over his fingers and the net as he closed his eyes. His maw opening, he curled his fingers. Dark magical smoke curled off the net, resisting Intoh's magic. A loud snap resounded through the fog, and Intoh fell back, panting.

"Did it, but dizzy. Must take break. Too much magic," he said, holding his chest.

"Yes, give yourself a break. You'll overwork yourself," Helai said. "You're already wounded." Magic was fickle. Some people produced more of the saelic chemical that produced magic, while others couldn't produce it at all. Perhaps it had to do with the gland that sat next to the heart and how hard that muscle could work. Not much research had been done on it or why the gland only existed in drikoty and humans. But she did know that muscles needed rest, and even brains required sleep.

"In fact," Helai said, looking around, "we should rest."

"I agree, but that horn made quite a bit of noise. We should find somewhere safer to rest. I can stay up and make sure we're not ambushed in our sleep," Cassius said, leaning down to pull the horn from the leader's corpse and strap it to his side. Rooster moved over to the net. He shoved it into his pack, then ran his hand over his patchy head.

"I will scout ahead and find us a safe spot. Wait here," Rooster said, slipping away into the fog as he pulled back the lever on his crossbow.

"I'm going to change just behind that tree," Helai told the others. Slipping behind the tree in question, she stripped out of her clothes and tugged the extra shirt, and pants Rooster had gotten from the dwarves on. A sigh of relief seeped through her lips at the dry clothes, and she pushed the wet clothes into her bag as she rejoined the others. Intoh pried an axe from one of the dyrvak's corpses, wrapping it in cloth, and Linda was back in the water, floating aimlessly with nothing but their snout above the surface.

Helai approached Cassius as he sat on a rock and cleaned his sword. His movement was fluid, an expert at work as he took a cloth to the steel to wipe the blood away. A small flask of oil sat at his side, and he did not glance up when she stopped beside him.

"Helai," he muttered quietly.

"Cassius." Helai was silent for a moment as she watched him work. "You saved my life. I just wanted to thank you." She still felt uneasy around Cassius, but she'd feel guilty until she thanked him.

"Your gratitude is unnecessary." His shoulders squared as he continued to work on his sword. A silence fell between them. Just before Helai thought it best to flee the conversation, Cassius sighed and met her gaze. Something tortured in his expression, but Helai was too frightened of him to pry.

"You think me a monster." She opened her mouth to reply, but he continued. "Perhaps I am. Or perhaps the stories your parents told you growing up were not entirely true. I could not stand idly by while you drowned. What kind of knight would I be?"

Shame colored Helai's cheeks as she fiddled with her fingers. "You told Ayla you were a knight of the White Dawn, and I have never heard of that order."

Cassius nodded, his gaze shifting back to his sword. "Their keep, the Dragon Keep, dwells within the Spine Mountains. The name 'White Dawn' is a cover, and their true name is the Sanguine Order. 'White Dawn' was a title given to the order's founder Ruxandra Albescu."

"Ruxandra." Helai mulled over the name as it rolled off her tongue.

"Ruxandra and her wife Louelle created the Sanguine Order long ago. Humans believe it is an order of knights that defend their code of honor."

Helai looked abhorred. "Vampires don't have honor."

Cassius' expression deadpanned as he met her gaze once more. "You are a cleric of Dalnor, no? You've certainly done things your mother would not be proud of. He is not even a god of Shoma."

Helai's fingers wrapped instinctively around the eye necklace around her throat.

The eye of the One will keep you safe, abib. Never take it off. Those were her mother's last words before she'd slipped Helai into a dark hole away from the men looking for them. Her mother had hidden Helai to give her a fighting chance.

Helai's heart ached at the reminder. If her mother had known her to stray from the path of their gods to worship a god of the west, she would have been devastated.

"I suppose." Silence encompassed them for a few moments. "You said Ruxandra founded the Sanguine Order. Did she contract vampirism from the deserts of Shoma? My people think it to be a curse of our god."

Cassius scoffed, setting down his sword. "It does not come from your god, Helai." Helai felt inclined to correct him—*Dalnor is my god, not Qevayl*—but she remained silent. It mattered little. Cassius picked up his sword again, resuming his cleaning task. "Why the sudden curiosity in vampire creation, Helai?"

Helai shook her head, holding up her hands. "No reason, just curiosity."

"Curiosity can be dangerous. You should be more careful," Cassius said as Helai rose. She retreated from Cassius' side without another word, leaving him to tend to his sword as she patrolled the perimeter.

Rooster returned not much later, hand gesturing for them to follow. The fog had thinned, but it still felt timeless in the marshes, and Helai despised the squelch of the wet ground beneath her boots. Exhaustion slowed her down, but she was eager to see the walls of Volendam, and that alone spurred her forward. *I hope you are waiting for me in an inn, Massoud.*

They set up camp fairly quickly into the night with no fire to warm them. They feared the wrath of more dyrvak should they see the flames. Helai found a small patch of dry ground to lay her bedroll out on as the others took their places too. The lizards slid into the water nearby to sleep, and Rooster propped himself up against a tree, one leg kicked up to rest an arm against his knee. Cassius stood guard at the outskirts, his hair pulled back neatly with a slick red ribbon. His hands were clasped behind his back, and he looked stoic, like a statue long forgotten.

Helai didn't say anything to any of them as she laid her clothes beside her to dry and settled down on her bedroll. There was no wind, no whispers among the flora, and the silence was haunting. She slipped a dagger beneath the bedroll under her head in case she needed it in the night. She'd been ambushed enough times in the sands of her home to know one could never be too careful.

Laying on her back, she found the fog too thick to see the stars. She often looked to the moon for guidance. She believed the moon to be something Dalnor had created, a beacon in the darkness and lighting the way for his clerics. It was so different from the beliefs of Shoma, which was thought to be the eye of Qevayl. The full moon's light was the holiest of nights in their eyes, a time when sinners were judged for their crimes.

There was no moon to wish upon tonight, and Helai rolled over on her side. The last thing she saw before she closed her eyes was a yellow and luminescent butterfly landing on Linda's snout as they rested just above the water.

Chapter Twenty-One
Cassius

Cassius stayed up to watch over the party, and the entire night was a restless one as the weight of the gun burned ever brighter in its shadowy home in his arm. It guided him towards Volendam, but he wasn't sure why or what he'd find there. He'd only been to Volendam a handful of times and not for a long time. He'd been human still, a young adult living with his uncle in Rovania. His uncle had sent him to Volendam to trade, and he had stayed for a week before traveling back along the river to his home. He could barely remember it.

Rooster stirred sometime in the early morning, and Cassius gave him a glance as the human sat beside him, staring up at the sky. The fog had cleared sometime in the night, and the stars twinkled brilliantly even as they faded with sunrise.

They said nothing to each other. Cassius had never been a man of many words. Isolated as a child due to his knightly training as a human, he'd only had his older brother to talk to. Over the years, even he and Markus had grown apart, and much of Cassius' adult life had been spent completely and utterly alone.

"What's it like?" Rooster asked, his fingers threading together behind his head.

"What?" Cassius turned to meet his gaze. He could feel Rooster's heart thundering under his shirt and taste the dried blood of a scab at his temple. Hunger clawed at his throat, but like time and time before, he ignored its demands.

Rooster shrugged. "Being a vampire. I've heard night-walkers have no souls to speak of and only care about blood and power." Rooster's gaze challenged Cassius, but Cassius gave him no satisfaction.

Instead, Cassius stood, offering Rooster a hand. "It is more complicated than that." As Cassius helped Rooster to his feet, he brushed his hands together. "I do not know about souls, but I have been alive long enough to see the cruelty of mankind. If they can have souls, then why not the best of vampires?"

Rooster thumbed his chin in thought as the others began to stir. "You bring up a fair point."

"I tend to have them from time to time."

Rooster's smile was faint as the conversation concluded, leaving Cassius to dwell on his thoughts. It was not the first time someone had asked him what it was like being a vampire. Cassius couldn't speak for low vampires, whose resurrection included a ritual to reanimate their corpses through necromancy. High vampires had been cursed for hundreds of years by the dragon Nelfta. When high vampires turned mortals and immortalized their bodies. Whether their soul stayed in their death remained to be seen.

Cassius turned as Helai rolled up her bedroll and Rooster spoke with Intoh, who was rousing Linda from sleep.

After gathering their things, they walked for the better part of the day. The transition from marshland to the forest was drastic and sudden. They walked on the dry ground now, their boots caked in dried mud, and autumn was in full bloom around them. The leaves were vibrant shades of gold and red; warm light seeped through breaks in the trees. The smell of the ocean grew more potent, and Cassius pointed out the walls of Volendam as they peeked over the trees on the horizon.

"We could make it to the gate but should probably make camp. It will be more difficult to get into the city after nightfall," Cassius said.

"This seems as good a place as any, and I can hear running water nearby. We can light a fire tonight, too," Rooster replied, hefting his pack off his shoulder and setting it on the ground.

Helai nodded. "I can go hunt for some food." The rations the dwarves had given them were getting low. After setting out her bedroll and placing her bag next to it, she disappeared into the woods, her steps silent.

Intoh settled down near the fire Rooster had made, his fingers drawing over the ax he had grabbed off the dyrvak's body. A low hum of dark light pulsed under the cloth, and Linda watched curiously.

Rooster stood at the edge of the meadow and then turned. "I'll be right back."

"I am going to go wash up at the creek I hear, so do not be surprised if I am not here when you return," Cassius called out to Rooster's retreating form. Rooster gave a thumbs up in acknowledgment without glancing back.

Linda huffed. "I come too," they said.

Cassius shrugged. "Makes no difference to me."

Intoh waved his hand without looking up as they embarked silently, slipping through the trees towards the sound of water trickling over rocks. The forest was still but warm, providing a sense of comfort and safety. It was a welcomed relief after the unease in the marshes. Birds chirped, and squirrels were seen stocking up on food for the coming winter.

It didn't take long to find the creek, large enough for the water to come up to Cassius' waist after he removed his armor and waded in. A sigh of relief passed his lips. He was growing hungrier, but it was easily ignored as the water washed over him and removed the blood and grime from his skin.

Linda dove into the water in front of Cassius, their snout the only thing above water as they waded around. They left Cassius alone with his thoughts, and he sank until only his head was dry.

Cassius... a woman's voice, soft and sultry, called out quietly to him, riding the wind. Cassius ignored it. *Cassius...* it called again, insistent, pulling him towards the city.

Grinding his teeth together, Cassius sank lower until he was completely submerged with nothing but the rushing water to be heard. Fish swam around him, light glinting off their scales as they rushed away from Linda, who hunted them. Linda swam by, trapping several fish in their mouth, and when Cassius rose out of the water, the voice that had called out to him was silent. He was relieved by it and stood to sit upon the bank, letting the sun dry his skin before he donned his clothes again.

"Come on, Linda. Surely Helai has returned with some food for you all to eat," Cassius said.

Linda hissed, diving into the water a few more times before they ascended onto the bank on all fours. The immense size of Linda was a force to be reckoned with all its own. Still, the sun had begun its descent over the trees, and Cassius knew better than to think they were safe just because it felt so.

"Rather eat fish," Linda said but raised on two feet and followed Cassius back into the line of trees. A flash of green light illuminated the trees before fading away. Cassius prepared for an attack, but then Rooster stepped into their line of sight, gripping a small branch. He nodded at them as they approached.

"I was just about to make my way back as well," Rooster said, stepping in line with Cassius. His blood smelled intoxicating, like sea salt and alcohol, and Cassius stopped breathing, a furrow on his brow.

"What was that?" Cassius asked, gesturing to the tree.

Rooster held up a branch. "A gift from the forest. Gonna make a bow out of it."

Cassius nodded. "I will need to find someone to feed on soon," he said. The older he got, the less he needed to feed, but he hadn't fed since Emberfoot Refuge, and he grew weary at the thought that he might not be able to wait until his first night within Volendam. If he waited too long, he'd black out and kill the nearest person to feed on. The lifeless eyes of the lovers in his estate haunted him at the thought.

"Why don't you just find some animal to drain?" Helai materialized next to Linda, a doe thrown across her shoulders.

Cassius scoffed, running a hand through his hair as it dried. "Only uncivilized vampires drink from animals. Animal blood is raw and natural, but drinking from an animal will cause the vampire to fall prey to the nature of the beast. Vampires who drink from animals rarely have their minds intact. If I wish to keep my mind, I can only drink from a human. The vampiric curse wills it so."

Helai's nose crinkled, but she said nothing.

Linda clapped Cassius hard on the back, startling everyone. "Sometimes eat people. Sometimes necessary. I get it." Cassius glanced up at Linda and nodded, gesturing to the others.

"See, the lizard understands. Be more like Linda, Helai."

Helai shook her head. As they neared the camp, they saw Intoh stoking the fire, the ax at his side. It was uncovered and no longer radiated dark magic. Helai and Rooster began preparing the doe for food. Linda fell onto their belly and promptly fell asleep, and Cassius propped up against a tree, a good deal away from the flame where the heat could not touch him.

The sun set on the party a couple of hours later. Light from the flame danced off their expressions as they ate. For the first time since they'd entered and left the marshlands, the atmosphere felt light, like no evil could touch them. Cassius was determined to stay up and take watch, but he could feel the edges of his soul crave rest.

"Once we get into the city, are we to part ways?" Rooster asked.

"I have business to attend to in Volendam, but I seek to find an inn in an affordable district if possible. The dwarves did not give us much skaels to split amongst ourselves," Cassius said. He did not know where in the city the voices urged him to, but he would not wait once they were inside the walls. He would seek out where the voices meant for him to go the moment he stepped into the city.

"I will be heading to an inn first. The poorest one, I imagine. I'm supposed to be meeting a friend in Volendam," Helai said, glancing at them as she chewed on strips of deer. "If he is not there, I'm not certain what I'll do. Wait, perhaps. Wait and hope he arrives."

Intoh rested against Linda, his food untouched. "Stay in Volendam. Study at college. Make money on side, perhaps?"

Rooster chewed thoughtfully. "I don't know about you all, but I am in fair need of skaels. I think we should stick together until we know why the rakken branded us and if there are any consequences to it." He shrugged, and Cassius stared at him silently. "I cannot deny that strange things have occurred since it happened. Linda, yours looks to be infected," Rooster said, gesturing to the brand on their leg.

A spider web of red shot out from their brand, ugly and festering. Cassius' brand ached; with it, he could feel the emotions of those around him, the quiet rage weighing on each of them in some capacity or another. It was a strange sensation, but whatever the brand was, it had connected them.

Intoh muttered to himself in drikotyian and rushed to Linda to look over their brand. Linda tried to wave him away, but he insisted, snapping at them in his native tongue. Linda grumbled but showed the brand to him.

"Looks magical—don't know how to heal it." Intoh patted Linda's leg. "College might have mage doctor."

Linda shrugged. "Doesn't hurt. Don't care."

"I have matters to attend to," Cassius said, waving his hand in dismissal. If he continued ignoring the urge that carried him forward much longer, he might lose what sanity he clung to. The others meant little to him, even as the brand ached in a reminder that they were all connected.

"I do as well, and we don't have to pretend we're a team, but—" Helai paused, her expression thoughtful. "We could at least stay in the same inn in Volendam, and we can go about our business. Eventually, we should see if these brands will be a problem, though."

"Will have to see what mage college says. Might stay there," Intoh said, turning away from Linda's leg to look at Helai. "Have to learn. Why I traveled here."

Helai nodded. "Of course."

Rooster thumbed his chin. "No harm in staying in the same inn. The ones closer to the docks are where I'm heading first—they'll be the cheapest, most likely."

Cassius sighed but nodded. It was going to take a miracle to get rid of the company of these strangers.

As if to mock him, the brand on his back burned.

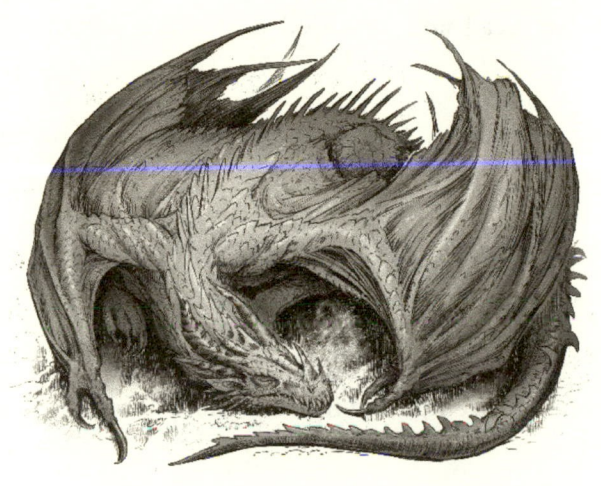

Chapter Twenty-Two
Rooster

The next day was as pleasant and sunny as the previous, and they woke up with little trouble. They approached the city gate within a few hours. The lizards had their rings twisted, masking them behind their humanoid facades, and it was a relief to see the walls close up.

Helai twisted her hands nervously. "I always hate this part," she said.

"What?" Rooster asked.

"Speaking with the guards to enter the city. Massoud was the talker; he'd charm his way into any city or bed he wished."

Cassius snorted. "You speak of this Massoud a lot. He sounds like quite the character."

Helai shook her head and chuckled under her breath. "That's putting it lightly."

Rooster held his hands up. "Just let me do the talking. Guards love me."

Helai side-eyed him. "Why don't I believe you?"

Laughter echoed from Rooster as they approached the guards. "It's a trading port city, and they don't require papers. I'm sure they'll ask for our names for the records and move us along. Nothing to worry about, Helai."

People came and went from the city, pulling carts and livestock behind them. One was pulled aside to be questioned, the guards searching through barrels of what looked to be wine. Volendam's walls were massive, their sigil draped over the edge to rest against the stone. Rooster took a moment to study it—a ship's wheel with kraken's tentacles of blue-green wrapping around it. Two guards were posted at the gate as they fell in line with the other travelers waiting to get into the city. Rooster bounced light on his feet as they approached.

The guards wore simple plate armor. A man stood next to the door, clipboard in hand, as he scribbled on it with ink and squill. Stains covered the man's shirt; if he was trying to grow a mustache, he was failing at it miserably. It made Rooster stroke his chin in silent sympathy.

"Next," the man shouted, and Rooster put on the kindest smile he could muster. His memory was gone, but this felt natural, charming the people around him.

"State your name and business," the man continued, glancing up. He held his quill poised at the ready.

"The name's Rooster. These are my compatriots, and we're traveling down from Emberfoot Refuge to look for work."

The man narrowed his eyes. "What's your *real* name, sir?"

"Rooster's my slave name. Freed myself, but the ol' noggin' don't quite work," he said, tapping his head. "So Rooster it is." He gestured to each of the others. "This is Cassius, Linda, Intoh, and Helai. We mean no trouble in the city."

The man took down their names, his eyes darting behind thin spectacles. "Linda's a woman's name, and he doesn't look like a woman," he said, gesturing to Linda.

Linda snorted in frustration. "I am Linda. Name is name."

"It is the name they have chosen for themself." Rooster leaned over, covering his mouth as if he meant to share some secret. "Lad's from Vangbar. The folk down there... Well, you understand."

The man hummed hesitantly, then tapped his clipboard with his quill and stepped aside. "You may pass."

Rooster nodded in the man's direction, then paused. "This is our first time traveling to Volendam. May you offer some direction? We are looking for an affordable inn to stay at, and I'd like to know who is in charge of the guard."

The man, who'd already moved on to the next travelers, refocused on Rooster. Turning, he gestured to the left within the city. "You'll want to find The Broken Arrow Inn. It's in the Hull District—not the best part of town, but the food's cheap and the board is cheaper.

Captain Booker runs the guard. I'll warn you, though—he doesn't like having his time wasted."

Rooster nodded. "'Course not. Thank you."

As they passed into the city, Rooster leaned over to Helai. "That wasn't so hard. Confidence is key."

Helai shook her head. "Easy for you, maybe."

They took a moment to take in the city. The roads ran along canals, where small boats traveled, and plenty of bridges to pass over them for easy movement. The road was coated in wet mud, but no one seemed to complain. The gate opened to a plaza where merchants sold their goods. Most of the booths had grand displays of fish, with the odd jeweler and leatherworker selling their wares. The buildings were tall and thin, pressed together in lines that overwhelmed the city. There was no castle in the distance, and the people wandering the streets wore simple clothes and did not reek of nobility.

"I am going to go and find that Broken Arrow," Rooster said.

"Perhaps we should all go and then split? I need to go there too. If Massoud is in the city, he'll be at the most run-down inn," Helai said.

Cassius stared off into the distance towards where the city started to improve. His gaze was far away, and he hummed and cleared his throat. "I have to attend to some things. I will find my way to The Broken Arrow later." He was gone before anyone could think to protest.

Linda shrugged. "Sound good."

Intoh nodded, and they set off in the direction the man at the gate had pointed. A pair of children laughed as they kicked a ball in an alleyway, and the air was ripe with humidity as clouds formed. It looked like it was going to rain soon.

"Wait—feel magic coming from here. Should go in there," Intoh said, stopping at a door. It looked just as worn and sun-soaked as the rest of them, paint peeling from the wood as the salty air claimed it. There was something subtle radiating off it, a hum of magic, and Rooster reached forward to press his palm against the wood. It was warm to the touch, and red scrolling text showed up against the frame the moment he knocked.

"Looks Eldrasian," Intoh said, craning his neck to study the text. "My people do much trade with them. Never learned."

"Wait—I know it," Rooster said quietly, pointing to the text. "It reads 'Arathanae.' I cannot remember what it means." The moment the word left his lips, however, the door swung open, and hot air brushed against their cheeks.

Rooster turned to the others. "Well, it would be rude not to go in now," he said. He was the first to step inside, followed closely by the others. A strange feeling passed over him, and he felt the effects of teleportation magic pulling him apart and putting him back together. It didn't hurt, but he felt woozy when they landed.

They had stepped into a blacksmithing forge. The floor dipped and swayed, and as Rooster looked around, he found they had come aboard a ship. It was immaculate, with dark oak swirling designs of leaves and flowers adorning the walls. Weapons and shields decorated the room, beautifully crafted with master skill. A forge sat to the right, and as Rooster stepped forward, the ship rocked again. A strange nostalgia pulled at his belly.

A man bent over the anvil and swung a hammer, hitting metal as it cooled. He was barrel-chested, and sweat gleaned off his bare skin. The man turned his head, revealing ears that curved to points, and Rooster realized the man was eldrasi. His humanlike appearance must have meant he sailed from the Isles of Míridan rather than the forests of Daesthara. Those that dwelled within the forest were bound to the trees of their ancestors and bore little semblance to humans.

Only when he seemed satisfied with his work did he acknowledge them. Setting his hammer down, he wiped his brow and tucked a strand of deep red hair behind his ear. "Welcome to the Fireband, my friends," he called out, running his hands over the beak of a giant, sleeping bird in the corner. The beast wings were a deep, rustic red and blended into the wall, its bottom half and tail bearing the appearance of a black jaguar. Heat rolled off of it in waves, and it stared at them with one massive, piercing amber eye. Part of its beat was chipped away, and the eldrasi stared up at it fondly as it fluffed its wings and resettled.

Rooster leaned over to Helai. In a hushed tone, he said: "I think this man is far out of our budget."

Grabbing a pint, the blacksmith chugged its contents down, sighing happily as he wiped the froth from his lips. "The dwarves truly make the best ale, do they not? You all can call me Velius, and I can assure you that whatever budget you may carry, I can adhere to it."

Rooster opened his mouth to speak, only to cock his head to the side. "Velius? Isn't that a well-known eldrasi forge master? The greatest one to have ever existed? He forged weapons from dragon scales, ultimately leading to his demise."

Velius smiled. "You know your eldrasi history, friend."

"Not sure how, to be honest. Must have heard it somewhere," Rooster admitted.

Velius' smile turned coy as he approached Rooster. Heat rolled off the eldrasi's skin as he offered Rooster a drink of his ale, which he took gladly. He hadn't had a taste of alcohol for several days.

"My craft is unmatched. Some might say I am Velius incarnate." As he studied everyone, Helai snorted, then quickly coughed. She gestured to the bird in the corner.

"What is it?" she asked.

Velius glanced over at it, smiling fondly. "A gryphon. Many believe they are extinct, hunted to death by alchemists for their feathers. While that claim is mostly true, my friend here is one of the last of his kind. He helps me forge the weapons you see here."

Velius winked at Helai, whose cheeks heated as she turned to study the daggers lining a table. The gryphon was large, so large that Rooster wasn't certain how truthful Velius was being with his claim, but how was he to know when his mind was lost?

Velius glanced back at Rooster. "Alas, I can't give away my things for free, but perhaps we can work something out." He walked around each of them, studying their forms and the weapons they had already carried. "I may be able to apply magically infused gems to your existing weapons to enhance their strength, and that will cost less. I will need the gems, of course...." He trailed off, mumbling as he studied the group with his arms folded across his chest.

"You would do this for us. Why?" Rooster eyed Velius suspiciously.

Velius waved his hand, drinking the rest of the ale in several gulps. "I will require a favor from all of you, of course." His words ran through Rooster, an unease that seeped through his pores and ran down his back. He didn't like owing people favors.

Velius held his hands up, seeing the expressions on everyone's faces. "A part of it would be gathering the materials I need, and I do not have time or resources to go and get them myself. Otherwise, I would."

"...and?" Helai asked, turning on her heel to stare at Velius.

Velius smiled, a radiance of gleaming white teeth. "And then you would just owe me. I don't have anything else now, and I won't ask you to risk your life for me, but one favor, and it's all I ask."

A silence passed around the room. Helai hesitated, her hand wavering in the air before dropping to her side before she nodded. "One favor then."

Linda shrugged. "One favor. Seems fair."

Intoh glanced around the room. "If acquiring crystals doesn't affect ability to get into mage college, then one favor." He nodded and held up a finger. "One."

Rooster bit his lower lip. He couldn't. Not without knowing Velius better. "I'm sorry, but I cannot. I'll find the materials for you to help my friends, but I have only just met you. You must understand."

Velius nodded, an easy smile gracing his features. "Of course. No harm! Come back with some more skaels, and I can offer you the full price on whatever you may need. I do not judge, my friend." A knowing expression crossed his face. "I would love to know how a greka and a krok'ida came across illusioned rings."

Hands flew to their weapons as Velius held his hands up in mocked surrender. "No harm, truly. You won't find me riddled with judgment, and I am merely curious."

"How can you see through the illusions?" Helai asked, her hands still curled tightly around two daggers.

Velius gestured to the rings. "These are not the first illusion rings I've seen." A sense of unease settled on Rooster's shoulders, but he pulled his hand off his sword as he straightened.

"You are a very strange blacksmith," he said.

The room was thick with tension, but Velius seemed unaffected by it. "Yes, I suppose so," he said, turning to run a hand alongside the gryphon's face as he laughed. The gryphon chirped in its sleep.

Rooster reached out to offer Velius his hand. "The name's Rooster, but my friends call me Cock." That earned quiet laughter from Velius, and Helai stepped away from the wall, her daggers tucked away.

She shook her head. "We do not call him that," she said. "I'm Helai."

Intoh pointed to himself and then Linda. "Intoh, and this Linda." Linda sniffed the air, and it looked strange in Linda's human form.

Ambling forward, Linda patted him on the head. "Good, sir, good," they said, much to everyone's surprise. The tension seemed to leave the room, and Helai picked up a small dagger off the table, balancing its hilt on the tip of her finger.

"Do your skills go beyond the simple make of a blacksmith? Could we ask for magically imbued items?" Helai asked.

Velius turned to look at Helai. He nodded, folding his arms across his chest. "I do." He shook his finger at Helai, his expression thoughtful. "There's an alchemist down the road, across the street from The Broken Arrow Inn. He and I don't see eye to eye, but if you could purchase some mithril dust from him, I can make you a sheath for your dagger."

That answer seemed to satisfy Helai as Linda shook their head. "Really want hammer."

Velius looked at Linda. "I can make you a war hammer with a simple steel for forty skaels."

Linda rumbled in excitement as they looked over to Intoh, who nodded, pulling out a small bag of skaels and counting them. Pressing it in Velius' outstretched hand, he strapped the small sack back onto his belt and looked around nervously. "Have any healing rings? Can only do the bare minimum. Need something to channel it."

Velius retreated to the opposite wall, where he plucked a silver necklace from a glass cabinet. There was a socket for a gem in the middle, but the socket was bare.

"There's a club up north in the Sails District, where the wealthy dwell. It is called the Silver Moon Club. You can't miss it. It's a vast boat, overly flashy, and super exclusive. If you can acquire a sapphire from there, I can socket it inside this necklace. It should be the thing you need."

"How can we acquire it if we don't have the funds?" Rooster asked.

Velius smiled innocently. "You all look like a talented bunch. I'm sure you'll figure it out."

Rooster and Helai exchanged looks, and Helai gave Rooster the faintest shrug. She did not seem all that worried about the thought of stealing; if Rooster was honest with himself, he wasn't either.

"Why Silver Moon Club? Is it close to mage college?" Intoh asked. Rooster could understand his hesitation.

"The club is upscale, and the owner is notorious for his love for gems. The man calls himself the Captain, and his love for the sea makes him partial to sapphires," Velius said. "The mage college is relatively close, so I'll leave it up to you, my friend."

Intoh stared at the necklace Velius offered to make him in a state of longing. "Will think on it. Need necklace. Don't want to get caught."

Rooster ran a hand through his hair. "You don't have the best of morals, do you?" He said with a lopsided grin.

Velius shrugged. "You seem in need, and the rich won't miss it. Do you need anything, Rooster?"

"I will find a bowyer in the city. I need nothing for now."

Velius nodded in agreement, turning to pick up his forging hammer. He swung it delicately in his hand. "If you manage to find me a ruby, I'll be all the merrier, but that's all I require for now. Or actually—" he held a thumb to his chin, then looked at Rooster.

"It's a favor, but a simple one at that. The club deals in the shadow market. They have a silver locket, and it's made of eldrasi silver. You'll be able to tell."

Rooster nodded. He could do that easily.

"I am here if you need me, but I must get back to work. It was quite a pleasure." Velius winked at Rooster.

As the party turned to leave, Velius called out to them. "Oh, and before I forget—I don't know which of you speaks Eldrasian, but I will only open my door to the phrase you read on the frame. Don't forget it."

Committing it to memory, Rooster ushered everyone out. The sky had turned angry and dark, thick clouds threatening to open at any moment.

"I will catch up with you," Helai said, head turned towards a nearby alleyway.

Rooster didn't question her. "We'll see you at The Broken Arrow then."

Helai nodded dismissively and pulled her hood up, slipping between merchants packing up and heading home for dinner. Torchlight donned many of the buildings, and those out on the street had a quickened pace, their faces turned towards the sky in concern.

"Make haste. Looks to pour at any moment," Intoh said.

"Yes, yes," Rooster said. "The inn can't be too far away."

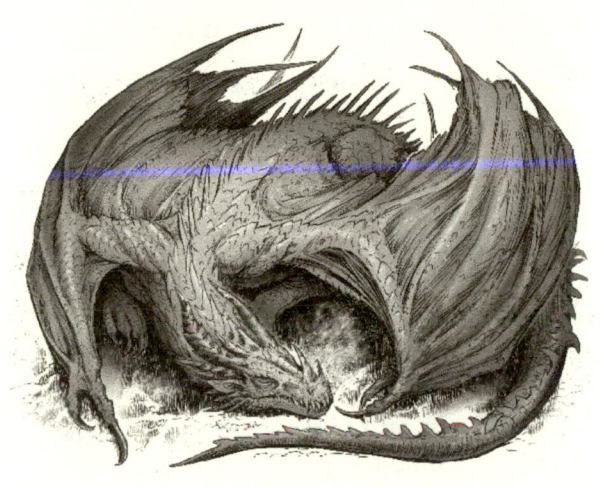

Chapter Twenty-Three
Cassius

When Cassius had broken away from the others, he'd headed down the dirt streets, following the canals until they were clear of grime and the people wore clothes of nobility. He did not know when he crossed into the Sails District, but there were subtle changes. Booths were decorated and took up permanent residence on the streets, and the storefronts were lined with gold. It tugged at Cassius's love for this culture, but he ignored it, the demands of his curse forcing his attention to an alleyway out of sight.

Luckily, he found someone to feed on with ease, a drunk sleeping off her hangover in the back of the alley. His fangs sank deeply into her neck as his hand slipped over her mouth to stifle her screams. Her blood was intoxicating as a wave of dizziness and elation ran through him. He wanted to stop, his honor demanded him to stop, but he couldn't. He wouldn't. He never wanted to feel the aches of starvation again.

As he drained the woman of her blood, he could hear Vera in his head chastising him.

"Cassius." She'd always used the same tone with him as his father when he was a child—disappointment with a hint of exasperation. "We don't need to kill them. If you keep yourself fed and hunt daily, you only need to take a little at a time." A part of him disagreed. A part of him enjoyed the kill, and that part warred with his guilt.

Cassius dropped the body to the ground and felt life return to the color in his cheeks. His fingers tingled as the blood pooled at their tips, and his chest rose and fell as he inhaled a breath of fresh air. As a human, he had thought vampires to be animated corpses, nothing more. It wasn't until he'd contracted the disease and returned that he'd discovered the curse to be much more complicated than that. He could still eat food in small doses if he was well fed on blood, could still drink wine, and could still fuck. The longer he went without blood, however, the more his body decayed and rotted, robbing him of those human pleasures. Another reason to argue consuming as much blood as he did. Feed the curse, and he could continue his life the same as always.

He leaned against the wall as blood rushed through his head. He was thankful for the cloud cover and its shield from the sun. Pushing away from the wall, Cassius leaned down and pulled a dagger from his hip. He slammed it into the woman's neck, right over the two bite marks, hiding them beneath the cut. Although it wouldn't fool a

Blodrägr due to the lack of blood in the corpse, it would deceive the local guards, making them less likely to call one in. The last thing he wanted was a vampire hunter on his heels.

Just as he was about to step out of the alley, a pain pierced him. Cassius took a shuddering breath as it intensified from the inky dark wound at his forearm. It slithered up his fingers, casting shadows as the woman from his estate materialized.

"Hello, Cassius," the woman said, a coy twist of her lips etching itself into a smile. His arm still burned, and he clutched his head, dizzy from all that had just occurred. The woman before him was fairly solid, only shadowy at her edges. Her form was fitted with the same thin black kimono as before, and her hair was held back, twisted in a bun, and stuck with two obsidian hairpins embellished with rubies. She stepped forward, and Cassius held his ground, his brow furrowed in question.

"Why am I here?" he asked.

"Why *are* you here?" she asked, playfulness coloring her tone.

Cassius remained silent. He would not play her games.

"Cassius," the woman purred, reaching to press her fingers gently underneath his chin. "You are so tense."

"Who are you? What do you want?" Cassius asked. He did not flinch away from her touch. To his surprise, he could feel her skin as if she were there.

"What do *you* want, Cassius?" The woman did not answer his questions. Backing him into the alley wall, her hand moved to rest on his chest, her fingers splayed over his heart. Jeweled clawed rings decorated each finger, attached by a chain that met at a bracelet around her wrist. The bracelet was adorned with a massive ruby, the band dressed with the ornate visage of an animal he couldn't make out, worn with age.

The woman's breath tickled Cassius' throat as she drew close, pushing herself up to rest her lips at his ear. "You strive for greatness, Cassius, and I have given you this gift because I believe you deserve this greatness. I am here to remind you not to stray from chasing that glory. You are so close; you need only to reach out and grab it." She turned, gesturing out of the alleyway where the roof of an opera house touched the horizon. "You know where your destiny lies, so why not seek it out?"

Cassius threaded his fingers through her hair and tugged back, rough and unamused. The woman did not make a sound, but her mouth opened to reveal sharp fangs as her hair was freed from her hairpins, her face contorting to show her monstrous rage.

"I was content tending to my estate in Wilhaven," Cassius hissed.

The woman's tongue clicked against the roof of her mouth in disagreement as her features softened. "Forgive me for not believing you, Cassius. You thought you were content in the castle you stole from your uncle, but you were a bomb—restless and waiting to unleash your curse upon the town. You would have left it in ruin. I gave you purpose."

"And what purpose is that?"

The woman pulled away, reaching out to cup his cheek in her jeweled hand. Her smile was kind, but there was something devious in her expression. "I urge you to find out." And with that, she began to fade, curling into smoke as she slipped back into the skin at his forearm.

Cassius let out a shaky breath, his illusion breaking momentarily as he growled and turned, punching the wall behind him. The brick shattered upon impact, but he barely felt it as he stood with his forehead pressed against the wall. Her words haunted him, and he did not wish to find The Broken Arrow until he saw the opera house himself.

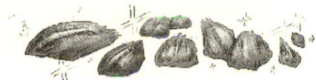

He wasn't sure what he'd expected to find, but a ruined opera house was not it. He stood at its edge, staring at the shell of its former glory. "Why hasn't the city torn you down?" Cassius questioned. Something felt off about it, a haunting he couldn't place. A sadness built up in his chest that he couldn't quite explain. There was anger there, too, old grief secreting from its walls. That feeling called to him again, like it had so many times before since waking from his imprisonment, only it was accompanied now by the burning of the brand on his back, urging him forward.

Before Cassius could take a step, a silver sword rested against the base of his throat.

"That place is condemned, and you are not allowed to step foot on the property." A voice, sharp and quick, halted his step. Cassius turned his head slowly. *Why can't I hear the man's heartbeat?*

The man was garbed in dark clothing that sheathed the hint of silver armor underneath. His beard was gray, and a thick banded scar ran across his nose, marring the flesh.

At first glance, there seemed little of the man to be concerned about, but then Cassius saw the silver-hilted stake strapped to the man's hip. Stakes were a standard weapon used against low vampires. An average stake couldn't kill high vampires and would merely immobilize them for a short time. Stakes dipped in lunaetium poison could kill high vampires, but that poison was only accessible to...

A Blodrägr, Cassius realized. One of the first things the Sanguine Order taught recruits was how to cover their vampiric presence from Blodrägrs; the second was how to deal with them if they resorted to such measures. Blodrägrs were a faction of Inquisitors, demon hunters based out of Hestia to hunt vampires.

"My apologies, sire. I only wished to get a closer look, and I find old abandoned things quite fascinating," Cassius said, raising the kindness in his tone and shifting his expression to an innocent one. Small laughter danced on the edges of his tongue.

The man ran a thumb over his thick mustache, slowly lowering his sword. "Quite the thick accent you have there. That is Hestian, no?"

Cassius nodded, stepping back from the opera house and onto the road. The moment he walked off the premises, he ceased to feel grief-stricken and full of rage. "You have a good ear, my friend. I have not been to Verenzia in some time, and I often wonder if I have lost the accent."

The man tilted his head, narrowing his eyes. "You do not look old enough for that to happen. Our homes refuse to be shaken from us so easily."

A tiny flicker of fear passed through Cassius at his small mess up. He had been turned into a vampire when he was twenty-seven years old, but he had been alive for so long that he sometimes forgot what he looked like to others. "Course not. I only jest." His heart thundered in his ears. He thought about reaching for his sword, but that would make him look suspicious. Blodrägr were trained vigorously to see through vampiric illusions and coax them into sharing their true natures. He would not fall into his trap. It was not surprising for a Blodrägr to be in Volendam. Cassius was almost sure it was a city frequented by low vampires. Still, he was confident in his abilities to keep the Blodrägr from recognizing him and forced himself to calm.

The Blodrägr studied him for several minutes, discerning whether or not he believed him, before gesturing down the street. "If the guards see you, they'll chase you from the property if they don't arrest you. They'll leave you to your fate if you manage to make it inside." It did not look like the Blodrägr meant to harm Cassius at that moment, with his stake still planted in its sheath at his hip, but he did not smile. Not that Cassius had ever known a Blodrägr to smile.

"What happens to those who get inside?" Cassius asked.

A wail rattled the windows, but Cassius was used to ghosts, and the noise did not frighten him. "No one that goes in comes out, so not entirely sure. I've done my research where I can. The locals say the place is haunted."

Cassius had looked up at the building with silent contemplation. He would have to be careful the next time he came back; it seemed the Blodrägr watched the building closely. The brand on his back cut through him with such intensity he gritted his teeth. The pain mingled with the ache to go inside, but Cassius knew the Blodrägr would stop him if he tried. Whatever was inside was more significant now than what initially called him here. He could feel a presence within. It filled him with a fair sense of fear, and as he turned back, he found that the Blodrägr was watching him closely.

"I appreciate your warning, but I must return to the inn I'm staying at," Cassius said, bowing his head respectfully and stepping away. The more distance he put between himself and the Blodrägr, the better.

"Take care. There are whispers of things crawling out of the shadows."

Cassius left, refusing to turn and look back even though he felt the Blodrägr's eyes on him until he turned down one of the streets. He quickly crossed the bridge into the Hull District and found The Broken Arrow. He was surprised to find that the others had not yet arrived. Rain began to fall the moment he walked through the door, and he hailed down the barkeeper the moment he could.

"Please, sir, I need wine."

He had a lot to contemplate. What did the woman behind his mysterious gun want? What was in the opera house? Was it his last stop, or was she going to pull him around the whole bloody world? Why was there a Blodrägr in Volendam? Why had the rakken branded him and the others?

Chapter Twenty-Four
Rooster

It began to rain the moment they saw the inn. A sign swung on the hinges of two ales clinking together, pierced by an arrow broken at the tip. Lightning shot across the sky, and thunder rattled Rooster's bones. They all rushed inside before the rain could soak them through.

The inn wasn't upscale by any means, but there was a sense of warmth and comfort. A fire roared in the fireplace against the wall to the left, and several fishermen sat at long tables, bent over pints and exchanging stories. As dinnertime rolled around, it brought the crowd in from the rain. The place grew packed rather quickly, and a woman bard strummed on her lute in the corner. Off to the right sat Cassius in a dirty booth, and Rooster waved. Cassius gestured with the glass of wine he nursed.

An older woman whisked around the room, her hair white and braided down the middle of her back. Wrinkles aged her face gracefully, her eyes kind as she slipped plates of food on the table in front of the fishermen. They all seemed to know her, thanking her and patting her on the back. She returned to the bar, where a young man frantically attempted to hand out drinks. His hair, once curly, was plastered around his face in sweat, and he kept thumbing his chin as if he longed for there to be a beard to stroke.

"I'll order us food," Rooster said. As Linda and Intoh broke away to sit with Cassius, Rooster approached the bar. The man was now cleaning dirty mugs with a questionable rag, and Rooster offered the most genuine smile he could muster as he leaned against the counter. "My friends would like to order some food and drink if it's not too much to ask."

"'Course! The name's Felix if it interests you. Welcome to The Broken Arrow. Do you need room and board as well?" Felix was young, now that Rooster was close enough to take note, his eyes a soft auburn brown with flecks of green. His accent was slight but strong enough to hint at Hestian roots.

"Yes, the cheapest you have. I'm pretty low on funds and looking for work. Does your inn have a notice board?" Rooster sighed happily as Felix set a pint of ale in front of him. The ale was too light for his taste but refreshing all the same.

"That'll be two skaels," Felix said before pointing to the wall to his left, behind Cassius. "Notice board is over there. There's quite a lot to choose from. Are those your friends?"

Rooster looked to where Felix gestured. Intoh sat silently, and Linda looked awkward in the booth as if they didn't know how to sit correctly in their human form. Helai had returned and sat next to Linda, her fingers ringing out her braid as her clothes were soaked through with rain.

"Yes, indeed." Rooster replied, taking his ale and heading towards them. Felix slipped past the bar with paper and quill, a bounce in his step that Rooster envied. The boy hadn't seen the woes of the world.

"Hello. The name is Felix. I'm the proud owner of The Broken Arrow and wanted to introduce myself. It's usually three skaels a day per room, but if you would like to stay the week, it'll be eighteen skaels each. Can I interest you in some food?"

Rooster slipped into the booth next to Helai, who scooted a bit to give him space. "I'll have whatever is warm," he said. Felix scribbled on his paper and then looked up expectantly.

Helai held up two fingers. "Make that two. Also," She leaned forward, her eyes scouring the inn. "Have you seen a Shoman man here? His name is Massoud, but he might be using a false name."

Felix's face turned crestfallen as he shook his head. "Afraid not, miss. I would have recognized him if he had, though. Don't get a lot of folks from Shoma around here. They prefer to trade with Hestia, not Volendam, but I'm sure you know that." He cleared his throat as Helai sat back, disappointed.

Felix looked down at his paper and then at Cassius. "You?"

"Nothing."

He glanced at the lizardfolk still dressed in their illusions. "And what for you two?"

Intoh didn't glance up from where he was staring at the table. "Linda and I will have some raw fish."

Confusion flickered across Felix's face, his quill poised on his paper. "Raw fish, you said?"

"A lifestyle choice," Linda affirmed, staring Felix down. Felix swallowed loudly and wrote it down, tapping the quill's tip against the paper. "Right, I'll have Hilde bring it out to you when it's ready. Our cheapest ale is one skaels each, and Patrina is our bard. She leaves the music open to requests if you have any. Just holler if you need anything." And with that, Felix scurried off to aid Hilde behind the bar.

Linda turned to Helai. "Teach word."

"Word?" Helai asked, confused.

Linda nodded. "Your word."

Understanding flickered over Helai's features. "Oh… a word in Shoman?"

Linda nodded again, more insistent. "Word."

Helai thought for a moment. "Okay… repeat after me—*bidic*."

Without hesitation, Linda replied. "Big dick."

A snort fled Intoh before he could contain it. Rooster inhaled his ale as Helai wheezed, her fingers pressing into the table's wood. "No, no, Linda," she said, "*Beh-dic*."

Linda cocked their head to the side as they attempted to hear better. With more enthusiasm, they shouted. "*Big dick!*"

Several patrons went silent and looked over. Helai slid further down in the booth, her face hidden in her hands. Rooster beat his chest with his fist, quelling his coughs as his ale dislodged itself from his throat. Intoh patted Linda on the shoulder. Cassius looked like he was ready to murder someone.

"We'll get there," Helai assured Linda, who was saved by Hilde bringing their food. A giant swordfish sat on a bed of rice on each of their plates, raw per Intoh's request and seasoned with butter and herb. Lemons embellished the sides, and Intoh looked at his plate hungrily. Large bowls of soup were set down in front of Rooster and Helai. They seemed to have some form of meat, a beefy brown broth, and several vegetables. There was a piece of bread to go with them, and Rooster's stomach rumbled at the sight.

"And more wine for you, dear," Hilde said in a sweet tone, setting another glass of wine in front of Cassius. He took it eagerly, shifting out of his seat to study the notice board.

"Where did you disappear off to after we left the Firebrand?" Rooster asked, looking at Helai. She shoveled food into her mouth eagerly, so she did not answer immediately.

"I've never met someone out of Shoma who uses spices in their food so... correctly," Helai said, sighing happily. "This is delicious, Felix," she said as he approached, carrying another round of drinks for everyone.

"Dirk's the cook. Don't know what I'd do without him," Felix said, grinning. He retreated to the bar as Helai turned to Rooster.

"I saw a shrine to Dalnor in the alley and needed to pay homage to it." Her gaze would not meet his, and Rooster opened his mouth to respond when Cassius returned, swirling his wine.

"There are a lot of useless jobs—lost cats, bread thieves—the like. But a few caught my eye–if we're to be around to partake. Someone is saying a mermaid dragged an exclusive member of the Silver Moon Club to their death, so the owner is offering a decent reward for the mermaid's head. Doesn't say it has to be the same mermaid that killed the person," Cassius said, reclaiming his seat.

"Do mermaids exist?" Helai asked.

It was Cassius that nodded. "I've seen them before off the coast of Hestia, and they usually like warmer waters, so I'm not sure why they're so far north."

"Speaking of Silver Moon Club, we met an eldrasi named Velius. He's a forge master on a ship called the Firebrand. His door is just up the street, and he uses teleportation magic to get you onto his ship. You should go meet him; I bet he can make you a shield," Rooster said, bouncing his knee as he ate his soup. Helai was right—the taste was divine. "He isn't requesting much skaels, just reagents. Some of them are at the Silver Moon Club."

Cassius' eyes narrowed. "If we haven't got the skaels, how can we get into a place called the Silver Moon Club? How are we to obtain these reagents?"

Rooster grinned. "By utilizing our charm, my friend."

Helai rolled her eyes and pushed her empty bowl away. "For having no memory, you're confident in your seduction skills."

"I may not have a memory, but I have looked into a mirror." Rooster grinned as he caught her gaze, trying to gauge her feelings about sharing the heist plan with Cassius. A part of him wondered if he shouldn't tell Cassius. A knight was a knight, first and foremost, and the vampire might be too noble for such a task.

Helai gave the fairest nods. "We'll visit the owner, and maybe we can negotiate our reward by bringing mermaid heads. Instead of skaels, maybe we can convince them to hand over some sapphires," she said.

Cassius waved his hand in dismissal. "Why not kill the mermaids, turn in their heads, collect the skaels, and then steal the sapphires on our way out?"

The four of them went silent as every head at the table turned to stare at Cassius. Rooster's brow furrowed, his head cocked to the side. "Aren't you a knight? Their nobility is what they pride themselves on. I thought you would be above stealing."

Cassius laughed and gestured to Felix for more wine. "The Order I was a part of held their own sense of honor. We seek honor in how we fight, but not whether or not the rich deserve yet another pile of gold." As another goblet was set down in front of him, Cassius took a moment to drink deeply, sighing happily as his expression turned serious, and leaned forward. "I've been to enough noble parties to know how unnecessarily wealthy the rich are."

Helai's mouth shut, her shock still written clearly across her face. Clearing her throat, she folded her fingers atop the table as she leaned close and lowered her voice. "Then we are to steal?"

"Most you will get from me is lookout–do not want to get on mage's bad side," Intoh said. His plate was still half full, and Linda stared at it mournfully as their plate sat empty and devoured. If Intoh noticed, he did not react, pulling his plate closer to chew on some of the fish bones left over.

"Not very sneaky," Linda said sadly, hesitantly turning away from Intoh's plate. "Will try best."

Rooster was still staring at Cassius. The vampire was so challenging to read. When Rooster thought he could gauge Cassius' morals and personality, he surprised him. Still, Rooster couldn't judge too harshly. He still didn't know what kind of man he was before he lost his memory. The sound of stealing from the club did not carry any weight of guilt, so perhaps he wasn't the best of men either.

"Right then. So we're to hunt some mermaids and steal some jewels. That will get us some decent weapons, at least. I need to find a bowyer once I have the skaels for it," Rooster said, watching sailors thank Felix and Hilde and leave for the night.

"I cannot linger too long. I was not traveling to Volendam for holiday," Cassius uttered behind his wine.

"Why *did* you come here?" Rooster tried to keep the accusation from his voice, but it slipped through anyway. His brand burned as anger closed his throat, and Cassius' anger reflected in his expression.

"My reasons are my own."

"Huh." The observation hummed against Rooster's lips as he raised his eyebrows in question but didn't say anything more. Tension thickened the air in the room, and Helai cleared her throat and changed the subject.

"Any other jobs we should worry about? I do not mean to stay in Volendam too long, but it would be nice to make as many skaels as possible before I head back south."

The tension remained for several more moments before Cassius downed the rest of his wine and visibly calmed. "There's a post about a missing child. She was tracked so far as the docks, but that's where the trace of her ends. There's speculation she fell into the bay, and a fish got her."

"Would a fish even eat a human? Are there fish large enough in the bay to do that?" Helai asked, disgusted.

Cassius shrugged. "There are a lot of strange things in this world. Could be possible. Could also be the mermaids. There's also a fishing vessel that got lost near the Isles of Bara, a few days' travel from here. There is reason to believe that tribesmen who worship false gods have something to do with it. The reward is for the leader's head, and the guard captain offers two hundred more if we bring back the vessel, assuming it's still in one piece."

"I wonder if that correlates with the cultist sightings or the rakken and dyrvak suddenly showing up." Rooster pondered, tipping his bowl back as he finished his soup.

"Perhaps. Will do some research when I go to the college," Intoh said, pushing his empty plate away from him towards the middle of the table. "Eager to go. Eager to learn."

"What have you been reading, anyway?" Helai asked, gesturing to the book Intoh had resting beside him.

"You wouldn't understand it," Intoh said, pulling the book closer. "In drikotyian. Theory about gods."

"You would be surprised," Helai protested.

Intoh cocked an eyebrow. "Speak drikotyian?"

Helai shook her head sheepishly. "No."

"Do we want to do these tasks together and split the skaels up five ways?" Rooster asked, eyeing Intoh curiously. The book did not look to be in drikotyian from the pages he had snuck glances at, but he wasn't sure why Intoh would lie.

"The jobs will go quicker if we stick together," Cassius said.

"I have to visit the alchemist tomorrow to get some mithril dust. Do we know anything about hunting mermaids?" Helai asked.

Rooster didn't.

"Will visit mage college tomorrow. See if library knows." Intoh piped up, pushing his seat back and standing. "Must retire. Much to do tomorrow." As he trailed off towards the stairs, Linda wordlessly got up, stole the rest of Intoh's fish, and gobbled it down as they followed Intoh up to the room. The tension returned as he, Helai, and Cassius remained, and Rooster tried to work over in his head why he felt a sudden unease and why there seemed to be a quiet urge to go somewhere. He hadn't thought about it much until now, but it always accompanied the burning of his brand.

"It is decided then," Rooster said, ignoring the urges and standing himself. "I'm going to introduce myself to the guard captain tomorrow, but we should meet back here when we can. Maybe Intoh will have information for us on what to do about the mermaids." Helai and Cassius nodded in agreement, so he left them to retire as well. As he climbed the stairs, he grew weary about his lack of memories. Was his memory loss temporary? Or would he wake one day and suddenly remember who he was? It was frustrating not knowing.

Only time would tell.

Chapter Twenty-Five
Helai

Volendam was unlike the deserts of Shoma. The people were hardy, and dampness clung to the air threatening to frizz Helai's hair. Helai slipped out of her room early that morning before the sun peeked through the window. Ease settled within her when she left the silent inn and returned to the alleyway she had found the day before.

The alley was littered with trash, and a couple of men lay in small makeshift homes near the back. Helai paid them no mind as she knelt in front of the shrine where a couple of skaels rested. Like yesterday, the closer she got to her shrine, the more the brand on her back burned, but she gritted her teeth and ignored it.

The shrine was an altar to Dalnor. His altars always bore the sculpture of a raven, its mouth opened to receive trinkets or skaels. The shrine itself wasn't enormous, nor was it fancy by any means. Dalnor would have hated his disciples worshiping at a lavish statue, given he hated anything in excess. He was a god for the common man, not the rich or the plentiful.

Helai leaned down. Wiping the grime away from the bowl where skaels already resided, she added more to the pile, then pressed her hands together in prayer.

Blinking, she stood on a hill in front of an ivory temple, not so large as to show off immense wealth but rather grand in its own right. It sat in the middle of a large city bathed in warm light. A sense of calm washed over her. She should have been afraid—this had never happened before—but she felt nothing but peace. Whatever this place was, it felt like she belonged.

"Hello, Helai," a voice said behind her. "Do not turn around," he instructed, taking her hand. Helai wondered why she did not fear him, but his voice drenched her in a sense of calm, and she did what she'd been told to as a cold breeze caressed her face. A raven landed on her shoulder, and still, she did not turn.

"Not many get to look upon the City of Stars until it is their time. You should count yourself lucky," the voice said. His voice was deep, echoing in a way that made it feel otherworldly.

"Who are you?" she asked.

A chuckle sounded from behind her. A key was left within her grasp as he pulled his hand away. "You were always my favorite. The most devoted, the most kind, the most determined. I grant you this key. You will know what door it opens when the time comes."

Before Helai could respond, a white light enveloped her, forcing her eyes closed. It was but a moment more, and she was standing back in the alleyway, rain hitting her face.

Was that...? she wondered, staring at the key. It wasn't fancy by any means. Black in color, it had no distinguishable features and no guesses about what it opened. Dalnor did not care for flare. He was the god of shadows, after all.

Helai pocketed the key and fled the alleyway, glancing back at the shrine one last time. The raven statue had not moved, but gold now spilled from its beak, piling onto the ground below. The homeless in the back of the alley were already rushing the shrine to grab at the skaels, their movements frantic. Helai knew it was Dalnor who was aiding them in their desperation.

As she headed for The Broken Arrow, she searched for Massoud in the streets and felt the burn of disappointment when she did not see him. She would have loved more than anything to have his advice right now. She wondered where he might be. There was no way he'd be holed up in the Sails District. He didn't have the skaels for it. He had spent the last of it gambling on cards just before they parted ways, and even though he was resourceful, he hated the rich more than anyone.

The inn was nearly empty when Helai re-entered. Felix was awake at the bar with Hilde, who frequently retreated to the back room to bring out Dirk's food. Whatever he was cooking made Helai's mouth water, and Helai waved at Felix as she took a seat at the booth they'd been sitting at the night before.

"Can I have one of whatever Dirk's making?" Helai asked Felix.

"Of course. It will be out soon."

Helai nodded, contenting herself with the warmth of the inn and the comfort of solitude. She was glad to be off the road and sleeping in a bed for once but would trade it without hesitation if she could relocate the other Ghosts.

"This seat taken?" Patrina, the bard, walked up, gesturing to the empty seat across from Helai, and sat when Helai shook her head. A dimpled smile graced her face as she stared at Helai. Her skin was dark and rich with cool, jewel undertones. She wore a faint dusting of silver glitter on her cheeks, and her eyes were so brown the pupil was almost lost in color. Her hair was an afro of curls embellished by several glints of silver-toned jewelry. She was breathtakingly gorgeous, and Helai took a moment to just appreciate the view, despite her reservations about bards.

"Don't usually see people from Shoma here," Patrina said.

"Most of my people have no reason to leave our home. It isn't the way of our culture," Helai said, taking great care to keep her tone neutral despite the pounding in her chest. "Only those who seek to wander and can do so leave the sands." Partial truths slipped from Helai's lips as she ran her finger over the wood. Her people had been prisoners of Mohalis' rule since before Helai had been born. A sultan in his own right, he had murdered all those who had defied him and now ruled Shoma with an iron grip. Helai and the other Ghosts of Light had been attempting to overthrow his rule for nearly a decade now, but their efforts were lost at theeldr moment as they had been forced to separate, flee, and hide when their efforts began to get noticed.

Mohalis' men had captured and murdered Zahra, and since then, the Ghosts had fled in separate directions to throw Mohalis' men off their trail. They were supposed to wait a year before returning to Shoma to regroup.

Patrina pressed her fingers against Helai's wrist. "I did not mean any harm by it. It is in my nature to be curious, is all," she said, gesturing to her lute in the corner.

"Sorry," Helai said, shaking her head. Bards were too nosy, and Helai had never liked them. "I often find bards using people's pain for their desire for success."

"Perhaps some do," Patrina agreed. "I do not find that to be of good taste. I assure you, our conversation stays between us," Patrina assured, crossing her leg over her knee. "May I be so bold? You know my name, but I do not know yours."

"Helai."

Patrina dipped her head in response. "Pleasure. I saw your friend eyeing the notice board last night. If there are any epic stories to be told, I'd love to hear them sometime." Helai nodded, remaining silent, and Patrina smiled. "I won't keep you. I merely wanted to introduce myself. If you ever have a request for a song, do let me know."

Patrina retreated, and Helai watched her go. Patrina seemed genuine, but Helai had seen the evil bards could commit in their lust for skaels.

Felix brought her breakfast not long after, and Helai's stomach growled as the aroma of breakfast potatoes assaulted her nose. It was some form of omelet with fish mixed in with eggs and vegetables, and Helai scarfed it down in record time.

Cassius and Rooster descended the stairs as she finished up, and she waved at them as they crossed the inn towards the front door.

"We'll meet up here later, yeah? Cassius is going to accompany me to the city guard," Rooster called out, and Helai nodded. They departed, and Helai retreated to Intoh and Linda's room to see if they were awake, knocking softly on the door.

"Come in," Intoh said.

Intoh sat at the windowsill in his human form, watching the rain hit the windowpane. As he read, the book was propped in his hand, the pages flipping magically. Linda still slept, their face pressed in the crook of their elbow. They were in their lizard form, barely able to sleep on the small bed they curled up on, and Helai glanced at Intoh, wondering if it was a good idea for Linda to brave their true form in the middle of the city. Still, she said nothing.

"We go and see alchemist. Gather mithril dust. Then I go to mage college. You are to wake Linda," Intoh said, not glancing up from his book.

Helai approached Linda hesitantly. "Perhaps you should wake them."

Intoh spared a glance over his book with a shake of his head. "They like you more. By my calculations, you are less likely to get bitten. Happened to me once. Don't want it to happen again."

"You've traveled with them longer. It's implausible they like me more." Her shoulder ached, likely from the rain due to an old injury she sustained from falling off a building running from Shoma guards. She rotated it as she sighed. "But fine. I've had to wake sleeping men before. A sleeping krok'ida should be no more difficult."

Pushing her sleeves to her elbows, Helai blew a strand of hair out of her face and stepped up to Linda. Hot air expelled from their nose, and Helai called out quietly. "Linda? Linda, it's time to wake."

"Have to rub their nose. The only way to wake," Intoh said.

Helai looked at him with the faintest of hesitations. Touching Linda while they slept seemed like a terrible idea, but she couldn't discern whether Intoh's tone was sarcastic or not. When she locked eyes with him, he held her expression like a challenge.

"You jest. They will think it is you," Helai said.

Intoh shook his head. "No, no, no. The only way," he insisted, shutting the book to move closer. "Small motions on tip of nose."

A soft frustrated sigh left Helai, but she scooted closer, her fingers moving out to draw small circles on the tip of Linda's nose. "Linda," she called again, a bit louder this time, "Time to wake up." Helai snatched her hand away as Linda moved to bite her hand, their jaw snapping shut as they blinked and pulled away once they noticed it was Helai.

Linda yawned, their mouth stretched wide to reveal sharp teeth. "No, I sleep," they said, flicking their tail at Helai but missing. Helai straightened and folded her arms across her chest. "I will tell you what I always told my friend Aryan when he didn't want to wake up either. The sun does not wait to greet the day, and there is much to do. If you come and meet the alchemist with us, we can get you breakfast before we go."

"What breakfast?" Linda asked, curious. "More fish?"

"I'm sure Dirk would be more than happy to prepare some fish for you, but we must go now," Helai agreed.

That seemed to catch Linda's attention, and they stood after a little more persuading. Linda twisted their ring, and Intoh grimaced as he slammed his book shut and hopped down from the windowsill.

"Still have scar from when I woke you. You treat Helai better. Will remember this," he said, his eyes narrowing.

Helai laughed as they exited. "Don't take it too personally, Intoh. Maybe they were just having a bad day when you woke them."

"Thought you bad. Not my fault," Linda said, shrugging. As they descended the stairs, the inn was bustling with life. Hilde balanced plates of potatoes and sausage on her arms as she wove through the tables, setting them down in front of hungry patrons.

Linda's stomach protested so loudly that Helai felt it in the soles of her feet.

"Come on, Linda. Let's get you some food," Helai said.

They sat at the bar to eat, and Helai ordered a drink made from Rolias beans soaked in honey and cream. She felt warmth from the drink almost immediately, and she curled her fingers around the mug as Felix set two plates of raw fish down in front of Intoh and Linda.

"Here you go," Linda said, pulling off a piece of their fish and offering it to Helai.

Helai smiled and held up her hands, shaking her head. "Oh no, thank you, Linda. I'm not a fan of raw fish."

Linda blinked at Helai. "Suit yourself."

"How old are you, Felix?" Helai asked as Felix wiped down the counter nearby. He looked barely old enough to call himself an adult, his face free of worry. He kept glancing over at Patrina, sitting in the corner, strumming her lute.

"Ah, what?" he asked, forcing his gaze away to settle on Helai. "Oh, I am nineteen years young! I was lucky to inherit this place from my parents when they passed."

Helai's face fell as she looked from Patrina to Felix. "Oh... I am sorry to hear that." Helai's parents had passed away when she'd been young too. She couldn't even remember what they looked like, only shattered memories that danced in and out of clarity. Massoud was the closest thing to family she had, a big brother in his own right. He had found her and Aryan, dirty children fighting for survival in the streets and took them in as his own. He had only been a ten-year-old boy at the time, and Helai had never found a way to repay him for keeping her alive all those years.

"Sadly, illness took them, so it's just me and Hilde running things, but I don't mind." He was younger than she'd thought, five years younger than herself. She could not help but admire Felix's hard work and positive outlook on the world.

"You're doing a fantastic job," she said, smiling at him.

His grin was radiant. "Enjoy your drink, Helai. I appreciate your business." As he returned to cleaning up, Helai finished her drink. It did not take Linda and Intoh long to complete their breakfast, so they headed out.

As they departed, the sun broke through the rain clouds, and the street in front of The Broken Arrow bustled with life. Children ran past, their faces dirty, fresh bread clutched between their fingers. A man shouted as he ran after them, and Helai took a moment to conveniently place herself in the way, gasping dramatically as he slammed into her.

"Oh, *ana aasif!* I was not watching where I was going," she said, forcing the man's attention on her. The man grunted, rubbing the back of his bald head, and his brows furrowed in anger.

"Damn kids," he uttered, and Helai noted with satisfaction that the kids had managed to get away. "Watch where you're walking next time, lady." He eyed Helai for a moment. "And if I find you stealing my bread, I'll take your hand as a consequence. The guards don't give two shits about what goes on down here. Stay away from my booth."

Helai watched him walk away, wondering bitterly if he'd said what he had because she was in the poor district or because she was from Shoma.

"Saw what did. Nice of you," Linda said, watching the old man amble back to his cart. The aroma of bread wafted over, soaked in sweetness, and it made Helai's mouth water.

Helai said nothing, just winked at Linda.

"Could send his booth flying. Just say word," Intoh said, electricity slipping through his fingers. Helai was confident he was serious, and she laughed, and it filled her with warmth, the protective nature of the drikoty.

"I did not know you to care so much, Intoh," Helai said. Intoh shook his head.

"Don't like bullies. Why I will hunt Amir one day."

Helai studied Intoh more closely as he glared at the old man and his cart. She prided herself in being a good judge of character, but she wasn't able to get a sense of Intoh's motives or why he stuck around. She knew him to be looking for something in magic, that much was clear, but she did not know greka well enough to know if Intoh's behavior was normal.

"He's not worth the trouble," she muttered. The alchemist was right across the street, where 'The Secret Ingredient' read out in gold letters above the door. Tall windows adorned both sides, and potions of various shapes and sizes sat on shelves, advertising the wares. A gentle hum emanated from the door, pulling Helai in.

"Go to college now. Much to do. Keep eye on Linda," Intoh demanded, turning away. Helai watched him disappear around the corner before glancing at Linda and entering the alchemist.

The inside of the shop was chaotic—multi-layered, shelves upon shelves embellished the walls. Papers scattered every inch of the place, and vials and bottles of liquids lined the shelves, their names scribbled hurriedly in front of them. To the immediate left was a staircase. Where it led to was unclear, as it veered to the right and disappeared upstairs.

Before them sat a giant desk littered with more papers. There was no organization to the madness, and the soft mutterings came from the store owner as he sat at the desk and read over a piece of paper. He was short in stature with large luminescent blue eyes and ears that tapered to points. They kept twitching, and he drank deeply from a bottle holding a stack of papers. Helai had never seen anything like him before, and when he spoke, it was at a faster pace than she was used to.

"Welcome to The Secret Ingredient; name's Golbin, whaddya want?" Golbin didn't glance over at them when he spoke, his fingers weaving over an alchemist's table carved right into the desk. Runes floated above the alchemist's table and sizzled a deep green.

"We require some mithril dust," Helai said, clasping her hands behind her back. She did not trust herself here. Linda was at the wall, studying each drawer and the words marking them.

Golbin looked at Helai, his small spectacles resting at the tip of his small bulbous nose. Ears darting, he climbed down from his desk at speed Helai could not follow, and before she knew it, he was at her side. The top of his head only reached her waist.

Helai held up her hands, uncertain. "Please, I can pay."

Golbin was stranger up close, his skin secreting a thin film of some sap-like substance. Soft chirps rumbled from his throat. He stared at her for a moment, silent. "Forty skaels."

Helai frowned. "Are you certain?"

Golbin folded his arms across his chest. "*Fifty* skaels."

Helai spluttered, then deflated in defeat. "I will have to come back."

A loud crash sounded behind Golbin, and then a plume of smoke enveloped Linda. Golbin shrieked a shrill, high-pitched noise and scurried over to Linda. "Out, out, get outta my shop before you break something. Do you know how long it took me to find those? You're lucky it wasn't its cousin plant—very explosive." He pointed an accusatory finger at Helai. "Will pay for that. Thirty skaels."

Helai opened her mouth in protest. "It was just an accident. That will be all the skaels I have. Please–Velius sent me–"

"*Velius*?" Golbin questioned, his demeanor relaxing. He retreated away from Linda, who looked contemplative like they were wondering whether to react to Golbin's outburst. Instead, they sat, a loud thump against the ground as Golbin pressed his hand to his forehead in frustration.

"Tell you what," Golbin said, sweeping the broken glass under the desk. "I will count your debt paid if you harvest a bom shroom for me. They've very important for a lot of potions I need. If you get me more than one, I'll pay you thirty skaels for each one after your debt is paid."

Helai eyed him suspiciously. "That's quite a bit of skaels for one mushroom."

Golbin chirped, staring between her and Linda. "Last guy died gathering for me. Didn't know touching the gills was very dangerous. Make you shit until you die."

Helai winced. Shitting herself to death did not sound like the best way to go. Still, she had dealt with poisonous plants in Shoma before. Handling deadly mushrooms couldn't be too difficult. "Where do I find them, and what do they look like?"

Golbin scowled, snapping his fingers as the flask on the desk appeared in his hand. He drank deeply from it and wiped his mouth with the back of his hand. Clapping his hands together, he scampered up the desk and searched through his mess of papers. Several flew to the floor as he pushed them aside until he found what he was looking for. "Here." He held a watercolor drawing of a mushroom. It was short and plump, the top bearing dark circles. The rest of the cap was a deep blue, and its stalk was bone white. The gills underneath the top looked like fish gills, and they shared the dark color of the circles on the cap. "This is a bom shroom." He turned it over to show a few paragraphs of text. "Tells you how to harvest, must be very careful," Golbin warned again, "do not touch their gills."

Helai grimaced, then nodded. That sounded less than ideal. "I will refrain from touching the gills," she confirmed, taking the paper from Golbin and pocketing it. "Where can I find bom shrooms?" she asked.

Golbin took another long draw from his flask. "They like moist, dark places. You will have the best of luck in the sewers below the city, as caves are too far away."

"Thank you for the information," she said.

Golbin waved his hand at her. "Don't die like the last guy, and we'll talk."

She was less than pleased at the thought of going anywhere underground after dealing with the rakken. She grimaced as the brand on her back burned, urging her to go down into the tunnels. It was followed by a different feeling, a quiet hunger. The hunger felt different from normal hunger, as if she hungered for something other than food. Her heart plummeted into her stomach as she watched Linda stare out the window at butterflies that landed on flowers in a flowerbox by the front door.

"Come on, Linda," she said, nodding at Golbin. "I'll return soon with your shrooms."

Golbin waved his hand in dismissal, already turned back to his alchemist's table as Linda followed Helai back outside.

Helai thought about going into the sewers by herself, but a twist in her gut urged her not to. Looking up at Linda, she smiled. "Want to go with me to collect some mushrooms?"

Linda shrugged, then nodded. "Sure, why not."

Chapter Twenty-Six
Intoh

It felt strange, being in a large city primarily made up of humans where no one paid him any mind. He still wasn't accustomed to looking like a human, his ring warm against his finger, and no one stared at him like he didn't belong.

He found the college with little trouble, crossing bridges and dodging people doing their business. The college teetered on the outskirts of the Sails District, near the northern docks. It was tremendous in size, built on the edge of a cliff. White spires shot up towards the sky, and stone waves embellished its sides, etched into marble and dusted with blue. Intoh could feel the magic built up here, and he shivered in anticipation as he neared the courtyard.

Students and mages walked about, conversing amongst themselves. A few studied books and others sat on benches around a beautiful fountain. The sculpture at its center was a woman wielding magic, guiding the water around her and into the pool below. Several people turned to look at Intoh when he entered, but their faces were kind and welcoming.

"If you come to learn, you'll want to speak with Tidebeard," a girl said, gesturing to an older gentleman across the courtyard. "He's our head teacher. You won't find anyone else better in the arts of hydromancy." Intoh bowed his head in gratitude as he hurried across the courtyard. Best not to waste any time. If he was going to unlock the ability to live forever, he needed to make haste. He wasn't getting any younger.

The man the girl had spoken of, Tidebeard, finished speaking up with a student and then turned to Intoh. "You come to seek knowledge?" Tidebeard was old, wrinkles aging his face. His expression still held life in them, and his walk was steady and sure-footed. His skin was dark, spotted with sunspots, and his beard was black and peppered with gray, not yet turned.

As Intoh gazed at him, the brand on his leg tingled, filling him with rage. He swallowed it, letting it burn and die in his belly, and then nodded.

Tidebeard gestured for him to follow. Intoh quickened his pace to catch up.

"I am Tidebeard, head professor at this college. What knowledge have you come to seek?" As they passed through the doors of the college, Intoh took a moment to marvel at its beauty. The waves were also carved into the walls as they stepped inside. Sculptures of people acted as pillars, their hands beckoning the water to weave around them in specific ways. Students spilled out of the hallways and into the main room. Many of them bowed their heads respectfully at Tidebeard as they passed. Intoh had never been to a place like this. His teachings in Lyvira had been condensed to drikoty knowledge and were done so in temples and coliseums, not in massive colleges.

Intoh knew the others would expect him to seek information on the mermaids, but selfishness gripped him. "I come seeking what you are willing to show me," Intoh admitted, biting his tongue. Many thought the search for immortality was immoral, an insult to the natural order of magic, and he did not know if he could trust Tidebeard with the truth.

Tidebeard stared at him for a moment before gesturing to his left side, where Intoh could see books lining the walls. *A library*, he thought as they neared. When they stepped through the threshold, Intoh realized the inside was larger than the outside, and he glanced up, noting several different floors. People read quietly in nooks, and a man stood at a podium near the door, reading from an old tome.

"Castis, this young man would like to check in and use the library. I believe he can learn a lot here."

Castis nodded and glanced out at the library. "Do be careful. If you don't remember the way out, it is easy to lose your way here."

Intoh gave a curt nod. Tidebeard patted his shoulder and turned. "If you need me, I will be teaching a lesson in one of my classrooms.

Direct him to my office once he's finished," he said to Castis before leaving with a wave of his cloak.

"Do you have a book on vampires?" Intoh asked, watching Tidebeard leave. Many races in Vilanthris lived long periods, but ancient races like the eldrasi and dwarves did not like giving up knowledge of their kind. Intoh's recent interactions with Cassius had him curious—maybe vampires were the secret to unlocking his desire for longer life.

Castis gestured down the winding stairs behind him to the floor below. "You'll find what you are looking for by going down those stairs and looking at the aisles on the right. I will not leave this podium, so if you have any questions, come here to find me." As Intoh headed past him, he noticed Castis was favoring one side to compensate for a missing leg and that he sat, not standing.

A few other students walked about the library, but Intoh was left to his own devices as he skimmed over the names of various titles, none of which he recognized. Some tomes were frequently pulled from their shelves, their bindings clean and shiny, whereas others were coated with a thick layer of dust.

Many of the books he pulled led to dead ends, and his frustration was evident when he threw down the fifth book he panned through. It appeared the vampires were just as secretive as the others, and while Intoh understood their secrecy, his bitterness preyed on his brand as he grew angrier and angrier.

Pacing down the aisles, he pressed a closed fist against his forehead in anger. Tears threatened the corners of his eyes, but he shoved them back, steeling himself against an overwhelming emotion.

What if this all is for naught? The thought was intrusive and weeded its way into his brain despite himself. He had sacrificed much to get here with little to show for it.

"No," he said out loud, angry at himself. "I can't give up now." A shimmer of scales stopped him when he turned back to the shelves of books. He turned to look, and next to him sat another greka poured over a small book. Her scales were a yellow-gold dipped in deep forest green, and around her eyes were rings of black that spiraled out to stretch over the sides of her head.

"Ekalas?" Intoh asked, his throat constricting. "What are you doing here?" His head spun as he grabbed the nearest shelf to steady himself. It had been a year and a half since he'd seen her.

"Minding after you. You never knew how to take care of yourself," Ekalas muttered absently in drikotyian, thumbing through the book in her lap. "You doubt the mission, but the mission hasn't changed just because I'm dead."

Shame filled his belly. Ekalas was right. This was a journey they'd begun together three years ago. They'd promised each other that no matter what, they'd see it to the end. Intoh hadn't calculated the possibility of Ekalas dying before they found the path to immortality.

"More difficult without you," Intoh admitted.

Ekalas looked up, staring at him with large green eyes. "Who said I left? Look, Intoh—you just have to look harder." He looked to where she gestured; a book he had overlooked caught his eye. It was a tiny thing, its spine barely wider than the width of his finger, but when he pulled it out and opened it, it spoke of correlations between the ancient dragons and the vampiric curse. His heart thundered in his ears as he turned to Ekalas, but she was gone.

Looking back down at the book, he ran a finger over the lip of the cover. He wasn't confident it had all the answers he needed, but as he shoved it into the inside of his shirt and headed back towards the front of the library, he felt something blossoming in his chest. There was a flicker of hope.

"Have book on mermaids?" Intoh asked, returning to Castis. He almost left, his excitement chasing any thought of the mermaids away. At the last minute, however, he remembered and turned back to stare up at Castis expectantly.

Castis did not reply for a time as he scribbled with ink and quill in an open book, but eventually, he dropped the quill against the podium and turned to gesture at the first row of shelves on Intoh's left.

"You'll find what you seek down that aisle towards the end on the right. I will warn you—stealing will result in permanent exile from the library." Castis made eye contact with Intoh and held it, his lip pursed in a thin line.

Intoh rubbed the nape of his neck and nodded three times in quick succession before hurrying off. If Castis knew he had a book in his possession, it would not be wise to leave with it.

He stopped where Castis suggested, reaching up to run his hand over the titles. "Ah," he muttered, his finger landing on a book titled *Mermaids, Sirens, and Other Demons of the Sea*. Pulling it from the shelf, he sank to the ground where he stood, opening the book to a random page and skimming over its contents. The binding cracked as he opened it, and shimmering, luminescent eyes stared up at him from the illustration on the page. He stared into the mermaid's eyes; a strange longing to go out to the bay and throw himself into the water pulled at him. He shook his head, trying to clear his thoughts, and forced his gaze to the words on the page.

The paragraphs depicted mermaids as creatures of demonic possession, simple sea life that had been twisted and mutated into a cross between humans and fish. They compelled themselves with the visages of humans, men, and women alike. Their voices carried across the sea, luring sailors to the ocean's depths so they could feast on their souls. Once the illusion broke, they manifested their rage, transforming into creatures with several rows of teeth and a sweeping fin that's edges were sharp as daggers. They rarely hunted alone. They usually hunted in the south, near Rolias off the coasts of Kythera.

Shutting the book, Intoh ambled up to the podium, where Castis was still reading his book. "Can't steal but borrow this?" Intoh asked, holding the book up for Castis to see.

"Absolutely not," he said without looking up. "If we allowed it, books would go missing."

Intoh's mouth opened, preparing to hiss at Castis, but then he remembered he was supposed to pass as a human. Shutting his mouth, he found a nook in the library and reread parts of the book, trying to commit the more critical bits to memory. He also read over the book he had intended to steal, not wishing to risk being barred from the library just after gaining access to it.

After researching mermaids until his head started to pound, Intoh returned the books to the shelf and got up to leave. The library's windows were stained glass, depicting famous times in history involving the sea, and they cast shades of blue over the shelves and tables as Intoh walked by.

Approaching Castis, the greka splayed a hand over his podium. "Direct me to Tidebeard. I wish to speak," he said.

With Castis' direction, Intoh scurried back the way he'd come, and it wasn't long before he could hear Tidebeard's booming voice coming from one of the classrooms.

"Now remember, magic is but a chemical that flows through us, much like energy flows through everything else. If you overextend the muscle, you will force your body to compensate, sometimes causing irreversible damage. It can, at times, be fatal. When you practice this magic, start small. Let that muscle strengthen. Nurture it, and it will treat you kindly. I expect to see everyone's progress when we meet up again. Class dismissed."

As students piled out of the classroom, Intoh waited patiently at the door. Several people smiled at Intoh, one even muttering, 'Hello' as they brushed past him. Tidebeard was at the front of the classroom. Separating him from the row of students' desks was a stream of water running from wall to wall, and the classroom itself was round. Plants grew near tall open windows to bathe in the sunlight. The water flowed through a small opening in the wall to travel outside, it's sound soothing.

"Hello again, Intoh. Did you find what you were looking for in the library?" Tidebeard asked, waving his hands over his desk. The papers there organized themselves in a neat pile, and Intoh stared at them in awe.

"And then some," Intoh said, clearing his throat. "Could spend forever in library. Not enough time. Must ask—what does one have to do to become student? Eager to learn." Grekas were lucky to live past two or three decades, and Intoh was already eight. If he was going to find a way to live longer, he needed to learn the arts of all magics quickly.

Tidebeard's lip twitched, suppressing a smile. Stroking his beard, he sighed and stared out of the window. The window was frosted; warped sunlight and shadows danced over the glass. "You are already gifted in the arts of magic, yes? It can be unwise to learn more than one type. The energy within can become chaotic and overpower the wielder. Those who lust after too much power are likely to die of a heart attack or burn themselves from the inside out." Peering over spectacles, Tidebeard's gaze fixated on Intoh. "It's not impossible, however. You will be allowed to study here if you promise to abide by my instructions and rules."

For the first time since Intoh left Lyvira, Intoh felt the clutches of excitement clinging to his belly. This was what he had abandoned his homeland for, why he'd murdered his leader. Off to Tidebeard's right, Ekalas stood with a nod of encouragement. "Of course. Will do everything you ask. Will not push too much. Do not wish to die."

Tidebeard nodded curtly. "Excellent. You will be required to come to the college three times a week for the foreseeable future, from morning until midday, unless you wish to board here."

Intoh shook his head. "Staying at Broken Arrow. Would like to remain."

Tidebeard moved to his desk. "I do not tolerate tardiness. You will be expected to work hard, but we treat each other like family at this college. Fighting will not be tolerated either. Do you understand?"

Intoh nodded.

"Good," Tidebeard said with a ring of satisfaction. "I shall see you in a couple of days then. For now, I must seek out my studies, and we're always learning, Intoh."

A thought struck him before Tidebeard could exit the room. Intoh called out. "Have you heard of the name Gorvayne?" Intoh called out.

Tidebeard halted, and when he glanced back at Intoh, his expression was mingled with curiosity and something Intoh couldn't quite place. Fear, perhaps?

"Why do you ask?"

"Heard name. Wondered what it might be," Intoh said. He didn't lie, but the whole truth danced just out of sight.

Tidebeard sighed, pressing his hand to the doorframe. "Gorvayne is a name written in the scripture of eldrasi legends, Intoh. It is the name of a dragon, long since dead. We do not utter their names here; names have power, and speaking it in excess would not be wise. Please do not bring it up again. I will see you in a few days."

Tidebeard dismissed Intoh, and he retreated from the college. The sun was still high in the sky but starting its descent, and Intoh's stomach protested loudly. He could not wait for Dirk's cooking.

As the college faded behind him, he couldn't help but wonder: what were dyrvak doing worshiping a dead dragon?

Chapter Twenty-Seven
Linda

"Come, Linda. Quickly now." Helai called out to Linda in hushed tones as they traveled through the city. Merchants closed up their stalls and headed home, lit lamps in buildings to bring warmth to the city. The taste of salt was in the air, and Linda reveled in the soft chill of the wind.

Linda grumbled in response but quickened their pace as Helai pulled them around the corner towards a canal that led to a massive entrance barred by several iron bars. The water was not plentiful like some other canals where boats traveled, but it still made a noise as they dropped down, and Helai glanced above them to ensure they had not been seen.

Gripping two iron bars between their hands, Linda pulled them apart. The hole created was large enough to slip through, and Linda peered into the darkness. As the stench of the city hit them, Linda nearly buckled, growling in disgust.

"Don't like that," they said. "Want go back. Hear Patrina sing."

"Come on," Helai urged, slipping in front of them and pulling the scarf around her neck up to her nose. "We'll get you the biggest plate of fish when we are done. I bet Patrina will sing you whatever song you'd like."

Linda hummed in contemplation. "Okay," they finally decided. They liked Helai well enough to help her, even if it meant going into shit-infested waters.

Helai started to braid her hair as she moved forward, then stopped. "I can't see a thing," she muttered, digging into her bag.

But the dark was no problem for Linda, who could see in the dark as well as if it were daytime.

"Bom shrooms? What like?" Linda asked, shifting the ring on their finger to slip into their true form. They shook their head from side to side, glad to be free of the illusion. The murky water came up to Linda's ankles as they moved forward, their tail trailing through it.

Pulling out the ball of light from her sack, Helai used it to study the walls as she bent low to the ground. "Don't worry, Linda. I'll find them if you watch for guards or anything else that might be crawling down here. If you see any mushrooms, just don't touch their gills." Helai glanced at Linda, who was looking further down in the tunnel. "He said you would shit yourself to death."

A shiver rolled through Linda. "Don't want that."

"I agree, so be careful where you step."

Linda turned towards Helai. There was something off—a strange feeling that coursed through them. They felt like something pulsed further down in the sewers, a heartbeat in the ground. It swept through them, filling their head with anger. They thought about bashing Helai's head in with a rock and chewing on her bones, sending a flurry of rage through them.

Shaking their head, a loud exhale left Linda's maw.

Helai turned, her expression sharp. "We must be quiet, Linda."

"Linda not sneaky. Linda doesn't know," Linda said in frustration, reaching out to squeeze the life out of Helai for chastising them, but Helai did not seem to notice as she turned away in excitement.

"Found one," she announced, kneeling next to a small mushroom that glowed faintly in the dim sewer. Helai also unsheathed the knife at her thigh, pulling out a small cloth. Her hand was steady as she cut the mushroom from the root and wrapped it in the fabric.

Linda seemed to be pulled out of a trance as the urge to kill Helai faded. It left dizziness in their gaze as they shook their head again, turning to peer towards the entrance. It did not seem like their actions were heard, but a scurry of movement deeper in the tunnels sent a wave of unease through Linda as they drew close to Helai.

"Hear that?" they asked, but Helai was too busy slicing through the mushroom where it stuck out of cracks in the stone. Linda smothered their fear when a small noise echoed through the tunnels, so faint it could have been imagined. Linda decided it would be best to stick close to Helai and ambled closer to her.

They were silent as they searched further down the tunnel, stopping where the tunnel split into different directions. The darkness seemed to spill around them like it wanted to drown them. Chills rolled down Linda's back as if eyes were on them, but when they looked behind them, they saw nothing.

"*Shit*," Helai hissed, clutching the small of her back. Linda worried she had touched the mushroom wrong, but a cut of pain shot across their thigh before they could question her, their mark flaring up, and it threatened to bring them to their knees.

Low laughter echoed around the corner as if someone stood just out of sight and mocked them. Linda wasn't confident why their fear festered, but it grew like a seed in the bowels of their belly, unyielding despite Linda's best attempts to murder it. Peering around the corner, they saw nothing.

"Something playing tricks," Linda said, wishing for a weapon in their hands. They opened their jaw instead, hoping whatever messed with them in the darkness would see and be afraid.

"Here, Linda. Step back," Helai said, leaning around the corner and whispering something into her palm. A shadow shaped like a desert fox materialized, incorporeal, as it shot off her hand and ran ahead. It left behind a line of black smoke that remained tethered to her open palm.

A few tense moments passed. Fear cascaded through them as their brands continued to burn without mercy. Helai clenched her jaw to keep quiet, the skin of her cheek pulsating as she watched her palm for any sign of change in her magic. Linda held their breath for as long as they could as the air thickened in trepidation.

Helai clenched her fist and the shadow trail dissipated. "Whatever it was, it's gone," she whispered to Linda, but Linda wasn't so sure as they stared down the tunnel, trying to discern what lay in hiding there. Even with their dark vision, they could not see anything waiting to attack them.

Linda growled. "Want to leave."

Helai shook her head, turning farther in. "I must get more. Golbin needs them." She fell silent then, careful not to make a sound as she hugged the wall. Linda followed.

Helai collected four more mushrooms before she was satisfied and said they could leave. Linda's relief was immense; even though they had not encountered any trouble, there was something wrong, and Linda did not like feeling like they were being watched. They were glad when the opening out of the sewers came into sight, and the moon's light drenched them in a safe glow. Right before they exited the sewers, Helai stopped Linda with a brush of their hand.

"Your ring," she whispered.

Linda hesitated. Readjusting the ring on their finger, they tucked themself safely behind the illusion. Maybe one day, Intoh would get strong enough to rework the illusion magic, and make the illusion a visage of what Linda wanted. Intoh had told Linda the rings were already illusioned when he stole them, and he wasn't strong enough yet to weave new illusions on them.

One day, Linda. When I'm strong enough.

That's what Intoh had told them, but they were impatient. As they looked down at the human hands they hid behind, they were too large, too hairy. It felt odd like they were tucked away in a place they didn't belong. Some days it was so invasive Linda could hardly stand it.

One day they'd be free.

Only when they were a safe distance away did Helai pry open the sack she had stuck the mushrooms in to count them. She seemed untroubled by the unease felt in the sewers, though Linda could smell the fear that rolled off her. Linda's brand no longer hurt, but there was still a sense of urgency, a feeling that they had somewhere to be.

"Come, Linda," Helai said, turning. "We'll take these to Golbin, and then I owe you dinner."

Chapter Twenty-Eight
Rooster

Silence had settled between them when he and Cassius left The Broken Arrow. It was comfortable, and Rooster did not fret too much when left alone with his thoughts. He began to whistle as the city sprang to life around them. People had finished setting up their stalls, and trade wares dotted the streets: silks and spices from Shoma, woven baskets from Míradan, and furs from Kreznov. A woman threw fish into baskets, ignoring children taunting her from an alleyway. The smell of fish tugged longingly in Rooster's belly, begging him to turn towards the docks.

"My mother used to have a fleet for trade long ago," Cassius said. "There's something… *unforgiving* about the ocean, and I remember her rage when she lost several ships in a storm."

Rooster glanced over at Cassius as he spoke. The vampire's gaze was far off.

"Did you ever sail yourself?" Rooster asked.

Cassius nodded. "When I was human, but only every once in a while." A silence fell between them, but it was brief before Rooster felt compelled to fill the silence with conversation.

"So you are from Wilhaven?" Rooster asked, drawing his arms close to stave off the cold. They sidestepped a carriage pulled by a large workhorse, and he hefted his cloak more securely around his shoulders. When Cassius nodded, Rooster's expression turned thoughtful. "Your accent hints at Hestian."

"My mother was from Fraheim, and my father was a knight for Verenzia in southern Hestia. I went to live with my uncle in Wilhaven when I was in my twenties, and when he passed, I… inherited his estate." A flicker of bitterness crossed Cassius' face, but it was gone so quickly that Rooster decided he imagined it.

"Ah," Rooster said, pulling his flask out. After taking a long pull from it, he wiped his lips and turned to Cassius with a curious expression, but the conversation went silent.

After a moment or two, Cassius spoke again. "I've been around a long time, and your accent sounds like it could be from the Isles of Rolias. Perhaps once you have enough skaels to get out of here, you can seek the answers of your past there?" He gestured to Rooster's flask, where the C.W. was etched onto the side. "Maybe someone knows the name of those initials."

Before Rooster could answer, a young boy covered in dirt and rail thin bumped into Cassius. "Pardon me, sir." He started to scurry off, but Rooster reached out and snagged the boy's collar, pulling him close.

"Hey, not cool, mister! Let me go!" The boy's struggles barely registered. Grinning at a passing couple, he snaked his arm over the boy's shoulders. The couple did not stop, but Rooster hadn't expected them to.

"You need to learn new tricks. Next time, have a friend of yours distract your victim before you try and pickpocket, or learn to be quieter. Give my friend his coin purse, and I'll let you go on your way." His grip on the boy's shirt tightened when the boy hesitated. Shoving the coin purse back at Cassius, he squirmed, grunting as he struggled.

"All right, now lemme go," he cried. Rooster released him, watching him scamper around a corner.

Cassius re-clasped his bag to his waist, nodding his head at Rooster. "Thanks."

"It was a trick I might have attempted once upon a time. Little fool," Rooster said, shaking his head. "Come on."

They continued forward, silence falling between them once more. It wasn't long before the guard's quarters came into sight. A small courtyard was set up with dummies, and several recruits of various skill levels practiced their sword fighting and archery. A seasoned guard with a scar mangling the side of her face glanced over at them. As they approached, she stepped away from the recruit she was instructing.

"State your business. You do not look to be joining the guard." Her voice was gravelly, her hair shaved, and Rooster offered a daring smile.

"We wish to introduce ourselves to Captain Booker. We have just traveled from the Spine Mountains and have troubling news about the marshes southeast of here."

The guard stared at them for a moment and then grunted, pointing at the stairs leading up to the wall. "Up those stairs and to the right. I will warn you our captain does not like his time wasted. He should be in his office."

"You're not the first person to say that," Rooster said. He glanced over at Cassius, who was watching the recruits practice. He had a glazed look in his eye as if he were reliving a memory. Many still fought with vigor, having just started their daily routine as the sun rose. One of the recruits came at his sparring partner with aggressive movements, forcing the other to stumble back and fall. Cassius moved forward as if to intervene but stopped at the last second, shaking his head.

"You want to keep watching, or shall we go?" Rooster teased, and it earned a glare from Cassius.

"Let's go," he said, watching the recruit help his friend up from the ground before moving towards the stairs.

When they reached the top, Rooster sidestepped out of the way of one of the guards. The wall overlooked the forest they'd passed through. It stretched for miles, changing into marshlands farther than the eye could see. Beyond that, the Spine Mountains rose on the horizon. A small breeze brushed against Rooster's face, and he smiled. He could get used to a sight like this.

When Cassius knocked on the captain's door, Rooster moved to stand by his side. Cassius clasped his hands behind his back, his spine erect like a seasoned soldier. An easy smile graced Rooster's lips as he clapped Cassius on the shoulder. "You need to learn how to loosen up, Cassius. You look too tense all the time."

"Perhaps you need to be warier of the world. Your carelessness caused you to lose your memory," Cassius said, his voice low.

"Uh, ouch," Rooster complained. The door opened slightly in front of them to reveal a tall man with broad shoulders and thick eyebrows. He was graying at his temples, and his beard was full and dark.

"Who are you, and what do you want?" His Kreznovian accent was thick. Rooster couldn't remember if he'd ever been as far north as Kreznov, but he knew the men and women there were hardened by the harsh winters and their love for hunting the massive wildlife that dwelled in their thick forests. Thinking of Kreznov made him think of Ayla, and his heart twinged painfully at the reminder of her death.

"I'm Rooster, and this is Cassius." Rooster's hand gestured. Even with his lanky stature, Rooster only reached the captain's chin. Still, he met Booker's gaze with respect and a lack of fear.

Booker stared at him. "And what of your business?"

"We have come to share news of the road, as we have just traveled down the Spine Mountains after staying with the dwarves. Their king has just suffered a great loss, and we have reason to believe there is unrest that could affect Volendam."

Booker didn't say anything for several moments. He worked his jaw over, the muscles clenching in his cheek, and then he opened the door and stepped aside. "Come in."

The room was small, with a desk taking up the room's primary focus. Small holes in the stone were on the far wall to shuffle light through or offer archers a vantage point should the city be under siege. Although light poured through the windows, Booker illuminated the room with a few candles scattered about. Besides the desk and chair, the room was void of decorum or other furniture. Rooster stood in the middle of the room as Booker sat, and Cassius stood near the small fireplace on the opposite wall.

Booker said: "You have five minutes. He picked his quill back up from atop a half-written letter and began to write. Rooster glanced at Cassius.

"We've come to warn you about dyrvak activity in the marshes," Rooster said. The light flickered off Booker's face, warping his expression, but he looked less than pleased. Folding his letter, he heated a spoon of wax over a candle flame. The silence stretched as he sealed the letter with the hot wax and stamped the Volendam sigil in its center.

"Now you look to waste my time. Dyrvak don't come out of Daesthara," Booker said, placing the stamp down and turning his full attention to Rooster.

"Take a day's journey into the marshland, and you will find a battleground defying that logic. I did not think they would leave the forests either, but there was no mistake in what we fought," Cassius said.

"I don't have the men to send out on a fool's errand. If you wish to bring me proof, that's your prerogative, but I do not have the resources to rely on the words of men I've just met."

Rooster opened his mouth to protest, but Booker held up his hand to silence him. "I will not have any more of my time taken. I trust you can see yourselves out?"

Cassius was first to exit, not a word spoken. As Rooster followed him, he waved his hand dramatically in a circle. "Thank you for your time."

Rooster received no answer, and as he stepped out onto the wall, the sky opened. Rooster welcomed the rain, his face upturned towards the sky.

"Great," Cassius muttered. "I hate the rain."

"He was pleasant," Rooster said, smiling, changing the subject as they left the guard's quarters behind them and made their way back down the stairs. Everyone moved to protect their stalls against the rain, and the number of people out on the road thinned.

"He doesn't need to be," Cassius replied, stepping to the side as a man balancing several large crates in his arms walked past. "But we gave him the information we have. What he does with it is up to him, and I have business to get back to." An impatient urge pulsed through Rooster as Cassius spoke, his impatience clear.

"Wait," Rooster said as he caught sight of the sea between buildings. "Let's go to the docks and speak with the sailors to see if they know anything about the mermaids."

"Go yourself. As I said, I need to go." Rooster opened his mouth to argue when he was assailed with the intense need to go north. Something that called out to him was difficult to ignore as Cassius sighed and ran his fingers through his hair, plastering strands to his face.

"Come with me. I have to show you something," he said, his voice laced with the sweetness of honey. A wave of calm washed over Rooster as Cassius' tone echoed with urgency, and Rooster was eager to listen. It was almost as if his choice in the matter was robbed, but he didn't feel out of control. He *wanted* to follow Cassius.

A man sat at the edge of an alleyway they passed, his hands shaking, a hood covering his face from the rain. As they moved in front of him, he grabbed Rooster's arm. The skin on the back of the man's hand was stretched thin, and he had a wild look in his eyes. "Ever get addicted to the power, boy?" he asked, his voice raspy and wet like he was suffering from a head cold. His lips were cracked and bleeding. Sores oozed a yellow pus all over his arms and legs.

Pulling free with disgust, Rooster pulled away and quickened his pace down the street, Cassius close beside him.

"Sulfen will grant you that power! All you need is a drop," the man raved as they left him behind.

Rounding a corner, Cassius said, "Sulfen? Isn't that a shadow market drug? I thought the market for it died ages ago."

Rooster shrugged. "I don't know." Sulfen was a drug that enhanced magical ability, but it had been made illegal a long time ago. The only way to get it was from the blood of a living host, and the side effects for the taker were often addicting. It did make the drinker extremely powerful for a short time, but taking it for long periods was often fatal. Those who took it died painfully.

Cassius said nothing more on the matter as they crossed a bridge into the Sails District. The grim nature of rain could not pull away the immediate signs of wealth as soon as they stepped foot in the entertainment quarter. The streets were paved with cobblestone, kept in excellent care, and the buildings showed no sign of weather or wear as their vibrant colors were bright and flourishing.

Magical orbs lit the streets, gleaming against the rain. They swayed inside metal contraptions hanging from posts, and Rooster blinked the water from his eyes as Cassius halted in front of an abandoned building. The moment they stopped, a hold on Rooster was broken, and he shook his head, confused.

"What is it?" Rooster was underwhelmed at the sight of the building, which looked to have burned down in its prime. While the building still stood strong, the glass in the windows was gone and boarded up, and black ash coated parts of the walls where a fire had licked up the sides of the stone and could not burn.

"An opera house. I am not certain what happened here, but I've been drawn to this place for a while now. The longer I wait, the stronger the urge gets. Whatever calls me here is impatient, and I do not think I can wait much longer," Cassius said, pacing with his hands clasped tightly behind his back.

"Did you do something to me?" Rooster held his head as dizziness took hold. It was like the brand on his back took a heartbeat of its own. Thump. Thump. Thump. He grew nauseous as an invisible force drove him to step forward, but his instincts fought it with everything they had, screaming at him to turn away and never look back.

"You feel what I have felt every moment we have been in this city," Cassius admitted quietly. "I am certain you have felt it, too, in some capacity."

Rooster pressed the heels of his hands to his eyes so hard he saw stars as the wave of nausea retreated. He had been feeling on edge since arriving in Volendam; that was certain. He couldn't be sure how much of it was connected to the opera house, but as he pulled his hands away and stared at it, he felt threatened to be unmade, like he stood on the edge of some great evil that could utterly destroy him.

"I did not tell you before because I did not trust you," Cassius said, drawing close and lowering his voice. "Something festers inside there. I wish I knew what it was, but I do not. You must understand my urgency now."

Rooster forced himself to take a few steps away from the opera house. The further he got, the easier it was to bear the uncomfortable feelings that plagued him. "We should tell the others. Whether we like it or not, we are branded, and I do not think we'll be able to leave the city until we help you with–" Rooster vaguely waved his hand at the opera house, "whatever shit is going on in there."

Hesitation stitched lines into Cassius' forehead. "I do not know if that is wise."

"If I have felt this, the others have as well," Rooster argued. "They have as much of a right to know as I do, and this is bigger than you now."

A heavy sigh escaped Cassius' lips as he murmured a soft curse in a different language under his breath. "You are right."

Rooster tossed another weary glance up at the opera house. "Good. Now can we leave this place? It's giving me the creeps."

After several tense moments, Cassius nodded, and they turned to leave. As Cassius moved to fall in step beside Rooster, he noticed Cassius' hands were shaking.

Chapter Twenty-Nine
Cassius

The Broken Arrow was a welcomed relief from the rain as he and Rooster walked through the front door. The warmth soaked up the cold outside as they moved to their booth, where the others sat with untouched food. Everyone was quiet and solemn, and when Helai noticed them, she bolted to her feet.

"Something strange is happening," she said. Worry infected her tone as Rooster gestured to Felix for some food. Cassius was also hungry, but not for fish, and made a mental note that he would need to go out later to feed.

"Yes, we might have an answer to that," Rooster said, eyeing Cassius as he sat where Helai had been sitting. Cassius did not return his gaze nor meet Helai's as she studied him, then gestured for Rooster to scoot over. She sat as he did, and Cassius took the empty spot across from her.

"I was coming to Volendam because something called me from my estate in Wilhaven. It's been getting steadily more insistent the longer I avoid it, and I am almost certain that you all feel it, too, due to the brands the rakken gave us. When I got to Volendam, I followed the urge to an abandoned opera house."

Intoh peered up from the fish he had been picking through. "Called to you? Does not seem good. Do not know why it is our problem."

A surge of anger passed through Cassius, and the whole party winced. "There is something in that opera house. If it is something of power, it would be better for us to get it than someone who means ill will. Perhaps it can guide us to answers."

"If it's calling to you, then I'm not so sure it's anything good," Rooster said with some hesitation. "But you're right. Whatever it is, it isn't something we want in the wrong hands."

"Where is this opera house?" Helai asked.

"It's in ruin in the midst of the Sails District. Not sure why the nobles haven't demanded it be torn down. I ran into a Blodrägr when I tried to enter it the other day; he said it was haunted." Cassius leaned forward, watching the torchlight above them flicker against the wall.

"What is Blodrägr?" Linda asked.

"They are a small faction of the Inquisition, those who hunt demons. Blodrägrs specialize in hunting vampires." Cassius sighed, running a hand through his hair. He'd faced a handful of Blodrägrs in the past and did not care to deal with one now if they could help. Having one in the city was enough to put him on edge, but the urge to seek out whatever was in the opera house was stronger. Even now, he could feel it–instead of the unsteady quiet thum, it was a strong heartbeat at the center of his chest. Each pulse sent a wave of nausea and urgency through him.

"If it is that urgent, then perhaps we should make it our priority," Helai said, tracing the table's grain with her finger. Patrina played a soft tune on her lute, lulling Cassius into quiet ease that pulled away from the horrible feelings he had been experiencing as of late.

"I would be the first person to agree with you on that, but I haven't gone there myself because I am not equipped to deal with whatever is inside. I have been meaning to meet Velius but have not had the time," Cassius said, leaning back in his seat.

A quiet fell around the table as Hilde approached, slipping a plate of potatoes and fresh fish in front of Rooster and Cassius. He would have frowned in disdain had a goblet of wine not soon followed.

"Let me know if you need anything else, dears," Hilde murmured in a quiet, sing-song voice before moving on to the following table. Felix cast secret looks at Patrina as she played, cleaning mugs from behind the counter at the bar. Several sailors sang a low, mournful song to the beat of Patrina's music, and Helai waited a moment or two more before she leaned forward, her voice quiet.

"I do not know if I trust Velius. He seems up to something."

"What–he wants to equip us with nice weapons for little skaels, and you automatically distrust him?" Rooster asked, bumping shoulders with Helai. "It's because he thought I was pretty and you weren't, wasn't it?"

"Not at all," Helai protested.

"It's okay," Rooster said with a laugh. "He's not my type." Sobering, he shook his head. "I don't trust him exactly, which is why *I* don't owe him a favor." He gave Helai a stern look. "Still—if he's going to give us the weapons we need to deal with the opera house, then my trust will extend at least that far."

Helai twisted her braid as Linda shook their head and said, "Sewers feel bad."

"That too," Helai added, looking at Linda. "We were in the sewers collecting mushrooms for Golbin, the alchemist, and there was something down there with us. I do not know what, but…" she trailed off, shuddering.

Cassius recalled feeling uneasy all day. He had brushed it off as other reasons, but perhaps it was correlated. "Maybe just rats," he suggested. "Or it's not unheard of for crocodiles to find themselves in the sewers. Volendam *is* near marshlands."

"Given the rats we had to deal with in the mountains, I would fear such a thing," Helai said with a sigh. "But you are probably right. We looked, and we found nothing. Perhaps it was nothing at all."

Silence encompassed the party for a few moments before Intoh spoke up. "Spoke to Tidebeard. Says Gorvayne is name of dead dragon. Eldrasi legend. Maybe good to talk to Velius?"

Cold seeped over Cassius at Intoh's words. A dead dragon? It seemed difficult to believe. Much of the world called them false gods, a beast made to tempt you away from whatever afterlife the individual believed. Others thought them to be nothing more than myth, a creature eldrasi created to explain their solitude and secrecy. Cassius could claim their existence at one time because he knew vampirism to come from the skull of one. It was strange, though, to have heard the name on different tongues and doubted their claims.

"A dragon?" Helai asked in disbelief.

Intoh nodded and shrugged. "Don't know why he'd lie. Don't know why the dyrvak are worshiping it either. So many questions, so few answers."

"Too many questions," Cassius agreed. "We are to attend the Silver Moon Club tomorrow, are we not? Should we come up with a plan, or are we to just go inside and improvise?"

"Hunt mermaids first—*your* idea. Remember?" Intoh said, gesturing to Cassius.

Cassius had forgotten his suggestion. "Yes, you're right. If that's the case, Rooster and I will pose as hunters," Cassius said.

"Helai seems better suited to the hunter role," Rooster interrupted, gesturing to Helai. "I will pose as a dashing and handsome young vagabond that will woo the club attendees." Rooster stroked his chin in exaggerated thought. His hair had finally started to grow out, curling around his ears as his facial hair was not quite long enough to be considered a beard but covered his chin and cheeks nonetheless.

Helai deadpanned. "You're going to be a whore?"

Rooster grinned. "The ladies aren't ready for the Cock."

Helai groaned, pressing the heel of her hand to her forehead. "Okay, okay." She eyed Cassius and sighed. "So we'll turn in the mermaid heads while you whisper lies in girls' ears. What about Linda and Intoh?"

"Told you. Won't go in—don't want to get caught. Student of college now." Intoh shook his head, his eyes flickering to the space in front of their table as if he was looking to someone for confirmation. Cassius sensed no one there.

"Can't go alone. Need you Intoh," Linda said.

"Will be right outside," Intoh assured, patting Linda's arm. "You can do this. Will have others with you."

"I think you would be okay going inside, Intoh. Go under the guise of a student trying to unwind from your studies," Rooster suggested. "If things go south, it will be better with you inside than stuck outdoors."

Cassius held up a hand. "Doesn't matter. We might benefit from leaving someone outside, just in case. I assume the club has gambling tables, and Linda can pose as one of the guards posted at those tables." Getting Rooster and Linda inside would be half the trouble. Cassius had been to plenty of exclusive parties in his long life and did not worry much for Rooster—there was always a need for brothels at those parties. Linda, however, would be trickier.

"That's not a bad idea if we can sneak the clothes for it," Rooster said.

Helai's eyes lit up. "What if Linda sneaks in with us to collect the bounty? They look the part already. If we can swipe guard clothes once inside, all the better." She shook her finger in thought. "Or Linda goes with you, Cassius, and I can sneak my way in and pose as a guest."

"Will go," Linda said, looking at Cassius. He wasn't sure how they all would remain in the club once they turned in the mermaid heads to whoever owned the Silver Moon Club, but Cassius had sweet-talked his fair share of nobles. So long as the others did not warrant unwanted attention, he could see them pulling off the heist with relative ease.

Rooster knocked his fist against the table. "Then we fight mermaids at the end of the week. A few of us can scope the Silver Moon Club throughout the week and go then. Afterwards—" Rooster caught Cassius' eye. "We go to the opera house."

Felix had begun putting out the lights and dimming the fire in the fireplace, and Patrina played softly for the last few people mulling over drinks. A shiver ran through Cassius as the others retired for the night. He couldn't help but wonder:

Would the opera house let him wait?

Chapter Thirty
Linda

Linda woke a few mornings later, face shoved into the crook of their elbow. Intoh prodded them awake, and Linda thought about lashing out and biting him just to teach him a lesson. A huff escaped their lips as they rolled out of bed and stood, stretching. It was still dark outside, the moon bright and low in the sky as hints of the sun dusted the horizon. Rooster sat with his feet kicked up on a bucket turned upside down, his fingers molding wax into small circles. A candle had been pulled from the wall and mutilated, carved away by Rooster's knife. He and Helai had gone to the Silver Moon Club the day before to scout it out and returned with promising news. The club was active and thriving, and no one had claimed the bounty for the mermaid heads, which meant they were still good to hunt them.

"It is time for you to go, Linda," Intoh said as he scurried out of the room.

"He is strange. Have you two traveled together long?" Rooster asked, picking up all the wax balls and slipping them into his pocket.

"Maybe year—maybe two," Linda admitted with a shake of their head. Thinking about their time in Lyvira was unsettling, a quiet and cold weight in their belly. "What doing?" They asked, gesturing to the wax.

"Hm," Rooster hummed, straightening to his feet. "Not sure if this will work, but mermaids use their voices to lull their prey into the water." He held up one ball of wax. "Maybe we can prevent that by sticking some of this wax in our ears."

Linda shrugged. They had never fought mermaids before, but the logic made sense. "Works for me."

Rooster brushed the front of his jacket, freeing the wrinkles and excess wax, and stepped forward. "After you," he said, gesturing to the open door. Linda ambled into the hall and descended stairs, where people nursed hangovers and ate breakfast before the day began. Hilde laughed at something Patrina said, and Felix was nowhere to be found.

Helai, Cassius, and Intoh sat at their booth. As Linda approached, they crinkled up their nose in disgust. The rotting smell was faint, but it radiated off Cassius all the same, even with the new life shined in his eyes and smooth skin.

"You stink," Linda said bluntly.

Cassius glared. "That's not very nice, Linda."

Linda scoffed a guttural sound that settled in the back of their throat.

"If you showered, would it rid you of the smell?" Rooster asked as they stepped out onto the street. Other than the occasional fisherman heading to the docks, the streets were vacant, small bugs with flickering lights dotting their spines flitting between buildings.

"Unlikely. Decay comes from within—not external," Intoh said, weighing in.

"Fucking mortals," Cassius groaned, pressing a palm to his gaze in exasperation. "Moving on, did you get those earplugs made? I fear we will be useless without them."

Rooster nodded, pulling the wax out of his pocket and handing a pair of them to everyone. Linda followed by example as Helai and Cassius pushed the wax into their ears, and the world's sounds grew muffled. It did not block out the noise completely, but the voices grew quieter.

"This just might work," Helai said as they crossed a canal. A young man guided a small, thin boat through the channel with a long pole, and Linda could smell the sweet treats and flowers he carried with him. The aroma distracted Linda, but Intoh pressed his hand to their side and directed them down the streets towards the docks.

Intoh stopped as they neared. "Will not be joining. Have lessons at college. Can't miss it."

Rooster raised an eyebrow. "We do not expect this to take long. Are you sure?"

Intoh nodded, already stepping away. "Will monitor things. Don't know how long you'll take–don't know where mermaids are. Please– will be fine. Will study hard. Can use teachings for further use."

Linda patted his head as he hurried off. They ignored the urge to follow him as they turned instead towards Rooster and the others as they made their way down onto the docks.

Large sails peeked over the rooftops as they got close to the bay, and the thick, pungent smell of fish wafted up from the sea. Salt etched Linda's tongue as lamps swung in the wind, fire flickering against the homes. Linda watched a man in an alley sniff and tug the rags of his clothes more tightly around himself, and his gaze was hard and cold when their eyes met.

The docks were already bustling with life, packed with fishermen prepping their boats to take out to sea. Rooster approached the first woman he saw bent over the knots that tied their fishing boat to the dock.

"Mornin' ma'am. We don't mean to bother you–but there would be skaels in it if you take us out with you," Rooster said. The sailor brushed back the dark hair from her face and squinted at them, her mouth drawn in a scowl.

"Oh yeah? An' why's that? None of you look like fishermen–'cept you," she said, pointing at Rooster, then Linda. "An' maybe you."

Rooster looked around and lowered his voice. "We've heard there are mermaids in these waters, and we want to see if the stories are true."

"Mermaids don't come this far north. Too cold–" the sailor protested, pulling the knots free from the dock. Confliction crossed her face as she shrugged. "Though—would love to know what mermaid tastes like. Never 'ad mermaid before."

"We'll work that into the deal," Rooster said, eyeing the others. Cassius stood with his arms folded across his chest, and Helai's eyes darted out to the open sea as she bit down on her lower lip.

A buzz of excitement coursed through Linda, being so close to the water. The desire to ignore everyone and dive in was almost too great to ignore, urged on by the tension to seek the opera house that coiled in their belly. Linda still didn't know what they thought about all of that. Sitting with Patrina at The Broken Arrow eating fish sounded more desirable than seeking out a haunted opera house.

"Thirty skaels for the trouble, and I want a piece of the mermaid," the sailor said, holding her hand to shake.

"We only need their heads," Helai pointed out, and after a moment, Rooster nodded, taking the sailor's hand.

"You have a deal," he said.

"Name's Tiku. Get on."

They all ambled onto Tiku's boat. It wasn't large, by any means, no bigger than the average sloop, and handled them all comfortably as they came aboard. A small crew of sailors worked the ropes and sails, prepping the ship for departure, and Linda watched on with a vague interest.

Helai was the last to enter, her hesitation noticed by Tiku, who gestured to a bucket.

"If you're going to vomit, best do it overboard," Tiku said, prepping the boat for departure. The sun had begun its ascent over the horizon, but its warmth had not yet touched the world, and Linda suppressed the urge to shudder.

"I won't," Helai assured. Sweat gleaned from her brow. Linda wasn't sure they believed her.

As dawn broke over the horizon, the sun's warmth was subtle. The small bob of the boat was a comfort for Linda and reminded them of their journey over from Lyvira. The sea had been far more unforgiving, with storms that tried to swallow their ship. Tiku was an excellent sailor, and the riding was reasonably smooth as they pushed out into the bay. Other boats sailed by them, some bigger than Tiku's, while others were mere small rowboats for some of the small fish near the shore.

"What's my course?" Tiku asked.

A strange expression came over Rooster's expression, and he glanced out at the water, his eyes unfocusing. It was as if he were reliving some memory. "I believe they hole up in underground caves and nothing too close to cities—they'd be hunted to extinction if they did."

Cassius thumbed his chin in thought. "Perhaps cave systems? We could try baiting them out if we know where to look."

Tiku grunted, gesturing to the netting near the front of the boat. "We can catch some fish an' throw it overboard."

Helai sat with her back flush against the side of the boat, her knees hugging her chest. She looked up, giving Tiku a confused stare. "Won't that attract other predators?"

Tiku shrugged and nodded. "Yes."

Cassius paced the ship, his hands clasped tightly behind his back. His gaze was far off, and he looked back towards Volendam as conflict coursed through his expression. A soft hum settled against Linda's chest, an unease that tightened the further they got away from Volendam. Sudden darkness inside Linda urged them to snap Tiku's neck, turn the boat around, and move further into the city. They resisted as Cassius ran a hand through his hair and sighed, pressing his fingers to the side of the ship so hard the tips turned white.

"Linda?" Rooster's voice pulled Linda away from their observations. They trained their gaze on Cassius as Rooster drew close. "Keep an eye on him, yeah? He looks—impatient. I can feel it too." Linda's brand burned with Rooster's words.

"Can do that," Linda agreed, a low growl pressing against their lips. It was becoming tiresome how often the brand burned. It was a constant reminder that Linda and the others were marked for something. Quiet anger shot through Linda at the thought of being chosen once more against their will. They felt imprisoned to its nature with no choice but to obey, and that thought alone was infuriating.

Rooster smiled and clasped Linda's shoulder, pulling their anger from them as quickly as it appeared. It was as if he had pulled a string in Linda's chest, undoing a tense knot that wove through Linda's shoulders. "Thank you. I do hope we find the mermaids soon."

Linda looked out at sea. It was calm this morning, with gentle waves crashing up against the boat, and Linda couldn't help but agree with Rooster.

They hoped the mermaids were worthy fighters.

Nearly a week passed, and tensions were high. Helai had gotten over her seasickness by the third day, but Linda had never seen someone relieve the contents of their stomach so much. Cassius was fading quickly, his hunger pulling his skin gaunt over high cheekbones, his eyes flashing red if the sun caught them right. He nearly drained Tiku, but Rooster convinced him against it. He spent much time muttering and pacing as he attempted to keep himself collected as Linda sat near the edge of the boat, staring longingly overboard. It was true torture being so close yet so far away from being in the water.

They had checked every cove and cave they'd come across to no avail. Rooster had to convince Tiku to stay out with extra skaels. Tiku had begrudgingly agreed.

"One week is all I'll give you," Tiku had said. "And we stay close to Volendam's waters. I've heard pirates are gathering up north." Linda was familiar with pirates who liked to raid the coasts of Lyvira and thought it best they did not come into contact with them.

"What those?" Linda asked, sitting down next to Helai. It was mid-afternoon, the sun tucked behind rain-soaked clouds. Helai sat near the front of the ship with her leg propped up, a few cards spread out in front of her. She shuffled the rest of the deck in her hands, and Linda stared at the cards curiously as they drew close. The boat swayed as they fell to sit beside Helai, and Helai held up a few cards. Someone beautifully decorated them with lines of gold. The edges were highly frayed, and some cards were so worn they were almost indiscernible about what illustration illustrated each card, but that told a tale of how much love Helai had given them in the past.

"It's a card game the kids of Shoma like to play on the streets. Your opponent picks three cards. You shuffle them and then lay them out in front of them." She set three cards face down in front of Linda. "After that, your opponent is supposed to guess which card is which. One point each." Helai flipped them back over, and Linda stared at them curiously. One was the sun draining into two goblets—one wreathed in gold, the other worn down and decrepit. The second one was a krok'ida, their scars tinged in silver. One claw raised delicately as a blue butterfly landed, wings outstretched. The last card was a dragon soaked in magic sleeping upon a sea of sand. It bore no front feet, its wings curling to a long claw on each end. The dark amber hue of its scales pulled Linda in closer, marveling at it.

"I think I sense something," Cassius said, startling Linda. The fog had settled over the water, but Tiku seemed accustomed to it, her fingers expertly handling the wheel as they cut through. Her crew adjusted sails, raising them as the boat slowed.

Helai quickly shuffled her cards back into her bag, her eyes trained at sea. Worry lined her brow as silence encompassed the boat. A quiet hush shot through the crew as Rooster settled next to Linda at the front of the ship. The coast was nothing more than craggy rocks and cliffside, and a shiver ran through Linda as cold air wafted through them.

"Keep a sharp eye," Rooster muttered quietly, pushing the wax more securely into his ears. "Something doesn't feel right." Linda felt it, too, a thick trepidation in the air. Something bumped against the bottom of the boat, strong enough to be noticed but not so strong that anyone lost their balance. A quiet giggle echoed through the fog, and Linda tried to spot movement in the water, but they couldn't see anything other than the faint splash and something slapping against the surface.

A soft singing sank over the water, only it was wrong. Even muffled behind the wax Linda had shoved in their ears, the music sounded like a mixture between utterly beautiful and something sharp scraping across rocks. A sailor stepped up next to Linda, slack-jawed and eyes fogged over. At first, Linda wasn't sure what he was doing, and then he pushed himself up onto the railing of the boat and jumped.

Helai gasped, her fingers pressed to her lips as more and more of Tiku's crew followed suit. Chaos erupted as the few not affected by the singing attempted to stop others from jumping overboard. It mattered little—they fought until they could throw themselves over. Linda grabbed the arm of a sailor and shook her. "No," Linda said, but the woman lashed out, biting down on Linda's hand. Beads of red seeped through her teeth. "No," Linda said again with more force, hitting the sailor on top of the head so hard it knocked her out. "Sleep." They were gentle as they laid the woman down, turning as Rooster grabbed a spear from the floor of the boat and chucked it at a mermaid. It hit its mark, and the mermaid went silent as she squirmed in the water and then died.

Linda looked over the side of the boat to see the water was stained red as dorsal fins cut through the surface. The mermaids were feral in their attacks and did not look like the ones Linda had seen off the coasts of their home. These mermaids barely clung to the humans that they were and were more fish than man. The ones in Lyvira still bore the upper half of a human man or woman, their bottom half beautiful scales and fins, but most of these mermaids took characteristics of sharks or water snakes. One jumped out of the water, her shriek high-pitched as she slammed into a struggling sailor in the water, her jagged teeth digging into his neck.

"We can't let them feed and leave," Rooster called out. It was true. The frenzy was fading as the water calmed, and Cassius sighed, staring sadly over the side of the boat. Untying his belt, his sword clambered to the ground as he reached up to tighten his ponytail.

"Linda, with me. Rooster, Helai—if you get nets in the water, perhaps Linda and I can draw them into traps."

Tiku grunted, striding forward. "Got some nets right over there," she said, gritting her teeth as she looked at the massacre. "Took me forever to get those number of men. Now I gotta start over." She shook her head and hit the boat railing as Rooster looked at her, astonished.

"How were you not affected by the songs?" he asked.

Tiku gestured to her ears. "Mostly deaf. Learned to read lips when I was a little girl. Don't even affect me much anymore."

Admiration ran through Linda. They couldn't imagine being unable to hear when their enemies were near. That would be like taking away Linda's sense of smell, which would be detrimental to their ability to fight. The thought sickened Linda as Helai hurried over to the other side of the boat to grab the nets as instructed.

"Let's go," Linda rumbled, looking to Cassius before jumping feet-first into the water. Their lungs squeezed painfully as the chilly water overcame them, and Linda reached over to twist the ring on their finger. It felt good to be back in their skin as the water rushed over their scales.

The water was clear as Linda swam around the boat, watching Cassius' form sink several feet below. The actual songs of the mermaids echoed clearly under the water, more haunting and monstrous than they were above water. It did not take long for Linda to notice the mermaids as they clicked at each other in quick succession, their tails creating waves of bubbles through the water as they ripped into one of the sailors. They fed in a frenzy, and none immediately noticed Linda as their focus remained on their meal.

Cassius and Linda locked eyes as Cassius gestured in a circular motion around the mermaids. If they could surround at least two mermaids and lead them back towards the boat, Rooster and Helai could work at capturing them with the nets. It seemed like a simple enough task as Linda swam towards them, careful to keep their distance until Cassius could flank. The water was colder than Linda was used to, but they still swam through it with ease, their eyes trained on the mermaids as they fed. One ripped the arm off the sailor's body, a pool of blood surrounding them in a haze of red.

As Cassius swam closer, a form shot towards Linda in their peripheral. Unable to dodge, the mermaid slammed into Linda's side, screeching in tongues Linda did not understand. The mermaid's teeth scraped over Linda's scales as the mermaid grabbed at Linda's arm with webbed fingers, her eyes wild and feral with anger. The anger reminded Linda of the dyrvak in the marshes.

Lifting their arm, Linda propelled the mermaid towards their mouth, but the mermaid dodged easily, circling away and using its shark-like tail to swim off. Linda did not follow as another mermaid hit their side, gnashing her teeth in Linda's face. Off in the distance, Cassius' face transformed into a decayed and horrifying monster, his eyes blood red as his fangs sank into a mermaid's neck. The mermaid thrashed as several of her kin turned away from their meal to hiss at Cassius, but he drank the mermaid's blood until her eyes rolled into the back of her head, and she died, her arms going limp.

A sharp pain ran through Linda's arm, and they hissed, lashing out at the mermaid that bit them. The mermaid was nearly too fast, darting away as Linda shot out with their teeth. They closed their mouth over the tip of the mermaid's tail, and the mermaid wailed as Linda turned, dragging them back towards the boat. Blood seeped through the water as their teeth dug into the mermaid's flesh, and they sailed underneath Tiku's boat and let go.

The mermaid flung a slur of angry words at Linda as they shot off into the water, only for a net to hit the surface and sink over her. The mermaid cried out as the net tightened around her, pulling her towards the surface.

The mermaid's cries got the attention of the others, who halted their feeding frenzy to hiss and dart towards Linda. Cassius was nowhere to be seen in the commotion, and Linda knew better than to stay still as they shot through the water, darting through coral and past fish to keep out of the reach of the vengeful mermaids.

They chased, and Linda lured them away as Cassius came into sight, carrying two dead mermaids under one arm. Their necks were bloodied and mangled, their eyes fogged over, and their mouths twisted in wordless, eternal screams. Cassius had tucked himself behind a mask of humanity once more as he swam towards the boat's surface to hand the corpses off to Rooster and Helai.

Linda turned away as several mermaids snapped at their tail, outpacing them all as they turned around a large coral reef. How quickly Linda outswam the mermaids in the water was almost too easy. It was exhilarating, too, an elation Linda hadn't felt since their days in Lyvira, fighting alongside their kin against the forest's darkness or chasing fish through lakes and off the coast. A terrible sadness overcame them, followed by a merciless wave of anger. Were they doomed to be plagued by this loneliness forever?

Turning, Linda found the mermaids had stopped pursuing them. Confusion swept through them, drowning the anger, and as they swam back towards the boat, all traces of the mermaids were gone. The corpses of the sailors had disappeared as well. Linda rose to the surface as Rooster's head poked over the side of the boat.

"Those mermaids are tougher than shit. Whipped Tiku with her tail. Helai says it's not fatal, but we should get her back to Volendam," he said, glancing back over his shoulder as Helai said something Linda could not catch. "Where's Cassius?"

"Not with you?" Linda asked, puzzled.

Rooster's gaze turned to Linda as his brow threaded with worry. "No. He went back down to see if you needed aid."

"I go look," Linda said, diving back into the water.

Linda looked everywhere for Cassius, but it was no use.

He was gone.

Chapter Thirty-One
Cassius

Cassius woke to the sound of humming—haunting and beautiful. He was wet, sand coating his body as it rubbed against his skin in discomfort. His hair was undone from its ponytail and fell in clumps around his face. His mouth tasted of sandpaper, and he was tempted to groan; it felt like a pick was being driven through his eye. As his vision cleared, he realized he was in a cave, the reflection of the water shimmering against the damp walls. He sat on an island of sand in the middle of the cavern, and Felix lay next to him, unconscious. He had no idea how Felix got caught in the thralls of mermaids, but he did recall not seeing Felix in the inn that morning.

Cassius dared not move as he saw a woman sitting on the opposite bank, webbed fingers wielding a knife over the corpse of a child. With startling clarity, Cassius thought the corpse might be the missing child from the postings board inside The Broken Arrow. The drawing on the posting matched the child's appearance. So it wasn't a large fish, after all.

She sang softly as she plunged her knife into the corpse and cut, almost as if she were lulling her child to sleep. Cassius felt dizzy as the singing washed over him, urging his eyes to close. It felt much the same as when he was a child, sitting on the shores of Verenzia with his brother, the waves comforting and warm as they swept over his feet. He fought off the compulsion to sleep; he had to.

Felix stirred, a soft groan emitting from his lips. It pulled Cassius back from the shoreline. Before his eyes could truly open, Cassius reached over and clamped a hand over Felix's mouth as tightly as he could. Felix's eyes shot open in panic, darting around as he fought against Cassius' hold. Only when he recognized Cassius he calmed, his gaze lighting up in confusion and fear.

Cassius raised a free finger to his lips, mouthing *don't scream* to Felix as he slowly pulled his hand away from Felix's lips. The sound of Felix's heart thundered in his throat, beckoning him to feed while simultaneously putting Felix's fear on display, and Cassius looked around in a vain attempt to seek a way out. He remembered being pulled off the boat, a woman's face, and then nothing.

The mermaid still sang as she desecrated the tiny corpse, cutting it into several pieces. As Cassius studied her, she pulled a large, purple scale from her side and slipped it inside the carcass, humming as it lit up in a dim glow.

Draugmin? Cassius wondered. How did a mermaid have her hands on dwarven gems? It was only a matter of time before she fixed her gaze on her next prize.

Don't move, he whispered to Felix, who nodded. His face was white as a sheet, and he shook, refusing to move as his eyes darted to the other sleeping mermaids. Cassius could count ten of them together, and his heart sank despite his refusal to give up. He knew there had to be a way out somewhere; he'd just have to find it without alerting any mermaids.

Linda burst out of the water, their scales shimmering as water dripped off them. He never thought he'd feel so relieved to see a krok'ida in the water.

"Stay in the middle until I can speak with Linda. It seems like they move slower on land," Cassius told Felix, who nodded and scooted closer to the middle of the island.

"I spoke with one of the sailors on the docks about fish prices. I don't—" Felix spluttered, wiping his hair out of his face. "The singing—it filled my head. I don't know what happened after that."

Cassius pressed a hand to Felix's shoulder. Luckily, the mermaids hadn't killed him immediately, and it was a miracle Felix was still alive. "It doesn't matter. We're here now, and the important thing to do is to stay calm."

"Stay calm? There are mermaids and—and a krok'ida in the water," Felix protested, his finger shaking as he pointed at Linda, who was fighting with a struggling mermaid in their mouth. "You said that's Linda?"

Unease coursed through Cassius. "There will be a lot to explain when we're safe." Krok'idas weren't widely accepted in this part of the world, seen as nothing more than brutes and monsters.

Still, Felix's fear overshadowed his curiosity as he curled his fingers in the sand and swallowed, his adam's apple bobbing. Dark blood spurt out from between Linda's teeth as the mermaid went limp. Another mermaid stabbed Linda in the back with a small dagger as Cassius drew forward, wishing for a weapon of any kind. He did not want to leave Felix, but Linda struggled as two more mermaids joined the first, attacking the krok'ida without mercy. Cassius looked down, spotting a rock in the sand. It was the size of his palm, and he threw it with such force that when it hit a mermaid in the back, one of her ribs cracked. It was just enough distraction for Linda to reach around and grab the mermaid by the throat. They lifted her and slammed her down on the bank. Several more of the mermaid's bones snapped, the sound echoing off the cave walls.

"Go—" Linda said, ignoring the mermaid's futile attempts to pry their hand away from her throat. "Will take care. Hole that way." Linda pointed in the water towards the wall, and Cassius looked at Felix.

"Can you swim?"

Felix's face was pale as he shook, glancing at the water. "Yes, but… aren't there mermaids in there?"

Cassius' answer was drowned out by the wailing of a mermaid as she crashed onto the shore, scrambling to grab Felix's foot. She was horribly mutated—one leg bore the resemblance of a woman's, the other twisted and forged into a flipper. A jagged dorsal fin jutted out of her spine, and her eyes were black as she opened her mouth, revealing several rows of razor-sharp teeth.

Felix screamed as he scrambled away on all fours. Cassius reached him just before the mermaid bit down on his ankle. He grabbed her by the back of her head and threw her back into the water. Linda burst out of the water and caught the mermaid in their maw, biting down. The mermaid's cry was cut off as Linda killed her, blood shooting out and seeping into the water as Linda disappeared back underneath.

"Thank you," Felix sobbed, tears running down his face. "Thank you." He scrambled to his feet, trembling as he drew close to Cassius. "I would like to leave now." His heartbeat was a cascade of temptation in Cassius' ear as he tugged Felix forward near the water's edge.

"Swim in front of me. Linda said there is a way out over there," Cassius said, gesturing to the opposite wall. It wasn't too far of a swim, but while he did not need to breathe underwater, Felix did.

The water was thick, dark, and chilly as Felix jumped in, followed closely by Cassius. It was not within Cassius' comfort zone as heartbeats cascaded around him. Linda shot through the water somewhere off to his left. The exit might have been lost to a human in the darkness of the water, but Cassius made out its outline in front of Felix. No mermaid was in sight; they must have been preoccupied with Linda's attacks.

It was disorienting being underwater, and it took most of Cassius' focus to slip through the exit without issue. The mermaids were humming something dangerous behind him, taunting Linda in harsh, deadly tongues that cut through the water with little mercy. It sent shivers running up Cassius' spine.

Barely making out Felix's feet in front of him, they swam through a small tunnel with no light in sight. If they did not see the light soon, Cassius feared Felix would drown. When all hope seemed lost, Cassius glimpsed a break in the darkness, a small shimmer of light way off in the distance. At that exact moment, a webbed hand clamped down around his ankle. With a shrill shriek, the mermaid began to drag him back towards the cavern. Her fingers were slimy, like seaweed pressed against a leg in the darkness, and Cassius' anger lashed out.

You will not get me again, you bitch, he thought bitterly as his human visage was disillusioned and his vampiric form was unleashed. Lips slipped back over jagged, pointed canines, his undead nature shining as he curled in on himself and sank his teeth into the mermaid's wrist. It stank of fish, and its blood was bitter and foul, but Cassius drank until the mermaid stopped struggling and was exsanguinated. He pulled away as her heartbeat stopped, moving through the darkness towards the light. He could feel the weak heartbeat of Felix somewhere in the dark, and soon enough, he brushed up against his body. Tucking him under his arm, he swam up until his head broke the surface.

Helai was pacing in Tiku's sloop just left of the entrance. Rooster leaned over the side of the boat as if contemplating whether or not he wanted to jump over.

"Thank Dalnor, you're both—oh gods, is that Felix? Is he alright?" Helai worried her lower lip with her teeth as Cassius pushed Felix towards Rooster, who pulled him up into the boat. Pulling himself up next, Helai moved to Felix's side as Rooster approached Cassius.

"What is Felix doing here?" Rooster asked.

Cassius shrugged, ringing the water from his clothes. He could feel a headache forming as his hunger became unbearable. The mermaids he had done little to soothe his cravings, and he was desperate for human blood and a bath. Oh, he'd kill for a bath. "Felix said he was talking to a fisherman about fish prices on the docks this morning when he was lured in by a mermaid."

Felix threw up water as he came to, coughing violently. Helai urged him onto his side. Linda crashed to the surface, water droplets shaking off their scales as they grabbed onto the side of the boat with both hands. Several scales had been ripped out of their side, and blood pooled in the water around them, but they appeared uninjured.

"All mermaids dead," Linda announced, a growl of approval rumbling the base of their throat. "Stole teeth. Will make necklace." Climbing over the side of the boat, Linda slapped their tail against the surface as they opened their maw, and several small teeth fell out of their mouth.

Cassius glanced over at Tiku's unconscious form. "Linda, your ring," he said, gesturing to his finger. Felix stared wide-eyed at Linda's massive bulk as they grumbled and twisted the ring on their finger, shaking away the lizard form and donning their human one.

"You guys have a lot of secrets," Felix rasped, pushing his hair out of his face. He was pale and shaking, but his heartbeat grew steadier as time passed.

"You don't know the half of it," Helai muttered, slipping vials back into her bag. Tension settled in the air, thickening like a tightened cord as Cassius clenched his fist. Four dead mermaids lay in a pile atop the boat's nets. Rooster had already gotten to work decapitating them, their eyes caught in eternal terror. Afterward, he adjusted the sails to turn the ship back towards Volendam.

Cassius found his belt and sword near the wheel and reattached it to his hips, forcing his hands to still. He would have to eat soon.

It took three days to travel back to Volendam, but the travel was smooth sailing. Felix had barely spoken, and Tiku was still unconscious, her brow thick with sweat as she muttered in her sleep. Cassius had been unable to sit still for the entirety of the trip; his hunger, mingled with his desire for the opera house, had all but consumed him.

Linda had spent the better part of the first day forging their tooth necklace with the help of Helai and Rooster, who worked patiently to whittle small holes into the teeth Linda had collected. It was nothing more than a thin rope lined with teeth, and it took several tries to get it long enough to fit around the thickness of Linda's neck, but Linda hummed with pride when it was finally finished.

Rooster had assumed control of the boat and managed it with ease as Cassius stepped up to Felix. The barkeeper looked better than when

Cassius had found him, and the color had returned to his skin, and his eyes were kind when they turned to greet Cassius.

"At first, I was terribly frightened. Not only of the mermaids but of Linda too." Felix went quiet for several moments, and Cassius said nothing. It was unlike Míridan, where the eldrasi welcomed trade from the drikoty. Humans were bred to suspect anyone different than them, and it was their biggest flaw.

"But my parents always told me to welcome everyone at the hearth—no matter their walks of life. 'Try to be nice,' my mother used to say. 'Help where you can,' said my father." He turned to Linda first but then looked at all of them, a small smile gracing his face. "Thank you for saving me."

A shiver ran through Cassius as the wind caught against his wet clothes. Helai grinned at Felix as she leaned her head against the mast. Linda patted Felix on the head. "Good sir, good."

Felix laughed, a breathy laugh that carried itself away in the wind. For a moment, for just a moment, Cassius was able to let go of all of the tension and desires and just feel the salty sea air hit his face. It only lasted a moment before the ache in his chest returned before the hunger rose to his throat before the brand on his back itched, but it was a moment he treasured as they pulled back into the bay of Volendam's port.

Cassius fled the docks the moment they pulled in, his hunger demanding he feed. Rooster waved him away, told him to meet back at the inn, and that's what he did after finding some poor fool in one of the alleyways.

The familiar warmth was a welcomed relief when he stepped through the door. The Broken Arrow was thick with entertainment as sailors beat their fists against the table as Patrina played a lively tune on her lute, dancing around the tables as Hilde wove around her to hand off plates of food. Felix sat at the booth they frequented rather than behind the bar, and Cassius approached the table as the others sat around it. It was strange, but the inn had begun to feel a bit homey. Cassius had never felt such comfort in his entire life.

"Thought we'd invite Felix for a drink to warm his blood before he got back to work," Rooster said, patting Felix on the back.

"No one questioned you being gone for a week and a half?" Cassius asked, pulling a chair over.

Felix nodded quickly, pulling a mug of ale to his lips. "Oh, they did, but after I told them you all saved me and that tonight deserved some celebration, they got everything in order real quick. I am the owner, after all." He grinned as he drank deeply, sighing happily as he watched Patrina gracefully weave around the tables, her smile radiant as she played.

"You know what you'd benefit by building, Felix?" Cassius shook his finger at him. "A bathhouse. My mother owned one in Verenzia. They bring in a fair profit if you do it right."

Felix laughed, waving his hand at Cassius. "You know, I'd say you run on a madman's ideas, but it might not be a bad idea. All bathhouses are in the Sails District and not accessible to the poor." He thumbed his chin, a soft sigh passing his lips. "I do not think I can afford the investment, I'm afraid."

Cassius tapped the table. "Think about it."

Felix nodded. "You know I will."

"Would love bath," Linda commented quietly as Intoh pushed through the crowd and approached the table.

"Gone for long time. Waited. Waited some more. Worried but did not know where to find you, so I waited." Intoh's endless mutterings were quick and anxious as he ran his hands through his hair. "Learned much at mage college but did not like being alone. Will not stay behind again," he said.

Intoh stank of magic as Helai slid out of her seat so that he could sit next to Linda.

Linda patted Intoh on the head as Rooster leaned forward, his eyes gleaming with interest. "Say—could you teach me some of that magic?"

Intoh nodded. "Will teach where can. Find mermaids?"

Rooster gestured to the stairs leading up to their rooms. "Got four heads in my room, and we'll take them tomorrow." He eyed the group, but no one said a word. Felix was oblivious to their plans to steal from the wealthiest place in Volendam, and it was best if it stayed that way.

Patrina grazed past the table, halting to press her lips to Felix's cheek.

Cassius gestured between them, his brow furrowed. "When did this…?"

Felix grinned up at Patrina with such fierce adoration it made Cassius' heart ache. "When I got back. Almost dying puts things in perspective, I suppose. I would have never forgiven myself if I had died without telling Patrina how I really feel."

The warmth radiating through Patrina's expression left comfort in the air, and Cassius reveled in it as Patrina laughed, leaning to press her fingers to Felix's jaw so she could turn him and kiss him properly. Cassius averted their eyes to nurse his wine.

"Pint for you, Felix. Glad you're still with us."

Cassius looked up as a sailor approached. A small, balding man, he offered Felix the ale in his hand. His smile was missing a few teeth, and Felix took it with gratitude.

"Thank you, my friend! I wouldn't be here if it weren't for these guys," Felix said, raising his glass to the table. It was far from the isolation and high-class parties Cassius was used to attending. The kind and genuine nature The Broken Arrow bled gave Cassius a sense of home, something he wasn't sure he'd felt before in his life.

"Ah yes—the docks have been talking about you. Calling you the Misfits we are. I got a full day at sea without fearing I'd get pulled under by mermaids." The sailor tipped his head at the table. "Made enough extra selling fish this morning to afford this drink for our bartender. Good man, Felix." He grinned again, patting Felix on the back as he ambled back over to a table with his friends.

"Misfits, huh?" Patrina's eyes glinted in the torchlight as she straightened up. "Careful–keep it up, and people will start singing songs about you."

"Wouldn't that be a shame?" Rooster said. His voice was drenched in sarcasm as he raised his mug to his lips. "Oh no, here comes the dashing young leader of the Freeman Misfits. Don't you just want to touch his muscles and tell him how pretty he is?"

Felix snorted into his drink and shook his head, looking up at Patrina. "How modest."

"Come, love," Patrina said, laughing. "Come and sit by the fire with me."

Cassius watched him go, and he couldn't stop a small smile, however brief, from piercing his lips. He had wished for what they had once. It was such a simple joy to see it blossoming between two people who persevered, despite all of the world's horrors.

"Well, Misfits. You ready to steal some jewels tomorrow?" Rooster asked, leaning into the name. It sounded strange, but a comfort overcame Cassius as a foreign feeling blossomed in his chest, combating the blood woman's constant reminder that he was to seek out whatever was in that opera house. It was the sense of belonging, a feeling he hadn't experienced since his days at Dragon Keep.

"To stealing jewels," Cassius said, raising his mug as he turned back towards the table. Tomorrow would bring its own dangers, but tonight was for celebrating. As Felix and Patrina kissed again and the night wore on, Cassius allowed himself a moment to relax.

Chapter Thirty-Two
Rooster

"How do I look? Can you see my ass through these?" Rooster twisted and turned towards Helai, who struggled not to roll her eyes and laugh. They stood a block away from the Silver Moon Club as the sun began to set. Cassius and Linda were dressed in their standard attire, a bag with the mermaid heads thrown over Linda's shoulder. Intoh was nowhere to be seen, camouflaged somewhere safe where he could watch on. Rooster was dressed in as little as possible, using clothes they already owned and desecrating them so that he could pass off as a whore. He had convinced Helai to sweet-talk Patrina into borrowing some of her glitter, and Helai had put it to good use on Rooster. He was convinced he'd die with glitter still tucked away in hard-to-reach places for weeks to come. Helai was dressed similarly, having agreed to accompany Rooster until she could get inside and steal some employees' clothes.

"No one can see your ass," Cassius said, his agitation evident as he scoured the streets for any signs of discourse. No one glanced their way as they took a moment to marvel at the club. Velius hadn't been kidding when he boasted that the place was upper class. Docked near a small fancy building was an enormous boat, connected to it by a pedestrian bridge. Magical globes floated around it, bathing it in an ethereal glow. Soft music pulled them in, and Rooster felt it hard to resist its charm. Those around them were dressed in silks and glittering dresses from foreign lands, and Rooster nodded at the others as they all split away. It would be strange to the club if they all showed up together.

"Hmph," the front guard was dressed in a silk tuxedo, his beard neatly trimmed. He rivaled Cassius in body mass, and Rooster looked at him with a shit-eating grin as the guard looked over him with poorly concealed disdain, then flickered his gaze to Helai.

"Straight to the tables with the likes of you, and if I find you making trouble, you'll be quick to regret it."

Rooster curtsied and moved inside, marveling at the pristine nature of the place. A flurry of magic slipped over them as they walked through the door. When he looked down, his clothes were freshly washed, and his skin had no dirt. He glanced behind him to see those behind him had also been refreshed.

The clubhouse was enormous, large enough to sport a dance floor and a bar, where an eldrasi handed out drinks at speeds Rooster could barely keep up with. The lights were low, setting the mood. As the bard sang and played their instruments, magical dragons stretched their wings and took off, spreading their music as far as possible. On the other side of the dance floor was a wooden bridge embellished with silver and gold loops along the railing that led out to the boat. It looked like the bridge could be moved to allow the ship to sail out to sea, should it wish.

"This is hard to look at," Helai said through gritted teeth, her tone hushed. Her hand was shaking at her side, eyebrows slanted as she frowned. "The people of the Hull District suffer while these—" She waved her hand in a circle, frustrated. "I can't think of the word in vilris. Eh...*ya kalb*," she uttered, switching to her native tongue before switching back. "They drink and dance and throw their money at chance." Her words were hissed with such hostility Rooster felt compelled to flinch. Her hand gestured to the card games played at tables in the corner. Several men and women sat on the players' laps, and smoke unfurled from cigars that sat on the lips of some. Rooster couldn't say he blamed Helai for her anger.

"Can't change the nature of humanity, I'm afraid. There will always be those who wish to exert their powers over others. That's what people like you are for—why people like you are important. Make them pay for it when you can," Rooster said. Breaking away from Helai, he gave her the subtlest nod before heading for the card table while Helai sauntered up to the bar.

"Hello, everyone," Rooster said, mustering a radiant grin. The smell of smoke was thick in the air as several men and women holding cards glanced up. Some of them already had the company of whores on their laps, and the card dealer shuffled cards as one man with a burly mustache, and hard eyes patted his knee.

"Well, aren't you a pretty thing," the man mused as wandering hands slipped over the curve of Rooster's ass. Rooster shifted on the man's lap—his interest in men was nonexistent, but he gave a soft smile and leaned closer. "Come sit on Cornelius' lap."

"I've also been told I'm good luck, so you've let the right whore onto your lap." Rooster winked at him and pulled away as the games resumed. It was a fast-paced game, and at one point, one of the players got so angry he threw his cards down and left, red-faced and stumbling. The others laughed.

"Poor bastard's gonna go home to his cheating wife and realize he's lost everything," one of them said. Another clicked his tongue against the roof of his mouth in disappointment. Cornelius shook his head, puffing at his cigar.

"No matter. Louie will be back tomorrow, no doubt."

"He's not going to get to the big tables losing like that. Been waiting for the day the Captain finally lets us join the big ranks," the man to the right of Rooster said. That piqued Rooster's curiosity, and he leaned against Cornelius, turning his mouth to the cusp of his ear.

"Is the Captain the owner of this club?"

Cornelius nodded. "High-stakes games are in the hull of his ship, and only the best are invited to play there. It's where the real rewards are betted on." He patted the side of Rooster's hip. "Nothing to trouble yourself with."

That's exactly what I want to trouble myself with, Rooster thought as he danced his fingers along Cornelius' forearm and moved to stand. "I'm going to go use the bathroom. Care for a drink on the way back?"

Cornelius grunted, his attention already back to the cards in his hand. The music lulled as Rooster wove through the crowd on the dance floor. There was subtle energy that zipped through the air, filling his chest with an excitable glee that forced a pep in his step as he made his way to the bathroom. On the way, he locked eyes with Helai as she chatted with the bartender. Rooster's eyes flickered to the bathrooms for the briefest moments before moving away.

A coat room sat next to the bathrooms as Rooster strolled by, whistling a tune under his breath. Other than distasteful or interested stares from the other club members, Rooster was left alone as he halted in front of the coats.

"Excuse me." Helai's voice sounded behind him as she sidled up next to him, hands moving through the coats as if she sought out her own. The fabrics of the coats were exceptionally made of various silks and leathers, and Rooster marveled at a blue jacket that captured his attention.

"I believe the ship's hull is where we need to be. High-stakes games go on down there, but if the owner has treasures, they'd be down there," Rooster whispered, glancing over Helai's shoulder to make sure they were alone. "We need to figure out a way down there."

"The bartender says the Captain is the name of the owner. No one knows his real name. Hopefully, Linda and Cassius can get some information from him. Here—" she pulled down a coat—red silk embellished in black furs–and pulled it around her shoulders. Pulling the band out of her hair, she pushed her hands through her braid, freeing strands to frame her face.

"Take it," Helai urged as Rooster stared longingly at the blue coat. "We need to blend in if we're crossing the bridge." No further urging was needed from Helai as Rooster pulled it off the rack and shrugged it on. The warmth that seeped into his skin was almost magical as Helai offered him her arm, and he took it.

"Let us hope we can get to the boat without needing an invitation," Helai whispered. The music had started back up, and it was a cascade of swaying bodies on the dance floor as they wove through the crowd, taking care to stay away from the card tables. Rooster fleetingly wondered if Cornelius would simply forget about him.

'Silver Moon Club' was etched in beautiful script on the boat's side. Lights dazzled the water below, dancing in small formations just above the surface. A memory edged to the forefront of his mind of glow bugs that illuminated a forest, chasing the horror of darkness away, but it faded almost as quickly as it came, giving Rooster no time to ponder it. People stood on the bridge, pointing at the water and swirling wine in their glasses as they spoke amongst themselves, and Rooster felt barren in his simple clothing. Rooster heard a splash somewhere far off as if someone had jumped off the boat, but no one stirred. Perhaps he was the only one to hear it.

As they stepped aboard the ship, two eldrasi stood guard at the captain's quarters. He leaned over to Helai. "Strange, seeing so many eldrasi in Volendam. I would think there would be more dwarves, being so close to the mountains."

Helai shrugged, tucking a strand of hair behind her ear as she stared at the ship deck. Another bard played, but this one was quieter, with a calming voice that was more soothing than energizing. "With all the trade Volendam does, maybe they have a good relationship with Míradan."

"Hmm," Rooster hummed, straightening. The eldrasi guards were identical in appearance, with dark hair twisted into buns atop their heads. Small flowers grew out of their temples, dotting the curve of their cheekbones, and their eyes were green so light it almost looked white. They both lowered their spears and stepped to the side as Cassius stepped out of the door, followed closely by a short man with piercing blue eyes and a balding head. He walked with a cane and shook Cassius' hand. They laughed about something, and when Cassius noticed Rooster and Helai, he gave a small wave.

"Ah, Helai. I was looking everywhere for you," Cassius said, his voice unnaturally light. Linda was nowhere to be seen, and Rooster tried to search for answers in Cassius' eyes when they made contact. "I see you found a friend."

Helai tugged Rooster closer. "His name is Rooster, and I thought he might be good company for the evening." Understanding struck Rooster as an easy smile crossed his face.

"Rooster? What a funny name. Cassius has told me all about you, Helai. I told him you two are welcome to remain and enjoy the evening on the ship if you'd like." The balding man held his hand out. "Just call me the Captain. I have some matters to attend to below decks, but please—feel free to use the bar and join some of the card games, should you wish."

"Thank you, Captain," Cassius said as the Captain tapped the tip of his cane against the deck and turned away. As Rooster watched him go, Cassius turned his back on the Captain and stared out along the river. As the day came to an end, the magical lights that fluttered about grew brighter.

"While I was inside, I managed to see a small safe situated under the Captain's desk," Cassius uttered, smiling at a couple that passed by and caught his eye.

"It would be worth it to see if what we need is in there," Helai said, pulling away from Rooster to press a hand to Cassius' arm. It was strange to see Helai so comfortable around the vampire, but they had all grown more relaxed around each other as of late. "If not, we'll have to go to the hull. Rooster said the high-stakes games are down there."

"Where is Linda?" Rooster asked quietly.

Cassius pointed to where Linda approached from the front of the ship. "Checked ship. Only two guards," Linda said, nodding their head at the guards standing in front of the Captain's quarters. If they were the only two guards on this ship's deck, that would make their thievery all the easier.

"Drink?" A voice interrupted their conversation as a woman dressed in black waltzed up to them, a silver tray of sparkling drinks balanced in one hand. Relief trailed through Rooster as he grabbed one of the glasses. The drink was sweet and light on Rooster's tongue as the others declined, and the woman moved away to serve the nearby members.

"If you can get me inside, I can open the safe. We just need to be able to get the guards away from the door without arousing suspicion," Helai said, watching the guests dance.

"Could possibly provide distraction."

A soft voice called out from beside Linda, who did not flinch. It took Rooster a moment to recognize it as Intoh's, even though Intoh was nowhere to be seen. A whisper of wind sailed past Rooster's leg as the end of Intoh's tail brushed against his ankle.

"What are you doing?" Helai asked, turning her face towards Cassius as if she were speaking to him. The ship's guests were ignorant of anything amiss as they danced around the mast, laughing and drinking.

"*Weilsta,*" Intoh whispered from his camouflaged state.

A puddle of water appeared on the dance floor, so small the dancers did not notice until it was too late.

A tall, lithe man's foot came down on the water, forcing him to slip right into a woman beside him. His face fell into her breasts as several drinks went flying. The woman cried out, shoving the man away and yelling obscenities at him as her date squared her shoulders, walked up to him, and punched him in the face.

Chaos broke out after that as the fighting escalated to the point where the guards watching the Captain's quarters took one look at each other and then drew forward, shouting their protests. Rooster stifled a grin as Intoh's quiet laughter could be heard somewhere off to his right.

"Humans so easily angered. Just have to push them in the right direction," Intoh said. "Hurry now—should take quite some time to break things up."

"We'll stay outside and keep watch," Cassius said, gesturing to Linda.

"We'll make quick work of it," Helai promised, tugging Rooster towards the door.

The inside of the Captain's quarters was immaculate; not a single speck of dust rested on the surfaces, and nothing was out of place. To the left was a bed, freshly made with a long, black coat hanging next to it. A large desk sat in the opposite corner, atop a quill made from a raven feather nestled next to a pot of ink. Inside a square glass container was a tooth similar in shape and size to the one that rested around Rooster's neck. Staring at it sent Rooster into a state of deja vu, and Rooster quickly looked away as Helai knelt behind the desk.

"We should hurry—I'm not sure how long Linda and Cassius can keep the guards distracted."

"It's a complicated lock, and it's going to take some time for me to work it over," Helai said, pulling tools out of her bag. "Just stay quiet. I need to be able to listen." Rooster was never any good at keeping quiet, but he did his best as he padded around the room, looking at what kind of person the Captain was.

His love for tidiness bordered on overbearing as Rooster trailed around the room. Not an object was out of place, and maps of Volendam and the surrounding seas were framed and hung on the wall. A bookcase rested just behind the door, filled with books on water magic. "I wonder if the Captain is a hydromancer," Rooster uttered to himself.

"Shh," Helai warned, glancing up at him. Her fingers moved two picks expertly within the lock, where she began a series of turns. Rooster had faith she would be able to break the lock; he only hoped she did it before the Captain returned.

A silver locket stole Rooster's attention from its place on the bedside table. It was in excellent care, with swirling designs and eldrasi etched in fine letters in a circular pattern. Perhaps it was the locket Velius wanted them to steal. Rooster reached out to grab it, intending to study it closer, but the moment his fingers curled around the locket, a strange feeling tugged at his belly.

He stood aboard a ship and a massive one at that. Three masts stood tall upon the deck with billowing white sails that carried them forward through the sea. Crew members bustled about him as an exceptionally tall woman with broad shoulders, raven locks, and a stern expression shouted orders.

She's from Volreya, Rooster realized. Volreya was a country in the far north, and many of its inhabitants had migrated south and fought for land control with Kreznov.

"Sigrun, please. We know you'll carry out your threat, and if you kill all of the crew, there will be no one to man the ships." A familiar voice sounded from above Rooster at the wheel. The deja vu made his head spin, and he watched the dark-haired woman, Sigrun, throw up her middle finger before he dared to take several steps forward and look up.

He locked eyes with the eldrasi woman from the sailboat in his last flashback. *Igraine*, Rooster thought to himself as he got lost in the endless blue of her eyes. *Her name is Igraine.* He opened his mouth to call out to her, to compliment her fire-soaked hair or perhaps the fierceness in her eyes, but before a word could flee his lips, he blinked, and he was back inside the Captain's quarters as Helai exclaimed quietly in excitement.

"I got it." Her gaze flickered to him, not knowing what he had just witnessed. He looked down at the locket and swallowed hard, closing his fingers around it and slipping it into his pocket. It was definitely the locket Velius had asked him to get, but what did Velius want with something that caused Rooster to see something like that?

Rooster closed his eyes as nausea cramped in his belly. There was so much he didn't understand. Was that a memory? Or was it a dream, something his mind made up to comfort him in his amnesia? None of it made sense.

"Are you alright?" Helai whispered. Rooster opened his eyes to see her staring at him in concern. "We need to hurry. I don't think we have that much time."

Rooster nodded and moved closer. "I'm fine," he whispered back. "Does the safe have what we need?"

Helai's eyes gleamed as she opened the safe door wider. "You tell me."

Skaels upon skaels piled inside the safe, and sitting on top of them were two sapphires, a ruby, and several smaller gemstones, all begging to be taken. Besides the piles of skaels were several rolled-up papers, but before Helai could take them, commotion sounded on the other side of the door.

"I'm telling you—I sensed water magic on board. Find whoever cast it and bring them straight to me." The Captain's voice was muffled for a moment before he opened the door. Helai and Rooster both froze, but a shouting followed by screaming forced the Captain to look away from his quarters.

"I will not have foul play going on on my ship," he called out, shutting the door again.

Rooster met Helai's gaze, and they both nodded simultaneously as they pulled all of the skaels and jewels out of the safe and shoved them into Helai's bag.

"Time to go."

Helai closed the safe and tucked away her tools as Rooster's heart plummeted to his stomach. He didn't know he would leave this club with more questions than he'd arrived with.

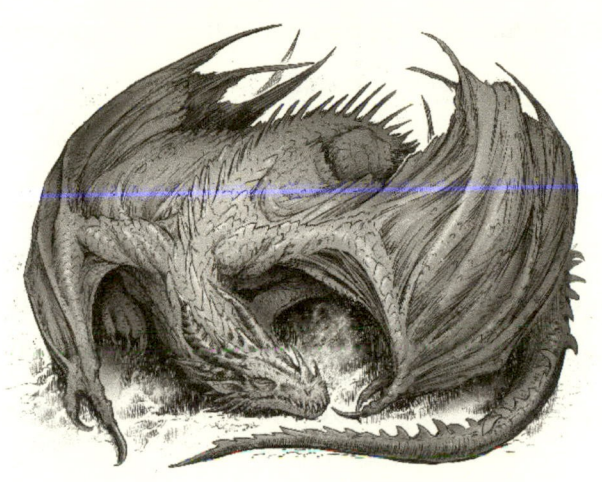

Chapter Thirty-Three
Linda

Linda had to admit—the vampire knew how to throw a punch.

Some time passed with little issue. The fight that Intoh had caused traveled through the ship's deck like a forest fire and the Captain's guards were occupied with trying to break up the fight. It sang to Linda's nature, and they had to wrestle with the urge to join the fight and teach every human there that they were the strongest warrior. At one point, Cassius must have felt their desperation because his hand came to rest on Linda's forearm. Intoh had disappeared again. Linda often didn't know when Intoh was there or when he was gone when he was in his hidden state, but he hadn't spoken in quite some time if he was still nearby. A man punched another in front of Linda with such force he sent the man to the ground, but the fight was winding down quicker than Linda thought it would.

How disappointing, they thought. *No one killed each other.*

The Captain ascended a set of stairs near his quarters, his face red with rage. A few others followed behind him, leaving the ship with worry stitched into their brows. To Linda, they all looked like ants after a boot had descended upon their home. Various parts of the deck were bloodstained, and those not interested in fighting had already fled the premises.

"What the *fuck* is going on?" The Captain hissed, tapping his cane against the floor. Once calm, the river grew angry, brushing up against the ship's sides as a storm waged in the Captain's expression. Linda recognized magic but didn't think the Captain was capable of it.

It caused the entire ship deck to still, the soft whimpers of those suffering from losing fights a song on the wind as Linda glanced nervously at Cassius. He seemed calm behind his silence.

"I will have order," the Captain seethed, straightening. The guards solemnly returned to his side as they headed back towards the Captain's quarters. They spoke to the Captain in hushed tones as people shuffled off the deck back over the bridge.

"I am truly sorry, Linda," Cassius whispered as the Captain opened the door to his quarters, his head turned towards one of the guards in distraction. Linda turned to question Cassius' apology and was met with the white-hot pain of his closed fist crossing their jaw.

"Why hit?" Linda groaned, holding their jaw with one hand.

"Because you called my mother a whore." Cassius growled and barreled into Linda. The vampire was so quick that Linda had no time to react as they both crashed to the ground. Linda's brand burned as anger consumed them, sending waves of strength through their arms as they rolled, putting Cassius on his back. They managed to headbutt him before a water current washed over them and carried them away. They hit the railings of the ship some feet away, and Cassius was slow to move to his feet as he coughed up water. The Captain stood between them, the vein in his head moments away from popping.

"You have precisely ten seconds to get off my ship," the Captain said. Behind him and the guards were the slightest movements at the entrance of the Captain's quarters, the quick opening and closing of the door. Linda's jaw hurt as they rose to their feet, and they did not look at Cassius. The Captain's eyes burned into the back of their head until they left the Silver Moon Club.

"I am sorry for your face, Linda," Cassius said, approaching. "We had to keep the Captain from catching Helai and Rooster."

"It okay. I understand," Linda said.

Cassius nodded, urging them both away from the front of the club. Many guests had gone home, and perhaps only a handful remained in hopes they could re-enter. The night was frigid, and Linda shivered against the soft wind that brushed against them. They missed the warmth.

They found Intoh under a lamppost, using the light of the darting orb to read a book. "Rooster went to meet Velius, and Helai went back to The Broken Arrow. Think we should do same," he said, slamming his book closed.

"I could not agree more," Cassius said, groaning. "Linda broke my nose, and while it has since healed, I could use some wine."

Satisfaction sank into Linda's chest as they returned to The Broken Arrow.

The inn's warmth had Linda in a daze, their eyes at half-mast as Helai and Rooster conversed in their corner. A current of excited energy coursed through them as they poured over the table, splitting up the skaels they had managed to snag from the boat. Rooster wore a new coat, deep blue, that was long and sweeping. Rooster had dropped off the jewels with Velius.

"He said he'd get started on your weapons right away," Rooster had told them. The news filled Linda with simple happiness. Soon they would have their war hammer.

"We each got seventy-three skaels from bringing in the mermaid heads, plus eighty-two from what we stole." Five piles of skaels were separated on the table by Cassius, with one pile being slightly smaller. That pile was pushed over to Intoh.

"Why smaller?" Intoh protested.

"You were absent for most of that heist," Cassius said, lowering his voice as Hilde swept by. "It is only fair."

"Went inside last minute. Caused distraction," Intoh argued.

"I think that warrants slightly more skaels," Rooster agreed, looking at the others. Linda didn't care. Intoh had always held onto their skaels for them.

Rooster pushed forward two skaels from his pile, and after a brief hesitation, the others followed suit. Linda pushed their pile over to Intoh and leaned back, struggling not to fall asleep as the evening wore on.

"I know it's late, but we made extra and thought you could enjoy some." The quiet sing-song of Hilde's voice roused Linda from dozing off as a plate of fish was set in front of them.

Intoh leaned forward a little to look at the offer, then sat back and shook his head. The greka preferred his fish raw, but Linda was growing fond of the way Dirk spiced it, and the aroma cradled their nose, making their mouth water. An ale was set beside the plate, packed to the brim with dark contents, and Linda grinned up at Hilde, hitting the table roughly with their fist. Cassius lifted his glass, startled, and Hilde clutched her chest with laughter.

"Meal, good," Linda shouted.

"A simple *thank you*, Linda. That's all that's required," Helai murmured.

Linda tilted their head, confused. "What thank you?" they asked. Humans were so strange.

Hilde smiled warmly. "It's a way to express your gratitude, dear. Come now, enjoy your food. I'm retiring for the evening, but Felix and Patrina are still staying up for a while." Hilde retreated, and Linda dug into their food as Cassius nursed his wine, a hand threading through his hair.

"Now that we have completed the tasks at hand, it is high time we paid a visit to the opera house," he whispered, leaning forward. The mention of the opera house sent a shiver through Linda, ending at their brand, which began to burn. Disgruntled, they shifted in their seat and took a long drink from their ale, savoring the taste as it hit their lips.

"It would be better to wait until Velius has completed making our weapons. You spoke of needing a shield, yes?" Rooster asked.

"The opera house remains abandoned. Before we visited the Silver Moon Club, Rooster and I checked out the opera house ourselves." Helai hesitated, glancing at Rooster as she tapped her mug absently with her fingers. "It would be best that we are the most prepared we can be."

"Did someone say opera house?" Patrina strolled by, halting at their booth. Her hair was in two buns atop her head today, and her eyes glittered with excitement as she pulled up a chair and sat down. "Do you mean Volelle Opera House? I have a story if you have time to hear it."

"I don't think—" Cassius started, but Linda spoke over him before he could finish.

"Linda love story," they said, leaning forward. They loved listening to Patrina's stories.

Patrina nodded enthusiastically as Felix cleared one of the tables beside them. "It's a love story," she started.

"Ah, I think tragedy would be more of an apt description, my love. He was more obsessed than driven by love," Felix interrupted, his head tilted to the side in indecisiveness.

"Love story, tragedy, whatever you want to call it, all started with a vampire." Patrina waved away Felix's argument as she continued, scooting closer to the booth as she leaned in. "No one knows what brought him to Volendam, but he loved the Volelle Opera House and frequented it quite often. Some say it was his love for Esmée Driessen, the lead opera singer."

"Vampires can't love," Felix cut in again, earning a stare from Patrina.

"He could have loved her," she said. "It's never been proven if vampires are capable of love or not. I suppose it depends on whether or not they have a soul."

"A vampire I've spoken to in the past told me they're just as capable of having souls as humans who do good or evil," Rooster said, staring directly at Cassius as he spoke. Cassius ignored him, staring at his wine as Linda finished the last of their fish. They stared at the empty plate mournfully, wishing for more.

"I think so. But regardless, he saw all of her shows. All of them. And then one day, in a fit of rage, he burned the opera house to the ground and sat in his booth while everyone burned."

"That's horrible," Helai said, pressing her fingers to her lips.

"Don't like ending," Linda said in agreement, picking pieces of fish out of their teeth with their finger. Felix sighed and grabbed everyone's plates, shrugging his shoulders sadly.

"It's a sad ending, and that's why that place houses so much pain. I've been near it once, and it made me feel so awful I never want to go there again." Patrina shuddered, wrapping her arms around herself.

"Come, Patrina. Enough of ghosts. Leave the Misfits to their celebrations," Felix said softly, carrying the empty plates away. Laughter ensued from the booth next to them as sailors told tales of their own, and Linda watched them pat each other's backs and toast their ale to some celebration.

Patrina tapped the table lightly before she stood. "I hope you have a good rest of your evening, Misfits." As Patrina left the table, a strange feeling pulled at Linda's belly, a feeling they couldn't quite place or understand.

Linda gestured to Rooster's hands. "What that?" they asked, comforting themself with conversation. A silver locket turned between his fingers as he watched it absentmindedly. While the chain looked worn, like it had been well-loved, the pristine locket was marked with simple swirling designs. It was nothing like the tooth necklace Linda bore around their neck, which meant something.

Rooster smiled and closed his hand around the locket, slipping it into his pocket. "Nothing–it's nothing. Just something I nabbed at the Silver Moon Club."

Linda huffed. "Like jewelry? Make tooth necklace."

Rooster laughed and shook his head, tugging the large tooth that hung from his neck out from under his shirt. "I have one, remember Linda?" Linda eyed it closely. They remembered hearing Obrand explain it to be a hydra tooth, but they'd never seen a hydra before. It could be a krok'ida tooth for all Linda knew.

"Might take to mage college. Might know more," Intoh suggested, pointing to the tooth.

"Hmm," Rooster hummed, tucking it away again. "Perhaps."

"What of your homeland? What is it like?" Helai asked, her gaze flickering between Linda and Intoh as she sipped her ale.

Linda thought for a moment. "Warm," they decided.

"So is mine." Helai sighed, sinking into her seat. "I miss the warmth."

Linda agreed. The cold was too hard on their joints, making them feel slow, which was dangerous for a fighter like Linda. Their growing fondness for ale and the warmth it left in their belly kept them from completely losing their mind.

The rest of the night was full of lively conversation. They lost Intoh first, murmuring something about studying, but it wasn't long after that Cassius retired too, saying something about leaving to find dinner. Helai and Rooster remained for a while after. Helai shared many stories of her time in Shoma. Linda had heard her mention the Ghosts of Light in passing, but it was the first time they understood that they had been a group just like the Misfits. Helai seemed to miss them terribly.

I'd miss Helai and Rooster if they left, Linda thought. *Cassius, too. Even if he does stink.*

Chapter Thirty-Four
Cassius

Cassius couldn't bear it. Every moment was agony, the silent screams of the woman possessing his blood more and more difficult to ignore. With every step he took he faced the roads leading him to the opera house. He knew if he didn't do something about it soon, the woman would drive him to madness.

He could tell it affected the others too. Rooster was never seen without a mug of ale in his hand. Helai's eyes were constantly trained to the exits of The Broken Arrow as if someone were going to come through at any moment and take them.

"We need to go," Cassius urged them one morning. The desperation clawed at the back of his throat, so insistent it drowned out all cravings of his bloodlust. He feared the power the blood woman wrought.

"We still need our weapons," Rooster said, tipping his mug against his lips. A few sailors came into The Broken Arrow, shaking the rain from their hair as Hilde greeted them at the door. "It's been a few days. We should visit Velius."

Cassius failed to keep his impatience and irritation from infecting his expression, but Rooster was right. It would be foolish to enter the opera house without proper preparation. "Let us be done with it, then," he said.

The rain fell harder as the group stepped out of the inn, but it was not a far walk to Velius' forge. Rooster knocked on the Firebrand's door. "Arathanae," he whispered. The door swung on its hinges, and they all disappeared inside. Cassius took a moment to gather his stomach as he was teleported magically onto a ship. He steadied his feet as the ship shifted in the water, and curiosity gripped him as he appeared in a forge.

The forge was of master craft, as pristine as it could be aboard a ship, and Cassius marveled at the steelwork decorating the walls. He had enough skaels to purchase himself a new sword and shield if he wanted, and he wandered the walls as Rooster moved towards the forge master, who was hard at work at the anvil.

"Velius—what news of our things?" Rooster asked arms open wide in dramatics. Helai stayed near the door, her foot kicked back as she leaned against the frame with her arms folded across her chest.

Velius set his hammer down as sweat gleaned his brow. His hair was tied back into a loose bun, but a few stray hairs had escaped and clung to his face. Cassius took a moment from admiring the swords on the wall to stare at their maker. He was easy on the eyes, his smile a radiant sun. Still—the scream that felt lodged in Cassius' throat whenever he thought of anything other than his hunger or his drive to the opera house prevented him from appreciating Velius for too long.

It didn't stop Velius from doing the same, however.

"You must be Cassius," he said, stepping around his anvil to approach. His blood was soaked in the scent of fire and honeyed bark. His heart was slow and steady, as most eldrasi heartbeats were, and Cassius met his gaze as he straightened his back and offered a smile.

"I hear you are forging weapons," Cassius said.

Velius flashed a toothy grin and glanced at the others, gesturing to all of his work on the walls. "It is what I do here." Pointing at Rooster, he winked at Cassius. "When Rooster dropped off the items I requested, he said you needed a sword and shield. I have many forged already if you don't want anything fancy. Many to protect that pretty face of yours."

Cassius' cheeks flushed at the compliment, and he defied his unease and took a moment to really study Velius. He was by no means unattractive—Cassius felt that familiar pull to reach up and tug Velius close—but irritation sank through him despite those desires. An impatience tugged at his belly to retreat. He knew it to be the blood woman, and his expression turned sad as he pulled away from Velius and shook his head.

"I'll take a look at what you have to offer. I'm not picky."

Velius lowered his head in respect and backed away. Cassius caught Rooster's eye, his expression curious as he looked between him and Velius.

"May I?" Cassius asked, gesturing to a small shield on the wall.

Velius nodded but gestured to the other wall, his gaze lingering over Cassius' broad shoulders. "I think a bigger shield would suit you better." The other wall housed various types of kite shields, large diamond-shaped shields, and tower shields, which were long enough to protect Cassius' legs, but Cassius shook his head.

"I'm looking for a kite shield eventually, but for now, a small, round one will do." Cassius gripped the small buckler in his right hand and tested it, bringing it in front of him. It wasn't exactly what he was looking for or what he was used to using, but the weight was nice, and so long as it blocked attacks, he didn't care.

"Seventy-five skaels for that one," Velius said.

Linda growled. "Hammer?" they asked.

Velius laughed, stepping up to a table where he moved aside cloth, revealing a war hammer, and gestured Linda closer. "I thought the name *Volroth* would suit the name of your hammer, Linda. In Eldrasian, it means 'supremacy,' but you're welcome to call it whatever you'd like."

Linda grabbed the war hammer tightly in both hands, swinging it slowly through the air to test its weight. The handle was made of a light material that looked like eldrasian steel with etches of white gold curling around it in an elegant design. The end of the handle formed into the claw of a krok'ida holding a sapphire. The head of the hammer was carved with sharp depictions of lizards and simple lines.

Twirling it, Linda hummed in approval. "This will do," they said, patting Velius on the back. "Kill many."

"That's the goal, but only the ones that deserve it," Velius said, his laugh lighthearted.

"I pity anyone that gets in Linda's way," Rooster agreed.

Cassius brought the shield over to Velius, setting it down on the table. "I will buy the shield and make do with the sword I've got. Seventy-five skaels, you said?" When Velius nodded, Cassius pulled his coin purse from his side and counted the coins, offering them to Velius. A small current of electrical tension passed through him when his fingers grazed Velius' palm, and he quickly pulled away.

Velius pocketed the skaels and turned to Helai, beckoning her closer. "I will not bite, Helai. Not without anyone's permission, that is." He winked at Cassius, who took care to study his shield. The eldrasi was relentless—that much Cassius could claim. Cassius would have thought it charming had he been liberated from the blood woman's intrusion.

"We must make haste," Cassius said, lowering his voice to Rooster as Helai brushed past him.

Rooster nodded. "In all due time. Patience," he urged, turning to see what Velius had forged for Helai.

Cassius sighed and turned to look as well.

In Velius' hand was a dagger sheath made of dark leather, inlaid with mithril trimming. Helai was hesitant to take it at first but eventually reached a hand out to study the sheath more closely.

"I imbued it with magic. See there—" Velius pointed to the inscription on the front, written in the Eldrasi scripture. "*A flower's fatal thorn.* Whatever dagger you place inside it will be coated in poison the moment you pull it out." His smile was soft as he stared at Helai. "So do be careful when you use it. The poison comes from a flower deep within Daesthara, and I'm afraid the antidote is quite hard to get."

Helai nodded, clipping the sheath to her belt. "Thank you, Velius. I have needed something like this for quite some time."

Confusion and curiosity crossed over Velius' face as he pointed at Helai. "That key—where did you get it?"

Helai stilled, her hand instinctively closing around the key hanging around her neck. It was the first time Cassius noticed it, but it did not seem worth noting. There was nothing special about it.

Helai's lips pursed as she slowly uncurled her fingers around the key, using the string to pull it away from her body. "I don't know why it captured your attention."

Velius hummed, staring at it a few moments longer before shaking his head. "Matter not! I'm sure you'll figure out what door it opens when you're meant to."

"Yeah…" The suspicion had returned to Helai's voice as she shoved the key under her shirt and quickly retreated towards the front door.

"Ah–that will be fifteen skaels. Just for the time," Velius said, raising his hand to stop Helai. After she paused and handed them over, he smiled and turned to Intoh, pointing to the pendant on the table.

The pendant held a sapphire embellished in silver waves that crashed against the stone. "You can store healing magic—or whatever magic you wish, I suppose, within it. You'll be able to pull from it without overexerting yourself. I call it Lithri Menlui or the 'Vision of Life's Water.' I hope it serves you well."

"Appreciate it. Will help," Intoh said, grabbing the pendant and slipping it over his head. It rested comfortably around his neck, hitting the middle of his chest where it gleamed when the light hit it right.

"I hope it does. It's fifty-two skaels," Velius said. As Intoh counted out the coin, impatience rang through Cassius, tempting him to leave. Unable to remain still, he paced. Denying the opera house was almost impossible now–he feared he would not be able to wait much longer. Now that they had their weapons, the urge to go was even more so. It choked panic into his lungs and stole away his resolve.

"I can see the pretty one does not wish to linger, and I have my own business to attend to," Velius said, pointing to Cassius. An eager smile graced the eldrasi's features, softening Cassius' ire. Velius waved his hand and pointed to the door.

"I am here if you need me."

As the door to the Firebrand closed behind them, Rooster hit Cassius lightly in the shoulder. "Pretty boy, eh?" He laughed at Cassius' stoic expression. "Not your type?"

Cassius sighed. "Not the *time*."

"Looked like he wanted to eat you," Intoh said, patting Cassius' arm sympathetically. "Do not think you would taste very good."

Cassius refrained from wincing. "Thanks?"

Their conversation was cut off by teeth chattering against one another. A woman, hooded and cloaked, stood in an alley, her back to them. A foul smell came off of her in waves, and her heartbeat was slow and unsteady, like she was sick.

"What is she...?" Helai asked, her question cut off as the woman turned unnaturally quick and hissed. Her teeth were stained dark as her eyes, bloodshot and wide, locked onto Cassius. Anger tugged at his belly as their expressions met, and she lashed out, her fingers torn and bloody as she pushed past them to disappear down the road. With her, the anger dissipated. Confusion rang through the party.

"Look—something carved there," Intoh said, pointing at the alley wall. The marking was covered in blood, but Cassius did not doubt that it was the same mark as the brand that they all shared. "The mark of Gorvayne." Intoh's confirmation sent a current of fear down Cassius' spine, but he turned, his brow furrowed.

"We have no reason to believe that. They are the markings of a mad woman. Come—we have our weapons. I will wait for the opera house no longer," he said. He had no time to contemplate the actions of cultists—not when a woman was infesting his blood, demanding he claim an armory he wasn't sure he wanted.

Rooster nodded, pressing a comforting hand to Cassius' shoulder. "You're right. To the opera house."

Chapter Thirty-Five
Cassius

"I changed my mind. I don't want to go in there," Rooster said as they stood in front of the double doors leading into the opera house. Intoh hid behind Linda, who had Volroth at the ready, and Cassius readjusted his shield. Its weight was both familiar and new to him, and he felt he would need it the moment they stepped through those doors.

"Strange," Cassius uttered quietly as they stopped. "I do not sense the Blodrägr." That knowledge made Cassius uneasy, but he did not sense the man's heartbeat and had not seen him since they drew close. While he was thankful for the easy entry, something did not sit right.

The grounds must have been beautiful once, enclosed in an ornate half-stone, half-iron fence. A cobbled half-circle path offered a private approach to the front stairs. But now, the massive trees on the property housed no leaves, their branches twisted and reaching towards the sky as if begging the gods to take them. Shutters hung on rusted hinges, and the brush was brown and curled. It was a desolate wasteland, and the moment Cassius stepped past the gate, he felt it—an endless sorrow.

Walking up to the door, he reached a hand out. The grief and anger he had felt when he first visited this place bled off the building in waves, a thickness that choked the air from his lungs. He pushed through it, anchored his feet, and peered over his shoulder.

"Stay back until I get this door open." Taking a deep breath, he pushed. The doors swung open with a groan, the wood creaking with protest. What little light daytime provided filtered through the door, sifting through the dust kicked up by the door's movement. Cassius stepped inside, followed closely by the others.

The door swung shut behind them.

Unsheathing his sword, Cassius held it and his shield out in front of him. A chill rolled through him, settling at the brand on his side. It burned without mercy, pulsating as if it had a heartbeat. Helai grimaced, her gaze catching Cassius' as she rubbed the space where her burn was under her armor.

Intoh went invisible, but his feet could be seen walking through the dust on the floor.

They all spread out, each of them with their weapons drawn. Hints of the opera house's former glory snuck through the burn scars, written in the architecture and decorum. Red rugs trailed through the hall, their vibrancy hidden under a thick layer of dust. Reaching the end of the corridor, they entered the Grand Hall. A crystal chandelier lay shattered in the middle of the floor. Torchlight glittered off it as candelabras lit up around them, seemingly on their own. A grand staircase at the opposite end of the room ended at a doorway Cassius could only assume led to the main theatre. Each side of the room branched out to a different hallway, turning off towards multiple separate rooms.

"She's beautiful," Helai whispered, standing near the stairs, her gaze turned up at a painting.

The woman's hair was pulled back and twisted into a braid, with extravagant loose curls softly framing her face. She wore a dress that was large, black, and poofy. An elegant string of pearls adorned her throat. Her lips were painted a dark red and pulled into a youthful smile full of pain. The haunted look in her green eyes had been perfectly captured. Below the painting was a gold plaque that read 'Esmsée Driessen, the pearl of Volendam.'

"No wonder the vampire fell in love with her," Cassius said softly.

"Theatre up here. A lot of chairs and piles of ash. The fire was not kind to this place," Intoh said, reappearing out of thin air at the top of the stairs. The doors leading into the theatre were gone, and Intoh poked his head through, twisting his ring to reveal his greka appearance. He raised his snout in the air and sniffed, his nostrils flaring. "Still smells like smoke—not sure how possible."

Rooster knelt on the ground, looking at something on the floor. "There's a hoof here… maybe dyrvak?" He turned to Linda as they rummaged through a series of framed paintings, all of which had been torn through by something with claws.

"See hoof too," Linda said, gesturing to the floor. "Don't like it."

A gust of wind blew through the hall, sending Cassius' hair into disarray. He felt like eyes were on him, but no one was looking when he turned. It put him on edge, and he gestured for Rooster to follow. "Come with me."

Rooster raised his head and nodded, moving to stand. Following Cassius up the stairs, Rooster called out to Helai. "The hoof marks lead down the hall to the right. If you investigate, be careful."

"Right. I'll take Linda with me," Helai said. Linda nodded, hefting their war hammer over their shoulder and following Helai down the hall as Cassius, Rooster, and Intoh walked through the doorway into the main theatre. A hole in the roof let in a bit of the moonlight. The place was massive, going up at least three floors in viewing booths. Chairs lined up in rows, leading up to the stage, charred and coated in dust. Two pillars wreathed in lines of gold rose on each side of the stage.

A slight frown graced Cassius' lips. "Something does not seem right. Do you feel that?"

It hit suddenly, a current of electricity that buzzed through the air, raising the hair on his arms. Intoh clung to one of the chairs, a low chirping noise leaving his lips.

"Not good. Feels like him," Intoh said, pointing to Cassius.

As the vampire opened his mouth to protest, a red colony of bats crashed into the three of them. Cassius gasped as the magic hit him like waves of the sea. Dizziness struck him, forcing him to blink several times to will it away, but it was a moot point. His head swam, a strong current and Cassius groaned and gripped a charred chair beside him for support. Magic hummed in the air, and a man appeared on stage. Other than his glowing red eyes, it was difficult to discern his features through the shadows, but he caught a glimpse of the sigil on the man's breastplate: The top view of a flying dragon drowning in the sun's rays. It was the sigil of the White Dawn, the Sanguine Order that Cassius once served.

The vampire stepped forward, his face revealed in the dim lighting. He did not care to cloak himself as Cassius did, the true visage of his vampirism out for the world to see. His face had all but caved in on itself, his skin but tattered remains as it stitched itself across the height of his cheekbones and clung to the corners of his eyes. He wore his hair down—black strands reaching his shoulders. His armor had seen better days, and he carried a lance that pulsated quietly with magic. The moment Cassius caught sight of it, the hunger in his chest became unbearable, urging him to claim the lance, to take it away.

Claim your right. The woman behind the gun commanded him forward. A slave to her word, he moved.

The vampire laughed his fangs reflecting in the light. "You have five seconds to run," he warned, his voice echoing in an ancient tone. His fingers flexed around the handle of his lance as Cassius turned, locking eyes with Rooster and Intoh. Fear coursed through them as Cassius' brand throbbed, a low chanting echoing quietly in the theatre's darkness. Every step towards the others felt like he was stuck in wet mud, and it wasn't long before the weight of whatever magic the vampire had asserted over Cassius proved too strong, and he was brought to his knees.

Cassius opened his mouth to call out, but words failed to come. He could not ask Rooster or Intoh to run, could not ask for their help. He could merely stare at them helplessly as his cheek hit the floor and he was slowly dragged backwards.

Another colony of bats flew past Cassius, hitting Rooster and Intoh in the chest. Both of them were flung through the theatre doorway. Their cries were silenced as Cassius was pulled to his feet and turned to stare at the vampire opposite him. He steeled himself, his expression hardening.

This was what he had come here for.

Chapter Thirty-Six
Helai

Helai stood in a room down the hall, studying the skeletons of dyrvak. They were stationed within a thick layer of cobwebs, their jaws open in some wordless scream, and she reached forward to touch a skull, but it crumbled the moment her fingers brushed the surface.

"How long do you think they've been in here?" She turned to Linda as they pulled away from a door situated on the opposite door they'd entered through. There was nothing special about the door—it looked much the same as every other door in the establishment—only the moment Helai looked at it, she felt a strong sense of unease curl in her belly.

"Let's get away from there, Linda," Helai said, reaching forward to tug at Linda's arm.

Linda hummed in agreement as they both retreated. "Door feels weird," Linda said.

As they turned to leave, a current of red mist trailed through the doorway and hit both of them in the chest. It knocked the air from Helai's lungs, making her gasp as momentary blindness overcame her. Panic swelled inside her as she reached out to feel where she was, only to have the floor feel like it dropped out from under her. A familiar feeling tugged her down, a twist in her gut; It felt similar to entering the Firebrand, like she was teleporting. She floated, suspended in nothingness, and then plummeted.

Helai's vision was slow to return. She blinked against the dim light of the room they were in. Linda stood a few feet away, reaching out to cling to something. They stood inside the skeletal structure of a large dressing room. The room was destroyed, the charred remains of chairs and mirrors in disarray around the room. The corpse of a jester sat crookedly in one of the mirrors. He was not burnt like he should have been. Half of his face was missing, skin grafted over bones. He wore a clown outfit free from damage, red and black checkered with a hat that jingled at the points.

"Where are we?" Linda asked.

"I don't know," Helai whispered. She wasn't sure why she was whispering, only that fear tugged at her belly as she stared into the blank gaze of the jester. "I think we're still in the theatre, but I don't know what happened."

"Stay close," Linda said, moving towards Helai. They reached her side as the jester giggled, head turned to the side as his limbs reanimated and cracked when he raised from the chair.

Horror crossed Helai's face as the jester pointed at her. His smile stretched unnaturally on his face, and a chill rolled down Helai's spine. "We're gonna play a game, and it's gonna be so much fun," He said, clapping gleefully as he rose from his seat. "Sigvald says if I win, I get to drink you dry."

His laughter was maniacal but fell short as Helai pulled a dagger from her hip and flung it expertly between three fingers. It struck the jester's shoulder, and as black ichor oozed from the wound, the jester frowned.

"Oh no. Oh, no, no, no! You're cheating—you aren't supposed to hit me before I tell you the rules." The jester cried in anger, prying the dagger loose from his shoulder. It clanked as it hit the floor, and clown music played from an orchestra in the other room.

"Go on–play with your friend," the jester sneered, wiggling his fingers at Linda. Linda growled, raising their war hammer, but before they could strike out, a wave of magic hit their chest and sent them flying through a door, where the orchestra's music grew louder.

"Linda," Helai cried out, but the door pulled shut, leaving Helai alone in the room with the jester. Laughter ensued from the jester once more as he grew bigger, magic shimmering in the surrounding air. His fingers flexed in preparation, and Helai stifled the fear that festered in her belly as she darted forward, pulling two more daggers from their sheaths as she drew close. He held a dagger of his own, and black energy seeped into the blade as his laughs grew more unhinged. He threw the dagger at her, and it moved too quickly for her eyes to follow.

Pain shot through her chest so quickly that it took her breath away. She looked down. The dagger's hilt was embedded in her chest, right above her heart. She swayed for a moment until understanding caught up, and she collapsed. The jester clapped again, bouncing forward to pull the dagger out. She coughed as blood cascaded from the wound and reached forward as if to grab the jester's foot. Her fingers went numb at first, but the cold was quick to spread through her entire body. Was this how it was to end? She did not want to die here. No, she would go down fighting. She would take the jester with her. He had bested her too quickly.

The gods truly cared little about her wishes as unconsciousness came to claim her the moment her cheek hit the carpet.

The last thing she saw before the darkness took her was Zahra's grief-stricken face. Helai was too weak to mouth the words, but she thought them all the same.

I'm sorry.

Helai did not know how much time had passed. It felt like mere moments as she woke, gasping for air. The pain from her chest was gone, and Helai rolled over on her back, staring down at her chest in horror as the wound, ugly and red, stitched itself up. The pain was unbearable, but dark magic forced her to her feet as her fingers tingled in weakness. Tears sprang to the corner of her eyes.

"Now you know how the game works." The jester laughed eagerly, snapping his fingers as he used magic to pull her closer. Her feet dragged against the floor as an invisible rope tugged her through the room, and soon the jester was skipping around her in untamed glee. "Best two out of three—loser gets eaten!"

Helai exhaled as one finger grazed over the crude stitchwork at her chest. Slipping the dagger from the sheath Velius made for her, she pulled it out and stabbed it into the jester's neck. He cried out in pain as black blood oozed down the jester's collarbone, and Helai pulled out the dagger and jumped back, out of range of the jester's retaliation.

The jester pressed his fingers to the wound as his veins turned black. The poison worked through his system, spider-webbing throughout his shoulder and down his arm. Crumbling to the ground, blood poured from his lips and seeped through his teeth, where the skin no longer existed. Yellow sap secreted from every orifice, collecting with his blood, and Helai stared on in horror and disgust.

Her fingers gripped the hilt of her dagger so tightly that her knuckles turned white. "Two out of three," she uttered to herself, using the momentary reprieve from the fight to shuffle around her bag. She pulled a vial of dark blue smoke from her waist, popped the cork off, and inhaled deeply. Her legs cramped almost immediately, but she could feel the energy returning to her limbs. When she moved, she was now quicker, stronger.

The jester twitched erratically on the ground, his wounds stitching themselves up. "One for me and one for you," he rasped, rolling over his belly. Spreading his fingers out, he pushed himself off the ground. "You're preeeeetty good at this," he cried, laughter bubbling out of his mouth as he circled Helai. He shot forward, charging at Helai at a speed that matched Cassius. Helai stumbled back, hoping the wall behind her would block his dagger, but it mattered not as the jester tripped and fell flat. The blade slipped from his grasp on impact, and Helai shot forward as he attempted to grab it. She brought her dagger down onto the jester's wrist to stop him from retrieving it. The dagger cut clean through, but Helai pulled away before complete amputation could occur. As the jester screamed in agony, he pulled his arm back. A few strands of skin and tendon still attached his hand to his wrist, dragging it across the floor as he crawled away. Despite thriving in chaos and violence her whole life, Helai resisted the urge to throw up as she reached down to grab the jester's dagger, ignoring his protests.

"No, no, no, that's mine. Give it back—give it back," the jester wailed. His voice grew shrill with each passing word. His wound gushed blood as Helai studied the dagger's hilt, which bore two masks, one smiling and the other frowning. The masks were tarnished, and Helai could barely read the words carved into the side, caked in her blood: The Last Laugh. Sheathing it, she moved to sink her dagger into the jester, but he was too quick, dodging away and tossing a foot out to sweep Helai's feet out from under her.

She hit the ground hard, unable to breathe as the wind was knocked from her lungs. A force pushed her away, sending her flying back through the door Linda had disappeared into. A whimper escaped her as she slammed into a wall, and she blinked the tears from her eyes as the jester skipped into the room. He was unflinching as he stared at her with unnaturally large eyes, his fingers wrapping around his broken wrist to pull it the rest of the way off.

"Naughty, naughty." The jester's tongue clicked against the roof of his mouth as he approached. To Helai's left, Linda fought what looked to be an orchestra conductor. She was tall with broad shoulders, her head nearly reaching Linda's shoulder. Her locs were tied together behind her head, and she wielded a two-handed axe as she swung expertly as the orchestra played in a fervor behind their fighting. The orchestra shuddered as the music rose in the air, its magic materializing a transparent winged creature above them. Helai didn't recognize the dragon until it opened its maw and breathed flame. The flame was a cluster of stars that poured out to scatter across the ceiling, and a sense of fullness struck Helai. It brushed up against her skin as it beckoned her to reach out towards the dragon.

"Eyes on the main attraction," the jester cried, and Helai's gaze flickered back to him in just enough time for her to dodge the dagger he flung at her. The metal whistled as it flew past her ear, hitting the wall and clanking as it hit the ground. As the intensity of the music rose, a sadness swelled within Helai. Tears pricked the corner of her eyes, and she grunted as the jester drew close and attempted to pin her against the wall. She rolled away, ignoring the ringing in her right ear, pulling another dagger from its sheathe and sinking it into the jester's side. As the jester cried out, his fangs descended. For the first time, Helai realized the jester was a vampire.

Twirling away from them, Helai uttered under her breath. A giddy thrill sang through her as magic pooled at her fingertips, beckoning smoke. It would not hide her completely, but the dark fog would be enough to disorient the jester. Or so she hoped.

"I will have my freedom," the woman snarled across the room as Linda pushed her away. "I will earn it by devouring your essence."

Linda frowned sadly, raising their war hammer. "Linda tastes bad."

Charging, Linda feigned to the left, then swung to the right. Their hammer slammed into the woman's chest with enough force to throw her back. The wood cracked as her body hit the wall behind the orchestra.

The woman growled in anger as she rose to her feet. Blood dripped from her lips as Linda roared. Spittle flying in all directions, the krok'ida charged again, lifting their war hammer and ignoring the pain from their various wounds. They swung, bashing the vampire's head in with their hammer as they skidded to a stop. Blood seeped over Volroth and onto the floor. Dizzy with bloodlust and rage, Linda heaved as they pried their war hammer from the gore of the conductor's head.

The orchestra vanished, turning to black smoke and drifting away in some invisible current. Helai's heart pounded in her throat as the jester giggled somewhere in the darkness of her smoke. "Come out, come out wherever you are. You are much more fun to play with than those stinky little rats."

Helai exhaled quietly. *Rats?* A scream lodged in her throat as the jester's face appeared in the fog. Helai stumbled away but was not quick enough as another blast of red magic slammed into her. She hit her back several feet away from the fog and had no time to scream before the jester had her pinned to the ground. His smile mocked her as he laughed with glee.

"Tasty little human." The jester moved to sink his teeth into Helai's neck, but something forced him to pause and look behind him.

Helai looked up to see Linda moving slowly out of the fog. It was terrifying, watching the krok'ida unfurl from the smoke. Their maw opened to a row of razor-sharp teeth. They moved with such force that the jester didn't even have time to call out before Linda's war hammer slammed into his side, flinging him off Helai. He hit the wall, and several bones cracked as Linda slammed their hammer into his head, his laughter mingled with screams. Blood and flesh shot out in different directions as the jester's body sank to the floor. Stained in blood, Linda turned, ambling over to help Helai to her feet.

"Thank you, Linda," Helai said. "You were terrifying." The silence was deafening, and Helai's stomach rolled painfully as her gaze fell on the jester's corpse. Linda patted her head, pulling her attention away from the bloodshed.

"Linda like hammer," Linda said, sheathing their war hammer at their side through a loop in their belt. "Linda also sneak."

Helai nodded, grinning up at Linda. "You did sneak. You would be very scary if you learned how to use that advantage in battle, Linda."

Linda hummed in contemplation, shrugging. "Maybe."

Helai looked around the room, her heart plummeting to her stomach. "We should find the others." As they turned back the way they came, Helai couldn't help but feel something was wrong.

Chapter Thirty-Seven
Intoh

Intoh swam in a sea of stars. He looked down to lush forests and stone temples, the home of his kind in the heart of Lyvira. His elders looked at carvings in ancient stones of the gods, breathing life and scripture into their way of life. He reached out to touch one of the scripts of a walking tree that drank from a sun-soaked goblet. Before his fingers could brush the cool stone, a voice called out to him.

"Come Intoh—you are one of the six. Perhaps you will fare better than the dyrvak that preceded you." The woman's voice coaxed Intoh away from memory into consciousness, and after blinking several times, he pushed himself into a seated position. Pain split across his head as Rooster pressed a hand to Intoh's shoulder, and the greka groaned. They were still in a theatre, but this stage was much more intimate with far less seating. A vampire stood on the stage, her hair a twist of blonde curls that cascaded down over one shoulder. She wore a beautiful blue dress glittered like starlight when the light struck it. Her face was a desecration of skin with rot and decay blossoming over the hollow of her cheeks. Her nose was no more, a large hole at the center of her face that exposed bone. The flash of fangs betrayed her vampiric nature. A giant orb floated beside her with swirls of blue energy that she beckoned small tendrils of water from.

"I'm not sure what happened. I woke up just a few moments before you," Rooster uttered, ducking behind a chair. It seemed to matter little—the vampire's eyes burned into Intoh as he lowered himself close to the ground beside Rooster. His heart fluttered in his chest, his fear a butterfly forging its way out of its cocoon.

"Need to find Cassius. See way he looked at lance?" Intoh urged. He didn't get to see much, just a flicker of movement from the vampire that had materialized in front of Cassius, but there was no denying the lance was what had been calling to Cassius. It was why they were here. "Plus—need Cassius' blood. Need to study vampirism more closely," Ekalas said beside him, her dorsal crests twitching along her spine as she glanced up at the vampire on stage.

Intoh looked at her and nodded. Of course, he did. He needed to know if vampire blood was the key to immortality. There were no records of vampires being able to turn greka, but Intoh's quest encouraged the impossible.

"Don't hide from me." The vampire's laughter darkened the room, and as Intoh raised his head to peek over the chairs, the air dried, like the moisture was being pulled from the room. Rooster remained bent behind chairs, his eyes trained on the vampire as he moved towards the side of the room. His hand rested on the hilt of his sword, and he met Intoh's gaze. Distract her, he mouthed.

Lightning shot out Intoh's fingertips as a water whip snaked out to hit him. The electricity used the water as a path, traveling through it to electrocute the vampire, who screamed and flinched away. The water whip made contact with Intoh just before the vampire dispelled it, and he hissed as he went invisible, ducking behind a burned chair.

"You cannot hide your heart from me, mage," the vampire called out, water hitting the chair he hid behind. He uncloaked, his heart beating wildly, and curled his fingers, beckoning forward a ball of electricity. He longed to use water, as Tidebeard had been teaching him, but there was not enough in the air to call to, and the orb ignored his instruction when he reached out to utilize its energy.

Throwing another orb of electricity at her like a bomb, Intoh slithered forward close to the floor to the other end of the row of chairs. His heart leaped to his throat as a vine of water wrapped around his tail and tugged him backwards, dragging him out into the aisle. Twisting, he saw a tendril of water had shot out of the orb and had his tail, carrying him towards the stage. His sphere of electricity must have missed, so he shot another one now. The lightning made contact with the woman this time, and she screeched, bolting away too quickly for his eyes to follow. The water dissipated, sinking into the velvet carpet of the aisle, and Intoh scrambled to his feet–he had lost sight of Rooster.

The vampire appeared before him, grabbing him around the neck before he could bolt away. Her eyes were wild, and no longer was her hair in a state of order—it still cascaded around her shoulders, but it was rough and untamed, frizzed from the electricity that had struck her.

"You crave knowledge. I can taste the different energies of magic that surround you. Such danger for such a little soul," the vampire whispered, squeezing her fingers around his throat. "Are you not afraid that your succulent little heart won't explode?" She caressed his cheek with her free hand, a soft sadness radiant in her expression. "Have you ever tasted the power of necromancy, I wonder?"

It began in his toes. She was not strangling him, not really, but she had cut off his ability to speak, and the tips of his fingers and toes grew cold. He watched with horror as she reached out to lift his arm and show him. Something did not feel right, a tension in the air that urged Intoh to flinch away, but he could not move as his hand deteriorated. It was slow as his skin peeled away to reveal tendon and bone at his fingertips. It was painful, exceptionally so, but he could not cry out. No matter how hard he struggled, the vampire was stronger.

Ekalas, he cried out silently. *I'm so sorry I failed.*

Intoh felt his tail go as his eyes grew heavy. All the energy had fled his limbs, and he was exhausted. It may be time for the Long Sleep. He was ready to find Ekalas in the Sun City, where drikoty go when they die. He'd come to her a failure, but at least he'd be with his friend again.

"Oi—fangy bitch." A voice—Rooster's—cut through the air, and the necromancy was pulled from Intoh's lungs. He gasped as life returned to him all at once. Warmth blossomed through his belly like newly awakened spring, and the vampire dropped him as she hissed and turned away.

He hit the ground, landing on top of his dead tail, and he stared at it mournfully as he crawled away. Rooster stood on the stage with his sword, an arrogant grin on his face despite the vampire that moved towards him.

Pulling a dagger out of her side, dark blood seeped from the wound. Rooster must have thrown it, and she threw it to the floor as she lashed out with her hand. A whip of water dashed out of the orb that hung by her side, wrapping around Rooster and tugging him closer.

"I'm going to peel your skin off and drink the marrow from your bones," the vampire seethed, reaching a hand out to Rooster. His arms were trapped beneath the ropes of water that curled around him, and Intoh scurried to his feet, pressing his hand to the flat of the vampire's back.

"*Asmit*," he cried, sending torrents of electricity through the vampire. His head felt like it was filled with angry bees as the vampire screamed. Bruises webbed up her skin, purple and delicate as the electricity coursed through her, and the orb pulled the water back to it, dropping Rooster to the floor.

Standing, Rooster unsheathed his sword and decapitated the vampire. Her head rolled, and Intoh caught the orb before it hit the ground. It pulsated with a soft white glow and was cool to the touch. Running his fingers over it was like trailing the surface of the water, and he marveled at it for only a moment before tucking it safely away in his bag. He'd have to study it later when they were safe at The Broken Arrow.

"Are you okay?" Rooster's voice caused Intoh to look up. He gestured to Intoh's back, where the absence of his tail was barely recognized.

"Oh, yes," Intoh said, nodding. "Happened before. Will come back." It would take time for the tail to grow back, but Intoh had lost it several times. It was strange, and his balance felt slightly off, but he would survive.

Flexing his fingers, he looked behind him at the exit. "Would just like to leave. Find Cassius now. Get lance. Get out."

Rooster sighed and patted Intoh on the shoulder. "I couldn't agree more."

Chapter Thirty-Eight
Cassius

Silence drenched the theatre in a deceitful calm—the vampire stood a few feet before him but did not move to attack. His stillness set Cassius on edge as they now stood atop the stage. A chill rolled down Cassius' spine as it felt like a ghostly hand tickled the nape of his neck, but he dared not look behind him.

"Cassius," a voice said behind him. It was the woman of his blood. He felt her hands on him now, her lips pressed to the cusp of his ear. He shuddered, but she only laughed. "Sigvald holds the lance—but it is yours. Why don't you be a good boy and take it?"

"Ahma will grow to poison you," the vampire said. "You come for the lance, yes?" Recognition struck Cassius. He had seen Sigvald's portrait in the Dragon Keep library when he was a knight there. He was renowned in the Order for his cavalry skills on the battlefield. Cassius had never met him, his disappearance occurring years before Cassius became a vampire.

"Do not listen to him, Cassius. Your blood sings for the Ebony Fang," Ahma circled him, her eyes soft and seductive as she ran a hand over his chest. "Collecting them all will grant you the ability to prevent the return of the dragons." She 'tsked,' her head tossed to the side in sympathy. "Their blood runs through our veins, but their return would bring about the end of days. It would be unwise to wake them."

A slow panic gripped Cassius. "Prevent their return? So it is true? Some mean to wake them in the first place?" Things were beginning to make sense. The sigils scratched into the walls of Volendam and on that tree in the marshes. The brand on the Misfits' backs. The cults praising a dead dragon named Gorvayne. Cassius swayed with the implications.

Sigvald growled. "Enough! She speaks in partial truths. Something woke me from my long sleep, a sleep I wish to return to. I urge you to leave this place, for I will not allow you to take the lance."

Ahma's laughter was cruel as she dashed away, gesturing to Sigvald with her hand. "The temptation to claim the lance will not silence until you do so, Cassius. I will not stop you if you decide to live with the torture."

Cassius raised his sword. He wasn't sure what to believe, his head a storm of conflicting emotions. If some meant to bring back the ancient dragons, it could mean nothing good for Vilanthris. Their awakening would rip the world apart. Cassius had only ever seen bits and pieces of the long-lost dragons in black market sales and estates and could not truly imagine how big they were. If finding and claiming all fragments of the Ebony Fang would prevent such an apocalypse, then perhaps he should bear the burden.

Sigvald's eyes grew sad as he lowered his head. "So be it." The lance slipped back into his skin, a mess of black and red smoke that spiraled into his forearm as he raised his sword and shield. "Honor me, brother."

It was unkind for those of the Sanguine Order to fight against each other. They became brothers in arms when they took their oaths with the Order. The knowledge guilted Cassius into hesitating, and Sigvald utilized the advantage, breaking past Cassius' defenses and slicing along Cassius' arm. Cassius hissed and flinched away, managing to bring up his shield before Sigvald's sword could connect.

Bringing his shield forward, Cassius threw it towards Sigvald's chin. Sigvald's head slammed back as a fang knocked loose. It fell to the floor as Cassius twisted his sword, aiming for Sigvald's weak points. His plate armor left him near impenetrable, but Cassius was used to wearing plate armor himself and knew where the weaknesses were. Cassius managed to strike Sigvald's armpit, which wounded Sigvald enough to retreat, crying out in anger.

"This lance will be nothing but a tool. It calls out to more than just you, Cassius. Something is festering here, an evil that chants in the darkness. It stirred me from my grave. I drank dyrvak blood for the first time in my long, undead life. They usually do not stray from their forests but have sensed a stirring with their god. I have heard and understood their dark tongues; Mot seeks to return." The name sent unease through Cassius, who paused.

"Who is Mot?"

Sigvald growled, using his shield to knock Cassius back. "The god. He goes by many names. The dragon dwells at the center of this world. A change is coming. I've been stuck in this opera house for a long time, yet I can sense it." He gestured to Ahma. "That part of her story rings true."

Planting his feet, Cassius felt the ghost of his father's glare on his back, urging him to loosen his knees, to grip his sword differently, to work hard, and move faster... he lunged out, knocking Sigvald's sword aside and bashing Sigvald in the face, breaking his nose. Black ichor oozed down his mouth and over his chin before it had a chance to heal, and Sigvald's gaze was stern as he backed up.

"A myth," Cassius said in disdain. "You spin lies."

"What reason would I have to lie?" Sigvald asked. His nose had already healed. "I urge you to pay closer attention. The signs have been growing. The end is coming."

Cassius hesitated again and looked to Ahma, who watched the fight with interest. She said nothing, but her eyes spoke volumes; she believed Sigvald.

"If you believe it, then why not claim the Ebony Fang yourself?" Cassius asked, dodging Sigvald's blade.

"The Silent Fox prepares his kin for the coming storm. Locating the Ebony Fang before it falls into the wrong hands has been a task appointed to me, but I cannot leave the Palace of Thorns. My father has forbidden it."

Understanding struck Cassius. "You are the Emperor's daughter?" Emperor Aikawa had not left his home in a long time. Not much was known about Amajin or its people, and many who entered the Bamboo Forest surrounding Amajin's borders never returned.

Ahma nodded, her voice sweet as honey. "It is why I ask for your aid now, Cassius. Claim the arsenal for me. Bring it to me in Amajin. Sigvald's stance is just, but he is nothing more than a ghost, a hollowed husk of disappointment. He could not claim it for me, so that right has been passed to you."

Unease passed through Cassius. He never asked for this. He did know he wanted the urge to seek out the lance to stop. If he had to kill Sigvald to do it, he would.

Sigvald did not grant him the chance to ponder as he charged forward. "I will not make it easy for you," he said. The strength of his arm was underestimated, cutting through Cassius' defenses and slicing deeply into Cassius' right arm. His shield fell as he cried out in pain, dodging another attack as Sigvald swung his sword with expert and grace. Cassius forced his breathing to even as he watched Sigvald's movements. His brand burned fiercely, stealing that breath away, but with it came a flooding of strength.

Cassius danced forward, circling Sigvald's sword arm and disarming him completely. Stepping back, Cassius raised his sword in stance and planted his feet once more as Sigvald cried out to him in rage. Raising his hands, he became a maelstrom of bats, chirping and shrieking as a plume of red smoke swallowed the knight and carried him away.

Cassius turned, but he did not see where Sigvald had gone. The pain in his arm faded as the cut stitched itself together, and a swoop of air brushed his back before he was kicked to the ground by a plated boot.

Cassius' sword flew off the stage as he hit the ground. Pain shot up his arms and legs as he caught himself, but a boot against the small of his back forced him to the floor. Sigvald said nothing, but he didn't have to. Cassius knew what came next.

Taking a deep breath, Cassius mustered the rest of his strength, even as it flourished through the brand, and used it to push back against Sigvald's boot. He rolled to the side just as Sigvald's sword came down to pierce Cassius through the heart. It hit the surface of the stage instead, embedding itself into the wood.

"The gun, Cassius," Ahma purred from across the stage. Her voice rattled in his head, but the moment he thought about it, the gun materialized, slinking down his arm in dark ichor form only to harden into a gun that fit perfectly within his grasp. Sigvald stood above him, eyes glowing bright red as his face contorted and twisted in ire. He pulled his sword out of the stage in one swift thrust, but before he could bring it back down, Cassius pointed the gun at Sigvald and pulled the trigger.

Time slowed as a bullet of dark red energy shot out from the gun. A shiver of power coursed through Cassius as it fired, sending a wave of pleasure down his spine. Sigvald's eyes widened as he looked down to where the gun had managed to pierce through his plate armor and hit his heart.

"I'm sorry," Cassius whispered as Sigvald fell. Cassius raised to turn him onto his back, and Sigvald's breathing was shallowed as he looked at Cassius.

"I urge you—do not trust her. Protect the lance—do not let her reclaim the arsenal." Sivgald whispered, his voice weak. The tips of his boots began to fade away, turning to dust, and Cassius pressed his hand to Sigvald's chest, right above his heart. Blood coated his fingers.

"By the blood of the dragon we were born," he said.

"By the blood of the dragon, we will die," Sigvald finished just before he faded to naught but ash. All that was left behind was the lance. Gentle grief momentarily incapacitated Cassius as he pressed his fist to where Sigvald died. "Take it," Ahma whispered as she approached.

"Take it and be free of its temptations." Cassius reached out and pressed a light touch to the stock of the lance. The lance sank to the ground in dark ichor and trailed up Cassius' arm, disappearing into the skin. The hum of power that drenched his blood now was intoxicating. Cassius had never felt so alive, even in his undeath. He shuddered, but soon everything went quiet.

Ahma faded as the other Misfits burst into the theater, but Cassius was too distracted by the silence to turn to them. His brand did nothing more than the pulse in a dull pain, and the lance was now tucked safely away in his arm alongside the woman and the gun. No more urges, no more quiet hunger lodged between his lungs.

Still, he thought as he turned to the Misfits, *why does it still feel like something is wrong?*

Chapter Thirty-Nine
Rooster

Relief sat heavily on Rooster's shoulders as he and the others drew forward towards Cassius. The echoes of vampiric screams still rang in his ears, and he halted a foot or so away from Cassius as the lance he had fought the other vampire for sank into the vampire's skin.

"What the fuck just happened?" Rooster asked, gesturing to Cassius' arm. Helai looked equally confused, her brow pressed together in a worried line. Even with the fight over, the air still buzzed with magic. Intoh sat on Linda's shoulder in greka form as Linda strolled around the room, sniffing the air. There was something inherently wrong, but Rooster could not place it. Cassius had killed the other vampire, but something still felt off.

"Feel strange," Linda said.

Cassius sighed. "It's a long story–" he said, gesturing to his arm. "One that should be told when we're in the safety of The Broken Arrow."

Helai shook her head. "I think, considering we just risked our lives for you, we deserve to know some truth." She wrapped her arms around her abdomen, her expression hard. "You do not have to tell us everything now, but are we in danger? I have enough of my own to worry about."

"I do not think we're in any immediate danger. I was… approached by a woman who wanted me to find the missing pieces of an armory." Cassius' reply was slow as he looked down at his arm.

"And this–" Rooster waved his hand to where the lance had disappeared, "this is the armory? I don't know how to say this… weapons aren't supposed to go inside us." The whole premise filled Rooster with unease. Vampires carried their own politics, and most of the time, it involved their own personal gain. It wasn't necessarily a good thing if someone was trying to amass a unique arsenal of powerful magical weapons. He had grown to trust Cassius, but depending on a vampire could be like trusting a double-edged sword.

"I do not know if I want to collect them all," Cassius said. He looked troubled, his gaze far off. "I do not feel the call for another one."

"What does that–" Helai's question cut off as a shot of pain hit them all at once. It was so sudden it took Rooster's breath away. The flares of pain from the brand had paled in comparison, and Rooster's eyes watered as he gritted his teeth.

The key around Helai's neck pulsed in a soft, tangible glow as the pain swept through the Misfits. The moment the key glowed, a door on the side of the theatre also glowed. It was subtle, etching the lines of the door, but it was strong enough for Rooster to look at Helai and point at the door.

The moment they acknowledged it, the pain disappeared. A bitter taste flooded Rooster's mouth as he bent at the waist. Phantom pains were still coursing through his arms and legs, but it was getting better as Cassius and Helai went up to the door. A wave of heat rolled under the door, and Intoh raised his hand and chirped in distress.

"Feel that, Ekalas? That's magic," Intoh said, staring at empty air from Linda's shoulder. "No, no, no. Don't want to go in there. Bad—something bad festers. We must go, turn back, flee. Please, Linda." Intoh tugged against Linda's neck as if the motion would turn them, but Linda was quick to ignore Intoh as Cassius pressed his hand to the doorknob and turned it.

"Locked," Cassius whispered in hushed tones as if they were not alone. As Rooster approached the door, a faint chanting etched the air, forcing the hair on his arm to stand on edge. Chanting was never a good sign, and his stomach plummeted in sudden fear as Helai pushed her key into the door. It was a perfect fit, and Rooster's exhale got silenced by the creaking of the door as it swung open. How Helai had gotten such a key was lost on Rooster, but he knew it was the same key Velius had pointed out. Wherever she had obtained it from seemed important.

There was no time to ask as the chanting grew louder, and a purple light bathed them. Gnashing teeth and low hums met them as they entered the room and were greeted with a hideous sight.

Somehow, the room was larger on the inside than it appeared within the theatre. They stood before four massive marble pillars, each veined with the same purple light pulsating through them. In the center was a nest made from stones, their roundness unnatural. Rakken and dyrvak shared places around a circle they made, and in their center lay a single tooth. The tooth was the size of Rooster and stained with reddish-brown. When Rooster spotted the altar, he realized it was blood smeared over the tooth.

"The Blodrägr," Cassius said. He looked at the altar fabricated with bones. The altar bore little design other than one large bone structure that went straight up and two smaller ones that branched off to form a 'Y' shape. A human man rested on the altar, murdered and gutted, his intestines spilled out and lifted to wrap around his neck in some sick form of rope, which had him tied to the altar. Nails pierced his hands to the smaller bones, his eyes carved out. His mouth drooped open in a scream. Nearly all his teeth were missing, and fresh blood still dripped from his fingertips. Nausea flooded Rooster at the sight of it.

"Leave now?" Intoh asked, tugging more desperately against Linda's neck. The fear pumped through them as a silent agreement formed: they needed to leave.

It was too late, though. Their entrance had been noticed by several dyrvak and a rakken overseeing whatever unholy ritual was taking place.

The air buzzed with magic, and Rooster felt almost like something was pulling at his skin, an attempt to peel him away, bit by bit.

"Oh, no-no. Scurry-kill-maim," the rakken shouted, pointing at the Misfits. Cassius pushed in front of them, shield brought up to his chest, his sword wielded again. One of the dyrvak stomped the floor with its hoof and charged, its ax raised and ready. Linda ambled beside Cassius and roared, spittle flying in all directions as they gripped their war hammer and twirled it.

As Linda moved to attack, Intoh slunk down their back and scurried away, electricity etching his fingertips as he stared at the other rakken and dyrvak in the circle. Something foul and misshapen jutted out of the middle of the nest as tendrils of purple magic trailed out of the pillars and poured into the bone.

Rooster ducked as a dyrvak's sword swung over his head, his hand reaching at his hip to unsheathe his sword. He cursed himself for not having it out sooner as he dodged the dyrvak's attack again, using the hilt to thrust forward as he pulled out his blade.

The dyrvak swept aside, lashing out to punch Rooster in the nose. Blood gushed as it broke, and before Rooster could cry out, the dyrvak grabbed Rooster by the throat and raised him. "The Whispering Lords will be resurrected, and a new dawn will break when they rise. Those who defy them will meet a most gruesome end." Panic sang through Rooster as he struggled to breathe, dropping his sword to grasp at the dyrvak's hand. Stars popped into the edges of his vision, his face a fire of pain as he looked into the hateful expression of his enemy. With every last bit of strength, he spat the blood that had poured into his mouth straight into the dyrvak's face.

The dyrvak growled, raising his sword to pierce Rooster with it.

"*Asmit!*"

A bright light bathed Rooster as the dyrvak dropped him. A light current swam through the dyrvak's veins as he curled over and stopped moving. Intoh ran up as Rooster gasped, his eyes watering as he gingerly touched his nose. He hissed at the pain and pulled away; it was broken.

Intoh pointed to the chanting circle. "Have to break it. Can't let them finish." Rooster forced himself to his feet as he grabbed his sword off the floor. Clanks of metal sounded behind him, but he ignored them as he drew forward with Intoh, struggling against a current of magic that tried to push them back. His back was on fire, the brand pulsating with the rhythm of the chanting, and as Rooster raised his sword to run it through the back of a dyrvak, Helai stood opposite him, her face reflecting off the light of the magic. The blade of her dagger glinted, and two dyrvak fell as the circle was broken. The air went taunt as the magic grew unsteady, a tightness that squeezed Rooster's lungs as he killed the dyrvak in front of him. The remainder of the circle cried out in anger as they were immediately unmade; their bodies were torn apart by magic, leaving nothing but their bones behind.

Rooster squeezed his eyes shut as the wave of magic drew near, but when no pain came, he opened his eyes. Drenched in purple light, he stared at Helai with a questioning expression. Unable to move, the tooth in the center of the nest cracked, splitting apart down the middle.

A low, undiscernible whispering washed over the room as the magic faded, and they were left in silence.

Rooster heaved as his broken nose throbbed. Helai lowered her dagger but remained on guard, her hands shaking. His brand no longer pounded as he stepped away from the bones of the dyrvak that fell and shattered in front of him.

"We should leave." Rooster turned as Cassius spoke, his brow furrowed as he looked onto the failed ritual. Blood dried on Cassius' armor and across his face, but it did not look to be his as Linda lowered their war hammer and raised their nose to the air to sniff.

"I think they were trying to bring back a dragon," Rooster uttered, reaching up to wipe the blood from his face. He winced at the pain as Helai approached, rummaging in her bag.

"Take this," she said, handing over a vial of swirling green.

Rooster took it after a moment of hesitation: healing potions were a common thing sold in apothecaries, but they could hold addictive properties, and Rooster never liked taking them. Still, his nose hurt, and they had far bigger things to worry about. The taste was sweet, like maple syrup and sugar, and the pain quickly faded as a pinching sensation hit his nose, followed by some itching and then nothing.

"We stopped it, though," Helai said. She didn't appear so sure as she took the empty vial from Rooster and slipped it into her bag. Anxiety crept through the Misfits as they fled the room. It had all seemed too easy.

"For now," Cassius said. His expression seemed troubled as they entered back into the main theater. "I was nearly killed by a cultist before I rode out for Volendam. 'The Whispering Lord must rise' was her words, if I remember. And the vampire I just fought? He spoke of dragons."

The news was troubling. The outcome wasn't good if there were other cultists elsewhere performing the same types of rituals. "Are we certain we believe they can even bring the dragons back, assuming they ever existed in the first place?" Helai asked. No one had ever seen a dragon. The eldrasi spoke of them in their legends, and their skeletons were scattered about in various parts of the world, but the proof was too small for Rooster to believe them to be real.

"One of the dyrvak spoke of 'the Whispering Lords.' It has to be correlated," Rooster said.

"Sounds like the rakken I killed. He said something about a 'coming storm.' I think we need to speak to the city guard. If there are cultists in Volendam trying to bring back a dragon, they should know about it," Helai said, pulling strands of stray hairs out of her face. They had reached the front door of the opera house, and Rooster's stomach plummeted as they left.

As Rooster reached the front door, a softness cradled the back of his neck, a low whisper etching goosebumps into his skin. It was too quiet to hear, and as he turned back to look, no one was there.

Chapter Forty
Cassius

They stumbled out of the opera house with a quickened fervor. Despite everything they'd just witnessed, Cassius felt a lightness on his chest he hadn't felt since before he had been imprisoned in his tomb. The woman in his blood was silent and no longer pushed him towards anything. The lance was tucked safely in his arm, alongside the gun; even if it was only momentary, he was free.

Helai clutched the eye pendant around her neck as they moved down the stairs. It was raining, and a soft drizzle sent goosebumps over Cassius' skin. The moment they stepped foot over the threshold of the opera house, a hunger gripped Cassius so tightly momentary blindness came over him. He gasped as his skin sunk in on itself and his heart squeezed painfully once before it stopped beating.

"Cassius, are you alright?" Rooster asked somewhere off to Cassius' left. His voice was drenched in concern, but all Cassius could hear was the sound of Helai and Rooster's blood pumping through their veins. The sound was delectable, and a whine curled at the back of his throat as he forced himself away.

"I need blood," he rasped, his fingers clinging weakly to a pillar of the opera house. He felt much like he did when he woke up in his tomb. "Get away from me," he demanded, forcing himself away from the others. He ignored their protests as he shot off into the night, his eyesight returning in shuddered waves.

He found a noble walking home alone, her umbrella keeping her safe from the rain. Cassius did little to mask himself as he grabbed her from behind, her scream cut off when he clamped his hand down over her mouth. The blood was sweet as it hit his lips, and he drank until he could not anymore, his eyesight sharpening first. It was elation when his heart started to beat, and he dropped the corpse as a heavy breath passed his lips. It was strange–it felt like he hadn't eaten in months, but they had only been in the opera house for a couple of hours.

After hiding the body, Cassius returned to the others. The rain had turned to snow, which also felt odd. It was too early in the year to be snowing, but flakes hit Cassius all the same as the others came into sight, and his shame burned flames in his belly.

"I apologize. I do not know what came over me," Cassius said.

"It would be wise to eat more often, friend. I fear you may take a bite out of one of us someday if you don't," Rooster said, gesturing between himself and Helai.

"It did not seem like a long time had passed between feedings. I fed only last night, and we were only in the opera house for a few hours. Does something seem off?" Cassius raised his hand to catch snowflakes as Intoh shivered and drew closer to Linda to steal some of their heat.

Helai's brows pressed together. "It does seem strange, but I don't think we'll get any answers standing here. If what the rakken say is true, we need to speak to the city guard if something is coming."

The grotesque image of whatever the rakken and the dyrvak were attempting to resurrect resurfaced in Cassius' mind's eye. Unease threatened to shake his core, but he swallowed and nodded. "We have spoken to Booker only once, and he seemed less inclined to believe us about the dyrvak, but we can always try."

As they approached Booker's office, the low sounds of argument could be heard. An eerie feeling had settled into the bones of Volendam as they traveled down the city's streets. The snow blanketed the sound, and it was coming down more heavily as Cassius knocked on Booker's door, the others behind him.

Silence overcame the room for a moment before Booker coughed. "Come in."

They entered the room. Booker sat behind his desk, which was piled with maps and other loose papers. Velius stood next to him, his hair down and glinting against the light of the flame in the fireplace. Obrand stood near the door, and everyone carried the expression like they had just been arguing passionately. The Captain from the Silver Moon Club was also there, his mouth open in surprise as he realized the Misfits were all together.

Obrand was the first to greet them as he rushed forward, his anger washing away. "I hear people are calling you the Misfits now. The name suits you." He reached forward to clasp Rooster on the arm, and Velius straightened, a dazzling smile crossing his face.

"I have heard such stories as well. Quite the title to live up to," Velius said.

As Obrand pulled away, a questioning expression crossed his face. "We overheard the bartender at the inn we're staying mention your names and how they haven't seen you for a month and a half. Where did you go?"

"A month and a *half?*" Helai asked. Disbelief struck Cassius. They'd been stuck inside the opera house for a month and a half? How was he still standing? How did Rooster and Helai not starve to death? Cassius' head swam with the implications.

"It was you all," the Captain hissed, working his jaw over and pulling Cassius from his revelations. The Captain raised his cane to tap dramatically against the floor. "You stole from me."

Rooster raised an eyebrow. "That's quite an accusation."

"I can see it," he said, pointing to Linda's weapon and Intoh's pendant. "Those are *my jewels.*" Cassius moved to step in front of Linda as the Captain stepped forward. A glare flashed in a warning.

"I suppose you have my locket too. Thieves," the Captain said, turning back to Booker. "I demand their arrest."

"Locket?" Velius asked from the corner. He looked at Rooster with a raised eyebrow. Rooster shrugged innocently.

A sigh passed Booker's lips as he pinched the bridge of his nose. "Silence. I will have one thing happening at a time. Do you have evidence that they stole those jewels from you?" Booker stared at the Captain as sweat dripped down his cheek.

"No."

Booker nodded. "Then we will launch an investigation. *In the meantime,*" he straightened in his chair as the Captain cursed quietly under his breath. "The dwarves are here with stories that an army amasses in the marshlands. They have given me no proof to believe them—"

Obrand's anger was quick as he turned to Booker, his finger raised to shake at him. "We do not go into the marshlands. It's a death sentence for dwarves, but I'm telling ya, lad—something stirs in the fog. The rakken have moved out of the mountains. We have been fighting them for the last several months. They want our cities to build their nests. Why abandon their cause now?"

Booker shrugged. "Assuming these rakken even exist. We have seen no signs of a siege."

Velius raised his hands as Obrand moved to protest. "Wait, wait—"

"If I may," Cassius interrupted. Everyone turned to look at him, and Cassius pressed forward. He was tired and craved a glass of wine. He had seen much in the last twenty-four hours… or a month and a half, if Obrand's claim was true. "We *did* warn you about the dyrvak in the marshlands. What reason would the dwarves have to abandon their king in his time of grief if not to speak the truth?" Cassius gestured to the other Misfits. "We have just left the opera house in the Sails District. Inside, cultists were attempting…" he paused, mulling over his following words. Booker wasn't likely to believe if he mentioned any word of dead dragons. "Dark magic. Dyrvak and rakken had their hands to play in the ritual, but we managed to stop them. I know you cannot send men out to the marshes, but I urge you to seek answers inside the opera house. If you are disinclined to believe the dwarves, it will take but a couple of hours to investigate my claim."

Helai moved to stand next to Cassius. He felt her eyes on him for a moment before her head turned to look at Booker. "What he says is true."

The Captain laughed, his hand running over his head in disbelief. "You cannot trust a word they say. They speak of madness!"

Booker leaned forward, threading his fingers together. He was silent before he leaned back and waved his hand. "I will send some men out to investigate."

Relief traveled through Cassius as Velius pushed off the wall to stand up straight. "If an army is forming in the marshlands, you all must be prepared."

A sudden silence shot through the room. The air was drenched in tension, and something did not seem right, like a scream was trapped in the hollow of Cassius' lungs. Panic stitched pathways along his arms, and everyone seemed attuned to the shift in emotion as they stopped talking.

"Do you hear that?" Obrand asked. Vibrations trailed through the stone and up Cassius' legs. It was subtle, so subtle Cassius wasn't sure if it was real, but it grew steadily louder.

War drums.

Velius and Booker were the first to react, moving towards the small window behind Booker's desk. Cassius spared a glance towards Rooster, who nodded ever the slightest. Booker wouldn't have to investigate the opera house after all.

"What is it?" Obrand asked, breaking the silence.

"An army," Booker said, his expression grim. "It's an army."

Pronounciation/Important Information

Characters

- Lindr'zkt (Lind-ar-zecked) – a krok'ida from Lyvira
- Intoh'gask (Een-toe-gask) – a greka from Lyvira
- Cassius (Cass-ee-us) – a vampire, originally from Hestia
- Rooster (Roo-ster) – a human from ???
- Helai (Hel-eye) – a human from Shoma

Places

- Amajin (Ah-mah-gin)
- Volreya (Vole-ray-uh)
- Kreznov (Krez-nov)
- Volendam (Vole-en-dawm)
- Nantielle (Non-tie-aye)
- Wolstadt (Wole-stat)
- Rovania (Row-vain-ee-uh)
- Kythera (Ky-th-ear-uh)
- Hestia (Hes-tea-uh)
- Daesthara (Day-es-thar-uh)
- Shoma (Show-muh)
- Míradan (Meer-uh-dawn)
- Lyvira (Lie-veer-uh)

Acknowledgements

I'd like to take a moment and thank my editor, Miranda. Without her sharp eyes and knowledge, this book would have been half of its greatness. I'd like to thank my family. Their endless support throughout the process of bringing this story to fruition has been noticed, and I couldn't have handled the downs of writing without them. I'd like to thank my tabletop party–without their help, the Misfits wouldn't exist. To my partner in crime, Matlin. Without his love and care, the story wouldn't have had its voice. And to my siblings; Ellie, you've read through all of the drafts almost as much as I have. You listen to my anxious ramblings when imposter syndrome hits hard. You created the best gentle giant an author could be privileged to use. Josh, you've been on board with me these last ten years developing this world, helping me work through inconsistencies in the worldbuilding, building me a map, making Rooster... I don't have the right words to express how grateful I am for the both of you.

And lastly, I'd like to thank you, the reader. Even if this wasn't your cup of tea, you made it this far. You read my story. That's all I could ask for.

If you would like to keep up to date with my writing, my most active account is on Instagram: @jordandugdaleauthor. There, you can keep up to date with my writing journey and future books in the Whispered Tales series.